Dear Reader,

It is with pleasure and pride that I present to you the paperback version of *The Man from Stone Creek*. Sam O'Ballivan is one of my all-time favorite heroes, a man of strength, integrity, humor and honor. His lady, Maddie, is his perfect match, however—a partner as well as a lover, his equal in every way.

I also wanted to write today to tell you about a special group of people with whom I've recently become involved. It is The Humane Society of the United States (HSUS), specifically their Pets for Life program.

The Pets for Life program is one of the best ways to help your local shelter—that is to help keep animals out of shelters in the first place. Something as basic as keeping a collar and tag on your pet all the time, so if he gets out and gets lost, he can be returned home. Being a responsible pet owner. Spaying or neutering your pet. And not giving up when things don't go perfectly. If your dog digs in the yard, or your cat scratches the furniture, know that these are problems that can be addressed. You can find all the information about these—and many other common problems—at www.petsforlife.org. This campaign is focused on keeping pets and their people together for a lifetime.

As many of you know, my own household includes two dogs, two cats and four horses, so this is a cause that is near and dear to my heart. I hope you'll get involved along with me.

May you be blessed.

With love,

Linda Lael Miller

Praise for the works of Linda Lael Miller

The Man from Stone Creek

"[Miller] paints a brilliant portrait of the good,
the bad and the ugly, the lost and the lonely,
and the power of love to bring light into the darkest of souls.
This is western romance at its finest."
—*Romantic Times BOOKreviews,* four and a half stars

"Linda Lael Miller is the Louis L'Amour
of western romantic fiction. Only better."
—*BookLoons*

"The plot is taut and moves rapidly,
pulling the reader into the lives of these characters.
Hidden currents explode to the surface and lives are forever
changed. Readers won't be able to put down this well-written
book from one of this genre's favorite authors."
—*Rendezvous*

McKettrick's Choice

"Miller's name is synonymous with the finest in
western romance. From the hard realities of life in an
untamed land to the passionate people who bring the
colorful history to life, she brings the best of the West
to readers, never failing to deliver a great read!"
—*Romantic Times BOOKreviews*

"Intrigue, danger, and greed are up against integrity,
kindness, and love in this engrossing western romance.
Miller has created unforgettable characters and woven
a many-faceted yet coherent and lovingly told tale."
—*Booklist,* starred review

McKettrick's Luck

"Miller's ability to bring a cast of characters to life is on full
display here…the veteran romance author doesn't disappoint
in her sizzling love scenes and fine sense of place."
—*Publishers Weekly*

LINDA LAEL MILLER

The Man from Stone Creek

HQN™

ISBN-13: 978-0-373-77198-1
ISBN-10:   0-373-77198-3

THE MAN FROM STONE CREEK

Also by Linda Lael Miller

And coming in July 2007 from HQN Books

For Kathy and Betty,
the Bannon girls,
with love

The Man from
Stone Creek

CHAPTER

ONE

Haven, Arizona Territory
Fall, 1903

THE PINT-SIZE CULPRITS, heretofore gathered around the well, scattered for the brush as soon as Sam O'Ballivan rode into the schoolyard on his nameless horse, but he'd seen enough to know they were up to no good. He caught glimpses of bowl-cut hair, denim trousers and chambray shirts as they fled. Pigtails, too, and a flash of red calico, bright as a cardinal rousted from the low branches of a white oak tree in winter. With a disgusted shake of his head, Sam reined in and dismounted, leaving the gelding to stand untethered while he strode toward the scene of recent mischief. A part of his mind stayed behind, with the animal—it was newly acquired, that horse, and the two of them had yet to form a proper acquaintance. All during the long ride south from his ranch just outside Flagstaff, he'd been too busy cogitating on the complexities of this

new assignment to consider much of anything else, going
over Major John Blackstone's orders again and again in
his head, sorting and sifting, weighing and measuring.

"Hold on," he called. The bucket rope was taut and quivering, and he recalled this particular trick from his own youth.

A male voice echoed from the depths of the water hole,
a shambling train of plaintive syllables rattling along a track
of hopeful goodwill. Sam recognized the keynote as relief.

*"I find myself in—obvious difficulties—and will—be
profoundly grateful for any assistance—"*

"Hold on," Sam repeated, the words underlaid with a
sigh. He was powerfully built—like a brick shithouse, the
boys in the bunkhouse liked to say—and seldom moved
quickly, except in a fight or when called upon to draw his
.45. He secured the rope with his left hand and reached for
the crank with the other, peering downward.

All he could make out, even squinting, were the soles
of two small, booted feet, bound at the ankles with what
looked like baling twine. Here was a dainty fellow, for sure
and certain—and most likely the incompetent schoolmaster Sam had come to relieve of his duties.

"I'm all right!" the teacher called cheerfully from the
pit. "Thomas P. Singleton, here!"

Sam felt chagrined that given the circumstances, he
hadn't thought to inquire after the man's well-being right
off, but kept cranking. He was a practical man, given to
engaging the crisis at hand and dealing with the conversa-
tional aspects of the situation later.

"That's good, Mr. Singleton," he said belatedly, and
when the ankles came within reach, he let go of the handle
and grabbed for them with both hands. Poor Tom resem-
bled a trussed gander, plucked and ready for the stew pot,
and he didn't weigh much more than one, either.

Sam hauled him out of the well and let him plop to the

LINDA LAEL MILLER

tinder-dry grass like a fresh-caught trout. He wasn't wet, so the water must be low.

Crouching, Sam pulled out his pocketknife and commenced to cutting the twine. The teacher's thin red hair stood straight up on his head, wild and crackling with static, as though it didn't subscribe to the law of gravity. The face beneath it was narrow, with pointy features and blue, watery eyes. The girlish lips curled into a self-deprecating smile.

"My replacement, I presume?" he asked, feeling for what turned out to be his pocket watch, still safe at the end of its tarnished chain, and tucking it away again with a relieved pat. Singleton was certainly a resilient sort; the way he acted, anybody would have thought the pair of them had just sat themselves down to a grand and sociable supper in some fancy Eastern restaurant instead of meeting the way they had. "I must say, your arrival was timely indeed."

Still resting on his haunches, Sam nodded in acknowledgment. "Sam O'Ballivan," he said, though he doubted an introduction was necessary. Up at Flagstaff, he'd heard all about the schoolmaster, and he figured the reverse was probably true. With a few pertinent details excepted, of course.

Singleton rubbed his rope-chafed wrists to restore the circulation, but he showed no inclination to stand up just yet. Poor little fella must have had noodles for legs, Sam reflected, after hanging upside down in the well like that. "Call me Tom," he said affably. "I am much obliged for your quick action on my behalf."

Sam let one corner of his mouth quirk upward. He was sparing with a smile; like names for horses, they meant something to him, and he gave them out only when he was good and ready. He made a stalwart friend, when he had a high opinion of somebody, but he took his time deciding such matters. He knew a little about Tom Singleton, much of it hearsay, but as to whether he liked the man or not... well, the vote was still untallied.

Small feet rustled the bushes nearby and a giggle or two rode the warm afternoon breeze. Valiantly, Singleton pretended not to hear, but there was a flush pulsing on his cheekbones. It had to be hard on a small man's dignity, being cranked up out of a schoolyard well by a big one, hired to take over his job. Sam wanted to tread lightly around what was left of Singleton's pride.

"You hurting anywhere?" Sam asked, rising to his feet and scanning the schoolyard. *Just you wait,* he told the hidden miscreants silently.

"Fit as a fiddle!" Singleton insisted. He tried to get up then, but Sam saw that he was fixing to crumple and withheld his hand out of regard for the fellow's self-respect. Sure enough, he went down.

"Best sit a spell," Sam said.

Another bush shivered, off to his left— No time like the present, he thought, and waded in, snatching up one of the offenders by his shirt collar and dragging him out into the open. The giggles turned to gasps and there was some powerful shrub-shaking as the rest of the gang lit out for safer ground. "And your name would be?"

The lad looked to be around twelve or thirteen, with a cap of chestnut-brown hair and strange, whiskey-colored eyes peering, at once scared and defiant, out of a freckled face. His clothes were plain, but of good sturdy quality, and he wore shoes, which marked him as somebody's pride and joy.

"Terran Chancelor," he answered, clearly begrudging the information. His gaze darted briefly to Singleton, who was just summoning up the gumption for another attempt at gaining his feet, and the sly pleasure in the kid's face made Sam want to shake him.

LINDA LAEL MILLER

Forbearing, Sam held him suspended, so the toes of his fine mail-order shoes just barely brushed the grass. "You the leader of this bunch of outlaws?" he asked.

"No," Chancelor snapped. "Put me down!"

Sam hoisted him an inch or two higher. "Maybe you'd like to hang upside down in the well for a while," he mused. It was a bluff, but the kid didn't need to know that. His eyes widened and he went a shade paler behind that constellation of freckles.

"I hope you're not the new schoolmaster," Terran Chancelor said with brave disdain. Sam wasn't sure how smart the kid was, but he had to credit him with grit.

He allowed himself a slow, wicked grin. "'Abandon hope, all ye who enter here,'" he quoted.

Chancelor frowned, gnawed at his lower lip. "What does *that* mean?" he asked, peevish. "Sounds like something out of some high-falutin' book."

Sam released his hold on the boy's shirt, watched as he dropped, swayed and found his balance. "It means, young Mr. Chancelor, that when you sit down at your desk bright and early tomorrow morning, here in the hallowed halls of learning, I'll be standing in front of the blackboard."

"Well, *hell*," the kid complained.

Sam suppressed a grin. "Peculiar that you should mention Hades," he said evenly. "That quote you just asked about is carved over the gate."

The boy's eyes widened again, but his color was high with fresh temper. He darted another glance at Singleton. "We were just having a little fun after school let out for the day, that's all. No harm done."

"I guess that depends on your viewpoint," Sam said mildly. "Whether or not there was any harm done, I mean. You tell your friends that I'll be happy to give any or all of them the same perspective Mr. Singleton here just enjoyed, if they're curious about how it feels."

Chancelor narrowed his eyes, looked as if he might be deciding whether he ought to spit in Sam's face. Fortunately for him, he didn't pursue that inclination. *Unfortunately* for him, he chose to run off at the mouth instead.

"You wouldn't dare," he said.

Quick as if he'd been wrestling a calf to the ground for branding, Sam hooked an arm around the boy's middle, tipped him over the rim of the well and caught a firm hold on his ankles. "There's where you're wrong, young Mr. Chancelor," he replied.

"My sister will have your hide for this!" the boy yelled, but his voice quavered as it bounced off the cold stone walls.

Sam chuckled. Singleton stared at him in horrified admiration.

"He's right, you know," Tom whispered earnestly. "Maddie Chancelor's got a tongue on her. She'll flay you to the bone."

"That right?" Sam asked. Bracing his elbows against the edge of the well, he let the kid dangle.

"The blood is probably rushing to his head," Singleton advised fretfully.

"Good for his brain," Sam said companionably.

"Get me out of here!" Terran sputtered, squirming. *"Right now!"*

"I wouldn't flail around like that, if I were you," Sam counseled. "Hell of a thing if you came out of those splendid boots of yours and took a spill. Fall like that, you'd probably break your fool neck."

The boy heeded Sam's advice and went still. "What do you want?" he asked, sounding just shy of reasonable.

"For a start," Sam answered, "a sincere apology."

LINDA LAEL MILLER

"What do I have to say 'sorry' to *you* for?"

Sam wondered idly about Maddie Chancelor and what kind of influence she might have in this little cowpattie of a town, plopped right along the border between Mexico and the Arizona Territory like an egg on a griddle. If she was anything like her brother, she must be a caution, as well as a shrew.

"Not a thing," he replied at his leisure. "But a kindly word to Mr. Singleton here wouldn't go amiss."

Sam felt a quiver of rage rise right up the length of that boy, then along the rope, like grounded lightning coursing back through a metal rod.

"All right!" Chancelor bellowed. "I'm sorry!"

"'I'm sorry, Mr. Singleton,'" Sam prompted.

"I'm sorry, Mr. Singleton," the boy repeated. His tone was neither as dutiful nor as earnest as it might have been, but Sam yanked him up anyhow and set him hard on his feet. The fury in the kid's eyes could have singed the bristles off a full-grown boar, but he held his tongue.

There might be hope for this one yet, Sam concluded silently, folding his arms as he regarded the furious youth.

"Go home and tell your sister," Sam said, "that the new schoolmaster will be stopping by shortly to discuss the calamitous state of your character."

The boy glowered at him in barely contained outrage, fists clenched, eyes fierce. "She'll be expecting you." He spat the words, simultaneously leaping backward, out of reach, ready to run. "Don't bother to unpack your gear. You won't be around here long."

Sam raised an eyebrow, took a step toward the kid.

He turned and fled down the road Sam had just traveled, arms pumping at his sides, feet raising little puffs of dust.

By then, Singleton had recovered his composure. "You're in for some trouble," he said with friendly regret, consulting his pocket watch and starting for the school-house. "Might as well show you around, though. I have an hour before the stage leaves for Tucson."

Leaving his horse to graze on the sweet grass, Sam followed. "Where will I find the formidable Maddie Chancelor?" he asked.

Singleton mounted three plank steps and pushed open the schoolhouse door, which creaked ominously on its hinges. "She's the postmistress, and she runs the mercantile, too," he answered with a note of bleak resignation. "When she hears how you hung young Terran headfirst down the well, she's not going to like it. They're alone in the world, the pair of them, and she protects that little scoundrel like a she-bear guarding a cub."

Sam digested the information as he crossed the threshold into a small, square room. There were long tables, rough-hewn, with benches, facing a blackboard on the east wall. A potbellied stove stood in one corner, with wood neatly stacked alongside. A few reading and ciphering primers lined a shelf next to the teacher's desk, and the place smelled of chalk. Dust motes danced in the light coming in through the high, narrow windows.

Singleton looked around wistfully, sighed.

Sam felt a twinge of sympathy, wondering if a lone incident had spurred those little hellions to act, or if anarchy was the order of the day around here. He wasn't about to ask, figuring the man had been through enough mortification as it was, but he'd have put his money on the latter.

"Your private quarters are back here," Singleton said after a long and melancholy pause, making for an inside door. "It isn't much, but the roof keeps out the rain, and there's a decent bed and a cookstove."

Sam was used to sleeping on the ground, wrapped up

in a bedroll. The accommodations sounded downright luxurious to him.

"Not that you'll want to stay long, even if Miss Chancelor doesn't get you fired," Singleton added. Two carpetbags waited at the foot of the bed and he stooped to fetch them up while Sam surveyed his new home.

"Looks like it'll do," he decided. The more he heard about Maddie Chancelor, the more he wanted to meet her.

Singleton stooped to pick up the satchels. Smiled gamely. "Good luck, Mr. O'Ballivan," he said. "And thank you again for your help."

"Good luck to you," Sam replied, a little embarrassed by the other man's gratitude. Anybody worth his bacon would have stepped in, in a circumstance like that.

Singleton set down one of the bags long enough to shake Sam's hand. "May God be with you," he added in parting. Then he crossed the room, opened the rear door and left, without looking back.

MADDIE CHANCELOR was measuring flour into a tin canister to fill Mrs. Ezra T. Burke's weekly grocery order, when Terran burst into the store, shirttail out, hair rumpled, face aflame.

"The new teacher's here," he blurted before she could ask if he'd been fighting again, "and he just tried his best to kill me!"

Instant alarm swelled within Maddie's breast, fair cutting off her wind, and her hands trembled as she set the scoop aside on the counter. "*Kill* you? What on earth…?"

"He would have drowned me in the well if I hadn't got the best of him," Terran insisted.

"Drowned you in the—"

"Well," Terran finished in furious triumph.

Maddie untied her apron laces as she rounded the

counter to examine her younger brother for injuries. He looked sound, and for someone who had nearly been murdered by drowning, he was remarkably dry, too.

"Tell me what happened," she said, grateful, for once, that the mercantile was empty.

Terran gulped visibly. "He got me by the feet and tried to drop me down the schoolyard well," he burst out. "I hid out in the brush, after I got away, or he'd have finished me for sure!"

Maddie's heart seized at the image of her brother, her only living relation, suspended from such a height. Haven was a wild town, a crossroads for rogues, scalawags and scoundrels from both sides of the border, but she hadn't expected the new schoolmaster to number among them. Anxiously she looked Terran over again. "You're certain you haven't been hurt?"

Terran nodded. "He said he'd be by here, real soon, to talk to you. He's going to tell you a whole passel of lies, Maddie. He'll say—"

Just then, the little brass bell over the door jingled and a man entered, removing his hat as he traversed the threshold.

Terran took one look at him and bolted for the stairs at the back of the store to take refuge in their rooms.

Maddie's face flamed. "You must be the new schoolmaster," she said.

He smiled, nodded. "Sam O'Ballivan," he replied. "And you must be Miss Chancelor."

Maddie gave a curt nod. Sam O'Ballivan was clean-shaven and muscular, probably six feet in height, with brown hair and shrewd blue eyes. He looked more like an outlaw than a schoolmaster, and she was sure the distinctive bulge under his long suit coat was the butt of a pistol. What had Mr. Callaway and the other members of the school board been thinking, to hire such a man?

LINDA LAEL MILLER

"How dare you assault my brother?" she asked evenly, when she could trust herself to speak at all.

Mr. O'Ballivan's mouth tilted upward at one corner. He kept his distance, though, which meant Maddie didn't have to go for the shotgun she kept under the counter in case of trouble. "Is that what he told you? Guess he's got a devious side, to go along with that mean streak of his."

Maddie felt like a kettle coming to a boil. "Terran is not a liar, nor does he have a 'mean streak,'" she managed to say. "And it's a fine how-do-you-do, your saying that, when you tried to drown him!"

O'Ballivan chuckled, and what looked like mischievous derision glinted briefly in his eyes. His blatant masculinity seemed to take over the whole store, like some ominous, unseen force. Maddie would have described him as rugged, rather than handsome, if she'd been thinking along such lines.

Which she most definitely wasn't.

"The truth, Miss Chancelor, is somewhat at variance with your brother's account of the incident in question," O'Ballivan said. "When I rode up, he and the rest of that pack of rascals had Tom Singleton hog-tied and hanging headfirst down the well. God knows how long he'd have dangled if I hadn't come along when I did."

Maddie blinked. *It wasn't true,* she told herself firmly. *Terran would never be involved in anything like that.*

"I don't believe you," she said.

"You don't *choose* to believe me," he remarked idly, examining a display of dime novels Maddie had spent much of the morning arranging. She disapproved heartily of yellow journalism, but the plain fact was, folks were willing to spend money on those little books, and she couldn't afford not to carry the merchandise.

At long last O'Ballivan's gaze swung back, colliding

with hers. Maddie felt a peculiar niggling in the pit of her stomach.

"You're not doing your brother any favors, you know, by taking his part when you know he's in the wrong," he said.

"Did you or did you not try to drown him?"

"If I'd tried to drown him," O'Ballivan said reasonably, "I would have succeeded. All I did was demonstrate that hanging headfirst down a well, while memorable, is not a desirable experience."

Maddie swallowed so hard it hurt. "What if you'd dropped him?"

"I wouldn't have," he responded, damnably self-assured.

She slipped behind the counter again, in case she needed the shotgun. "I will not tolerate that kind of rough treatment," she insisted, making an effort to keep her voice from rising. "Terran is a *child,* Mr. O'Ballivan."

He drew near enough to rest his hands between the pickle crock and a pyramid of bright red tobacco cans. "Terran," he said, "is a spoiled, bullying brat. And *I,* Miss Chancelor, will not tolerate the sort of behavior I witnessed today. I was hired to restore order in that school, and I will do it—however many times I have to hold your brother over a well by his feet. Do we understand each other?"

Maddie felt heat surge up her neck to pulse along her cheekbones, and her ears burned. "If you lay a hand on him again," she said, "I will have you dismissed."

He smiled slightly. "Then I guess we *do* understand each other. You're welcome to try to get rid of me, Miss Chancelor, but if what I saw in that schoolyard a little while ago is typical, I'd say I'm just the kind of teacher this town needs."

"You don't *look* like a schoolmaster," Maddie said.

"And you don't look like a storekeeper," Mr. O'Ballivan retorted. "I guess appearances can be deceiving."

Maddie resisted an impulse to pat her hair, which tended

LINDA LAEL MILLER

to be unruly and was forever coming down from its pins. "What does a storekeeper look like?" she retorted.

"What does a schoolmaster look like?" he countered.

Maddie sighed and glanced hopefully toward the door, wishing the man would leave and stop taking up all the room in her store. "If you have no further business here, Mr. O'Ballivan—"

"It happens that I do," he said, and she knew by the light in his eyes that he enjoyed baiting her. "I'd like to collect my mail. You are the postmistress, aren't you?"

Letters and packages came into Haven once a week, on the stagecoach, which had been and gone by four o'clock that afternoon. Busy with Mrs. Burke's order, which she had promised to deliver personally after closing, she'd told the driver to put the mail in the back room and promptly forgotten all about it.

"Yes," Maddie said. "I am the postmistress. But I haven't had a chance to do any sorting."

"There should be a parcel addressed to me," O'Ballivan told her, and showed no sign of moving away from the counter, let alone leaving the premises.

Maddie glanced at the large, loud-ticking clock on the far wall, above the display window. "I'm about to close for the day."

Again, that slow, thoughtful smile. "Well, then," Sam O'Ballivan said, "if you'll just point me to that parcel, I'll be on my way."

Maddie sighed. "I'll get it for you," she conceded, and turned away.

"It's bound to be too heavy," he argued, and came right around the end of the counter without so much as a by-your-leave. "Just show me where it is."

Impatient, Maddie tossed aside the curtain covering the entrance to the back of the store and gestured toward the

THE MAN FROM STONE CREEK

corner where the mail had been stowed. Sure enough, there was a very large box wrapped in brown paper and tied with heavy string.

Mr. O'Ballivan lifted it with one hand, tilted it slightly so she could see the large, slanted letters on the face of the package: S. O'Ballivan, c/o General Delivery, Haven, Arizona Territory.

He'd saved her the awkwardness of asking for proof that the parcel belonged to him before releasing it, but Maddie wasn't grateful. She just wanted him gone, so she could close the store, tally the books and deliver Mrs. Burke's groceries. She wanted the place to expand to its normal size, so she could breathe.

"Obliged," he said, pausing in the front doorway to don his hat again. He tugged lightly at the brim.

"Goodbye, Mr. O'Ballivan," Maddie said pointedly, right on his heels. She put one hand on the door lock, eager to latch it behind him.

He shifted the parcel from one hand to the other, as easily as if it were a basket of eggs. "Until next time," he said, and touched his hat brim again.

Maddie, already moving to shut the door, frowned. "Do you receive a lot of mail?"

"No," Mr. O'Ballivan replied, "but I expect we'll have a few more rounds over your brother."

Maddie gave the door a shove and latched it.

Mr. O'Ballivan smiled at her through the glass.

She wrenched down the shade.

As she turned away, she was certain she heard him laugh.

BACK IN HIS ROOM behind the schoolhouse, Sam built a fire in the stove, ladled water into the coffeepot that came with the place, along with the last of Tom Singleton's stash of ground beans, and set the concoction on to boil.

LINDA LAEL MILLER

If Miss Maddie Chancelor hadn't run him off so quickly, he'd have had time to lay in a few staples. As things stood, he'd need to take his supper at the saloon and bring the leftovers home for breakfast.

After school let out tomorrow, he'd go back to the mercantile.

Like as not, Miss Maddie wouldn't be all that glad to see him.

Sam smiled at the thought and turned his attention to the parcel. He'd packed the books himself, before starting the trip down from Stone Creek, and taken them to the stagecoach office for shipping. Now, he looked forward to putting up his feet when he got back from taking his meal, and reading until the lamp ran low on kerosene.

Of course, he'd have to shake Maddie's image loose from his mind before he'd be able to concentrate worth a damn.

After what the boy and Singleton had said, he'd expected someone entirely different. An aging, mean-eyed spinster with warts, maybe. Or a rough-edged Calamity Jane sort of woman, brawny enough to do a man's work.

The real Maddie had come as quite a surprise, with her slender figure and thick, reddish-brown hair, ready to tumble down over her back and shoulders at the slightest provocation. She couldn't have been much past twenty-five, and while that probably qualified her as an old maid, it was a pure wonder to him that some lonely bachelor hadn't tumbled right into those rum-colored eyes and snatched her up a long time ago. Women such as her were few and far between, this far west of the Mississippi, and generally had their choice of men.

Her temperament was on the cussed side, it was true, but there was fire in her; he'd felt the heat the moment he'd stepped into the mercantile and locked eyes with her.

He smiled again as he opened the stove door and stuck

in another chunk of wood, hoping to get the coffee perking sooner and wondering how long it would be before the lady organized a campaign to send the new schoolmaster down the road.

Satisfied that the stove was doing the best it could, Sam opened the box to unpack his books. Except for his horse, Dionysus, grazing on sweet hay up in the high country while a lame leg mended, he treasured these worn and oft-read volumes more than anything else he owned. Some were warped by damp weather and creek water, having traveled miles in his saddlebags, while others had been scarred by sparks from forgotten campfires.

All of them were old friends, and Sam handled them tenderly as he silently welcomed each one to a new home. When he got time, he'd find a plank of wood somewhere and put up a shelf they could stand on. In the meantime, they made good company, sitting right there on the table.

He'd attended to the gelding earlier, staking it on a long line in the tall grass behind the schoolhouse, where a little stream made its crooked way from hither to yon, and stowed his tack in the woodshed. Now, as twilight thickened around the walls and purpled the windowpanes, he lit a lamp and used his shirttail to wipe out the blue metal mug he carried with him whenever he left the ranch.

He'd just poured coffee when a light knock sounded at the back door.

Sam arched an eyebrow and checked to make sure his .45 was within easy reach, there on the rickety table next to the bed. He wasn't expecting anybody.

"Mr. O'Ballivan?" a female voice called, thin as a shred of frayed ribbon. "Are you to home?"

Curious, Sam opened the door.

The woman stood in a dim wash of moonlight, holding a basket and smiling up at him. Since no proper lady would

LINDA LAEL MILLER

have come calling on an unmarried man, especially after dark, he wasn't surprised by her skimpy attire. She was a dance hall girl.

She laughed at his expression. "I brung you some vittles," she said, and shoved the basket at him. "Compliments of Miss Oralee Pringle, over to the Rattlesnake Saloon. She said to tell you welcome to Haven, and be sure to pay us a visit first chance you get. I don't reckon I ought to come in?"

Sam cleared his throat, accepted the basket. It felt warm in his hands and smelled deliciously of fresh-baked bread and fried chicken. His stomach growled. "I don't suppose you ought to," he agreed, at a loss. "But thank you, Miss—?"

The response was a coy smile. "My name is Bird of Paradise," she said, "but you can call me Bird."

Sam frowned. Behind that mask of powder and kohl was the face of a schoolgirl. "How old are you?"

"Old enough," Bird replied lightly, waggling her fingers at him over one bare shoulder as she turned to go.

Sam opened his mouth, closed it again.

Bird disappeared into the darkness.

He stood in the doorway, staring after her for a long time. He'd pay a call on Oralee Pringle first chance he got, he decided, but he had more in mind than returning the basket.

CHAPTER
TWO

ESTEBAN VIERRA waited until well after nightfall before crossing the river from the Mexican side; he prided himself on his ability to move freely in the darkness, like a cat. Leaving his horse to graze on the bank, he made his way through the cottonwoods and thistly underbrush to the schoolhouse, pausing to admire the Ranger's mount. The click of a pistol cylinder, somewhere behind him, made him freeze.

It stung him, this chink in his prowess, and he felt more irritation than fear.

"Hold your hands out from your sides," a voice instructed.

Vierra obeyed calmly. "O'Ballivan?" he asked.

He heard the revolver slide back into the holster with a deftness that spoke volumes about the man at his back. "Yes."

He turned. "That's a fine horse," he said cordially. "I hope it's fast."

O'Ballivan's expression was grim, his craggy features

LINDA LAEL MILLER

defined by the play of light and shadow. "What are you doing here? My instructions were to meet you tomorrow night, on the other side of the river."

Vierra smiled. "I got curious," he said.

The Ranger parted with the briefest of grins, his teeth flashing white in the gloom. "You could have got *dead*," he replied. "And if you've no better sense than to come prowling around another man's horse in the night, this whole plan might need some review."

"Don't you trust me?" Vierra asked, his aggrieved tone at some variance with his easy smile.

"I don't know you from Adam's Aunt Bessie," O'Ballivan responded, one hand still resting lightly on the butt of his revolver. "Of *course* I don't trust you."

"That could be a problem. Maybe we ought to get better acquainted."

O'Ballivan looked him over. "Maybe," he said cautiously. "You're Mexican. How is it that you don't have an accent?"

Vierra shrugged. "I think in Spanish," he said. "And I *do* have an accent. I borrowed yours."

"What do you know about these outlaws we're after?" O'Ballivan asked after a long and pensive silence.

"Ah," Vierra said, folding his arms. "You just said you don't trust me. Why should *I* trust *you?*"

"I don't reckon you do," O'Ballivan observed dryly.

Vierra was pleased. Here was a worthy opponent, a rare phenomenon in his experience, one he could spar with. "I have been offered a very large reward, in gold, if I bring these *banditos* back to certain anxious *rancheros* in my country," he said. Often, he'd discovered, a superficial truth was the most effective means of deception. It made most people complacent.

Of course, O'Ballivan clearly wasn't most people.

"They've done plenty on this side of the border," the

Ranger said. "My orders are to turn them in to a certain federal judge in Tucson."

"Two men, working toward the same end, but with very different objectives," Vierra allowed, still smiling. "Tell me—are the *Americanos* offering a bounty? Is that why you are doing this?"

O'Ballivan shook his head. "A man I respect asked me to track the murdering bastards down and bring them in, dead or alive. That's payment enough for me."

Vierra spread his hands. "Then there is no misunderstanding," he said.

"No misunderstanding at all," O'Ballivan agreed. "Good night, Señor Vierra."

"You will be at the meeting place tomorrow night? The cantina in Refugio?"

O'Ballivan, turning to go, paused to look back over one brawny shoulder and nod. "Tomorrow night," he confirmed, and moved toward the schoolhouse.

Vierra watched him out of sight, then gave a low whistle through his teeth. The Ranger's horse came to him, and he stroked its fine neck with one hand before retreating into the darkness.

SAM ASSESSED HIS CROP of pupils as they filed obediently into the schoolroom the next morning and took their places without a word or a glance in his direction.

Terran Chancelor's presence surprised him a little; he'd half expected Maddie to undertake the remainder of her brother's education personally, if only to keep him safe from the fiendish new schoolteacher. But here he was, faced scrubbed, hair brushed, hands folded, sitting square in the middle at the front table.

There were four girls, of varying ages, the youngest barely larger than a china doll he'd seen once in a store

LINDA LAEL MILLER

window, the eldest nearly grown and already taking his measure as husband material, unless he missed his guess. The two in between, eight or nine years old by his estimate, looked enough alike to be sisters.

The boys added up to nine, and they, too, ranged from near babyhood to strapping.

When they were settled, Sam turned to the blackboard and picked up a nubbin of chalk. "My name," he told them, "is Sam O'Ballivan." On the board he signed his name the way he always did.

SO'B.

A few snickers rose, as expected.

Sam faced the gathering, careful to keep his expression sober.

The blond boy sitting next to Terran was still grinning.

"Your name?" Sam inquired.

"Ben Donagher," the lad replied.

"You're amused, Mr. Donagher?"

Donagher's grin widened. "Well, it's just that SOB means—"

Sam pointed the bit of chalk at him. "Yes?"

"Son of a bitch," the boy said.

Sam nodded. "You'd do well to remember that," he replied.

Donagher flushed and lowered his gaze.

Terran gave his seatmate a subtle jab of the elbow.

"You have something to add, Mr. Chancelor?" Sam wanted to know.

More giggles, mostly stifled.

"No, sir," Terran said, but his eyes glittered and it was clearly all he could do not to laugh.

Sam put down the chalk and rested a hip on the edge of his desk. "When I arrived yesterday," he began, "there was an incident under way. Mr. Chancelor had the misfortune to be caught, but I've got a pretty good idea who else was involved."

The smallest girl raised her hand eagerly. "I didn't do nothin', Mr. SOB," she spouted. "I went straight home, because my mama said she'd thrash my behind if the chickens didn't get fed."

Laughter erupted. Sam bit the inside of his lip, so he wouldn't smile, and waited it out. "Mr. O'Ballivan," he corrected.

Tears welled in the little girl's eyes; she seemed to shrink, as if trying to fold in on herself until she disappeared entirely.

"Violet's a tit-baby," somebody said.

"She makes water in her bloomers," added another voice.

"Her papa got hisself hanged for horse thieving."

Sam scanned the room. "Enough," he said quietly.

The resulting silence was profound.

He went to where Violet huddled at the far end of the back table and crouched beside her. A tear slid down her cheek and puddled on the slate resting in her lap. Up close, he noticed that her calico dress was faded and thin with wear, and she smelled pungently of urine, wood smoke and general neglect.

Sam laid a tentative hand on her small, bony back. "When you want to use the outhouse, Violet," he said, "you don't have to raise your hand for permission. You just get right up and go."

Violet nodded miserably, unable to lift her head. "Mr. Singleton made me wait," she whispered.

Sam patted her awkwardly on one small, hunched shoulder and straightened to address the rest of the class. "I will not countenance bullying," he said. "Ask Mr. Chancelor if you don't believe me."

Terran flushed vividly, keeping his gaze fixed straight ahead, but no one made a sound.

"Now," Sam said, "let's get down to business. How many of you know how to read and write?"

IT WAS THREE FORTY-FIVE by the big clock on the mercantile wall when Sam O'Ballivan strode in. Maddie felt his presence, even before she stole a glance to confirm it. She drew a deep breath and smiled at Undine Donagher, who had come to town to order ready-made dresses from the catalog.

There were no other customers; folks tended to stay clear of the store when the Donaghers stopped by, which was often, since they owned the establishment.

"Maybe this silk would do," Maddie suggested warmly.

Undine, the pretty and youthful wife of Mungo Donagher, a grizzled old rancher who probably tallied his land holdings in counties instead of acres, was someone Maddie dreaded rather than welcomed, even though Undine invariably spent a great deal of money when she went on a buying tangent. Because Mungo liked to keep the accounts straight, he made all his purchases like any other customer would.

Undine turned to look at Sam and her petulant expression went coquettish. Mungo, occupying himself with a display of rifles, seemed to sense the shift of his wife's attention and turned, frowning, to watch the exchange.

Undine tugged at her white gloves, with their rows of tiny pearl buttons, and smiled, ignoring her husband. "I don't believe we've met," she said, and walked right over to Mr. O'Ballivan as if they'd encountered each other at a soiree. "I'd have remembered anybody as handsome as you are."

Sam nodded with solemn cordiality, a flush darkening his neck, and took a box from the stack next to the door. "Howdy," he said, and his gaze skittered to Maddie.

She realized that her mouth was open, and closed it again, but not quickly enough, she saw, to fool Mr. O'Ballivan. The flicker in his eyes told her he'd registered her disapproval of Undine's bold behavior and found it amusing.

Recovering her manners, Maddie said, "Mrs. Donagher, this is Mr. O'Ballivan, the new schoolmaster."

Before she could introduce Mungo, he stepped between Undine and Mr. O'Ballivan, extending a work-roughened, pawlike hand in greeting. His manner was one of blustery goodwill, but Maddie wasn't fooled, and neither, apparently, was Mr. O'Ballivan. A muscle bunched in his jaw even as he shook Mungo's hand.

Undine, her flirtation thwarted, pushed out her lower lip and retreated to the counter, where she and Maddie had been poring over the catalog.

"You look like you might just be able to handle that bunch over to the schoolhouse," Mungo boomed, apparently determined to keep the conversation going. "One of those whelps is mine. Name's Ben. He gives you any trouble, you just haul him off to the woodshed and tan his hide."

A motion at the window drew Maddie's eyes, and she saw her brother peering through the glass. When he spotted Sam O'Ballivan, he recoiled visibly and hurried off down the sidewalk.

"I don't make much use of the woodshed," O'Ballivan said.

Maddie's temper heated. No, she thought. You just hang innocent children upside down in the well by their feet and scare the life out of them.

Mungo laughed, fairly rattling the canned goods on the shelves. It was not a friendly sound; Mungo Donagher was not a friendly man. In fact, most people feared him, along with his three older sons, who were, in Maddie's opinion, little better than criminals. She stayed close to the shotgun when any of them were in the store.

LINDA LAEL MILLER

"I hope you're a better man than poor Tom Singleton," Mungo said. "Those snot-nosed little devils stampeded right over him. Thought he might toughen up, but he didn't."

Maddie glanced at Undine, saw a faint blush rise in the woman's cheeks and the slightest tightening around the mouth. She wondered about that, but only briefly, because the exchange between Sam O'Ballivan and the patriarch was building up steam.

"Yes," O'Ballivan agreed mildly, selecting a cake of yellow soap from those on offer and dropping it into the box in the curve of his left arm, moving on, and then going back for another. This time, he chose the fancy, scented kind, French-milled and wrapped in pretty paper. It cost the earth, and Maddie's curiosity was piqued again. "I saw the evidence of that yesterday. I'll need two pounds of coffee, Miss Chancelor. A pound of sugar, too." He proceeded to add tins of peaches, tomatoes and green beans to his purchases.

"A man's got no business teaching if he can't ride herd on a few brats." Mungo thundered on. "'Course it's usually a woman's job. Teaching school, I mean. My older boys always favored a schoolmarm."

I'll just bet they did, Maddie thought, watching Sam O'Ballivan closely while trying to pretend she'd barely noticed him at all.

O'Ballivan didn't answer. Occupied with his shopping, he reached down for a shaving brush, then a razor, then tooth powder. Maddie wondered, as she had from the first moment of their acquaintance, why a man like that would want to spend his days writing on a blackboard in a border town like Haven. He must have felt confined in the schoolhouse, a place hardly big enough to accommodate the width of his shoulders, and his skin was weathered, as if he'd spent much of his life outdoors.

Maddie knew the salary allotted to the teacher was

paltry, since she attended school board meetings, and besides, Mungo was right. Most teachers were female. Mr. Singleton had been an exception, hired after his predecessor eloped with a medicine peddler three weeks into the school term. And now here was Sam O'Ballivan, who looked more like a hired gunslinger than anything else.

"I guess you didn't hear me say most teachers are female," Mungo said, sounding less jovial now as O'Ballivan set the box on the counter and proceeded to examine a large copper washtub hanging on the wall.

"Oh, I heard you, all right," he replied, hoisting the tub down from its peg. "It just didn't seem like the sort of remark that called for an answer."

The air fairly crackled.

Maddie debated whether or not she ought to stipulate that she didn't sell on credit, since the tub was one of the most expensive items she carried, but she didn't want to be the next one to speak.

Meanwhile, Undine had recovered her aplomb. "We'd be honored to have you come to our place for supper, Mr. O'Ballivan," she said. Mungo turned to glower at her, but she went right on ignoring him.

Sam set the tub on the counter. "I accept," he said.

Mungo seemed taken aback, and Maddie was a little surprised herself. A mite irritated, too, though she couldn't have said why.

Undine batted her thick lashes and posed, as if for a daguerreotypist about to take her likeness. "Would tonight be too soon?"

"Unfortunately," Sam said, "I have a prior commitment."

Undine was the image of sweet disappointment. "Tomorrow, then?"

"Tomorrow will be fine," Sam replied.

LINDA LAEL MILLER

Maddie risked a sidelong peek at Mungo, who looked as if his thick head of white hair might be about to fly upward and stick to the ceiling. Was O'Ballivan such a fool that he didn't know where he wasn't welcome? Or was he simply unable to resist Undine Donagher's undeniable charms?

"Seven o'clock, then," Undine chimed, twinkling. "The ranch house is five miles east of here, along the river trail."

Sam nodded. "I'll be there," he said.

"Bring Miss Chancelor here along with you," Mungo added. It wasn't an invitation. It was an order, thrust into the exchange like a fist.

Maddie opened her mouth to protest.

"That's a fine idea," Sam replied before she could get a word out.

Undine's face fell. Mungo took a hard grip on her elbow and ushered her toward the door. "I'll send a ranch hand back for the goods we bought," the rancher announced without turning his head.

"I was just being neighborly," Undine was heard to say as Mungo fairly hurled her outside.

Maddie stared after them, confounded.

Sam O'Ballivan helped himself to a towel, four cotton shirts and a shiny new bucket.

"This tub costs eight dollars," Maddie pointed out when she'd had a few moments to recover. "I don't—"

Mr. O'Ballivan paused, took a wallet from the inside pocket of his coat and inspected the contents thoughtfully. Even from where she stood, Maddie could see that he had plenty of money, and that made her wonder even more.

"I think I can cover it," he concluded, replacing the wallet.

"Who are you?" Maddie demanded. It was her nature, after all, to be forthright, and she'd held her curiosity in check as long as she could.

He added three pairs of socks to the pile. "You don't have much of a memory," he said. "I believe I've already introduced myself."

Maddie rounded the counter and advanced, setting her hands on her hips and forcing him to stop and face her. "I guess you didn't notice that Mungo Donagher doesn't want you coming to his house for supper."

Sam's mouth quirked again, though he didn't actually smile. "Now that hurts my feelings," he said. "The invitation sounded sincere enough to me."

Maddie gave an exasperated sigh. "Oh, it was *sincere,* all right. Undine meant every word of it. It's Mungo I'm worried about."

"Now why would you worry about Mungo or anything else, Miss Chancelor?"

Maddie knotted her hands in her apron, so she wouldn't box Sam O'Ballivan's ears. "You're new in Haven, and you obviously have the sensibilities of a hitching post, so I'll tell you," she said. "Mr. Donagher is a hard man. He's vengeful and he's rich, and when folks get on his bad side, they tend to meet with sudden misfortune."

"I do appreciate your concern, Miss Chancelor, but I'm not afraid of that old coot. Do you have any storybooks?"

Maddie blinked. "Storybooks?"

Sam's eyes danced. "For kids," he explained with the sort of patience one usually reserves for an idiot.

Maddie gestured toward a table in the far corner of the store, followed determinedly when Sam headed in that direction. She was about to pursue the subject of his identity again when she noticed the reverent way he chose and examined a volume of fairy tales. It made her throat tighten.

"My mother used to read those stories to me," she said, and then could have bitten off her tongue at the hinge. Mr.

O'Ballivan's gaze came straight to her face, and she felt exposed, as if her memories were no more private than the goods displayed in the window at the front of the store.

"Did she?" he asked quietly.

Maddie swallowed, nodded. Looked away.

Sam caught her chin between his thumb and the curve of his forefinger. His flesh was calloused, giving the lie, yet again, to his being a schoolmaster. He turned her head so she had to meet his eyes.

His touch made her nerves spark under her skin. She wanted to pull away, but she couldn't quite make herself do it. In fact, she couldn't even speak, so she just stood there, like a fool, astounded by her own weakness.

"How is it that you're not married, Maddie Chancelor?" Sam asked gravely, and let his hand fall back to his side.

Maddie moistened her lips. It was a forward question, one he had no right to ask. She was surprised when she heard herself answer. "I was engaged once," she said softly. "He was killed."

She waited for the pain that always came when she merely thought of Warren, let alone mentioned him out loud, but it didn't come.

"I'm sorry," Sam O'Ballivan said solemnly.

"It's been five years," Maddie answered, and was grateful when the bell jingled over the door. She'd been alone with Mr. O'Ballivan, or whoever he was, for much too long.

ONCE HE'D SETTLED UP his bill and Maddie had promised to send Terran around in a buckboard with the things he'd bought, Sam left the store. The basket Bird had brought him the night before was on the bench on the sidewalk, where he'd left it.

He'd return it to Oralee Pringle, with his thanks, and ask

THE MAN FROM STONE CREEK

her about Bird while he was at it. A good part of his mind stayed behind, though, worrying at Maddie Chancelor like an old dog with a soup bone.

She'd loved a man, five years ago, enough to say she'd marry him.

Why did it open a hollow place inside him, knowing that? Maddie was a beautiful woman, and she must have had suitors right along. Had she laid her heart in the casket, with her intended, and closed the lid on it for good? And why should it matter to him, anyway, when he was all but promised to the major's daughter?

He crossed the street, weaving his way between horses and wagons, and strode along the wooden sidewalk toward the Rattlesnake. The tinny strains of an out-of-tune piano spilled over the swinging doors and he paused outside, trying to shake off his melancholy mood.

An old, swaybacked horse stood at the water trough, square in front of the saloon, a little apart from the others, reins hanging loose. He was spotted, and his ribs showed.

Sam paused to pat him. "You look about as sorrowful as I feel," he said.

"You brought the basket back."

Sam turned his head, saw that Bird had stepped out of the saloon to stand on the sidewalk. In the light of day, she looked even younger than she had the night before. She wore a red dress that showed her legs and too much bosom, and her face was freshly painted.

"I'm obliged," he said, still stroking the horse. "That was the best supper I've had in a long time."

Bird smiled and took the basket. "I guess you meant to thank Oralee," she said. "She's gone to Tucson. Won't be back until tomorrow sometime."

Sam nodded.

Bird lingered. "That's Dobbin," she said, indicating the

LINDA LAEL MILLER

horse. "He's a pitiful old fella, isn't he? Belongs to Charlie Wilcox. Stands out here, patient as the saints, all day every day, waiting for Charlie to finish swilling whiskey and ride him on home. Charlie'd never get back to that shack of his if it wasn't for Dobbin."

Sam felt a pang of sympathy for the horse. Wished he could put him out to pasture, with Dionysus, come summer, and let him eat his fill of good grass.

He stepped away from Dobbin, stood looking down at Bird.

"You gonna ask me how old I am again?" she asked, smiling up into his face.

"I'd like to," he said, "but I reckon I'd be wasting my breath."

"I'm seventeen," she told him.

More like fifteen, he thought, sorrier for her than he was for the horse. "How did you end up working in a place like the Rattlesnake Saloon?" he asked.

She shrugged. "Just makin' my way in the world," she replied without a trace of self-pity. "We've all got to do that, don't we?"

"I guess we do," Sam agreed. "Don't you have any folks?"

"Just a sister," Bird said. "She's married, and I was a trial to her, so she showed me the road. You comin' inside?"

Sam shook his head, pondering. He'd never had a sister, but if he had, he wouldn't have turned her out, whether she was a trial to him or not.

Bird looked crestfallen. "How come you don't like me?" she blurted. "Most men take to me right away."

"I like you fine," Sam said. "That's the problem."

She went from crestfallen to confused. "I don't understand."

"I don't imagine you do." On impulse, he reached out,

took her hand, squeezed it lightly. "If you ever need help, Bird, you come to me."

She smiled sadly. "It's too late for that," she said. Then, carrying the basket, she turned and hurried back into the saloon.

Sam stared after her for a few bleak moments, patted Dobbin again, then headed back toward the schoolhouse.

One of these days he was going to stop wanting to save worn-out horses and misguided girls and a whole lot of other things. It would be pure, blessed relief when that day came.

CHAPTER

THREE

SAM WAS OUT BACK of the schoolhouse, splitting wood for the fire, when Terran rolled up at the reins of an ancient buckboard, drawn by two sorry-looking horses, one mud-brown, the other a pink-eyed pinto. Their hooves wanted trimming, he reflected, lodging the ax in the chopping block and dusting his hands together. If he'd had his hasp handy, he'd have undertaken the job right then and there.

Terran, perched on the seat, drew up the team, set the brake lever with a deft motion of one foot, and jumped to the ground. Sam's copper tub gleamed in the bed of the wagon, catching the last fierce rays of the setting sun.

The boy rounded the buckboard, lowered the tailgate with a creak of hinges, and scrambled in to haul the boxes to the rear, where Sam was waiting to claim them.

"Too bad you ain't a lady," Terran remarked, admiring the tub. "You could give Violet Perkins a sudsing."

Sam hoisted the box containing his coffee, sugar, canned goods and toiletries. "There are worse things," he observed, "than smelling bad."

"That depends," Terran replied, sliding back another box, "on whether or not you're downwind from her."

Holding back a smile, Sam set the first crate on the ground and reached for the second. "Is it true that Violet's father was hanged for a horse thief?"

Terran paused to meet his gaze. "Somebody lynched him, that's for sure," he answered solemnly. "Maddie thinks it was the Donagher brothers."

"I take it there's no law in this town," Sam ventured. He'd seen a jailhouse, walking back from the store the day before, but the windows had been shuttered and except for an old yellow dog sunning himself on the wooden sidewalk in front of the door, there had been no sign of habitation.

Terran shrugged, then squared his shoulders to move the copper tub. "Not since Warren Debney was gunned down five years ago," he said. "He was the town marshal."

The statement snagged Sam's attention. *It's been five years,* Maddie had said back at the mercantile when he'd offered his condolences on the death of the man she'd planned to marry. He wanted to ask Terran, straight-out, if his guess was right, but he couldn't think of a way to do it without prying into what amounted to family business.

"How did it happen?" Sam inquired, grasping the tub and lowering it to the ground.

Terran stood, tight-fisted, in the empty wagon bed, staring down at Sam. His expression was flat, giving away nothing of his thoughts. "Warren was walking Maddie home from a social at the church that night," he recalled, his voice so quiet that Sam had to strain to hear it. "Somebody shot him from the roof of the telegraph office. Maddie had blood all over her dress when they brought her home."

Sam closed his eyes against the image, though violence of that kind was nothing new to him, and if the boy had

LINDA LAEL MILLER

been standing on the ground he'd have laid a reassuring hand on his shoulder. "Did they ever run the shootist to ground?" he asked.

Terran shook his head, kept his eyes averted. Sam caught the glint of tears despite that effort. "He'd tangled with Rex Donagher the day before, Warren had, and some folks thought Rex was the one did it, but things never went any further than that."

"The town never replaced Debney? Got themselves a new lawman?"

Terran gave a bitter snort at that. "If there's a prisoner— and that ain't often—old Charlie Wilcox usually stands guard. If he's sober enough, anyhow."

Charlie Wilcox, Sam recalled, from his conversation with Bird out in front of the Rattlesnake Saloon that afternoon, was evidently the town drunk. Nothing much to recommend him, it seemed, save that he was the owner of a loyal horse.

Sam pulled a penny from his vest pocket—he'd left his suit coat inside the schoolhouse when he saw the need to chop wood—and extended the coin to Terran. "Thanks," he said.

Terran blinked. "What's that for?"

"Delivering my goods," Sam replied.

Terran's gaze strayed to the Colt .45 on Sam's hip, and his eyes widened. He advanced a step to take the penny. "Obliged," he said, but he was looking at the revolver, not the penny.

"You any good with that gun?" he ventured to ask.

Sam let one corner of his mouth tilt upward. "Just use it for shooting snakes, mostly," he lied.

Terran closed his hand tightly around the penny. Met Sam's eyes. "I never knew a schoolmaster to pack a .45 before," he said. "Mr. Singleton sure didn't."

"Mr. Singleton," Sam answered, "is a whole different kind of man than I am."

"We didn't mean to hurt him," Terran said.

Sam nodded. "I believe that," he allowed. "But a prank can go wrong, mighty fast, even when nobody intends for it to happen. And there are ways to do a man injury that don't leave any marks on his hide."

Terran's cheeks blazed, making his freckles stand out in bold relief. He hitched up his pants and then stood with his feet spread and his hands on his hips. "You mean to mete out punishment, Mr. O'Ballivan?"

Sam shook his head. "Not unless it's called for, Mr. Chancelor," he replied. He gave a sparing smile. "And I don't reckon any of you will take a notion to try putting *me* down the well."

Terran tried to look solemn, but it was a lost cause. He grinned. "No, sir," he said, "I don't reckon we will."

Sam put out his hand, waited.

The boy hesitated, then took it, and they shook on the bargain.

Terran was the first to speak. "Maddie says you aren't like any schoolteacher *she's* ever seen," he confided.

Sam chuckled and shut the tailgate. "Is that right?"

Terran hesitated a moment, as if he might say something more, but then he scrambled over the back of the wagon seat to take up the reins again. Looking back at Sam over one scrawny shoulder, he gave another grin. "She don't appreciate having to take her supper at the Donaghers's tomorrow night, neither."

"Why'd she agree to go, then?" Sam asked, honestly puzzled, as the boy cranked the brake lever forward.

"Said she was roped into it," Terran answered. Then, blithely, he added, "Maddie reckons as how if you're stupid enough to step right into a scorpions' nest, she'd better go along and see that you don't get stung."

"Kind of her to look out for me," Sam said dryly.

LINDA LAEL MILLER

Terran swung the wagon around in a wide circle in the grass, and when he pulled up alongside Sam, his expression had turned somber. "She looked out for Warren, too," he said, "and they still killed him."

Sam didn't know what to say to that, so he didn't say anything at all.

"See you tomorrow," Terran told him.

Sam saluted and watched with his thumbs hooked in his gun belt as the boy drove back toward the road. Once Maddie Chancelor's little brother was out of sight, he went back, took up his ax again and chopped the rest of the wood with more force than the job truly required.

MUNGO DONAGHER SURVEYED his bride as she dashed from one end of the ranch house kitchen to the other, grabbing down china plates from the cupboard and inspecting them for God-knew-what. She didn't bother with cooking— they had Anna Deerhorn to do that, along with the cleaning and other household work—but ever since she'd invited the schoolmaster out for a meal, she'd been in a fine dither of preparation.

"If I didn't know better," Mungo said sourly, "I'd think you were taken with that O'Ballivan feller."

Undine stopped her china-studying and turned to look at him, her eyes wide with innocent affront. "What a dreadful thing to say, Mungo Donagher," she protested, putting one hand to her glossy black hair and pressing the other to her throat. "There's only one man for me, and that's you."

Mungo knew he was being a damned fool, but he went ahead and believed her anyhow. It would have been hard not to, the way she was looking at him with those big purple eyes of hers. Lord, but she was a pretty thing, and lively in private, too.

THE MAN FROM STONE CREEK

He put out his arms, and she came to him with just the briefest hesitation and the smallest sigh. He ignored that, and held her close against him, filling his nostrils with the lemony scent of her hair.

Just then the side door swung open and his youngest, Ben, burst through from outside, clutching a speckled pup in both arms.

"Get that dog out of this house," Mungo commanded, loosening his hold on Undine and pretending he didn't notice how quickly she drew back.

The boy swallowed. His eyes were red-rimmed, and the way he was breathing, fast and shallow, usually signaled one of his fits. "Garrett and Landry," he gasped, "they said they was gonna drown him in the crick!"

"It'd be a favor to me if they did," Mungo growled. "Save me feeding him."

Ben held the mutt closer. "Please, Pa," he pleaded, gasping a little as he parceled out his words. "He's a good dog, and he's got a name, too. It's Neptune."

"Neptune," Mungo muttered. "That's a damn sissy name if I ever heard one."

Undine shifted, so she was standing just back of Ben. "Let him have the pup, Mungo," she said quietly. "It's not so much to ask."

Undine had a soft spot when it came to critters. Wanted one of those silly little dogs, small enough to ride in a reticule. She'd seen women carrying them around in the big city and been struck by the fancy ever since. Though just what "big city" that was, she'd never shared.

"Critters don't belong in the house, Undine," he said patiently.

She rested a light hand on Ben's shoulder. "The child's in a state," she pointed out, as if Mungo didn't have eyes in his head to see that for himself.

LINDA·LAEL MILLER

The boy shuddered. He was fragile, as his mother had been, God rest her soul. Elsie had died having him, and sometimes Mungo still felt a pang of grief when he recollected her. For the most part, though, he was glad to be shut of Elsie, same as he was his first wife. Hildy'd given him three strong sons, but she'd been good for nothing much besides. Tended to weeping spells and fits of sorrow. Always pining for the home folks back in Pennsylvania, that was Hildy. One day, with winter coming on, like it was now, he'd herded Garrett, Landry and Rex to town for boots. Hildy had taken his best hunting rifle, gone around behind the chicken coop, stuck the barrel in her mouth and pulled the trigger.

Blew the whole back of her head off, and he'd found her like that.

The memory made him set his jaw. "I don't like to encourage weakness in my boys, Undine," he said firmly. "That dog's small now, but he'll be big as a yearling calf before you know it."

Undine tilted her head to one side and gave him that look, the one she got when she meant to have her way. "Ben can keep him in his room for now. You'll never even know he's here."

By that time, Ben was staring up at Undine, open-mouthed, his eyes round with amazement.

"Say it's all right, Mungo," Undine crooned.

Ben was breathing easier. He turned his gaze slowly back to his father's face. "I'll take Neptune to school with me, come Monday mornin'," he said on a rush of air. "That way, he won't be getting underfoot around here all day."

"A dog's got no business in a schoolhouse," Mungo groused, testy because he knew he'd been bested. He'd never have given in to the boy, but Undine had ways of making a man wish he'd done otherwise if he went against her grain.

THE MAN FROM STONE CREEK

"I can't leave him here, Pa," Ben told him. "They'll hurt him if I do."

Mungo cursed. "All right," he said. "All right! But if I trip over that mutt one time—"

A smile lit Ben's face. "You won't, Pa. I promise you won't." With that he ran for the back stairs, still squeezing that infernal pup.

"He'll grow up to be just like that Singleton fella, if this keeps on," Mungo muttered. He shook his head just to think of one of his sons, with Donagher blood flowing in his veins, mewling over some stray bitch's get found by the side of the road. It would have been a far better thing, to his mind, if Garrett and Landry *had* drowned that useless hank of hair and hide and been done with it.

Undine stepped in close, put the cool, smooth palms of her hands to either side of his face. "You're too hard on him," she said, breathing the words more than saying them. "He's barely twelve years old, Mungo."

"When I was twelve years old," Mungo rumbled, "I was mining coal in Kentucky. Supporting my ma and two sisters." It still plagued him sometimes, the memory of those hard and hopeless days—never saw the sunshine, it seemed, or drew in a breath of clean air. One day, he'd just had enough. Laid down his shovel for good and headed west, working as a roustabout for the Army as far as Ohio, then taking whatever job he could to patch together a living.

In time, he'd saved up a good bit of money, and then, when he was twenty-one, he'd struck it lucky in the California gold fields and bought himself the beginnings of the vast cattle ranch he owned today. Still troubled his conscience, now and then, the way he'd left Ma and the girls to look out for themselves, but he reckoned they'd managed. He'd sent them money, when he could, but never got so much as a letter back to say thanks.

LINDA LAEL MILLER

It was like his mother to hold a grudge, and mostly likely she was dead by now anyway. He wondered sometimes how his sisters had fared, if they'd married and had children, but he'd long since resigned himself to not knowing.

Undine touched his top shirt button, brought him back from his somber wanderings. "Times are different now," she said. "Folks live gentler than they used to."

"You're in a kindly frame of mind today," Mungo remarked fondly, resting his forehead against Undine's.

She smiled, pulling back to look into his eyes. "Maybe it would be a good thing," she said, very quietly, "to send Ben away to school. There are some fine places in San Francisco. We could take him there, get him settled, and have ourselves a little honeymoon trip in the bargain."

Mungo frowned. "That would cost a pretty penny," he said.

"The boy would be making his own way in no time," Undine reasoned. Again she smiled, and even though Mungo knew he was being handled like a hog balking at a gate, he didn't mind. "And you'd never miss the money. You're the richest man in this part of the Arizona Territory, if not the whole of it. And I would *so* enjoy being fitted for some fine dresses, instead of ordering ready-mades out of Maddie Chancelor's silly catalogs." She sighed and her eyes glistened, wistful and faraway. "Sometimes I get such a loneliness for the city, stuck out here the way we are, it's like an ache inside me. Makes me just about frantic to get away."

Her words struck a chill in the depths of Mungo's crusty soul. Undine was like a brightly plumed bird, a spot of color in a grim landscape. Without her, the days would be a hollow round of hard work, and the nights—well, they'd be unbearable.

"You're not thinkin' about leavin' me, are you?" he asked, his voice so hoarse it felt like rusty barbed wire

THE MAN FROM STONE CREEK

coming out of his throat. He'd met Undine on a cattle buying trip up toward Phoenix, a year before, wooed her with what geegaws he could find in the shops, and brought her home as his wife. She'd been reluctant, until he'd shown her the size of the herd he and the boys would be driving back down to Haven.

"A lady thinks about all sorts of things," she admitted. "Please, Mungo. If I have to pass the winter in this place, I might go mad."

Talk of madness made Mungo profoundly uneasy, deep in his spirit. Undine didn't know about Hildy and the way she'd given up on living; he'd told her very little about his two previous marriages, other than to say that Garrett, Landry and Rex were by his first wife and Ben by his second.

"The boys can handle the ranch for a few months," Undine wheedled, looking up at him with imploring, luminous eyes.

Mungo huffed out an exasperated breath. "Leave them in charge," he said, "and we'd be lucky if we came back to an inch of land and a bale of moldy hay next spring."

"You've got that banker, Mr. James, to ride herd on them," she replied. He knew by her tone that she was stepping lightly, picking her way from one idea to the next, though she'd long since mapped out the route in her mind. She bit her plump lower lip. "I might just have to go by myself if you won't come with me."

Mungo was no fool. He knew that if Undine wanted to go to San Francisco, or anywhere else, she'd find a way to do it, with or without him. He'd never dared to ask how she'd wound up in Phoenix, but he was pretty sure it had to do with some man. "I'll think about it," he said in a low voice, but it felt as if the words had been torn out of him, like a stubborn stump wrenched from the ground by a team of mules.

She brightened, pretty as a pansy after a summer rain. "Good," she whispered. "That's good."

SAM SADDLED the nameless horse an hour after sunset, consulted the written instructions the major had given him before he'd left Stone Creek, even though he knew them by heart. Across the river, on the Mexican side, he was to find a certain cantina, order a drink and wait. He'd be told where to go from there, to meet up with Vierra.

The river was wide, shallow and washed with starlight. He made the crossing without getting his pant legs wet above the knee, though his boots filled to overflowing.

On the far bank, in a copse of whispering cottonwoods, he dismounted, emptied the boots and pulled them back on. He'd have to sleep in them tonight; if he took them off, he'd never get them on again. Best to let them dry to the contours of his feet, the way they had a hundred times before.

Sam swung back up into the saddle, headed slowly for the little cluster of lights where the trees gave way to open ground, and the village of Refugio. Here the buildings were mostly adobe, with a few teetering wooden shacks interspersed, and even though he probably could have hurled a stone back across the border, the two places were as different as Santa Fe and Boston.

He found the cantina easily, drawn by the sound of a guitar, and left the horse standing in the dooryard, among the burros and other mounts already there, nibbling on patches of grass. Two of the horses, he noticed, bore the distinctive Donagher brand, a *D* with a bar through it. Major Blackstone had sketched it for him, on the margin of his orders.

The lintel over the cantina door was low and Sam ducked his head as he entered. The clientele was mostly Mexican, as were the bartender and the girl serving drinks, but the cowboys standing at the bar were outsiders, like him. The pair of them turned their heads as Sam took a place at an empty table, their eyes narrowed with interest.

He nodded a greeting, wondering if the men were Mungo Donagher's sons, or simply rode for his outfit. A spread that size required a lot of range help.

The girl took her time traipsing over to him through the smoky gloom. She wore a white dress, set off her smooth brown shoulders, and her dark hair was wound into a tight knot at the back of her head. She smiled, with a virgin's shyness, and asked in Spanish what his pleasure would be.

Sam was briefly reminded of Bird, selling herself as well as liquor across the river at Oralee Pringle's saloon. His stomach soured around the light supper he'd made for himself, but he responded to the smile as best he could. He asked for whiskey, and the girl flounced away to fetch his order.

The pair of riders had turned back to their shared bottle, though Sam suspected they were keeping an eye on him in the long, dingy mirror behind the bar. Both of them wore side arms under their dusty coats, one a right-handed gun, the other a southpaw. He unsnapped the narrow leather strap that kept his own .45 secure in the holster.

The girl came back with his whiskey. Sam paid her and left the drink to sit on the table, untouched. The barmaid lingered, her brown eyes thoughtful and unblinking, and then suddenly plopped herself onto his lap, draping her arms around his neck.

Tentatively, Sam hooked an arm around her slender waist.

She nuzzled his neck, sending shivers through him before nibbling her way up to his ear to whisper, this time in halting English, "Vierra, he will meet you behind the church, beside the grave of Carlos Tiendos, one hour from now. In the meantime—" she tasted his earlobe "—you could come up the stairs with me."

Sam shifted uncomfortably. He'd gone a while without a woman, so the invitation had its appeal, but a particular storekeeper/postmistress had taken up squatter's rights in the back of his mind, and that ruined everything. Besides, he needed to keep his thoughts on the task ahead of him, meet up with Vierra and work out a plan.

"They are watching you," the girl persisted. "Those two *Americanos* at the bar."

Sam traced the outward curve of one of her breasts with one finger, so they'd have something to look at. He might as well have been running a hand over a wooden Indian outside a cigar store, for all the excitement he felt. Damn that Maddie Chancelor, anyhow. "Who are they?" he whispered back.

She trembled at his caress, though Sam felt as though the blood in his veins had turned to high-country slush. "Donaghers," she answered, confirming his suspicions. "Garrett and Landry. They don't take to strangers, so you must be careful."

Sam nodded almost imperceptibly. If what Terran had told him about the three eldest Donagher brothers was true, he'd have a run-in with them sooner or later, but this night, he didn't want to be bothered.

"Come upstairs with me," the girl reiterated. "They will guess that I am passing a message if you don't."

Sam forced a lusty chuckle, for the benefit of the Donaghers and anybody else who might be paying attention. "Lead the way," he said under his breath.

She bounced to her feet, grabbed his hand and hauled him toward a set of three stone steps, around the far end of the bar. He swatted her lightly on the bottom as they passed the Donaghers and she giggled mischievously.

"My name," she told him, closing the door of a dark room behind them, "is Rosita."

THE MAN FROM STONE CREEK

Sam stood warily, waiting for his eyes to adjust, taking a measure of the place with all his remaining senses. He'd been led into more than one trap in his life, usually by a pretty woman full of promises, and he was absolutely still until he was sure they were alone.

Rosita raised herself onto her toes, slipped her arms around his neck again and kissed him on the mouth. "We might as well make good use of the time," she teased in her native language.

Sam laid his hands on either side of her waist and set her gently away from him. Thin moonlight seeped into the room, through a single, narrow window, outlining a narrow cot, a washstand and a simple wooden chest with a candlestick on top.

He crossed to the chest, took a match from his shirt pocket and lit the candle. In the flickering light, he noted the crucifix on the wall above the cot, and wondered about Rosita.

"Is this your room?" he asked.

He must have spoken Spanish, because she understood him readily. She tilted her head to one side, her mouth forming a fetching little pout. *"Sí,"* she said.

He glanced at the crucifix again. "You bring men here?"

She nodded, took another step toward him.

He held up a hand, halting her progress.

Rosita looked as though he'd slapped her. "I am not pretty to you?" she asked softly, this time in English.

"It isn't that," Sam said, and thrust a hand through his hair. He'd left his hat at the table, with his glass of whiskey.

"You do not like women?"

He chuckled. "Oh, I'm right fond of women," he said.

She tugged at one side of her ruffly bodice, about to pull her dress down.

"Stop," Sam told her. Then, at her injured expression,

he drew a five dollar gold piece from his vest pocket and extended it.

Rosita was clearly confused, and her dark eyes rounded at the gleaming coin resting in his palm, then climbed, questioning, to his face.

"That's for keeping your clothes on," he told her gruffly.

She darted forward, snatched the gold piece from his hand and took a couple of hasty steps back, dropping it down the front of her dress. "Nobody ever pay me to keep clothes *on*," she marveled. Then, watching him closely, she blinked. "Downstairs…they think we—" Rosita flushed and fell silent.

"Let them think it," Sam said. Then he leaned down, put one hand on the cot, with its thin, lumpy mattress, and gave it a few quick pushes, so the metal springs creaked. The sound was loud enough to raise speculation downstairs, even over the melancholy strum of the guitar.

Rosita put one hand over her mouth and giggled.

Sam pulled part of his shirttail out and rumpled his hair.

"You have folks around here?" he asked, watching her face. He'd have bet his last pound of coffee beans that she hadn't seen her sixteenth birthday yet. "Someplace you could go?"

She shook her head.

"How about the padre, over at the church? Maybe he could help."

"Help?" Rosita echoed, obviously puzzled.

Sam sighed. "Never mind," he said. He consulted his watch. He was supposed to meet Vierra in twenty minutes. "This church you told me about—where is it?"

Rosita went to the window to point the place out, and Sam stood behind her. The adobe bell tower was clearly visible, even in the starlight. He could get there on foot, in plenty of time.

He was turning to go when Rosita caught hold of his arm. "Vierra," she said in an urgent whisper. "Do not trust him too much."

Sam cupped Rosita's small, earnest face with one hand. "Thanks," he told her, and headed for the door.

She followed him down the stone steps and he made a point of tucking his shirttail back in as soon as he was visible to the patrons of the cantina. He smoothed his hair, crossed to the table and reclaimed his hat. As an afterthought, he downed the whiskey, and it burned its way to his stomach.

He knew the Donaghers would follow, and as soon as he got outside, he ducked around the corner of the cantina, into the deep shadows, instead of heading for his horse.

Sure enough, Mungo's sons came outside a moment later.

"Where'd he go?" one of them asked the other.

"Maybe the outhouse," the other replied.

Sam waited. If they bothered his horse, he'd have to deal with them, but they were either drunk or just plain stupid, maybe both, and headed for the privy at the far side of the dooryard.

He watched as one of them slammed at the outhouse wall with the butt of his gun and bellowed, "You in there, mister?"

The second brother tried the door, pulling on the wire hook outside, and it swung open with a squeal of rusted hinges.

"Hey!" the first brother yelled, putting his head through the opening.

Sam eased out of his hiding place.

Both the Donaghers stepped into the outhouse.

Sam shut the door on them and fastened the sturdy wire hook around the twisted nail so they'd be a while getting out again.

A roar sounded from inside and the whole privy rocked

LINDA LAEL MILLER

on the hard-packed dirt. Sam grinned, mounted his horse and rode for the church to meet Vierra.

He could still hear the Donagher brothers yelling when he got where he was going. The graveyard was enclosed behind a high rock wall, and there was no gate in evidence, so he stood in the saddle and vaulted over, landing on his feet.

He took a moment to assess his surroundings, as he had in Rosita's room over the cantina, and spotted the red glow of Vierra's cheroot about a hundred yards away, beneath a towering cottonwood.

He approached, one hand resting on the handle of his Colt, just in case.

Vierra's grin flashed white and he solidified from a shadow to a man, ground out the cheroot with the toe of one boot. "There is some trouble at the cantina?" he asked, inclining his head in that direction. The sound of splintering wood, mingled with bellowed curses, swelled in the otherwise peaceful night.

Good thing I didn't leave my horse behind, Sam thought. They might have shot him out of pure spite.

He shrugged. "Just a couple of cowpokes breaking out of the privy," he said. "I reckon they would either have jumped me or followed me here, if I hadn't corralled them for a few minutes."

Vierra laughed. "The Donaghers," he said.

Sam nodded, took another look around. It was a typical cemetery, full of stone monuments and crude wooden crosses. He recalled the crucifix on Rosita's wall, and it sobered him. "What do you have to tell me here that you couldn't have said last night in Haven?" he asked.

Vierra reached into his vest and produced a thick fold of papers. "These are the places where the *banditos* have struck on this side of the border." He crouched, spreading a large hand-drawn map on the ground, and Sam joined him to have a look. "Here, at Rancho Los Cruces, " Vierra said, placing a gloved fingertip on the spot, "they stole some two hundred head of cattle and left four *vaqueros* dead. Here, in the canyon, they robbed a train."

Sam listened intently, committing the map to memory, just in case Vierra wasn't inclined to part with it.

"They used dynamite to cause an avalanche," Vierra explained, lingering at the place marked as Reoso Canyon. "The train, of course, was forced to stop. They took a shipment of gold, and the wife and young daughter of a *patron* were captured, as well. The wife was found later—" Vierra stopped, and his throat worked. "She had been raped and dragged to death behind a horse. There has been no word of the girl."

"Christ," Sam rasped, closing his eyes for a moment.

Vierra was silent for a long time. When he spoke, his voice was flat. "I was told that you would give me a map corresponding to this one. Showing all the places this gang has struck on your side of the border."

Sam nodded, reached into the inside pocket of his coat and handed over a careful copy of the drawing the major had given him. "Except for the woman and the girl," he said as Vierra unfolded the paper to examine it in a shaft of moonlight, "it's a version of what you just showed me. Rustling. Train robberies. They cleaned out a couple of banks, too, and killed a freight wagon driver."

"Our superiors," Vierra observed, his gaze fixed on Sam's map, "they believe we are dealing with the same band of men. Do you know why?"

Sam knew it wasn't a question. It was a prompt. "Yes," he said after a moment of hesitation. "They leave a mark."

Vierra folded Sam's map carefully and tucked it away inside his vest. "A stake, driven into the ground, always with a bit of blood-soaked cloth attached."

LINDA LAEL MILLER

Bile rose in the back of Sam's throat. He'd seen the signature several times, and just the recollection of it turned his stomach. He nodded, took another moment before he spoke. "I suppose you've considered that it might be the Donaghers," he said. That was Major Blackstone's theory, and, since his conversation with Terran Chancelor that afternoon, regarding the Debney shooting, the possibility had stuck in his mind like a burr.

A muscle bunched in Vierra's jaw. "*Sí*," he said. "But there is no proof."

Sam waited.

"The *patrons* who hired me, they want the right men. No mistakes," Vierra went on. "And I do not have the option, as you do, of shooting them through the heart and bringing them in draped over their saddles. The *patrons* want them alive. The streets of a certain village, a day or two south of here, will run with their blood."

A chill trickled down Sam's spine. He had no love for these murdering bastards, and would just as soon draw on them as take his next breath, but the law was the law. Unless one or more of them forced his hand, they would stand trial, in an American court, their fate decided by a judge and jury. He didn't give a damn what happened to them after that, but by God, he'd get them that far, whether Vierra got in his way or not. "I guess it all depends on who catches up to them first," he said moderately.

Both men rose to their feet. Vierra surrendered the map he'd brought with him. "There is a train making its way north in ten days," he said. "I have told a few people that there will be a fortune in *oro federale* aboard. We will see if the rumor reaches the right ears."

Federal gold, Sam reflected. Cheese in a mousetrap.

"And you've got a pretty good idea where they'll try to

intercept the train," he ventured, recalling Vierra's map in perfect detail. "That railroad trestle downriver from here."

Vierra smiled. "I am impressed," he said. "The new schoolmaster has paid attention to the lesson."

CHAPTER

FOUR

"YOU WANT ME to do *what?*" Maddie gaped at Sam O'Ballivan's copper bathtub, ensconced squarely in front of the schoolhouse stove. Terran had left the store early that morning, of his own volition, and she'd barely recovered from her brother's change of heart when back he came, breathless from running all the way.

"Mr. O'Ballivan says to come quick, if you wouldn't mind!" he'd cried.

Maddie had frowned, concerned. Elias James, the town banker and, for all practical intents and purposes, her employer, since he oversaw Mungo's investments, expected the mercantile door to be unlocked by nine o'clock sharp, and in the six years she'd been running the general store, she'd never failed to do that. It was now eight forty-five. "Is there some emergency?" she'd asked, already untying the apron strings she'd just tied a moment before.

"He says it's important," Terran had insisted.

And here she was, standing in the schoolhouse, staring

THE MAN FROM STONE CREEK

in consternation at Sam O'Ballivan and the bathtub she'd sold him herself.

"I want you," Sam repeated patiently, "to show Violet Perkins how to take a bath."

Maddie knew Violet, of course, and had sympathy for her. The poor child hung around the store sometimes, when school was out, hoping for a hard-boiled egg from the crock next to the counter, or a piece of penny candy. She mooned over the few ready-made dresses Maddie carried—most women sewed their children's garments at home, as well as their own—and huddled by the stove for hours when it was cold or rainy outside. Maddie often indulged her with a plate of leftovers from her own larder at the rear of the store, pretending the food would go to waste if Violet didn't eat it.

"Here?" she asked, noting that Sam had set out the bar of French-milled soap and the towel he'd purchased with the bathtub. "In the schoolhouse?"

"What better place?" Sam reasoned. He'd been sitting behind his desk, wearing spectacles and poring over a thick volume when she burst in. At Maddie's appearance, he'd set aside the glasses and stood. "A school is a place to learn, isn't it? And Violet needs to know how to take a bath."

Flummoxed, Maddie spread her hands. "What about the other students?" she asked. "You can't expect the child to undress in front of the boys—"

Sam smiled. "Of course not. The girls can stay—I suspect some of them could do with a demonstration. I'll take the boys down to the river for their lesson." He held up the cake of yellow soap from yesterday's marketing. "I've noticed that Violet is generally the first to raise her hand. Let her think she's volunteering."

Maddie glanced at the schoolhouse clock, torn. It was

LINDA LAEL MILLER

nine o'clock, straight-up, and the mercantile was still closed. At that very moment Mr. James was probably looking out his office window, the bank being kitty-corner from the store, wondering why the customers couldn't get in to buy things and whipping up a temper because of it.

"Why me?" she asked.

Sam smiled again. "You're the only woman I know in Haven besides Bird of Paradise over at the Rattlesnake Saloon. I don't guess it would be fitting to bring her in to teach bathing, though she'd probably agree if I asked her."

Maddie sniffed. "It certainly *wouldn't* be fitting," she said, wondering how Sam O'Ballivan had come to make the woman's acquaintance. *Damned* if she'd ask him, even if her life depended on it. She approached the tub and peered inside, already unfastening her cuff buttons to roll up her sleeves. "We will need water, Mr. O'Ballivan."

"I've got some heating in the back room," he said. "No sense in lugging it in here and pouring it into the tub if you weren't going to agree."

She sighed. "What about the store?"

"Well, I figured, as the owner, you could—"

Maddie flushed. "I am *not* the owner. I manage it for someone else, and I am accountable to Mr. James, at the bank, who serves as trustee."

Sam frowned. "Oh," he said.

"Yes," Maddie confirmed. "*Oh.* By now, there are probably people standing three-deep on the sidewalk, complaining because they can't get in to buy salt and tobacco and kitchen matches."

Sam brightened. "I think I have a solution," he said. "I'll take the boys to the river another day. In the meantime, they can learn how a mercantile operates. We'll make a morning of it."

"*You* intend to take over *my* store?" Maddie asked,

affronted. "Do you think it's so easy that any idiot can do it?"

The schoolmaster smiled. "I don't regard myself as an idiot, as a general rule. How hard can it be, filling flour bags and measuring cloth off a bolt?"

Maddie came to an instant simmer, but before she could tell the man what she thought of his blithe and patently arrogant assumption that keeping a thriving mercantile was something he could do one-handed, the pupils began to straggle in. She swallowed her outrage and stood as circumspectly as she could, letting her gaze bore into Sam O'Ballivan like a pointy stick.

When everyone was settled in their seats, Sam announced his plan. The boys would help him tend the mercantile, the girls would remain at the schoolhouse for a "hygiene" lesson.

The boys cheered and stomped their feet, and rushed for the door at an offhand signal from Sam. The girls sat, wide-eyed, waiting for enlightenment. Maddie would have bet not a one of them could have defined the word *hygiene,* but they *had* noticed the bathtub. They were all agog at the spectacle.

"Miss Chancelor will give the demonstration," Sam went on, looking worriedly from face to face. "But we'll need a volunteer to get into the tub."

Sure enough, Violet's hand shot up. "I'll do it, Mr. SOB," she cried.

"Mr. O'Ballivan," Sam countered easily. "That's good, Violet. I appreciate your willingness to take the initiative."

Violet beamed. "Can I go to the privy first?"

The other girls giggled and Sam silenced them with a ponderous sweep of his eyes.

"Yes," he said. "You do that."

While Violet was gone to the privy, he brought in four buckets of hot water and emptied them into the tub. The remaining girls watched, barely able to suppress their amusement.

When he'd set aside the last bucket, Sam turned to address them. "If even one of you makes fun of Violet," he said, "you'll find yourself writing 'I will not bully smaller children' one hundred times on the blackboard. Is that clear to everyone?"

The girls nodded, subdued.

Sam dusted his hands together. "Good," he said, and turned to Maddie. "Now, Miss Chancelor, if I might have the key to the mercantile—"

She surrendered it, slapping it down into his palm with a little more force than strictly necessary.

"Thank you," he said, tossing the large brass key once and catching it with an aplomb that made Maddie grit her teeth.

And so it was that Maddie came to illustrate the finer points of taking a bath, using Violet Perkins as a model.

MADDIE HAD BEEN RIGHT, Sam thought as he opened the mercantile for the day's commerce. There were eight women waiting on the sidewalk, shopping baskets in hand, tapping their toes in impatience. He greeted them with a nod and made his crew of boys wait until the ladies had swept inside.

It was the contrary nature of folks, he reckoned, that on this particular morning, everybody in town wanted to get their marketing done. Had Maddie followed her usual routine, there most likely wouldn't have been so much urgency.

He set the boys to sweeping and dusting canned goods while the female population of Haven made their various selections.

"Where," demanded a narrow-faced old biddy with hooded, hawklike eyes and a nose to match, "is Maddie?"

Sam opened his mouth to answer, but before he could

get a word out, Terran cut him off. "She's over to the schoolhouse, giving Violet Perkins a bath!" he crowed.

"Teaching a hygiene lesson," Sam corrected quietly.

"Well," huffed the Hawk Woman, "it's about time somebody look that child in hand."

"Yes," Sam said, opening the cash register drawer to tally the funds on hand. "It *is* about time."

The woman blinked.

Sam silently congratulated himself on a bull's-eye.

By ten-thirty, he'd taken in four dollars and forty-eight cents, and made careful note of every transaction, so Maddie couldn't say he'd fouled up her books. Then, figuring the hygiene lesson ought to be over, and Violet decent again, he dispatched Terran and young Ben Donagher to the schoolhouse to find out.

When they came back, Maddie was with them, the front of her dress sodden and her hair moist around her face. He couldn't rightly tell if that sparkle in her whiskey eyes was temper or satisfaction with a job well done.

"I see my store is still standing," she remarked.

Sam grinned. "I trust my school has fared as well," he parried, reaching for his hat.

"You'll have to empty the bathtub yourself," Maddie said, taking her storekeeper's apron down off a peg and donning it. "Violet fairly gleams with cleanliness. One of the other girls aired out her dress while she was soaking."

Sam sent the boys trooping back to the schoolhouse, lingering to take out his wallet. "Next time Violet comes in the store," he said, laying a bill down on the counter, "you outfit her with a new one. Say there was a drawing and she won."

Maddie regarded him solemnly. He still couldn't tell whether she was pleased with him or wanted to peel off a strip of his hide. "You lie very easily, Mr. O'Ballivan," she said.

Well, that answered *one* of his questions. "Kids like

Violet run into more than their fair share of humiliation, it seems to me," he replied. "If a lie can spare them embarrassment, then I'm all for it."

She had the good grace to blush.

He waited until he'd reached the doorway before putting on his hat. "We're due at the Donaghers's supper table at seven o'clock," he reminded her. "Best have Terran hitch up that buckboard you use for deliveries unless you want to ride two to a horse."

Maddie put the bill he'd left on the counter into the cash register and headed for a display of calico dresses, probably to choose one for Violet. "We'll take the buckboard," she said without looking at him.

Sam smiled to himself as he closed the door behind him.

Damn, he thought. It would have been a fine thing to share a saddle with Miss Maddie Chancelor. A fine thing indeed.

SCHOOL HAD LET OUT for the day and Sam was seated at his desk, going over the map Vierra had given him the night before, when a small, impossibly thin woman stepped shyly over the threshold. She wore a bonnet and a faded cotton dress, and he knew who she was before she introduced herself.

He refolded the map, set a paper weight on top of it, and stood. "Sam O'Ballivan," he said by way of introduction, and added a cordial nod.

"Mrs. John Perkins," Violet's mother responded, lingering just inside the open door.

"Come in," Sam urged when she didn't show any signs of moving.

She hesitated another moment, then thrust herself into motion. He noticed then, as she approached, that she was carrying a basket over one arm, filled with brown eggs. She

THE MAN FROM STONE CREEK

set the whole works on his desk, straightened her spine, and looked up at him.

"I guess my Violet had a bath today at school," she said.

Sam waited. She'd brought him eggs, which might be construed as a peaceful gesture, but you never knew with women. They could be crafty as all get-out. Most of the time, when they said one thing, they meant another. They expected a man to learn their language and converse in it like a native.

Mrs. Perkins drew herself up to her full, unremarkable height, the top of her head barely reaching Sam's shirt pocket. Under the brim of that bonnet, her eyes spoke eloquently of her discouragement and her fierce pride. "I came to thank you for making a lesson of it," she said. "Violet's real pleased that she was chosen for an example."

"Violet," Sam said honestly, "is a fine girl."

Tears brimmed along the woman's lower lashes and her pointed little chin jutted out. "It's been so hard since John was killed. I love my Violet, I truly do, but betwixt keepin' food on the table and a roof over our heads, I fear I've let some things go."

Sam wanted to lay a hand on Mrs. Perkins's bony shoulder, but it would be a familiar gesture, so he refrained. "Any time you want the use of my bathtub," he said awkwardly, "you just say the word. I'll fill it with hot water and make myself scarce."

Mrs. Perkins blinked, sniffled, looked away for a moment. "That's right kind," she said. "I can do better by my girl, and I will, too. I swear I will, Mr. O'Ballivan. Short of goin' to work for Oralee Pringle, though, I can't think how."

Sam took an egg from the basket and examined it as thoroughly as if he'd never seen one before. "I do favor eggs," he said. "I'd buy a dozen from you, every other day,

LINDA LAEL MILLER

and pay a good price for a chicken now and then, too, if you've got any to spare."

"Them eggs was meant as a present," Mrs. Perkins said, but she looked hopeful. "I sell a few, but folks around here mostly keep their own chickens."

"Bring me a dozen, day after tomorrow," Sam replied. "I'll give fifty cents for them, if you throw in a stewing hen every now and then."

For the first time since she'd entered the schoolhouse, Mrs. Perkins smiled. It was tentative, and her eyes were wary, as if she thought he might be playing a joke on her. "That's an awful lot of money, for twelve eggs and a chicken," she said carefully.

"I'm a man of princely tastes," Sam replied. His mouth watered, just looking at those eggs. He'd have fried half of them up for a feast if he wasn't dining at the Donagher ranch that night.

It would be interesting to see if those two fools he'd locked in that Mexican outhouse showed up at the table, and more interesting still to pass an evening in Maddie Chancelor's company.

"You want that chicken plucked and dressed out, or still flappin' its wings?" Violet's mother asked.

Sam took a moment to shift back to the present moment. "It would be a favor to me if it was ready for the kettle," he said.

Mrs. Perkins beamed. "Fifty cents," she said dreamily. "I don't know as I'll recall what to do with so much money."

Sam took up the eggs. "I'll put these by, and give you back your basket," he told the woman. She waited while he performed the errand, and looked surprised when he came back and handed her two quarters along with the battered wicker container. "I like to pay in advance," he said as casually as he could.

THE MAN FROM STONE CREEK

To his surprise, she stood on her tiptoes, kissed him on the cheek and fled with the basket, fifty cents and the better part of her dignity.

CHAPTER

FIVE

MADDIE DROVE UP in front of the schoolhouse promptly at six o'clock that evening, the last of the daylight rimming her chestnut hair in fire. She managed the decrepit buckboard and pitiful team as grandly as if she'd been at the reins of a fancy surrey drawn by a matched pair of Tennessee trotters.

Sam lingered a few moments on the steps of that one-room school, savoring the sight of her, etching it into his memory. Once he left Haven for good, and married up with Abigail, as it was his destiny to do, he wanted to be able to recall Maddie Chancelor in every exquisite detail, just as she looked right then, wearing a blue woolen dress, with a matching bonnet dangling down her straight, slender back by its ribbons.

He felt a shifting, sorrowful ache of pleasure, watching her from under the brim of his hat, and the recalcitrant expression on her face did nothing to dampen the sad joy of taking her in.

"Well," she called, after rattling to a shambly stop, "are we going to the Donaghers' or not?"

Sam bit back a grin, tempted to reach out and give the bell rope a good wrench before he stepped down, announcing to all creation that he was having supper with the best-looking woman he'd ever laid eyes on. But some things were just too private to tell, even though nobody but him would have known the meaning of that clanging peal.

His insides reverberated, just as surely as if he'd gone ahead and pulled that rope with all his might.

"Evening, Miss Chancelor," he said, approaching the wagon. She'd hung kerosene lanterns on either side of the buckboard, to light their way a little after darkness rolled over the landscape like a blanket, but she'd yet to strike a match to the wicks. She was a prudent soul, Maddie was, and not inclined to waste costly fuel before there was a true need for it.

She showed no signs of letting go of the reins so he could take them. He resigned himself to being driven through the center of town by a lady, and climbed up beside her, swallowing a swell of masculine pride.

"I don't mind telling you," she said, "that sitting down at Mungo Donagher's table is just about the last thing in the world I want to do this evening."

Sam smiled. The prospect wasn't real high on his list, either, but there was a possibility he'd meet up with Donagher's elder sons, and that was the only reason he'd accepted the invitation. Like Vierra, he was already half convinced that Mungo's boys were involved in the outlaw gang that had been plaguing both the Arizona Territory and the State of Sonora for several years, but he needed proof—a quantity that was most often gathered one small, seemingly unimportant fact at a time.

"Terran told me about Warren Debney," he said quietly,

LINDA LAEL MILLER

just to get it out of the way. If he hadn't spoken up, the knowledge would have remained a gulf between them, and he wanted as little distance as possible.

He felt her stiffen beside him, and she set the buckboard rolling with a hard slap of the reins and a lurch that nearly unseated him, since he hadn't braced for it. "Terran," she said, "sometimes talks too much."

Sam resettled his hat, needing something to occupy his hands, for it was obvious Maddie wasn't about to surrender the reins. "He said one of the Donagher brothers probably fired the fatal shot," he went on, slow and quiet. "What do *you* think, Maddie?"

She was quiet for a long time, so long that Sam feared she didn't intend to answer at all. Finally, though, she said, "I believe it was Rex. He's the meanest of the three, and he and Warren had had several run-ins just prior to the shooting."

"You were with him? Debney, I mean—when he was shot?"

She swallowed visibly, nodded, keeping her gaze fixed on the road into the main part of town. "He died in my arms," she said, so quietly that Sam barely heard her over the hooves of those worn-out horses and the rattle of fittings.

He wanted to put his arm around her, but he knew it would cause her to pull away, so he didn't. They rounded a bend and passed the mercantile, then the Rattlesnake Saloon. Charlie Wilcox's old nag stood out front, patiently waiting to bear him home on its swayed back. "I'm sorry that happened to you, Maddie Chancelor," Sam said.

"So am I," she replied.

Sam shifted on the hard wagon seat. "It must be difficult for you—sitting down to take a meal with somebody who might have killed your man. I didn't know about that when I roped you into coming along, and if you want to change your mind, I'll understand."

THE MAN FROM STONE CREEK

At long last she looked him in the eye. They were traveling east, with the setting sun at their backs, headed for the river road that led to the Donagher ranch. Sam reckoned that, after a mile or two, they'd have to stop so he could step down and light those lanterns, but for now, all he cared about was whatever Maddie was about to say.

"It makes me nervous when any of the Donagher boys come into the store," she said frankly. "Just the same, I wouldn't miss a chance to look them straight in the eye and let them know they're not fooling me for one moment. They got away with shooting Warren, and stringing up poor, harmless John Perkins, too. Maybe they fooled the law, but they can't fool God, and they can't fool *me*."

Sam sighed as they passed the row of businesses along the main street, all of them closed up and dark, like Maddie Chancelor's broken heart probably was. He didn't care for the idea of her drawing the Donaghers' attention, taunting them with her suspicions. It was akin to stirring a hornet's nest with a chunk of firewood.

"You probably ought to stay in town tonight. I'd be obliged, though, for the loan of your wagon."

To his surprise, and cautious delight, she favored him with a soft smile and a shake of her head. The subtle scent of her lush hair teased his senses. "I guess the team and buckboard would be safe in your keeping," she said, "and I do appreciate your kind concern. But I've looked after myself for a long time, and anyway, the Donaghers wouldn't dare bother me in Mungo's presence." Humor flickered in her brown eyes. "Besides, there is the question of *your* safety, Mr. O'Ballivan."

He straightened his spine. "I'm not afraid of any of the Donaghers, or all of them put together," he said.

"I know that," Maddie replied. "But there's one Donagher you'd be wise to look out for, and that's Undine."

LINDA LAEL MILLER

They were passing out of town, and Sam gave up on the hope that Maddie would change her mind and go back to her quarters above the mercantile, instead of venturing into the snakes' den, with him. "Undine," he repeated, confused. Unless the lady had a derringer tucked up the sleeve of her dress, he couldn't imagine how she'd do him any harm.

"She's set her sights on you," Maddie said. "Mungo won't take kindly to that. He's mean jealous, and he'd as soon kill any man she takes a fancy to as look at him."

Sam pondered that bit of information, then took a risk. "Did she 'take a fancy' to Warren Debney?" he asked. "Or maybe John Perkins?"

"Warren was dead and buried long before Mungo brought Undine to Haven as his bride," Maddie said, and her eyes took on a haunted expression. "As for Mr. Perkins, she wouldn't have given him a second look. But she *has* taken a liking to you. If you ignore that, it will be at your peril."

Sam rubbed his chin with one hand, as he often did when he was thinking. He'd shaved for the occasion, and his skin still felt raw from the stroke of the new razor. His new white shirt itched, too, so he shrugged inside it, in a vain attempt to find relief. "You sound mighty certain," he said at some length, "about Undine's flirtations being potentially fatal for the object of her attentions, that is. Something must have happened to convince you."

"It's just a feeling," Maddie said, narrowing her wondrous eyes a little upon the darkening road. "Woman's intuition."

"I think there's more to it than that," Sam persisted.

She met his eyes. "Haven is small. There are plenty of stories going around, and I hear most of them because just about everybody in this part of the territory makes their way to the mercantile on a regular basis. Mungo's temper is legendary—they say he once beat Landry, the middle son by his first wife, nearly to death for leaving a gate open. Ben—the little one—is a friend of Terran's, and sometimes passes the night with us if the weather is bad enough that he can't get home. That boy is terrified of his father—and his brothers, too. I always get the feeling, whenever I'm around him, that there are things he wants to tell me—tell anybody—but he's afraid to speak up."

"He was in on dangling Singleton down the well," Sam said. For the sake of the peace, he didn't add *along with your brother.* "I've been keeping an eye on Ben, trying to size him up. He's smart as hell, but he's skittish, too. Yesterday in class somebody dropped the dictionary and he about jumped out of his hide."

Maddie bit her lower lip. "I worry about Ben, out there alone with those rowdy men," she confessed. "Undine seems fond of him, though. If it weren't for her, I don't think I'd close my eyes at night for fretting about it. If she were to leave—"

It was all but dark by then, and Sam laid a hand over Maddie's, where she gripped the reins. "Better pull up," he said, "so I can light those lamps."

She complied ably, and he got down to attend to the lanterns. When he climbed back into the wagon box, she surprised him by handing over the reins.

"What else can you tell me about Mungo and his boys?" he asked mildly when they'd traveled a ways. The river twisted and wound alongside the narrow track, whispering stories of its own.

"They own just about everything in Haven, save Oralee Pringle's saloon," she said, sighing. Then, with reluctance, she reminded him, and maybe herself, "Including the general store."

LINDA LAEL MILLER

In the beginning, Sam had believed the store was Maddie's, taken comfort in the idea that she had a way to get along, to provide for herself and Terran. Singleton had said, that first day, that they didn't have any other family, and he'd assumed she must have inherited the mercantile from her father. Then she'd said she ran the place for somebody else and had to account to Mr. James, the banker. It hadn't occurred to Sam that that "somebody else" might be a Donagher.

"I work for Mungo Donagher," Maddie affirmed, sounding as if she'd just awakened from a bad dream only to find out it was real. "Mr. James, over at the bank, oversees the accounts, like I told you, but it's Mungo who pays my wages."

"I don't suppose you can afford to offend him by accusing his boys of gunning down Warren Debney," he said when he'd considered for a while.

"I'm not so sure he didn't do it himself," Maddie admitted softly, and when she looked up at Sam, he saw bleak resignation in her eyes. He'd have done or said just about anything, right then, to give her ease, but nothing came to mind.

"What makes you say that?" Sam asked when he'd absorbed the statement.

Maddie was silent for a long time and Sam was beginning to think he'd asked one question too many when she finally answered. "Until he brought Undine home from Phoenix," she said, "Mungo was courting me. He told me if I went ahead and married Warren, I'd have to give up managing the mercantile."

Something elemental and dark rose up within Sam, and he was a while putting it right. He felt as protective and as possessive of Maddie as if he'd been the one about to put a ring on her finger instead of Warren Debney. "And if you'd given in? Married Mungo instead of Debney?"

"He'd have signed the store over as a wedding gift," Maddie recalled, frowning. "A *plaything,* as he put it."

It made Sam's gorge rise, to think of Mungo Donagher touching Maddie, let alone bedding her. "Some women," he said in his own good time, "would have taken the old coot up on the bargain."

Maddie pulled her shawl up around her shoulders, against the chill of the evening, and Sam thought she moved a fraction of an inch closer to him. "I'd sooner take up residence upstairs at the Rattlesnake Saloon. It amounts to the same thing."

Sam hadn't thought any image could be worse than Maddie throwing in with the head of the Donagher clan, but sure enough, she'd come up with one. He set his jaw and tightened his hold on the reins. At the rate these horses were traveling, they might be on time for breakfast.

THE LIGHTS of Mungo Donagher's long, rustic house winked in the thick purplish gloom of the night. Normally, Maddie would sooner have been thrown to the lions than set foot in that place a second time, but with Sam O'Ballivan beside her, she actually enjoyed the prospect. She even hoped she would come face-to-face with Rex Donagher; she'd find a way to let him know what she thought of him and those cur brothers of his, even though she dared not insult their father. Without her job at the mercantile, she and Terran would be worse off than Violet Perkins and her mother, Hittie.

Mungo himself was waiting to greet them when they pulled up in the dooryard. The ground was unadorned by flowers and there were no curtains at the windows. Had Maddie lived in such a house, she would have planted peonies and climbing roses first thing, even if she had to carry water from the river to make them thrive. Her own

LINDA LAEL MILLER

plants were spindly and pitiful, and wherever she moved them, shadows followed, robbing them of light.

Mungo's stance was stern and his countenance unwelcoming. Maddie knew it was Sam he mistrusted, not herself, but she felt a quiver of unease in the pit of her stomach just the same. She'd warned Sam, though, and that was all she could do.

He climbed down from the wagon box, extinguished the lamps to save kerosene for the ride back to town, and then extended a hand to Maddie. All that time, Mungo neither moved nor spoke. She felt his displeasure, invisible but real, roiling in the space between them.

"Evening, Mr. Donagher," Sam said as cheerfully as if Mungo had been watching the road in eager anticipation of their arrival. "Mind if I unhitch these horses and let them graze on some of this grass?"

Before Mungo could form a reply, Undine slipped through the open doorway behind him, holding up a lantern that glowed almost as brightly as her smile.

"Supper's ready to be served," she called. "I cooked it myself, too."

In the spill of light from Undine's lantern, Mungo's face looked hard.

Maddie shivered inwardly and wished it wouldn't be baldly impolite to fetch her shotgun from underneath the wagon seat and bring it right inside with her. "I'm half starved," she answered, because Sam didn't say a word—he was busy unhitching the team—and neither did Mungo.

Undine blinked, as though she hadn't taken notice of Maddie until that moment. "That's fine," she said without conviction. "You come on inside now, Maddie. Let the men tend to those horses." She nudged Mungo with one elbow and he finally moved.

Maddie glanced in Sam's direction, and was strangely

stricken to see that he'd paused in his work to gaze thoughtfully in Undine's direction. In that moment, she would have given her meager savings, stashed in a coffee tin under a loose floorboard in her bedroom, to know what was going through his mind.

It irritated her that she was even curious—Sam O'Ballivan was nothing to her, after all—and she swished her skirts a little as she swept up the walk toward Undine.

"Did you send off for those spring dresses I wanted?" Undine asked, addressing Maddie in an overbright, over-earnest tone, eyes sneaking past her to devour Sam. "If I can't get Mungo to take me to San Francisco for the worst of it, they'll be the only gaiety in the whole winter."

Winters in that part of the Arizona Territory were mild; snow was rare and the temperatures seldom called for cloak or coat. Maddie didn't bother to point that out, since Undine knew it well enough. "I wired the order to Chicago this afternoon," she said, accidentally brushing against Mungo as the two of them passed on the porch steps. She paused to watch as her recalcitrant host strode toward Sam and the horses.

"That's fine," Undine replied, but she sounded distracted, and when Maddie looked at her, she saw that she was still fastened on Sam. Mungo might as well have been invisible.

"Are the boys home?" Maddie asked, referring to Garrett, Landry and Rex. Ben was visible in the doorway, holding a pup in both arms and taking in the scene in shy silence.

Undine gave a tinkling little laugh. "Why, Maddie Chancelor, have you gone and set your cap for one of my stepsons? Here you are, in the company of the handsomest man in the whole territory, and you're wondering about those ruffians?"

LINDA LAEL MILLER

Maddie smiled, even though her stomach rolled at the thought of "setting her cap" for the likes of the Donaghers. She'd sooner die an old maid or even throw in with Oralee Pringle, than have truck with any of them. Worried that Undine's last remark might have reached Mungo's ears, she slipped an arm through the other woman's and hastily squired her into the front room, with its plank floors, beamed ceiling, and tall stone fireplace.

"Are you *trying* to make your husband angry?" she whispered a moment later, when Ben had gone outside to join Mungo and Sam at the wagon.

Undine blinked, her eyes wide with innocence. "Whatever do you mean, asking a question like that?" she asked, one hand fluttering to her throat.

Maddie narrowed her eyes. "I meant exactly what I said. Mungo is covetous as a rutting buck, and you damn well know it."

Undine smiled slyly and batted her lashes. "I'm not sure *Mungo's* the covetous one," she purred. "Are you taken with Mr. O'Ballivan, Maddie?"

Maddie's temper simmered. "No," she said fiercely, "I am *not* taken with Mr. O'Ballivan. I just don't want to see anyone get killed over your silly flirtations, that's all!"

"Have a care, Maddie Chancelor," Undine advised. "One word from me, and you and that brother of yours will be on the streets instead of living over the store and collecting a generous salary every month."

After a deep breath or two, Maddie was able to speak calmly. "And one word from *me,* Undine, and Mungo will know all about those letters from Tucson I've been separating from the ranch mail so you can read them in secret."

Undine's cheeks pinkened and her eyes flashed. She bit down on her lower lip.

For a moment Maddie was afraid Mungo's wife might

hurl the lantern at her, since she was still holding it. Instead she extinguished the flame and set it aside. "Come and see how pretty the table looks," she said as cordially as if no hard words had passed between them.

The long trestle table at the far end of the front room did look festive, set with glistening china plates and water glasses of cut crystal gracing a pristine cloth edged with lace. Undine's fancy tastes had been the talk of Haven when *that* order rolled into town on the weekly stagecoach.

Maddie felt a hunger that had nothing to do with food as she took in the sight of that table. Silver candlesticks, with beeswax tapers waiting to be lit. Elegant flatware. A bouquet of wildflowers, spilling over the sides of an exquisitely painted china vase.

"It looks wonderful," she said, and she meant it.

Undine seemed pleased. "Mungo has promised me a spinet," she said, well aware, it appeared, of Maddie's secret yearning for a home of her own. "We'll have it sent from San Francisco, if I have my way."

You always do, Maddie thought uncharitably. Her fingers flexed, missing the smooth ivory keys of the piano she'd played at the orphanage in St. Louis and, before that, in the churches and tents where her father had preached the gospel.

Don't remember, she told herself firmly.

She was spared further conversation with Undine when Sam, Mungo and the boy trooped in. The puppy was missing and Maddie presumed Ben had left it outside.

She saw Sam sweep the well-set table with a glance as he passed, following Mungo toward the kitchen, and knew he wasn't impressed by the china and cut glass; he'd been counting the places.

Feeling remiss, Maddie did the same. The total was

seven, which meant that unless Ben was to have his supper in the kitchen, as children often did on such occasions, two more people would be joining the festivities. If the boy had already eaten, then Garrett, Landry and Rex might make an entrance at any time.

Maddie steeled herself for that. The exchange with Undine had shaken her a little, but she quickly recovered and followed the men to wash her own hands.

Anna Deerhorn, the Donaghers' cook and housekeeper, was in the kitchen, and sure enough, she'd put a plateful of food on the big round table by the windows. Ben took a seat.

Anna met Maddie's gaze and gave a nod of greeting.

Maddie smiled. "That embroidery thread you wanted came in on Wednesday," she told the other woman, and pulled a small package from the pocket of her skirt. She'd wrapped the bright floss carefully before leaving the mercantile to pick Sam up at the schoolhouse.

Anna took the package with another nod and a whispered, "Thank you," and Maddie glanced warily at Mungo, wondering if she'd somehow betrayed a secret.

Mungo, as it happened, was too busy keeping a suspicious eye on Sam to pay any mind to anything else going on in the room, but Maddie was still troubled. If she got a chance to speak to Anna alone, she would take it.

They'd all washed up, in the basin Anna kept refilling with hot water from the reservoir on the cookstove, and taken their places at the table in the next room—Undine had seated herself squarely between Mungo and Sam, Maddie saw, with rising trepidation—when a clamor arose in the kitchen.

Nobody moved, and Mungo, who had been glowering at Sam since they'd sat down, didn't look away.

Maddie felt a little trill of fear when the door between the two rooms swung open, and Garrett, Landry and Rex

THE MAN FROM STONE CREEK

strolled through, single-file, all of them looking as though they'd just come off the trail.

Garrett, the firstborn, was tall and broad through the shoulders, with dark hair and watchful blue eyes. If he lived to old age, which wasn't likely, given his reputation, he'd look much as Mungo did now. Any woman who didn't know him would mark him down as handsome, Maddie supposed, but he was no stranger to her, and she kept a careful distance.

Landry, the second son, was a plain man, smaller than Garrett, with a narrow face and small eyes that flitted constantly from place to place, like a rodent on the lookout for a hungry cat.

Rex, like his eldest brother, was at least six feet in height. The resemblance ended there, though; his features were oddly blurred, as though reflected in moving water, his skin pitted by an early case of smallpox.

When their eyes fell on Sam O'Ballivan, Rex and Landry came to a standstill. Garrett, seeing that his father's attention was focused elsewhere, winked at Undine, who blushed and lowered her gaze.

Well, Maddie thought. I should have guessed.

Sam stood, and Maddie wondered if he was still wearing his .45 under his suit coat, or if he'd left it in the wagon, as most dinner guests would.

"I'm Sam O'Ballivan," he said heartily. "It's a pleasure to meet you."

Rex and Landry didn't look as though they agreed, but they recovered soon enough.

"Howdy," Rex said grudgingly.

"You sure do get around," Landry observed. "I'd swear I seen you someplace before." The unfriendly expression on his face clearly indicated that he knew exactly where he'd seen Sam O'Ballivan before, and had hoped not to repeat the experience.

LINDA LAEL MILLER

Sam smiled, unruffled. "It's a small world," he said, and sat down again.

Undine watched out of the corner of her eye as Garrett took the place next to Maddie, reached for a cloth napkin and flipped it open.

"Anna's ready to serve that venison roast any time now," she said, oblivious to the tension snapping in the air.

Maddie suppressed an urge to move her chair an inch or two farther from Garrett's. It made her skin crawl, being that close to him, and in her agitation, she happened to snag glances with Sam, sitting directly across the table from her.

She'd have sworn he smiled at her, even though his mouth didn't move, and she felt reassured.

Meanwhile, Rex and Landry hauled back their own chairs, with a great deal of scraping, and sat themselves down. Both of them kept casting unhappy looks in Sam's direction.

How, Maddie wondered, had he managed to make their questionable acquaintance in the short time since he'd come to Haven? When the Donagher brothers came to town, word spread like a storm warning and, since the mercantile was the heart of the community, and thus the changing house for the smallest tidbit of gossip, she would have known they were around five minutes after they rode in.

How would a schoolmaster, new to this part of the Territory, know a pair of scoundrels like Rex and Landry?

She could hardly wait to ask him.

The venison roast proved delicious, as did the rest of the meal—a heaping bowl of mashed potatoes, freshly baked biscuits, green beans and corn and peach cobbler for dessert.

Undine spent the entire evening fawning over Sam, and Mungo glared the whole time. Landry and Rex were jumpy, and Maddie, hungry as she was, could barely get a bite down her throat. The whole place felt like one giant tinderbox ready to explode into flames at a spark.

Garrett appeared comfortable enough, filling and emptying his plate more than once and stealing the occasional telling glance at Undine. And Sam seemed impervious to the sullen hostility coming his way from Mungo, Landry and Rex. He listened to Undine's relentless chatter as though it had been written on a sacred scroll and carried down from Mount Olympus on a platter, and by the time the peach cobbler went around the table, Maddie's stomach was clenched tight as a fist.

Would this night never end?

It was nearly nine-thirty, by the fancy clock on the sideboard, when Sam declined a third cup of coffee from a devoted Undine, and announced that he and Miss Chancelor had better be getting back to town. After all, he said, he had work to do in the morning, and Maddie liked to open the store for business right on time. She kept it open every day except Sunday.

Maddie fairly knocked her chair over backward getting to her feet.

"Landry, Rex," Mungo said gruffly, "you go out and hitch up that team." It was the first full sentence he'd spoken since they'd all sat at the table. "Garrett, help Undine clear the table. I'm sure Anna's gone out to her cabin and turned in by now."

Maddie felt regret. She liked Anna, and rarely got to see her.

"Sure thing, Pa," Garrett said, and waited until his father had risen and turned his back before dragging his eyes slowly over Undine.

Sam and Maddie took their leave. They had gone a mile up the river road before Sam stopped the team, got down and inspected the rigging. Up until then, he and Maddie hadn't spoken.

"What are you doing?" Maddie asked. She was fitful,

LINDA LAEL MILLER

anxious to get home to Terran, lock the doors behind her and forget she'd ever gone to supper at the Donagher ranch.

Sam didn't answer. He just tightened everything and climbed back up to take the reins. Maddie figured he hadn't trusted the Donaghers' hitching job, and didn't pursue the subject.

"You know them," she said when they'd been rolling again for several minutes. "Rex and Landry, I mean."

Sam chuckled. "Not as well as I plan to," he replied, and left Maddie to go right on wondering who Sam O'Ballivan really was, and what he wanted with Mungo Donagher's outlaw sons.

CHAPTER
SIX

A LOW, MEWLING SOUND caught Sam's ear as he rounded the back of the buckboard, out behind the mercantile, hoping to help Maddie down before she went ahead and made the leap herself. He paused and peered into the wagon bed, waiting for a cloud to pass over the skinny moon so he could see more than a shadowy shape huddled in the corner behind the seat.

Just as the moon was unveiled—the side lanterns had winked out, one and then the other, halfway back to town—Maddie turned from her perch to look down. "Land sakes," she said, "it's Ben's puppy."

Sam sighed, resettled his hat, and reached over the side of the wagon to hoist the little critter out. He'd been nestled on a pile of empty burlap bags the whole way, without making a sound until now.

"Sure enough," he agreed, setting the mutt on the ground and watching dubiously as it sniffed the rear wheel and then lifted a hind leg.

LINDA LAEL MILLER

Maddie gathered her skirts and clambered deftly over the board backrest to stand on the floorboards, her hands resting on her hips. "Somebody must have put him in the wagon. He couldn't have gotten there on his own."

"Ben, I reckon," Sam said. The dog had finished his business and was now smelling his pant leg. He hoped the lop-eared little creature hadn't mistaken him for a wagon wheel.

"Looks like you've been gifted with a dog," Maddie said with a degree of satisfaction that was wholly unbecoming.

Sam rubbed the back of his neck with one hand. "Now what would I do with a dog?" he countered.

She sat on the side-rail and swung her legs over with a swish of skirts. Sam caught her around the waist just before she would have made the jump, and stumbled a bit at the unexpected solidity of that deceptively slender frame. The contact between their two torsos roused something inside him that made him set her away from him abruptly.

Remember Abigail, he told himself. Damned if he could bring her face to mind, though, right at that moment.

"You're heavier than I would have guessed," he said, and then wished he could suck the words back in and swallow them.

Maddie seemed flustered. She straightened her skirts and patted her hair and took her time looking up into his face. "I can think of a thousand things you could have said," she told him peevishly, "that would have been better than *that*."

Sam felt the fool, and that always made him testy. He cleared his throat and tried again. "I didn't mean—"

Maddie put up a hand to silence him. In the sparse moonlight, he saw that she was amused, not insulted, and his relief was profound. She stooped, all of a sudden, and swept the little yellow dog up into her arms. Smiled, instead of making a face, when the pup gave her cheek a tentative lap.

Something shifted inside Sam, watching her. Made him wonder what she'd look like holding a baby. He took an unconscious step backward. "I'd best unhitch this team for you," he said. He didn't see a barn, but there was plenty of grass for the horses, and a trough.

"No need," she answered, still cuddling the pup. "Terran can do it."

With that, she gave a shrill whistle through her teeth.

Sam grinned, in spite of himself. He'd always admired people who could whistle like that, and he'd never run across the talent in a woman before. There were lots of things about Maddie Chancelor, he suspected, that he'd never come across before.

Before he could ask how she'd acquired the skill, the back door of the mercantile slammed open and Terran bounded out. Catching sight of the pup in his sister's arms, he stopped short.

"That's Neptune," he said. "What's he doing here?"

"I'm not sure," Maddie answered, stroking the dog's back in a way that made Sam widen his stance slightly. "We just found him in the back of the wagon. Unhitch the team and see that they get a little grain, please."

Terran nodded, but he approached and put out a hand to touch Neptune's wriggly little body. "I reckon Ben was worried one of his brothers would drown him in the creek," he speculated. He looked up at Maddie with hope clearly visible in his eyes, even in that poor light. "Can we keep him?"

"You know we can't," Maddie said with some regret. "Mr. James would have a fit."

Terran looked so dejected that Sam almost reached out and ruffled his hair, the way a man does when he wants to

LINDA LAEL MILLER

reassure a boy. He refrained, because the truce between him and Terran was new, like a naked and fragile bird just hatched from the egg.

"I guess I could take him back to the schoolhouse," he said with considerable reluctance. Sam was trying to break the habit of taking in lost critters; he'd left them scattered all over the Arizona Territory and half of Texas and New Mexico, as well, always in a good home, and at some point, it had to stop. "Just until we get the straight of the matter. I'll ask Ben about it Monday, before school takes up."

Maddie smiled a little and shoved the dog into his arms. "That's a splendid idea," she said.

Terran gazed at Neptune with a longing that made Sam feel bruised on the inside, then sighed and went to work releasing the harness fittings.

Sam stood there for a long moment, as confounded as if he were suddenly thirteen again, while the pup chewed on the collar of his one good suit coat. "What am I supposed to feed him?" he asked.

Maddie indulged in another smile. "You're a schoolmaster," she said. "You'll reason it out." With that, she gave a little curtsy—there was something of mockery in it—and raised her chin a notch. "Good night, Mr. O'Ballivan. And thank you for a very…interesting evening."

Before he could shuffle the pup and tug at his hat brim, she was gone, disappearing into the mercantile through the same door Terran had just come out of.

While Sam was still standing there, oddly befuddled, Terran finished his work, hung the harnesses on a fence post and dusted his hands together. "He'd probably favor some jerked venison, being a dog," the boy said. He ran into the store and came out again, quick as the proverbial wink, and held out two hands full of dried meat, obviously purloined from a crock or a bin in the mercantile.

THE MAN FROM STONE CREEK

Sam had to shuffle again, to take the jerky. He stuffed it into his pockets and looked up just as Maddie's shadow moved back from a second-floor window. "Obliged," he said.

"You need something else?" Terran asked reasonably.

Sam told his feet to move, but they didn't comply right away. "No," he said, still looking up at that lighted window, where Maddie had been standing only moments before. "I'll be going now."

Terran waited for him to follow through. "You taken a shine to my sister?" he asked when Sam stood stock-still for another minute or so.

That broke the spell. "No," Sam lied, and thrust himself into motion. He felt Terran's gaze on his back as he walked away.

Back at the schoolhouse, he went inside, set the pup on the floor, lit a lantern and assessed the situation while Neptune gnawed on a strip of dried meat from his pocket. Coming to no ready conclusion, he checked on the nameless horse, out there in the grass-scented darkness, found it sound, and returned to his quarters, which suddenly seemed lonely, even with Neptune curled up in front of the cold stove.

"I don't have any good reason to keep a dog," he said solemnly.

Neptune laid his muzzle on his paws, closed his eyes and fell asleep.

Sam kicked off his boots, shrugged out of his suit coat and loosened his collar. He unbuckled his gun belt, set the .45 within easy reach on the bedside stand. His eyes wandered to the stacks of books, teetering in piles and taking up most of the tabletop. He crossed to the middle of the room, selected a favorite, sat in the solitary wooden chair and flipped through the thin leaves, but his mind wouldn't settle on the familiar words. It kept straying, like

LINDA LAEL MILLER

a calf separated from the herd, to the mercantile on the main street of town and thence to the woman he'd glimpsed at that upstairs window.

Like as not, Maddie was getting ready to turn in right about now. Taking off her clothes, putting on a nightgown, maybe letting down her hair. He wondered if it reached to her waist, and if she plaited it before getting into bed.

Sam's throat constricted, and his groin ached.

He slammed *The Odyssey* shut, rousing the pup from its slumbers, and set the volume aside, to rest beside his .45.

Neptune let out a little whimper of concern.

"It's all right, boy," he told the dog. It was a pitiful thing, when a man was glad for the company of a pup that had been foisted off on him.

Usually, reading settled Sam's mind and made it easier to sleep. Tonight, the time-worn way of corralling his thoughts was not going to work, so with a sigh, he left his chair, ladled some water into a basin and washed up for the night. He used his toothbrush and powder, spitting out the back door, turned down the wick on the lamp, stripped to the skin and crawled under the covers of his narrow, lumpy schoolmaster's bed.

It didn't surprise him much when the pup jumped onto the foot of the mattress and settled himself, with a dog sigh, between Sam's feet. He cupped his hands behind his head and stared up at the dark ceiling, reviewing the events of the evening in his mind.

It took some doing to get past Maddie—the way she'd looked in her go-to-supper dress, the gleam of her hair when it caught a stray glint of moonlight, the way she'd told him about Warren Debney's death and her suspicion that one or all of the Donagher brothers had been behind it, or even Mungo himself.

THE MAN FROM STONE CREEK

Maybe, Sam thought, not for the first time, the old man had ordered the killing, out of spite. He'd wanted Maddie for a wife, and even now, when all danger of that was past, the mere idea turned Sam's stomach sour. Come to that, he didn't care much for the idea of that Debney fellow touching her, either, God rest his soul.

Deliberately he shifted his mind back to the Donaghers, where it belonged.

Garrett was a charmer, and perhaps a little too fond of his stepmother, if appearances were to be credited. Mungo's eldest might or might not be part of the gang Sam and Vierra wanted to rein in; dishonorable as it was, outlawry was rough, dirty work, requiring some hard riding and a modicum of grit. Garrett seemed the kind to take the easy route. His kind weren't usually good for much when it came to ranching, either, in Sam's experience. They always had one eye out for a lady and one ear cocked for the dinner bell.

Landry and Rex, now, they were different. Tear off those homespun, misbuttoned shirts they'd been wearing at Undine's elegant supper and you'd probably find a mean streak painted down their backs. They'd recognized Sam, sure enough, as the man they'd meant to harass the night before, over on the Mexican side of the river, and he'd kept his coat pushed back, so his .45 would be handy, all the way back to Haven.

He figured it was Maddie that had kept them from coming after him, as soon as supper was ended and he'd driven out of sight of the ranch house. If her company hadn't been so downright pleasant, he might have regretted having her along for just that reason. He wouldn't have minded a little set-to with one or both of the Donaghers, but he was a patient man.

He could wait.

Neptune gave a low growl and got to his feet.

LINDA LAEL MILLER

Sam reached for the .45.

Maybe he wouldn't have to wait.

The door latch rattled.

The dog let out a sharp bark. His hackles were standing straight up.

Sam cursed under his breath, cocked the .45 and reached for his pants. Got into them one-handed and fastened the top button.

"Mr. O'Ballivan?" a familiar female voice called.

"Hush," he told the dog.

Sam opened the door, the revolver still in his hand, and found Bird standing on the step, looking up at him. Even in the pale light of the moon, he could see that one of her eyes was blackened and her chin was wobbling.

He reached out, caught hold of her arm and pulled her inside.

Neptune growled once more, then subsided, settling himself on the mattress again, satisfied that he'd done his duty.

"What happened?" Sam demanded, setting the .45 on the nightstand again and groping to light the lantern. In the glow of the lamp, he saw that Bird's face was streaked with kohl, her dress torn, and the shiner was worse than any he'd ever seen.

"Somebody got rough," she said, and sank into his chair as if her knees wouldn't hold her up for another moment.

Sam found a basin and emptied the water bucket into it, then reached for the one towel he owned. He and Violet Perkins had both used it, so it wasn't as clean as he'd have liked, but they'd have to make do.

"Who?" Sam asked, wetting a corner of the towel in the basin and dabbing at her upper lip with it. She'd been punched at least twice, and it would be a wonder if she still had all her teeth.

THE MAN FROM STONE CREEK

Bird shivered, and when she looked up into his eyes, it seemed like he could see the bruises on her soul. "Garrett Donagher," she whispered. "He came in a little while ago, in a real state. I don't mind liftin' my skirt, that's my job, but—"

A tremor of rage went through Sam and it took a few moments to ride it out. Donagher must have set out for town as soon as he and Maddie had left the ranch house, riding overland at a hard pace.

"You told me to come to you if I had trouble," Bird reminded him in a small, shamed voice.

"What brought this on?" he asked, and went on cleaning up her face. The answer wouldn't matter in the vast scheme of things, but he needed something to keep his mind on the task at hand, keep him from hunting Donagher down and taking his fists to him.

A tear slipped down Bird's cheek, trickling its windy way through rouge as thick as a coat of whitewash. "I don't know," she said miserably. "I went over it and over it in my mind, after I got loose of him and come running for your place, but I can't come up with a reason for what he did, 'cept simple meanness." She stopped, swallowed miserably. "I hit Garrett over the head with a lamp," she confessed. "Oralee ain't going to like that, my breaking her lamp. Least of all, on a customer's head. Knocked him clean out, too."

Sam smiled at the image of a Donagher prostrate on the floor of a whorehouse, though it probably looked more like a grimace to Bird. "Good," he said.

"Good?" Bird asked, blinking again. "Garrett's going to kill me when he comes around, if one of his brothers doesn't do it first." Another fleeting, brave little smile. "You said you'd help me, if I got myself into trouble, but right now, I can't for the life of me reckon how you'll go about it."

LINDA LAEL MILLER

Sam got his flask, the one he carried in his saddlebags when he was away from Stone Creek, and dampened a fresh corner of the towel with it. Bird winced when he touched it to the cut over her lip. "It's a conundrum, all right," he conceded. "You sure can't go back to the Rattlesnake. But if you spend the night here, I'll be out of work by morning."

Bird's shoulders slumped. She clearly expected him to go back on his word, like everybody else in her life had probably done for as long as she could recall.

She didn't know Sam O'Ballivan. What he'd go through to keep a promise was fitting stuff for the epic tales in those volumes over there on the table. He'd cut his teeth on Hercules, after all, but at times like this one, he felt like Prometheus, condemned to have his liver fed to an eagle on a continuous basis. It was the price of stealing fire, he supposed.

He must have voiced at least some of his thoughts, because Bird wrinkled her nose in confusion and asked, "Who?"

"Prometheus," he said, resigned to the explanation. "He was a Greek god. Among other things, he stole fire and gave it to humans, so they could keep warm and cook their food. Zeus wasn't too happy about it and sent this eagle—"

"I never heard nothin' like that at the preachin'," Bird said, confounded.

"Never mind." Sam sighed.

"Who's this Zeus fella?"

"Just somebody in a story," Sam answered. He'd done all he could, in terms of tending Bird's wounds. The finer points of Greek mythology would have to wait.

"What are we going to do now?" Bird asked. "I'd as soon take my chances with wolves and bears as go back to the Rattlesnake."

THE MAN FROM STONE CREEK

Sam strapped on his gun belt, slid his .45 into the holster, draped his coat over Bird's shoulders. "Only one thing we can do," he said.

Five minutes later he was knocking at the back door of the mercantile.

Maddie answered, bundled in a wrapper and holding a lantern high. He'd have bet the shotgun was leaning against the doorframe, within easy reach. She'd plaited her hair, the single braid resting over her right shoulder like a gleaming length of chestnut-colored rope, reaching past her waist.

Her eyes widened when she saw Bird, huddled in Sam's coat, shivering even though it was a warm night.

"I know it's late," Sam began, and then stopped, because he didn't know where to go from there.

Maddie's jaw clamped down visibly. She'd grind down her molars if she kept that up. She ran her gaze over the saloon girl again, then stepped back. "Come in," she said.

Sure enough, the shotgun was beside the door. Sam felt a little less flummoxed, having that settled, along with the way Maddie wore her hair when she went to bed. Beyond those two things, though, he seemed to be at a loss.

"You're hurt," Maddie said, taking another look at Bird's face in the lamplight.

"Garrett Donagher beat me up," Bird said, and Sam was thankful. He'd had the impetus to get here, but now that they were in the kitchen behind the mercantile, with Maddie naturally wanting an explanation, he was having a hard time finding words.

"Sit down," Maddie told her, pulling back a chair at a round table and setting the lamp in the middle. "Let me have a look."

"I can't go back to the Rattlesnake," Bird went on nervously, taking a seat and turning her face up for Maddie's

LINDA LAEL MILLER

inspection. "And Mr. O'Ballivan says I can't stay at the schoolhouse, either, or he'll be out of work by morning."

Maddie flung a glance in Sam's direction. He kept his distance and held his tongue, leaning back against the wall and folding his arms. He hoped the light wasn't good enough to reveal the flush he felt pulsing in his neck and rising to his ears.

"So he brought you here," Maddie said.

Bird swallowed and lowered her head before she nodded.

"Why can't you go back to Oralee's?"

"Because I clouted Garrett over the head with a lamp to get away from him," Bird said, looking up slowly. "He was bleedin' pretty good when I left him." She swallowed again, harder this time. "You don't reckon I *kilt* him, do you?"

Maddie sighed. "He's Mungo Donagher's son," she said. "His head is harder than packed dirt." She set her hands on her hips. "Where was Oralee while all this was happening?"

"She lit out for Tucson a couple of days ago, and she ain't come back yet," Bird answered, squirming a little. "She wouldn't take my part even if she was here, though. Garrett's a customer, and I'm just a…just a—"

Maddie laid a hand on Bird's shoulder, squeezed. "I could make you a cup of tea," she said with brisk kindness.

"I'd rather have whiskey," Bird replied honestly.

Sam bit back a grin.

"Sorry," Maddie said. "Fresh out."

About that time, Terran appeared, through a curtained doorway, sleep-baffled and clad in a long nightshirt. "Is she a dance hall girl?"

There was a stove in the corner and a sink with a pump. "Yes," Maddie said, sounding exasperated. She poked some kindling into the stove, along with crumpled newspaper, and lit a match to it. "And if you tell a soul she's here, Terran Chancelor, you'll be splitting firewood till your hands blister."

Terran came a step closer, peering curiously at Bird. "What's your name?"

"Bird of Paradise," Bird said, smiling a little now that she knew she wasn't going to be turned away.

"Tarnation," Terran said, awed. "You born with that name?"

Sam pushed away from the wall, took the teakettle from Maddie and pumped water into it at the sink.

"Nope," Bird told Terran. "I was Esther Sue before I came to work for Oralee."

"I like Bird of Paradise better," Terran said, dragging back a chair and sitting himself down next to the night visitor. "It's a pure mouthful, though."

"Just call me Bird," Bird suggested. "Like Mr. O'Ballivan here does."

Sam had his back to Terran, but he felt the boy's gaze boring into his spine.

"I'd like to know how you and Mr. O'Ballivan became acquainted," Maddie said. Her tone was cordial, but there was bedrock under it. She wrenched the teakettle out of Sam's hands and set it on the stovetop with a little bang of metal against metal.

Sam's ears burned.

"I brought him his supper," Bird said proudly, "first night he was in town. We got to be friends then."

"Isn't that nice?" Maddie responded. She didn't sound like she thought it was nice, but that seemed to go over both Terran's and Bird's heads. Sam wished it had gone over his.

"Nothing happened," he told Maddie, and then could have kicked himself, because it was none of her damn business whether anything *happened* or not.

LINDA LAEL MILLER

Maddie clattered down some cups from a cupboard, along with a tin of tea leaves. Evidently she and Terran had their meals down here and slept upstairs. Sam's eyes rose to the ceiling, and he was possessed of a powerful wondering where he had no call to wonder.

"Maddie won't let me go near the Rattlesnake," Terran confided to Bird. "Not even to deliver Miss Oralee's provisions. Not that she buys much from us."

"It's no place for a fine boy like you," Bird agreed. "You listen to your sister. She knows what's best for you."

"Do you have a sister?" Terran asked, still breathless with amazement at finding a dance hall girl in the family kitchen in the middle of the night.

"I did once," Bird said with a note of sorrowful nostalgia. "She wouldn't speak to me now."

Maddie waxed thoughtful. Now that she was over the shock of the encounter, Sam figured, she was sifting for solutions. He blessed her for that, though he knew she'd shoot a few blistering remarks his way the next time they were alone.

"Where does your sister live?" she asked Bird, measuring orange pekoe into a crockery pot and then adding more wood to the fire in the belly of the stove.

"Denver," Bird replied. The way she said the word, the place might have been on the other side of an ocean, instead of a week's travel by stagecoach and railroad. "She's married and lives in a big house with a porch that wraps almost the whole way around."

"You're sure she wouldn't take you in?" Sam asked, feeling that he ought to say something since he'd been the one to carry the problem to Maddie and drop it at her feet. Which, he noted, were bare under the hem of that wrapper.

He cleared his throat and looked away, forcing his gaze back to Bird and Terran, sitting close together at Maddie's table in a spill of lantern light, waiting for the tea water to boil. It might have been a cozy scene, if he hadn't known Garrett Donagher had probably come to by now and was fixing to turn over every stone in town until he found Bird and exacted vengeance.

"I don't know," Bird mused sadly, having taken so long to answer Sam's initial question that he'd forgotten what it was and had to do some catching up.

Maddie had a pencil and a scrap of paper, and sat herself in a third chair at the table. "What's your sister's name?" she asked practically.

Bird hesitated. "Mrs. Zebediah T. Roundtree," she said. "Her husband's a lawyer." She followed with an address, in a good part of Denver.

Maddie scribbled down the information and thrust it at Sam. "Send a wire, first thing in the morning," she told him. "If you give the telegraph operator a dollar, he'll keep it to himself. If you don't, you might as well print bills and post them all over Haven."

Sam nodded, took the paper and tucked it into his vest pocket.

Heat began to surge through the teakettle on the stove.

Maddie got up again, brewed the tea, and poured cups for herself and Bird, since Sam declined the offer, made with a raised eyebrow, and wished that, just once, he could get through an uneventful day.

Terran was sent back to bed, and went unwillingly.

Bird took a few sips from her tea, laid her head down on the table and went to sleep.

Maddie glared at Sam over the rim of her steaming cup.

"Well," Sam said, compelled to defend himself, "*you* made *me* take the dog home."

Maddie made a snorting sound, set her cup down and clapped one hand over her mouth. Sam was relieved to see

LINDA LAEL MILLER

that, one, she wasn't choking, and two, her eyes were bright with laughter.

Once she'd swallowed and caught her breath, she actually smiled.

"You'll be all right here?" Sam asked, thinking he ought to leave. Trouble was, Bird was still wearing his coat, and he didn't want to wake her up, given what she'd been through. On the other hand, he'd left most of his belongings up at Stone Creek, and he'd need that coat, if only to cover up his .45.

Maddie inclined her head toward the shotgun, still leaning against the wall next to the door. "I'll be just fine," she said, "provided you don't rescue anybody else before we can put Bird on the stagecoach come Wednesday."

Sam sighed and got to his feet, uneasy with leaving, and not just because Garrett Donagher might get wind of Bird's hiding place and come after her. Being around Maddie was like drawing close to a fire on a cold night. A man didn't like going back out into the blizzard.

"Terran will bring your suit coat to school in the morning," Maddie said. Evidently, mind reading numbered among her talents. "I'll wrap it in brown paper, so folks won't be speculating on how it came to here."

Sam nodded and put his hand on the door latch. "Good night, Maddie," he said. "And thank you."

She didn't smile, and that was probably a good thing, because then he'd have liked leaving even less than he already did. "Good night, Sam O'Ballivan," she replied.

He heard the lock snap into place as soon as he'd closed the door behind him, and it gave him a lonely feeling, standing out here on the back step. He didn't linger and took the long way back to the schoolhouse, passing by the Rattlesnake Saloon. There were plenty of horses tied up out front, including Charlie Wilcox's old nag, waiting wearily to plod back to the shack.

THE MAN FROM STONE CREEK

Sam resisted an urge to stop and commiserate.
He'd done enough of that for one night.

TERRAN TURNED UP at the schoolhouse the next morning, even though it was Saturday, and his eyes gleamed with secrets when he shoved a bundle into Sam's hands, out front by the well. Maddie had returned the suit coat, as promised.

"How's Bird faring?" Sam asked, watching as Neptune trundled through the deep, breeze-rippled grass in pursuit of a horsefly.

The boy looked around secretively, then whispered his answer, even though there was nobody but Sam and the dog around to hear. "She ate four hotcakes this morning," he confided. "Maddie says the way she's going, she'll eat us out of house and home before Wednesday ever gets here. Did you send that wire to Denver?"

Sam nodded. He'd taken care of that first thing, after feeding Neptune some more jerked venison and swilling enough coffee to get his eyes to stay open. It had cost him a dollar and a half to dispatch that message. His thoughts snagged on the hotcakes, though, and made his stomach rumble.

Terran fairly swelled with importance. "You think she'll take Bird in? Mrs. Zebediah T. Roundtree and her lawyer husband, I mean?"

Sam shrugged. "I hope so," he said. He frowned. "You don't miss much, do you?"

Terran's smile was smug. "Next to nothin'," he said.

CHAPTER

SEVEN

AT SUNSET, Vierra roused himself, disentangling his arms and legs from those of the woman whose bed he shared, groping his way upward, out of sleepy satiation, clumsily lighting the lamp on the bedside table and contemplating a cheroot.

The woman lay with her face hidden beneath a glimmering curtain of honey-colored hair, her body soft and warm from a long afternoon of lovemaking. For one disconcerting moment, he could not recall her name, knew only that she *wasn't* Pilar Montoya.

He shook off the melancholy that realization brought. He'd gone too deep and waded doggedly back to the shallower regions of his mind.

Oh, yes, he thought, sitting up to rub his face hard with both hands. This was Amadea Rios-Flores, luscious wife of a very old and very wealthy *patron,* imported from Europe and denied nothing, except lovers. If he was caught with her, he would be bound to a post, stripped of his shirt and lashed until he bled to death.

Not a pleasant prospect, though at least it would mean he felt something.

The lovely Amadea stirred on the pillows, turned sleepily onto her back, crooned his name as she stretched.

Footsteps thumped in the corridor.

Suddenly alert, Vierra swore, threw back the heavy linen sheet and swung both legs over the side of the bed.

A loud, husbandly rap sounded at the door.

Vierra snatched up his clothes and took refuge behind the silk changing screen in the corner, peering through the narrow crack between two artfully painted panels— peacocks, with their tail feathers spread—as he scrambled into his pants. Too late, he realized he'd forgotten his boots, and one of them was sticking out from beneath the bed.

Vierra held his breath and waited as Amadea sat up, yawned, realized the problem and pulled the sheet up over her breasts with a small gasp of alarm. Her eyes were wide as they sought him.

Silently he ran through the list of saints, seeking one he hadn't offended with some promise, hastily made and just as hastily broken.

"Come in," Amadea called in her strange Teutonic Spanish. Her gaze darted to the open window, with its lace curtains fluttering on the hot breath of the evening. No doubt she believed Vierra had already ducked out, the same way he'd come in, by way of the hacienda's sloping, many-leveled roof.

He crossed himself as Juan Rios-Flores opened the door and strode across the threshold, strutting like the vainglorious little rooster he was. Rios-Flores was barely five feet tall, with a balding head, gray mutton-chop whiskers, a belly and a wide nose that looked as if it had been flattened by the bristled side of a horse brush.

He sniffed the air as if scenting Vierra.

LINDA LAEL MILLER

St. Jude, Vierra thought. Perhaps he hadn't affronted the patron saint of the impossible—at least, not too seriously. *I will never again sleep with another man's wife,* he promised silently. He didn't believe the vow for a moment, of course, and neither, regrettably, would St. Jude.

"Our guests will be arriving soon," Rio-Flores told his pink and thoroughly satisfied wife. His suspicion seemed to be abating, but Vierra didn't breathe or move even the smallest muscle. If he could have willed his heart to stop beating, he would have done so. "Why are you languishing there in bed? The servants require direction."

"I had a headache," Amadea lied prettily. She stretched again, beneath the sheet, and made a kittenish sound of contentment. "I am better now." Her perfect face crumpled into a frown. On her, even that was attractive. "I thought you were in Refugio until tomorrow," she added.

Vierra had thought the same thing, which was why he'd availed himself to the pleasures of Amadea's sleek, succulent body in the middle of the day.

I'm getting too old for this, he told himself and the pertinent saint, whom he hoped was bending a kindly ear his way.

"I finished my business there early," Rios-Flores said, narrowing his little eyes and scanning the room. As his gaze passed over the changing screen, Vierra shivered. The distinctive scent of passion was subtle, but unmistakable, as well, and it would be a miracle if no one in the hacienda had heard Amadea's cries of release. Perhaps one of the servants had passed in the corridor at the wrong time, and reported to *el patron*.

Vierra closed his eyes and made another empty vow to St. Jude. *No more married women,* he reiterated. *I promise.*

"Get dressed," Rios-Flores commanded gruffly. And then, mercifully, he was gone, closing the door smartly behind him.

THE MAN FROM STONE CREEK

Vierra, who had been in many such delicate situations before and could not be sure of his standing with his favorite saint, waited. Amadea crawled out of bed, on the side closest to him, saw his boots lying on the floor and bit down hard on her lower lip. Her eyes came to rest on the changing screen and narrowed. Just as she opened her mouth to speak, the door flew open again and Rios-Flores dashed in.

Wrapped in the sheet, Amadea looked back at her husband over a bare shoulder, simultaneously employing one foot to slide Vierra's boot under the bed.

"You wanted something, darling?" she asked innocently.

Vierra was certain he'd succeeded at willing his heartbeat to a standstill.

Rios-Flores flushed, no doubt feeling the fool. He looked like a fat fish, tossed up onto the bank, straining to breathe. At last, he shook his head and left the room again.

Vierra's knees went weak with relief. He turned his eyes heavenward and crossed himself again.

Gracias, he told the patient saint.

Amadea, statuesque in her sheet, rounded the end of the bed, hurried to the door and turned the key in the lock.

"Get out!" she whispered as furiously as if Vierra were an intruder rather than a once-welcome guest. "If Juan finds you here, he will kill us both!"

Vierra slipped out from behind the screen, stooped to retrieve his boots and tugged them on. Thanking God, the Virgin, the angels and all the attending saints and martyrs, he planted a light kiss on Amadea's pouting mouth and made for the window.

He would not be back, he decided as he navigated the tile roof, his step as light as a cat's. No, indeed. From now on he would confine his amorous adventures to women who did not have jealous and powerful husbands.

LINDA LAEL MILLER

He paused, looked up at the black-velvet sky with its great river of diamonds flowing from horizon to horizon.

Unless, he amended, with a slight smile, the temptation proved too great for a poor, misguided sinner like him to resist.

IT WAS GOING TO BE a quiet, lonely night, Sam thought as he dragged the copper bathtub into the middle of the floor. He'd shot a rabbit for supper, eaten his fill and given the leftovers to Neptune.

The dog's owner hadn't shown up to claim him, and Sam was troubled about that, but the plain fact of the matter was, he'd been thinking about Maddie Chancelor ever since he'd left the mercantile the night before. Hadn't gotten any sleep to speak of, either, and he'd been in a fractious temper because of it.

He felt restless now, as though there was something he ought to be doing and wasn't. The major's orders had been specific. *Act like a schoolmaster. Don't stir things up too much before time—that'll make folks curious and they'll start flapping their jaws. When you've got those outlaws dead to rights, that's when you make your move.*

He took two buckets and carried them through the schoolhouse and on outside, to the well he'd pulled poor Tom Singleton out of his first day in Haven. Filled them both, taking some comfort in the laborious nature of the cranking required, and hauled them back inside to heat on top of the stove.

Things had come to a sorry pass, he reflected as he built up the fire, when the best a man could look forward to was a bath in two inches of lukewarm water. Even his old friend and companion Hercules couldn't be counted on to liven up the night. He felt too fitful to read; there was something on the wind, charging the air like a storm gathering force in the furthest hills, and he was damned if he could guess what it was.

While the tin buckets sat on the stovetop, taking their sweet time to warm, Sam went outside to groom the horse the major had given him, along with a princely sum of money. *You'll need bribes, dealing with them Mexicans,* the old man had said. *And have a care how you handle Vierra. Don't know much about him. Best we could do, though, so you'll have to keep your wits about you.*

Neptune, heretofore plaguing the patient old horse, settled his haunches in the deep grass and growled low in his throat. To hear him, a man would have thought he was a wolf instead of a squirmy pup who whimpered in his sleep.

"Hush," Sam told him, and paused from brushing the horse to listen.

A wagon, coming close.

He smiled to himself, and hope surged up his windpipe to swell in his throat. Maddie Chancelor, come to make a delivery? He hadn't ordered anything from the mercantile, insofar as he could recollect. Maybe she'd gotten tired of harboring Bird while they waited for an answer to the telegram he'd sent, and decided to toss her back in his lap. Maddie was taking a risk, all right, hiding a saloon girl in the rooms above the general store, and he knew she was chafing under the load. If Mungo got wind of the deceit, there'd be hell to pay.

Sam set aside the brush and waited. He'd left his coat inside, since it was a warm evening, and his gun belt was in plain sight around his hips. If his caller *wasn't* Maddie, it might be an awkward thing to explain. This was 1903, after all, a new and modern century, and the world had changed since the old days. Most men didn't wear a sidearm, at least in town, and that went double for school-masters.

LINDA LAEL MILLER

A buggy rounded the corner of the schoolhouse, a moving shadow in the light of a scant moon and a legion of stars. As it got closer, he saw that the rig was drawn smartly by a coal-black gelding, and there was a fancy woman at the reins.

"Sam O'Ballivan?" the lady inquired, pulling to a stop a dozen yards short of where he stood. She gave the buggy whip a decisive little flick before jamming it into its holder.

Not a social call, then, he decided.

"Yes, ma'am," he said.

Neptune didn't bark. Instead he seemed to be lying low in the grass, like a soldier dodging cannonballs inside a beleaguered fort.

"Oralee Pringle," the visitor announced. The whole buggy shook as she alighted. She was hefty, and dressed in what looked like brown bombazine. The heavy fabric rustled as she approached, and her dyed-yellow ringlets bounced, like her bosom.

"Evening," Sam said, thinking he might have to revise his previous decision that it was going to be a boring night.

Miss Pringle put out a hand almost as brawny as Sam's own, and he shook it as a matter of courtesy. Round eyes, probably dark blue, peered up at him from beneath piles of lacquered curls. Oralee had been a pretty girl once, he figured, but her best years were behind her, along with a whole slew of rich dinners, given the expanse of the backside he'd glimpsed as she climbed down out of that buggy.

"I've lost one of my girls," Oralee said forthrightly. "Wondered if you knew anything about her. Bird of Paradise, she calls herself." The brothel and saloon owner gave a little snort of derision. "Damn near not worth the trouble she causes me. Sent her over here with supper in a basket to welcome you to town, before I lit out for Tucson."

Sam held her gaze. There were times when a man had to lie, though he'd never favored it. "It was a fine supper," he said. "And I'm obliged, but I haven't seen the girl since."

Oralee pondered the reply, and Sam would have bet she didn't believe him. "Troublesome little thing, and too skinny by half for most of my customers. Skittish as all get-out. Split Garrett Donagher's head open with a lamp I had sent all the way from Boston. Once he came to, he fair took my place apart, looking for her."

"Maybe it's a good thing she isn't around then," Sam said easily.

Oralee narrowed her eyes to slits. "The other girls said Bird was all swoony, after she come back from fetching that basket over here. She took a liking to you, according to them."

"I'm flattered," Sam replied.

"You don't look like no schoolteacher I've ever seen," Oralee prodded.

"You're not the first person to say that," he said with modest regret. "What do I look like to you, Miss Pringle?"

"A lawman, maybe," Oralee decided. She glanced down at the .45 riding low on Sam's right hip before shifting her attention back to his face. "Or a gunslinger."

Privately, Sam indulged his habit of renaming folks for characters in the books he knew practically by heart. From that moment on, Oralee Pringle was Medusa. Those ringlets of hers could turn to snakes anytime, and with little provocation.

"You get a lot of gunslingers through here?" he asked.

Neptune whined and tried to climb up his left leg.

"Plenty of 'em," Medusa replied, watching him shrewdly. "And not a few lawmen, too."

Sam rubbed his chin thoughtfully. "Not likely I'll run into either, teaching school."

"Well, if you do," the madam said, jabbing a plump

LINDA LAEL MILLER

finger against Sam's chest, probably feeling for a badge, "whichever side of the law they're on, you tell 'em what I'm telling you right now. There ain't *nothin'* goes on in this town that Oralee Pringle don't know all about."

"I'll be sure and pass that on," Sam promised, quietly affable, "should the opportunity arise." He stooped and caught Neptune in the curve of one arm. The pup shivered.

"Next time you pay off a telegraph operator," Oralee shot back, "you'd better give him more than a dollar."

Hell, Sam thought, but he kept his expression still as a frozen puddle on a winter's day. He said nothing.

"Where'd you put her?" Oralee demanded. "Stage don't come through till Wednesday, and if she'd left town on horseback, I'd have heard about it from ole Dub, over to the livery stable."

"If I knew," Sam said, "I don't reckon I'd tell you."

Suddenly, unexpectedly, Oralee smiled. She had tiny white teeth, like a doll's, and the effect was jarring in a face the size of a full moon. "I make a real good friend, Sam O'Ballivan," she said, "and a real *bad* enemy. You got a yen for Bird, we can work something out. In the meantime, Garrett Donagher is making my life miserable, and that means Mungo ain't far behind. I don't need that kind of trouble."

"I certainly sympathize," Sam told her, watching with morbid fascination as Oralee's curls quivered around her head, fixing to sprout eyes, scales and fangs, "but I can't help you. And much as I'd like to stay out here and chew the fat with you, Miss Pringle, I've got something on the stove." He put the pup down and it raced for the back door of the schoolhouse like a rabbit for a hole.

"So do I," Oralee retorted. "My bustle. The Donaghers'll be stoking the fire pretty soon, too, if I don't do something about Bird."

THE MAN FROM STONE CREEK

Sam enjoyed the stove-and-bustle image for a few moments as he took the madam's plump arm and steered her in the direction of the buggy. "The way you talk, Miss Pringle," he said with easy cordiality, "a man would think Mungo and his boys were outlaws, instead of good, upstanding ranchers."

Oralee narrowed her eyes as she peered up at him, and they all but disappeared into the surrounding flesh. "Now that sounds like somethin' a lawman would say. If he happened to be fishin' for information, for example."

"You've got a fanciful nature, ma'am." Sam steadied the buggy, thinking it might turn right over on its side if he didn't, while Miss Pringle climbed aboard. Her pulling horse gave a snorting sigh as she took up the reins, and Sam gave it a comforting pat on the flanks. The poor critter would probably collapse from fright if it ever saw Oralee coming toward it with a saddle.

She snorted, sounding much like the horse. "We'll see who's fanciful," Oralee said. Then she slapped down those reins and trundled off into the darkness, putting Sam in mind of a ship departing over restless waters and listing distinctly to the left.

Neptune greeted Sam with a hopeful whimper when he stepped over the threshold into a wafting cloud of steam from the water on the stove. He shut the door, latched it, and bent to ruffle the dog's ears. "You can breathe easy now, friend," he told the animal. "She's gone."

He poured the simmering contents of the kettle into the tub, then lit a lamp in the schoolroom and appropriated the last of the day's drinking water, adding that to the bath so he wouldn't parboil himself, and took off his gun belt. He was naked as his first birthday, smoking a cheroot, and longing for his own comforts, up at Stone Creek, when the inside door suddenly sprang open.

LINDA LAEL MILLER

Sam had left his .45 on the table when he undressed for the occasion, and it was a good thing. If it had been close at hand, he'd have shot Maddie Chancelor on the threshold before he realized who she was.

"You've got to do something!" she blurted.

Sam almost swallowed the cheroot, and then he had to wait for his gizzard to shinny back down out of his throat and settle into its right place. His towel was draped over the side of the copper tub Maddie had sold him at a premium price, and he didn't reach for it. If she saw more than was proper, and embarrassed herself, well, it would serve her right for barging into a man's place of residence without so much as a knock or a rousing hail from the doorstep. The cheroot made a sizzling sound as he dunked it in his bathwater.

She froze, in the midst of revelation, and slapped a hand over her eyes. "Land sakes," she gasped. "You're not decent!"

Sam relished her discomfort, since it was so richly deserved, and for some less honorable reasons, too. "I don't usually bathe with my clothes on, Miss Chancelor," he replied. "And suffice it to say, I wasn't expecting company."

Maddie turned her back before lowering her hand so she could see again. "There was a light in the schoolroom window," she said with miserable dignity, "and the door was unlatched, so I just came in. I assumed you were working late."

Sam considered getting out of the tub, with the towel to cover his privates, and pulling on his shirt and britches, but he decided against it. He'd gone to a lot of trouble for that bath, and he meant to suds up and rinse, whether Maddie stayed on or not. "There are some things," he drawled, reaching for the soap, "that a lady shouldn't assume."

THE MAN FROM STONE CREEK

He watched her spine straighten under her trim cotton dress. "The schoolhouse," she said, "is a public building."

Sam soaped his neck, shoulders and armpits, then commenced to splashing. Neptune, lying in front of the stove with his muzzle resting on his paws, rolled a piteous look in his direction. "Worthless dog," he said with affection. "You're supposed to bark when you hear an intruder."

"I am *not* an intruder," Maddie said. She was gripping the doorframe now on either side, almost as if she feared she might turn around and look right at Sam if she didn't hold on to something solid.

"I reckon that's a matter of perspective," he replied with a private grin. "Did you come here to say something, or just to ruin my reputation as well as your own?"

Maddie sputtered for a moment or two before she got a coherent word out. "It's Bird," she said. "She's taught Terran to swear like a sea captain. Tonight, when I finished the accounts and went in to start supper, they were playing *poker.*"

"Saints preserve us," Sam said. "Not poker."

"Five card stud," Maddie confirmed, horrified.

"The devil," Sam replied with resignation, "has come to Haven and hung out his shingle."

She stiffened. "This is not a joking matter, Mr. O'Ballivan," she said. "I want my brother to grow up to be a gentleman. Gentlemen do not gamble and curse."

Sam smiled and settled back in the tub, even though the water was lukewarm by then, and didn't even cover his knees, much less the flagpole. He relented and covered himself with the towel, which put him in mind of the tents he'd slept in during his cavalry days. "If that's your definition of a gentleman," he remarked, "Terran's beat from the start. He could probably hold his own in the swearing

LINDA LAEL MILLER

department before he ever made Bird's acquaintance. In fact, I'd venture to say he's taught *her* a new word or two."

That was the final straw for Maddie Chancelor. She whirled in the doorway, her eyes fixed stalwartly on Sam's face and burning into his flesh like a pair of brands. "Come and fetch that—" she paused, swallowed visibly "—young *woman* before she corrupts my brother!"

If Maddie had been anybody but who she was, Sam would have stood, just to give her a start. Fortunately, taps had sounded by then, and the tent had flattened out some. Not that she'd have looked at that segment of his anatomy to save her very life.

"I am amenable to suggestion," Sam told Maddie, delighting in the pink flames on her cheekbones and the righteous glitter in her eyes. "I can't hand Bird over to Miss Pringle, or the Donaghers will get her. I can't bring her here without the whole town knowing and running the both of us out on a rail. I'm afraid I'm fresh out of ideas."

Maddie bit her lower lip. "It's a long time till Wednesday," she lamented. "Four whole days."

"Yes," Sam agreed. "By that time, Terran could have earned himself eternal damnation—if he hasn't already."

Miss Chancelor blinked, and Sam would have sworn she had something sour in her mouth and meant to spit it out. He was right, in a manner of speaking. "I do believe the devil *has* come to Haven," she snapped, "and passed himself off as a schoolmaster!"

Sam sighed, and Neptune gave him another sorrowful glance. "I suppose Terran could bunk in here for the time being," he said. "Tell him to bring a bedroll, though, because I'm not sleeping on the floor."

Maddie blinked again, and Sam wondered if she needed spectacles and was too vain to wear them. "I'm not so sure that would be an improvement," she answered, calmer now. He could tell she was weighing the nays and yeas of the matter. "You carry a sidearm. For all I know, you're a gunslinger. Besides, folks will know Terran left home, and they'll wonder why. They'll *talk.*"

"I reckon they're already talking," Sam mused. "It's dark out. You're an unmarried woman, and I'm an unmarried man. Here I am, taking a bath. There *you* are, watching me—"

"I am *not* watching you!"

"I don't reckon the gossips will slice the story that fine." He paused, savoring her indignation. "Do you?"

She trembled with the effort to contain a whole new burst of female fury. "I do wholeheartedly despise you, Sam O'Ballivan," she said with an evenness of tone that was clearly hard-won. "Perhaps you've fooled everyone else in this town, but you *do not fool me.*"

"I don't seem to have much credibility with Miss Oralee Pringle, either," Sam said sadly, repressing a grin. The bathwater was just plain cold now, and goose bumps swept over his flesh in nubby little legions.

Maddie's wonderful eyes widened. "Jupiter and Zeus," she spouted, "if you've so much as set foot inside the Rattlesnake Saloon, the school board will see that you're on the outbound stage with Bird!"

"Would that bother you, Miss Chancelor?" Sam asked, settling back just as if the water was warm and deep, fit for soaking in. "My being shown the road, I mean?"

"Bother me?" she countered, but she took a moment too long in doing it. "I'd get up a marching band and hold a parade!"

Like as not, Sam reflected, he'd be dead of pneumonia before that happened, and miss the spectacle. "Miss Pringle paid me a visit tonight," he allowed. "Fortunately, I was fully clad at the time, and chopping wood out back, like the gentleman I am."

LINDA LAEL MILLER

"What did she want?" The words were measured out carefully, like scoops of something precious, sold by the ounce.

"Bird," Sam replied with a slight but involuntary shiver that had nothing to do with the fate the girl would meet if she fell into Garrett Donagher's hands, and everything to do with the fact that the fire was dying down and a night chill was rising through the cracks between the floorboards. "The telegraph operator took my bribe and sent the wire to her folks up in Denver—I watched him do it—but he must have gone straight to Oralee after that."

"Tarnation," Maddie said.

"Did Bird teach you that awful word?" Sam teased.

She bristled again. God, he loved it when she bristled. It was almost worth freezing to death in a copper bathtub. "I'm leaving," she told him, as if she expected an argument.

"It's past time," Sam said.

Maddie disappeared in a twirl of skirts and he heard the schoolhouse door slam in the distance.

Neptune whined.

"Sorry dog," Sam said, hoisting himself out of the tub and tucking the towel around his middle like a loincloth so he could open the stove door and chuck in some more wood. After that, he pulled on his pants and shirt. He'd brew some coffee, he decided, take the chill off his bones.

Half an hour later there came a light rap at the back door.

Neptune managed a halfhearted growl, probably trying to make up for his earlier shortcoming.

Sam swore. He was in no mood for company, or somebody who needed rescuing. "Who's there?" he demanded.

"Me," a small voice answered.

Grumbling, Sam opened the door.

THE MAN FROM STONE CREEK

Terran was standing on the step, clutching a bedroll in his skinny arms. The lamplight gilded his hair, giving him a deceptively angelic aspect. "Maddie said to come and sleep over here to the schoolhouse," he announced. "And you're not to swear or play poker."

Sam stepped back so the boy could enter. "I reckon I can restrain myself from swearing," he said seriously, "but poker is another matter."

A slow grin broke over Terran's face. "Five card stud?" he asked.

"Deuces wild," Sam answered.

CHAPTER
EIGHT

MADDIE TOLD HERSELF she ought to get upstairs and go to bed, tired as she was, and with another hard day bound to roll in with the sunrise. The store would be closed, but Maddie wasn't a churchgoer, so Sunday was her day for housekeeping, baking and the like.

What stopped her from turning in was knowing that once she put out the lamp and let her mind slow down, she'd have to think about Sam O'Ballivan, over there at the schoolhouse, sprawled in that copper bathtub without a stitch on.

She flushed at the memory, and put it aside like she was sorting sales flyers from real mail after the weekly stagecoach had been and gone. She'd make tea, she decided. That would settle her a little.

She pumped water into the teakettle and set it on the stove with a slight bang, and when she turned to get the tin canister of orange pekoe down off the shelf, Bird was standing right there, like she'd sprung up out of the floor.

Startled, Maddie gasped and put a hand to her heart.

THE MAN FROM STONE CREEK

"Sorry I scairt you," Bird said contritely.

Maddie caught her breath and worked up a smile. "I thought you'd gone to bed," she said. She'd put up a cot in the pantry for the girl, and except for the swearing and the poker-playing, she'd proved a pleasant and unobtrusive houseguest.

Shyly, Bird sank into a chair at the table. "I tried real hard to sleep, but I couldn't," she said.

"I'm brewing tea," Maddie said, mostly recovered and bustling again. "Would you like some?"

"Only if you've got whiskey to put with it," Bird answered.

"No whiskey," Maddie told the other woman. After seeing Sam O'Ballivan bare as a harsh truth, she could have used a dose herself.

That night, Bird looked even younger than she was, with her dark hair down and brushed, and her face scrubbed clean of powder and paint. Her eyes were liquid with sorrow. "I guess it was on account of me that you sent Terran over to the schoolhouse to stay," she said, almost in a whisper.

Maddie stopped, put down the tea canister and laid a hand on Bird's shoulder. The girl had enough to fret about without the knowledge that she'd effectively put Terran out of his home. "It's all right, Bird," she told the girl gently.

"I ought to be the one to go," Bird said. "Not Terran. This here's his rightful place." Her face looked so forlorn that tears sprang to Maddie's eyes. She knew what it was to be alone, to look up at lighted windows on a cold night and long for a place where she was welcome. At the orphanage, too old to be a ward, like Terran, she'd washed dishes and scrubbed floors to earn her keep, and slept on a pallet behind the kitchen stove. And she'd have done considerably more just to be allowed to stay under the same roof with her young brother. With Mama and Papa gone, he was all she had left.

LINDA LAEL MILLER

"What will you do," Maddie asked, fair choking on the words, "if your folks up in Denver won't take you in?"

Bird looked forlorn, as though she'd long since resigned herself to certain disappointment. "I guess I'd do what I've been doing right along. I'd just be in another place, that's all." She gave a fragile little smile, full of grief, and a shrug to match. "If you fall in with a good outfit, it's not so bad. Almost like a family, when the other girls are nice and the madam is good to you."

Maddie felt an infinite sadness, just to think of Bird or anyone else being in such straits that they'd think of a brothel as home and its inhabitants as a family. Would she have consigned herself to that sort of a life, under any circumstances?

On her own, she'd have starved first. But she hadn't been on her own—she'd had Terran to provide for. And the truth was, she'd have married just about any man, if necessary, to provide for the boy. Including Mungo Donagher.

The thought made her shudder.

That would have been a form of prostitution, selling herself for food and shelter. Which meant she wasn't so different from Bird, and neither were the thousands of other women who'd made a similar choice. And she wasn't out of danger, by any means. If Mungo found out she'd hidden the woman who knocked his eldest son senseless with a whorehouse lamp, she would be looking for a husband in no time at all.

Warren's beloved face should have come to mind then, even though he was forever gone. Instead, the face she conjured up was Sam O'Ballivan's. Sam, with his wise, gentle eyes, his rugged and unhandsome features that somehow came together into a pleasing whole.

Bird looked at her curiously. "You cold? You're shiverin'."

THE MAN FROM STONE CREEK

"It's a little chilly tonight, don't you think?" Maddie responded with a brightness she most assuredly didn't feel. "A nice cup of tea will be just the thing. Are you sure you wouldn't like some?"

"I guess I'd better get up a taste for the stuff," Bird said. "Just in case my sister is in a forgiving state of mind. She's one for tea-drinkin', and that's the fact of it."

Before Maddie could reply, someone knocked hard at the back door.

"Hide," Maddie whispered frantically. It wasn't Sam, pounding like that, and Terran wouldn't have bothered with a knock at all. The lock was turned, but he had a key.

Bird darted for the inside door, which was really just a curtain separating the kitchen from the main part of the mercantile.

"Who's there?" Maddie called, smoothing her skirts and looking around for the shotgun. Then she remembered she'd put it back in its usual place that morning, under the counter in the store.

The door fairly rattled on its hinges. "Open up!" a man yelled. The voice was familiar.

One of the Donaghers, Maddie thought, and a trill of dread ruffled every nerve in her body. She took a few tentative steps toward the curtain, but she knew she'd never get to the counter, grab the shotgun and get back before whichever of Mungo's sons was out there kicked down the door and stormed inside.

"It's Sunday, and we're closed," she said with what was meant to sound like pleasant regret.

"Open this goddamn door!" the visitor bellowed. "I know you've got Bird in there, and I mean to get her by the hair for what she done to me!"

Garrett Donagher, then.

Maddie murmured a silent prayer that Bird had had the

LINDA LAEL MILLER

good sense to escape via the front door of the mercantile, then she put on a smile and a countenance of polite confusion, and released the lock.

Garrett loomed in the dark opening like a messenger of doom, his face contorted by rage, frustration and, from the smell of him, a good deal of alcoholic consolation.

Maddie blinked at him, though inside she was as alert as a hawk startled in its nest by a very large, very dangerous predator. "Garrett? What in the world—?"

Donagher pushed past her, into the small kitchen, sweeping the corners with a glare of suspicious fury. "Where is she? Where's Bird?"

"Bird?" Maddie echoed, and blinked again.

"I know she's here," Donagher insisted. He was standing entirely too close, so close that Maddie could feel the warmth of his quick, shallow breathing on the skin of her forehead. "That meddling schoolmaster brung her."

Maddie peered up at Garrett. Bird had hit him a good one, that was for sure. The gash, angry but healing, was visible through the hair on the right side of his head. "What *happened?*" she asked with an expression of sympathetic horror. She made a move to touch the wound, but he flinched away.

"You know damn well *what happened,*" Garrett accused. "Bird broke a lamp over my head. It a lucky thing she didn't kill me!"

Debatable, Maddie thought, but she was the picture of concerned bafflement. Had Bird bolted? And where would she go if she had? Would she have the presence of mind to go straight to Sam O'Ballivan?

"I don't know who told you that this woman—Bird, did you say?—was here, but she's not."

"You're a liar, Maddie Chancelor!" Donagher decreed, shaking a finger under her nose. "And you might want to remember that my pa *owns* this mercantile. You do as I say, or you and that brother of yours will be out on the street!"

Because Maddie wanted with every instinct that was in her to take a step back, she took one forward instead. "I do a good job, running this store. It's been turning a profit ever since I took over. *That* might have a little weight with your father, too."

Garrett reacted as if she'd struck him a blow to the forehead. He looked stupefied, then furious again. He shoved Maddie aside, staggered a little as he moved into the center of the room. "I'll find her, if I have to tear this place apart to do it!" he raged. "You hear me, Bird? Come out, right now!"

Maddie wrung her hands. "If you do any damage to the mercantile," she said bravely, "Mungo will horsewhip you for it!"

Garrett turned slowly, and Maddie thought she glimpsed hesitation in him, and fear. He stared at her.

"Search the building from top to bottom if you want," she said very quietly. "Just be peaceable about it."

He lingered for a few heart-stopping moments, evidently pondering the situation, then grabbed up the lamp in the middle of the table and headed for the curtain. Maddie followed, because she would have been left in the dark if she hadn't, and because she wanted to get closer to the shotgun.

She slipped behind the counter as quickly as she could.

The gun was gone.

Maddie took in a sharp breath, glanced anxiously around. Garrett, meanwhile, looked behind barrels of pickles, under display tables and behind the changing screen, where ladies tried on ready-made dresses. The front door was shut and bolted from the inside.

She swallowed hard. Bird *hadn't* escaped, then, hadn't

LINDA LAEL MILLER

gone to fetch Sam. She was hiding somewhere in the store, and she probably had the shotgun. Scared and cornered, the girl was bound to shoot Donagher dead if he confronted her, and the consequences of that didn't bear thinking about.

"You're making a fool of yourself, Garrett Donagher," Maddie said, bravado being the only weapon that remained to her. "I'll forgive you for calling me a liar, but I won't tolerate any more of this nonsense."

Donagher paused again, stared at her blearily. A sudden, wicked smile twisted his mouth, and the effect of it raced through Maddie's system like snake venom. "You know, you're a pretty woman," he said. "A little priggish, maybe, and not very mannerly, but with a little manly guidance—"

Maddie's gorge rose.

He took a step toward her, then stopped, gazing past her shoulder. At the same time, he groped for the handle of his pistol.

Sam.

Maddie's heart skidded and scrambled inside her chest, like a deer flailing for purchase on a patch of ice. Dear God, why had she wished for Sam to come? Now, most likely, Garrett would kill him, pick him off like a rat in the woodpile.

She closed her eyes, but the memories rushed in, as real as if she were living the tragedy all over again. A soft, summer evening. The crack of a rifle shot. Warren, struck down in the street. The gurgling sound he made when he tried to breathe, blood spreading crimson across the front of his white shirt. He'd squeezed her hand and died.

Dazed, Maddie gripped the edge of the counter to keep from collapsing. She couldn't bring herself to look back.

"I wouldn't draw if I were you," said the man standing just behind her.

It wasn't Sam.

THE MAN FROM STONE CREEK

Maddie turned, dizzy with fear and relief and a host of other emotions.

The man she recognized as Esteban Vierra stood with his arms folded. He spared a smile for her, but his dark eyes were fixed on Garrett and burning with challenge.

"I'm not scared of no damn Mexican," Garrett said.

"That's a pity," Vierra said easily. "Because I can drop you like a road apple from a horse's ass before you even clear leather."

Maddie laid her palm to her heart, fingers splayed. "Please," she said. "No shooting."

Garrett's neck and lower jaw went red, but he kept his hands wide from his body. Apparently he believed Vierra's assertion, though his expression and mien were defiant. "What the hell are you doin' here, anyway?" he demanded.

Vierra didn't move, but it was a dangerous sort of stillness, reminiscent of a panther poised to pounce on its prey. "I came to ask you to leave," he replied with no inflection in his voice at all. His ebony eyes gleamed in the thin light of the lantern.

"I have business here," Donagher argued. "I'm lookin' for a woman. A whore."

"No whores around that I can see," Vierra said with a lethal mildness that caused Maddie to wonder if she'd be any safer with him than Garrett Donagher. She knew little about him, beyond what Warren had told her—Vierra, who appeared in Haven occasionally, always briefly, always unexpectedly, and always leaving some kind of disturbance in his wake—had been both a *bandito* and a *federale*. According to Warren, he moved easily from one to the other, as the whim struck him. He'd come into the mercantile once or twice, to buy cheroots, and inspired Terran to ask for black *vaquero* boots for his twelfth birthday.

LINDA LAEL MILLER

Maddie had refused.

Donagher glanced disconsolately around the store, perhaps hoping that Bird would show herself so he could spirit her away and throttle her in an alley. "Bad enough you have truck with that schoolmaster, Miss Maddie," he said, sounding for all the world like a scorned suitor, once hopeful and now cruelly thwarted. "Vierra, here, he's nothin' but an outlaw. Only one reason he'd be on this side of the border, and that's cause somebody's after him on the other one."

"I'm sure he merely wants to purchase cheroots," Maddie said in a businesslike manner. "As for you, Garrett Donagher, you get out of here right this instant and don't you *dare* come back until you're stone sober and ready to apologize for barging in, scaring me to death and calling me a liar."

Donagher's gaze shifted from Maddie to Vierra. To her pure surprise, he sighed, strode to the front door, threw back the bolt and went out without a word or a backward glance. She watched as he moved past the display window, most likely headed for the Rattlesnake Saloon.

"I *could* use some cheroots," Vierra said.

Maddie faced him, feeling both grateful and alarmed. She kept the cheroots on the counter nearby, but she didn't reach for a packet and neither did he. "Thank you," she said.

He smiled. "I saw the light as I was passing the store. It looked as though you might be in a little difficulty—"

Just then Bird appeared on the stairway leading up to Maddie's and Terran's private rooms. She was hardly more than a spindly shadow, but she cocked the missing shotgun with an unnerving deftness.

"I ain't too sure about this fella, Maddie," she said. "I've seen him around the Rattlesnake, and I don't think he was up to any good."

THE MAN FROM STONE CREEK

Maddie's knees sagged. Mr. Vierra examined a packet of cheroots, apparently unconcerned with the shotgun and Bird's assessment of his character. "Land's sake, Bird," she said, "put down that gun before you hurt somebody."

Bird was a while responding. Finally, though, she lowered the gun, leaned it against the wall beside the stairs. She kept to the shadows, probably afraid Garrett might double back. "He'll never leave us be clear till Wednesday," she said miserably.

"What's happening on Wednesday?" Vierra asked, putting down the packet and reaching for the more expensive brand.

"The stagecoach comes through then," Maddie said, wondering why she was confiding in a man she barely knew. "Bird plans to be on it. She's going to Denver, to live with her sister."

Vierra considered that, though he still didn't look in Bird's direction. "I see."

"Garrett will kill me afore then," Bird lamented.

"Ah," Vierra said, as though that explained everything. And maybe, for all practical intents and purposes, it did. "The stagecoach driver will be no match for even one Donagher, let alone all three of them. What you need is an escort."

Bird sat on one of the steps and propped her chin in her hands. "What's an escort?" she asked.

Vierra's eyes danced as he met Maddie's gaze. "An able gunman with a little time on his hands," he answered. He turned to Bird. "Get your things. I'll take you as far north as I can. Put you on a train or a stagecoach—whatever we come to first."

Maddie gaped at him. "You'd do that? Why? Bird can't pay you, and neither can I."

"And we don't even know if my sister will take me in," Bird added sadly. "It'll be a miracle if she does."

"That's a chance you'll have to take," Vierra said. He still didn't turn in Bird's direction, maybe because, like Maddie, he suspected Garrett might be watching from outside. "If you stay in Haven, Donagher's going to have your hide, one way or the other. I suspect he'd make things hard for Miss Maddie, too. I'll pay your train fare, and you can send it back when you have it to spare." He smiled at Maddie. "Care of General Delivery."

"Bird," Maddie said firmly, "you don't even know this man."

"I've done a lot more than take to the road with men I didn't know," Bird pointed out.

Vierra laid out the posted price of the packet of cheroots he'd been examining and tucked them into his vest pocket. "I'll be on my way now," he said. "Fasten the bolt behind me, and put out that lamp. Be sure to lock the back way, too—that's how I got in. In an hour, I'll be in the pasture behind the store with a second horse."

"I'll be ready," Bird said.

CHAPTER

NINE

MUNGO WAS OUT OF BED and watching for dawn when he heard a rider coming. He hadn't bothered to light a lantern, since he knew the inside of the house as intimately as the bodies of any one of his three wives. He'd built it with his own two hands, after all, laid every plank, planed the bark off every tree, pounded every peg and nail into place. Only thing he'd had help with was hoisting the logs into place for the walls, and that had come from a pair of mules.

And now Undine wanted him to leave it—for California, of all places. Damn fool idea. He'd play hell shaking it loose from his bride's pretty head, though. Once she took a notion, that was that.

He swore and willed the coffee he'd started to brew faster. Waited for the rider to dismount, put up his horse and come inside.

The side door opened, squeaking a little on its hinges, and the new arrival stepped lightly, so as not to rouse the household. Mungo set his jaw, took his pistol down off the shelf, and waited, just in case he was wrong about who it was.

He was seldom wrong about anything, and when Garrett crossed the threshold, treading light as a sneak-thief looking to plunder the cash box, Mungo set the pistol aside with a thump.

"Dammit, old man," Garrett said, rubbing his whisker-bristled chin with one hand. "You savin' on lamp oil or something? You gave me a turn, lurkin' in the dark like that."

Heat rushing into the coffeepot on the stove was the only sound in the room, save the tick of the clock Mungo had bought off a squatter, some years back, for two buckets of milk and a sack of potatoes.

Mungo struck a match to light the glorified lantern Undine kept in the middle of the table. Sulphur mingled with kerosene and the aroma of strong coffee about to boil.

"Did you leave that horse of yours standing in the dooryard?" he demanded of his eldest son, keeping his voice low so as not to disturb Undine's rest. She was keen on getting more than her share of sleep, and their bedroom was directly off the kitchen.

"He's all right," Garrett said, sounding testy, but wary, too.

"Put him away," Mungo ordered. "I paid good money for that horse."

Garrett thrust out his jaw. "I'm plum wore out, Pa," he replied, his tone just short of a whine. "And in case you haven't taken notice of it yet, I'm hurt."

"You look sound enough to me," Mungo said. "Whatever's happened, it wasn't bad enough to keep you from carousin' most of the night. Put away the horse. I'll not tell you again."

Even in the poor light of Undine's prissy table lamp, Mungo could see Garrett wanted to spit in his face, but he didn't quite dare. He turned, grumbling under his breath, and slammed out the door.

That brought Undine yawning into the kitchen, with her hair down and her lace wrapper pulled snug around her full bosom. Mungo wished she wouldn't go around the house that way, take a chance on the boys seeing her half-naked. He didn't want another man's eyes coming to rest on her, even if that man was his own flesh and blood.

"I don't know how a person is supposed to sleep around here," she complained. She looked warm and flushed and rumpled, and Mungo felt himself stir.

"Garrett just rode in," he said gruffly. There were better things to talk about, he supposed, but the sight of her struck them from his mind. He longed to lay her out on their bed, open that wrapper and explore every curve and crevice of that luscious little body, but he wasn't a young man anymore. He couldn't depend on his own anatomy, and Undine was a demanding lover. Oh, he knew how to make her happy, with his hands and especially his mouth, but it was still humiliating not to be able to finish the job proper.

The coffee boiled over, sizzled on the stovetop.

Mungo lunged for it, moved the pot to the back, and scalded his hand in the process.

"Let me see," Undine purred when he cursed and strode to the sink to pump water over his thumb. She wasn't much for household duties, but she knew enough to sympathize. She traipsed over to peer around his arm.

Mungo showed her the hand.

"I'll get the butter," she told him.

"I'm fine, Undine," Mungo insisted, though he wasn't. He refused because he knew from experience that smearing grease on his seared flesh would make it burn like fire. It was a poor remedy, but folks seemed wedded to the idea. "Pour me a cup of that coffee if you want to help."

LINDA LAEL MILLER

She sighed and did as he asked, fetching a cup down from the cupboard and proceeding to the stove. With pointed motions, as if to demonstrate that *she* was smart enough to avoid injury while performing a simple kitchen task, she wadded up a dishtowel and used it like a pot holder.

Mungo pumped more water over his hand, but it seemed that would be a while working. He couldn't stand at the sink all day, so he decided to tough it out. He'd waited his way out of worse predicaments, that was for sure—like the time he was chopping wood and cut clean through his boot with a freshly sharpened ax. Damn near lost a toe that day, and one of the ranch hands finally had to cauterize the wound with a poker, since it wouldn't stop bleeding.

He sat at the table, feeling weary to the bone and three years older than the boulder that marked his property line at the northeast corner.

Undine set the steaming mug in front of him and bent to kiss the bald spot on top of his head. He was gratified, though he would have preferred to pretend that bare patch wasn't there.

"When we get to San Francisco," she said, "we'll stay in a fancy hotel and there'll be somebody bringing your coffee to you every morning, in a china cup."

She could have done that right there on the ranch, served up his coffee, that is, but Mungo wasn't fool enough to say so. Anna Deerhorn did the female work around the place, and Undine was content to leave her to it. She figured her job was to look pretty, spend money and perform the occasional bed favor. It hadn't been that way with his other wives—he'd required plenty from them—but then, he'd been younger, and they'd been plain, sturdy women, just glad to have a husband.

"Undine, who's going to run this ranch if we go off to California?"

THE MAN FROM STONE CREEK

She smiled and wriggled her way onto his lap. Time was, the feel of her warm bottom would have made him hard and straight as a fence post, but old Gus didn't even try to rise. She put her arms around his neck. "You've got four sons and at least a dozen drovers on the place. You think it's going to fall apart in a few months?"

When he didn't answer right away, Undine took hold of his injured hand, slid it inside her wrapper, to cup her breast. Mungo didn't even mind that it made the scald worse.

"Ben's going with us, unless your plans have changed since we talked about it last, and those brothers of his haven't got sense enough not to climb a lightning rod in a rainstorm. As for the ranch hands, well, they're mostly drifters, likely to ride on when the mood takes them, and rustle a few head of my cattle for good measure."

Undine made a murmury sound in her throat as Mungo played with her nipple. Let her head fall back, wanting him to kiss her throat.

Lord if he hadn't started something he might not be able to finish.

Abruptly he shoved back the chair and set her on her feet. "You go on back to bed, Undine," he said. "I have work to do and, anyways, Anna will be coming in here soon to start breakfast."

Undine wrenched her wrapper shut. "I'm packing my things to leave for California," she said. "If you won't come along, I'll go by myself. Take the stage as far as Tucson on Wednesday afternoon and make my way from there!"

She'd threatened to go before, but this was the first time she'd been specific. Mungo heard Garrett on the step outside the back door and knew they wouldn't be alone longer than another second or two.

"All right," Mungo said. "I'll take you to California, Undine. Soon as I've got these cattle to market, we'll go."

LINDA LAEL MILLER

. He could see her pulse pounding at the base of her throat, and her eyes were wide and hopeful.

"You promise, Mungo?"

Garrett opened the door, made a to-do about hanging up his gun belt on the peg in the little hallway, stomping his boots on the wooden floor.

"I promise," Mungo told her.

Undine's gaze darted to the entrance, careened back to Mungo's face.

"Go on back to bed, Undine," he said. Garrett was staring at her, nearly bare as she was; Mungo didn't need to look at his eldest son to know he was gobbling her up with his eyeballs.

Undine hesitated a moment, then fled.

"Anna says she's under the weather," Garrett announced. It came out sounding hoarse, and he cleared his throat. Set a basketful of brown eggs on the table. "She gathered these for breakfast and gave them to me, but she's keeping to her cabin for the day."

Mungo swore. He usually ate a stevedore's meal in the morning, but damned if he could rustle up an appetite, what with a winter in California ahead of him. He'd worry about the ranch every day they were gone, and it would take five years of good herds to pay off the bills Undine would run up.

He got to his feet, felt his old bones waver like a board shack in a high wind. "I'll be on the north range, lookin' for strays," he told his son. "You saddle up, as soon as you've had all you want of those eggs, and meet me out there. Bring those no-good brothers of yours, if you have to turn over their bunks to do it."

Garrett let out a huff of breath. "Pa, I told you I was hurt. And I ain't been to bed for two days."

Mungo took up his gun belt, thrust the pistol into the

holster and strapped the whole thing around his hips. Headed for the door, to claim his hat and coat. "Do as I tell you," he said, and left the house quietly, so as not to put Undine on the peck. By now, she was sleeping again, probably dreaming about San Francisco hotels, where folks brought a man's morning coffee in a china cup.

GARRETT GOT OUT A SKILLET and a tin of lard, even went so far as to crack a few eggs into a blue crockery bowl. He could see the barn door from the window over the sink, in the first thin light of dawn, and he watched until he saw the old man ride out at a good clip.

With a little smile, he set the bowl aside and turned from the window.

Undine stood in the bedroom doorway, one shoulder resting against the framework, the other bare where she'd pulled her wrapper down to entice him. All he'd have to do was cross the room, give that lacy trim a good yank, and her plump breasts would be there for the taking.

Undine stuck out her lower lip. "Your daddy worked me up into a dither and left me wanting," she complained pettishly. "What are you going to do about it, Garrett Donagher?"

"Plenty," he said, and went to her.

The bedroom was shadowy, though a little light crept in through the window over the washstand, with its china pitcher and bowl.

Garrett opened Undine's robe and feasted his eyes on her even before he thought to kick the door shut behind them.

"Turn—the—key," Undine gasped between hungry kisses.

"He's gone," Garrett told her. There were times when a man had to take his time to please a woman, but this wasn't

LINDA LAEL MILLER

one of them. Undine pulled out of his arms, laid herself sideways on the bed and opened her legs to him.

He unbuttoned his pants.

"Not yet," she murmured, shaking her head from side to side on the rumpled sheets. "Use your mouth on me, Garrett."

He'd sooner have rammed into her, satisfied himself, satisfied her, too, but if he refused her, she'd make him pay. So he knelt between her legs, parted her, and helped himself to the goods.

She moaned and hemmed him in with those legs of hers, her hands in his hair, holding him to her, making sure he took care of business.

Her hips began to rise and fall, and he reached up, took hold of her breasts, now fondling, now squeezing.

Undine whimpered and sighed and carried on, louder and louder.

If he'd had time, Garrett would have reckoned that was why he hadn't heard the door open behind him. He surely did feel the barrel of that pistol press into the nape of his neck, though.

CHAPTER

TEN

WHEN SAM SAW MADDIE crossing the schoolyard the next morning, he figured she'd come to make sure he hadn't taught Terran any new curse words or how to play cutthroat stud.

He could plead innocent on one of the charges, at least.

Watching her approach, he stopped cranking up that morning's drinking water, and wondered at the goings-on just beneath and back of his heart. The sunlight turned her chestnut hair to bronze, and her plain, work-a-day calico dress looked regal. As she drew closer, he saw the flash in her eyes and the flush on her cheekbones.

He reckoned she'd found out about the poker, then.

He pulled up the bucket and set it at his feet. Neptune, ever helpful, stuck his nose in and lapped.

"Bird is gone," Maddie said in a loud whisper, coming to stand square in front of him, like a petticoat general fixing to review her troops. She might as well have picked up that bucket and dashed him with the icy contents.

"What?"

Maddie set her jaw. "I had no choice but to let her go," she said, and he knew by her tone that her stubborn stance was nothing but show. "Garrett Donagher came to the store last night, looking for her. He was drunk and bound to find Bird if he had to tear down the walls to do it."

"You let him take her?"

The color flared brighter in her cheeks. "Of *course* I didn't! There wouldn't have been a thing I could do to save him, though, if Mr. Vierra hadn't interceded—"

Sam put up a hand. "Wait," he said sharply. "Save *him?* I thought it was Bird Donagher he was after."

Maddie thrust out an impatient breath. For all the gravity of the situation, Sam had a sudden and ferocious yearning to take that beautiful, rebellious face between his rein-calloused hands and kiss Miss Maddie Chancelor into stupefaction.

"It was Garrett who was saved. Bird had the shotgun, and she'd have killed him for sure. *That* would have made a fine snarl of things, now wouldn't it?"

Sam rubbed the back of his neck, unable to hide his consternation. "I reckon it would have," he agreed. He narrowed his eyes. "Where does Vierra figure into all this?"

"Right where I left off," Maddie replied crisply. "He's taken her north, to catch a stagecoach or a train for Denver." A new worry seemed to catch up with her just then; she paused to put a hand to her mouth and her shoulders stooped a little. When Maddie met Sam's gaze again, her eyes were full of trepidation. "Did she escape one devil only to find herself on the road with another?"

Sam reached out, hesitated, and squeezed her shoulder gently. A charge went through him, stirred up a riot in that strange new landscape that had opened up under his heart. He took a few breaths to steady himself. "Why didn't you come for me, Maddie?"

THE MAN FROM STONE CREEK

She sagged a little, but she didn't shake his hand off her shoulder, and that gave him a bleak kind of comfort. She gnawed at her lower lip, glanced down at her feet, and finally looked him squarely, resolutely, in the eye. "I was afraid," she said very softly.

Sam was chagrined. What had he been thinking, chiding Maddie for not coming to fetch him? Donagher had probably lingered outside awhile, watching for a second chance. "You made the right decision," he allowed. "You wouldn't have been safe."

"I wasn't worried about myself," she said with spirit and no little defiance.

"Then who—?" The words fell away, like pebbles from a limp slingshot, as the answer came to him, out of nowhere. "Me?" he asked, and for a moment or two, there was no sound save the birds, the rustle of cottonwood leaves and that damn dog slurping up the drinking water.

Maddie clamped her jaw down tight again, looked away and gave one unwilling nod.

Exultation swept through Sam, but he contained it. He had no right or reason to feel that way—he'd be riding back up north to Stone Creek, to Abigail, as soon as he'd completed his business in that part of the Territory, and like as not, he'd never lay eyes on Maddie Chancelor again. He'd set his course, tacitly promised to marry the major's daughter, and he couldn't go back on his word, even when it was only implied.

Neptune backed away from the water bucket, belched and ran off to chase a butterfly flickering yellow and crimson over the thirsty grass. Sam bent, emptied the pail, put the hook through the handle, and reeled it back down into the well as if it were the most important thing he'd do all day.

It seemed that even the birds and the trees went still.

LINDA LAEL MILLER

"Where's Terran?" Maddie asked when Sam had the bucket clear down and on the way back up again.

"I sent him for the eggs," he said. "I buy them from Violet's mama. Fifty cents a basket."

She touched his arm and he stiffened as surely as if she'd laid a hot poker to his flesh. Felt a flush of embarrassment heat the back of his neck. Damnation, he was acting like a besotted boy, not a full-grown man.

"Sam—" she began, but he never knew what she'd meant to say because just then Terran came bursting through the brush, egg basket in one hand, face contorted with excited horror.

"Sam!" he whooped. "Maddie! Come quick!"

Maddie took the egg basket from Terran, set it down and caught him firmly by the shoulders. Gave him a little shake. "What's happened?"

Terran's eyes were huge in his pale face. He made a few false starts before he managed to choke out the news. "Mungo Donagher just showed up at the jailhouse, driving a wagon—" He pulled free of Maddie's hold and gagged a couple of times before he could go on. "He's awash in blood. I've never seen so much blood. He said it's Garrett under the tarp in the bed of that buckboard—"

"Dear God," Maddie gasped.

"Both of you stay right here," Sam ordered, and headed for the main part of town. Neptune tried to follow, but he sent the dog back with a stern command, and when he glanced over his shoulder, he saw Maddie and Terran staring after him, Maddie with one arm around her brother, as though she was holding him upright.

A crowd had gathered in front of the abandoned jailhouse and, sure enough, there was a team and wagon out front. Sam looked into the bed, saw a bloody tarpaulin with a man's shape sprawled beneath it. He reached in, tossed back a corner of the canvas covering, steeled himself against the sight. The body was unrecognizable, a ludicrous tangle of gore where the head should have been. He'd seen that kind of carnage before, but he'd never reconciled himself to it, the way some men did.

He covered the corpse again and made his way through the gathering of whispering townsfolk to the open doorway of Warren Debney's office.

Mungo Donagher sat square in front of the desk, splashed from head to foot with blood and other matter, hands resting crimson-streaked on his thighs, staring bleakly into the maw of hell itself.

The yellow dog was there, the one Sam had seen often, lying outside on the sidewalk, taking the sun, but there was no one to take charge. Donagher sat alone, motionless. He'd gotten himself this far, confessed his crime in the street and hunkered down to await his fate.

Sam rounded the desk, opened drawers until he found a forgotten pint of whiskey, dusty and three-quarters full, brought it to Mungo. "Take a swig of this," he said, gruffly kind.

The man didn't reach for the vessel or even raise his eyes. He was watching the devil dance, it seemed to Sam, and could not look away from the performance. "I killed him. Killed my own boy," he told Sam.

Sam put the bottle in Mungo's right hand. "Drink," he said. "It'll steady your nerves."

"Caught him with my wife," Mungo said. His stained fingers trembled, but he took the whiskey, steered it to his mouth, took a deep draught.

"Did you kill her, too?" Sam asked, thinking of the feckless, pretty Undine.

Mungo shook his head, took another gulp of whiskey and shuddered as it went down. "I should have married

LINDA LAEL MILLER

Maddie," he said, like a man talking in his sleep. "She wouldn't have wanted to go to California. She wouldn't have spread her legs for another man."

Sam felt his back molars clamp together at the mention of Maddie, especially in that context, but he swallowed the furious protest that swelled in his throat. A figure moved into the doorway, from the street, and he recognized Oralee Pringle.

"Who's the law in this town?" Sam demanded.

Oralee made a contemptuous sound. "Ain't any," she said, watching him speculatively as she approached, laid a plump, beringed hand on Donagher's shoulder. "Is it true, Mungo?" she asked with a gentleness Sam wouldn't have imagined she was capable of. "Did you shoot Garrett? Truly?"

Mungo didn't look at her, but he nodded. "I shot him, all right."

Oralee's gaze collided with Sam's over Mungo's head. "If you ain't a lawman," she said calmly, "what are you doing in here?" She cocked a thumb toward the road. "Half the men in town are out there gawking in that street, but not a one of them had the guts to come in and see what was what. My guess is, they're afraid old Mungo will put a hole in them, too, the way he did his boy."

Mungo drained the whiskey bottle. "I'd do it again, too," he said.

"Is there a doctor around here?" Sam asked Oralee.

"You must not have taken a look at what's left of Garrett," Oralee replied. "I did. Ain't no doctor can help him. What he wants is the undertaker, and a whole slew of prayers said for his rotten soul."

"Reckon I'll hang for this?" Mungo inquired, but he was still watching the devil dance. From his rapt expression, it was quite the show.

THE MAN FROM STONE CREEK

"Could be," Oralee said matter-of-factly. She looked around the musty office, like she was familiar with it, even a little nostalgic, and marched over to take a ring of keys down off a peg. "You'd better lock Mungo up, Mr. School-master. Once he comes out of this stupor, a castrated bull would be easier to wrestle."

Sam took the keys. "Send somebody for the doctor," he told Oralee. "If there is one."

"Have to ride all the way to Tucson, unless you want a Mexican."

Sam's sigh came through his teeth. *"Send somebody,"* he repeated.

Her tiny eyes widened as best they could, given their obvious limits. "For him?" she asked, cocking a thumb at Mungo.

"Yes." Sam bit the word off like the tip of a cigar, spat it out. Hooked a hand under Mungo's elbow and urged him to his feet. For a big man, Donagher was docile, but Oralee was likely right to claim he'd be a sight less cordial when he came out of his daze. "Come along," he told the old man.

Mungo let himself be led to the single cell at the back of the long, narrow room. He took a seat on the cot wedged up against the wall and clasped his hands loosely between his knees.

Sam's stomach churned, watching Mungo, sitting there with his son's blood dried in streaks on his flesh, splashed like red paint over his clothes.

"He'll be wild when he realizes what he's done," he said, aware that Oralee was standing close behind him.

"Mungo?" Oralee scoffed. "He'd do it all over again. Just like he said before."

Sam turned to stare down into Oralee's round, upturned face. He'd never seen a colder woman, and given some of

LINDA LAEL MILLER

the places he'd frequented before he'd wound up at Stone Creek, that was saying something. "Get a doctor," he said, hoping the third request would be the charm. "And somebody with the backbone to stand guard while I'm gone, if you can find them."

Oralee didn't blink. "You sure give orders real easy-like, for a schoolmaster."

"Do it," Sam said, and pushed past her. He took the cell keys with him, just in case someone took it into their head to let Mungo go in his absence.

Townspeople milled and churned in the street, shaking their heads and muttering, one to another.

Sam scanned them, picked out a trail-worn cowpuncher with a go-to-hell look in his eyes and a .44 riding low on his left hip. "You ever guarded a prisoner?" he asked.

The cowpoke shook his head.

Sam tossed him the cell keys. "You've just been deputized," he said.

The man caught the keys deftly, nodded, and went inside the jailhouse without a word.

Maddie made her way through the throng and stood facing Sam.

"The undertaker's on his way," she said quietly, her eyes searching his face.

"I've got to ride out to the Donagher place," Sam told her. "I'd appreciate it if you'd look after Neptune while I'm gone."

She caught hold of his arm when he would have walked past her, headed for the schoolhouse to saddle his nameless horse. "I'd better go with you," she said.

Sam shook his head. "No telling what I'm going to find out there."

"All the more reason you shouldn't go alone," she insisted. "Undine will need a woman. And—" She paused, swallowed. "There's Ben to think about."

THE MAN FROM STONE CREEK

The boy. Sweet Jesus, he'd forgotten all about him.

"There's no time to hitch up your buckboard," Sam argued when he'd swallowed a throatful of sick dread and a wash of ugly memories from his own boyhood.

"I can ride," Maddie said. She turned to face the gathering of onlookers. "Who will make me the loan of a horse?"

CHAPTER

ⷮⷮⷮ

ELEVEN

UNDINE STOOD at the gate when Sam and Maddie rode up, one delicate hand shading her eyes from the midday sun. She looked so pristinely fresh in her white-eyelet dress that, for one marrow-chilling moment, Maddie thought she was seeing the specter of Mungo Donagher's young wife rather than the flesh-and-blood woman herself.

"I guess you've come about Garrett," Undine sang out in the tone she might have used to indicate that tea was about to be served in the formal garden.

Maddie stared so long that Sam had dismounted and come to help her off her borrowed horse before she managed to shepherd her scattered thoughts back into a flock. "We have," she said, avoiding Sam's upraised arms to put her left foot into the stirrup and get down on her own. Lord, how she despised riding sidesaddle, but her skirts and petticoats precluded the more sensible way.

"Anna Deerhorn is cleaning up the mess," Undine said with the merest wince of distaste. She was waxen, and her

THE MAN FROM STONE CREEK

smile seemed a bit fixed, as though it rightly belonged on some other woman's face. She added, a bit hastily, "Mungo was only defending my virtue, you know. I told him he oughtn't to turn himself in like a criminal, but he wouldn't listen."

Maddie, who had seen Mungo as well as what remained of Garrett, was not inclined to discuss Undine's virtue. Out of the corner of her eye, she saw Sam set his jaw. He'd related Mungo's story on the way out from town, and it differed considerably from Undine's.

"Where is Ben?" he asked.

Undine's eyelashes fluttered, as though she thought she should recognize the boy's name, but couldn't quite catch hold of it. "I'll ask Anna," she said, and swayed a little. Maddie reached out, took a firm hold on the other woman's elbow.

Sam was already headed up the walk. He disappeared into the shadowy interior of the ranch house, leaving the door ajar behind him. "Ben!" he called.

If there was an answer, Maddie didn't hear it.

Undine put a hand over her mouth, leaned on Maddie and let herself be led toward the front door. "It was awful," she whispered. "Garrett barged right into our bedroom— Mungo's and mine—and *forced* himself upon me."

Maddie slipped an arm around Undine's waist. "What happened then?" she asked very quietly.

"Mungo came back, just in time to save me," Undine said, and fetching tears brimmed in her eyes. "He…he put a gun to the back of Garrett's head and…and—"

"Maybe you should sit down before you finish," Maddie said, and eased Undine into one of the two rocking chairs on the front porch before taking the other for herself.

Undine began to rock, back and forth, back and forth, staring wildly into what must have been a truly horrible

LINDA LAEL MILLER

memory, whatever her own part in the making of it. "How will we go to California now?" she murmured.

Maddie drew and released a long, slow, deep breath before replying. "Mungo is in serious trouble, Undine. He has confessed to murder. He'll be tried, and he could be hanged, if he's convicted."

Undine's gaze shot to Maddie's face, heated and defiant. "But it *wasn't* murder! Mungo was only protecting me!"

It was not the time to point out, as the Territorial attorney surely would, if there was a trial, that Mungo had employed excessive force in freeing his wife from the unwanted attentions of his eldest son. Mungo might have been elderly, by some standards, but he was bull-strong, and even Garrett, for all his youth, would have found him a formidable foe.

Before Maddie could find words to state any of those things, Anna appeared in the open doorway. Her gaze skittered off Undine, who was back to rocking again, to land fierce on Maddie's face.

"Mr. O'Ballivan wants you," she said. "He said I shouldn't have took to cleaning that room."

Maddie rose from her chair, smoothed her skirts uneasily. Although her first instinct was to avoid the scene of Garrett's death, she would not give in to it. If Sam could stand the sight, so could she. "Will you sit with Mrs. Donagher?" she asked.

"No, ma'am," Anna Deerhorn replied.

Undine did not seem to hear her. She was rocking harder and muttering under her breath about California.

Maddie nodded, straightened her shoulders and marched into the house.

"Through the kitchen," Anna said, behind her.

Maddie's nerves leaped under her skin, and she felt perspiration gather between her breasts and shoulder blades, but she made her way toward the master bedroom. Toward Sam.

THE MAN FROM STONE CREEK

A mound of blood-soaked sheets and blankets marked the doorway. Maddie swallowed a rush of bile, stiffened her backbone, and proceeded.

A ludicrously graceful spray of crimson patterned the wall above the bed. Sam was digging, with one finger, in a hole in the equally grisly mattress. He brought out a spent bullet, held it up to the light pouring in through the nearby window. "It must have gone right through his head," he mused in a detached voice, entirely devoid of emotion. "Undine's lucky it didn't hit her."

Maddie's stomach roiled and she thrust out one hand to steady herself against the framework of the door. The smell of death was rife in the room, dense and cloying, with an edge of coppery sweetness. It seemed to seep into her very flesh, become a part of her. *Where in God's name was Ben? Had he heard the shot or, worse yet, witnessed the tragedy firsthand?*

"Undine claims Mungo was defending her," she said, feeling light-headed, struggling not to disgrace herself by vomiting or even swooning.

Sam didn't answer. He was still intent on studying the bullet.

"I'm—I'm going looking for Ben," Maddie went on.

At last Sam met her gaze and, for the briefest of moments, she glimpsed an old and elemental horror there, something that had nothing to do with the grim events of that dreadful morning. "Look behind the cookstove," he said. "Then in the barn and the chicken coop."

"There's no need to search," Anna Deerhorn said, and Maddie flinched, for she hadn't realized that the woman was standing almost at her elbow. "He's at my cabin."

Maddie nodded and turned, perhaps too quickly, to make for the kitchen door. She half expected Anna to accompany her, but the housekeeper went instead to the sink

LINDA LAEL MILLER

to pump water for the round washtub at her feet. There was explanation forthcoming, but Maddie didn't require one. Once the tub was filled, Anna would soak Garrett's lifeblood from the sheets.

The cabin stood well back of the main house, sturdy and small.

Maddie lifted her skirts in both hands as she climbed the plank steps and entered without knocking.

"Ben?" she called gently. There were two windows, with heavy burlap curtains, tightly drawn. She waited for her eyes to adjust to the change. "Ben, it's me, Maddie Chancelor. Terran's sister."

Nothing.

She squinted, and Sam's oddly knowing words came back to her. *Look behind the cookstove.*

Anna's stove was huge, taking up fully a quarter of the space in the single room. Maddie approached at a slow pace and said Ben's name again, gently.

Sure enough, he was there, huddled against the wall behind that stove, his arms wrapped tightly around his skinny knees.

Maddie crouched, reached out tentatively to touch his cap of fair hair. He jerked away from her and let out a small, despairing whimper.

Her eyes burned and her throat constricted. "It's all right, Ben," she said, very gently. "You're safe now. I'm here, and so is Mr. O'Ballivan."

Ben raised his head, stared at her with enormous, panicked eyes. Then, to her surprise, he grasped her arm and tried to pull her behind the stove. "There's been some shootin'!" he rasped, clawing at her in desperation. "You've got to hide, Maddie! You've got to hide!"

A raw sob escaped Maddie. She shifted to her knees and hauled the child into her arms, holding him close and then closer still. He clung, his hands knotted in the fabric of her dress.

"It's over now," she promised. "It's all over."

"Pa shot Garrett," Ben cried, burying his face in Maddie's bodice. "He dragged him through the kitchen, put him in a wagon. There was so much blood—"

Maddie held on to the boy as tightly as he held to her. "Shh," she whispered against his fever-moist temple. He had heard the shot. He had seen his father hauling his brother's decimated body out of the house and loading it into the back of the buckboard. What *else* had the poor child seen? It wouldn't do to ask him, not yet. "Shh."

"I can't stay here," Ben said fretfully. "Where am I going to stay, Maddie?"

"With Terran and me, of course," Maddie said with a certainty she didn't feel. Mungo Donagher owned the general store, and she, as his employee, was at his mercy. If he hanged or went to prison, she might not have a roof over her own head, and her brother's, let alone one to offer this shattered, frightened boy.

He pulled back far enough to study her face, but his hands were still fisted, gripping the cloth of her dress as fiercely as if letting go would mean being swept downstream in a violent river. "Could I? Could I really?"

Maddie bit her lower lip, nodded. "We'll go to your room right now and pack your things. When Mr. O'Ballivan and I head back to town, we'll take you with us."

The child's eyes seemed to take up his entire face, and he shook his head hard from side to side. "I won't go in there," he vowed. "Not ever."

Maddie let out her breath. "Then you can share Terran's things," she said.

"Is my pa coming home?"

She stroked his hair, damp with perspiration, clinging

LINDA LAEL MILLER

in tendrils to his forehead and the nape of his neck. "No, sweetheart," she told him. "Not right away, anyhow."

A great shudder moved through the small, wiry body, and Maddie tightened her embrace.

"Mr. O'Ballivan's here?" he asked, his voice muffled. She felt the tension seeping out of his frame, now that he'd taken in what she'd said before.

Maddie still held him tightly. Sam O'Ballivan represented safety to Ben and, she realized, to her, as well. It was an unsettling insight. Except for that brief and shining time when she'd believed Warren would be her protector, Maddie had been on her own since her folks died. The thought of depending on another person made her want to scramble behind Anna's cookstove and hide there with Ben.

"Is the boy all right?"

Maddie stiffened. She'd left the door open and Sam was standing just over the threshold. "As well as can be expected," she said moderately. She got to her feet, somehow managing to bring Ben along with her. He kept a death grip on her hand, stayed close to her side.

Sam was a sturdy shadow, rimmed in daylight.

"Anna's got some of your belongings together," Sam told the boy. "We can head back to town whenever you're ready."

Ben swallowed audibly. Nodded. "Maddie said I could stay at the store, with her," he said almost fearfully. Perhaps he was afraid she would rescind the offer.

"That'll be fine," Sam said. He looked past them, to the cookstove, and once again, Maddie thought she saw some dark recollection move in his eyes. "Come along, now. There's nothing more to be done here, for the time being."

Undine did not come out of the house to say goodbye, nor did Anna Deerhorn. Sam helped Maddie onto her waiting horse, then mounted his own, pulling Ben up behind him. The pitiful bundle tied behind Maddie's saddle represented what little was left of Ben's former life.

They made the five-mile journey back to Haven mostly in silence, and Maddie was relieved to see that Mungo's buckboard, along with its horrid load, had been removed.

Charlie Wilcox's patient old horse stood forlornly in front of the Rattlesnake Saloon, waiting to carry his master home, and folks had gone back to their usual pursuits. Only the smoke curling from the jailhouse chimney and the red splotches in the dirt, where Mungo's wagon had stood, marked this as anything but an ordinary day.

Maddie and Sam parted in front of the mercantile. He untied Ben's bundle from the back of her horse, handed it to her and leaned to take her horse's reins. It was understood that he would return the animal to its owner and she would see to her new charge.

"Thanks, Maddie," Sam said.

She nodded, watched for a little too long as he rode away.

THE COWBOY Sam had left in charge of the jailhouse in general and Mungo Donagher in particular sat back in the marshal's chair, his feet on the desk.

A squat man in a bowler hat stood nearby, looking consternated. His handlebar mustache twitched as he gave Sam a rapid up-and-down assessment.

"Sam O'Ballivan," Sam said.

"Elias James," came the reserved reply. "I run the Cattleman's Bank."

Sam went to shut the jailhouse door, and almost closed it on the old yellow dog, which slunk across the threshold, pausing to stretch himself midway.

"I manage Mungo Donagher's affairs," James announced, mustache wiggling again. Sure sign of a bluster

LINDA LAEL MILLER

building up. "I plan on sending to Tucson for a lawyer. In the meantime, I'd like to know by what legal authority—"

Sam crossed to the cell, looked in at Mungo. He was sprawled facedown on the cot, snoring like a man with a clear conscience. The blood of his son, covering him like a mantle, certainly belied that impression.

Banker James, cut off by Sam's lack of attention, tried again. "I was speaking to you, sir," he said icily.

"I'm aware of that," Sam said, turning away from Mungo. The cowpoke watched the scenario unfold with mild amusement and some curiosity.

"You are a schoolmaster," James pointed out.

"And a citizen," Sam replied. "As such, I can make an arrest."

James's shrewd, piglike eyes bulged with affronted disbelief. "This is *Mungo Donagher* we're talking about!"

Sam progressed to the stove, examined it. The door was rusted shut, but a good pull got it open. There was no wood, and no coffeepot on hand anyhow, so it was a fruitless effort. "I don't care," he said calmly, "if it's Ulysses S. Grant. The fact is, Donagher killed a man. And he'll stay right in that cell until a circuit judge or a U.S. Marshal comes along to say otherwise."

The cowboy put a matchstick between his teeth and shifted it from one side of his mouth to the other, but he offered no comment. Nor did he show any sign of rising from the chair behind that desk, which obviously chapped the banker's hide. Maybe he was used to people standing in his presence.

"For all we know," James said, gesturing impatiently in the cowboy's direction, "this man is an outlaw."

"Could be," Sam agreed. He glanced at the drifter. "You got a name, Cowboy?"

A slow, easy smile. Not a man in a hurry to show up

elsewhere, that was plain. "Yes, sir," he said. "Is somebody gonna pay me a wage for ridin' herd on that old man, or am I supposed to do it out of the goodness of my heart?"

Banker James bristled at the mention of wages. "Your name?" he prodded, whittling a sharp little point on the end of the question.

"Rowdy Rhodes," the cowpoke answered with an insolent tug at the brim of his hat, which rested loosely on the back of his head.

"Sounds made-up," the banker said huffily. "Mr. O'Ballivan here presumed to hire you. As far as I'm concerned, he can pay you."

Just then, the door opened and Oralee cannonballed across the threshold with a napkin-draped basket. The yellow dog sniffed hopefully and was ignored.

"Supper for the prisoner," Oralee announced.

The dog lay down with a sigh. Sam imagined he'd have to take the poor critter back to the schoolhouse and feed it.

"What are you doing here?" James asked, eyeing Oralee with clear disapproval.

"I'm on the town council," Oralee said. She sized up Rowdy Rhodes, who did not bother to rise from his chair. "Who are you?"

"I'm the deputy," Rhodes explained. "Do I get a badge?"

"There's probably one around here someplace," Oralee replied, and headed for the cell. "That Mexican doctor must have give old Mungo a dose of laudanum," she reflected, peering in. "If he wasn't rattlin' the cell door with them snores of his, I'd figure him for dead."

She backtracked and set the basket on one corner of the desk. Sam, Rowdy and the yellow dog all looked at it. Only Banker James did not seem interested.

LINDA LAEL MILLER

"This man," James said, indicating Rhodes with a jabbing motion of his thumb, "expects to be paid."

"Reckon that's fair," Oralee decided. She opened her velvet handbag, took out a fifty-cent piece and slapped it down next to the basket.

For a moment or two, it was a toss-up whether the cowpoke would go for the money or the food in that basket. Smelled like biscuits and fried meat.

Even with all he'd seen that day, Sam's stomach rumbled.

"You're paying this…this stranger out of your own pocket?" James demanded.

"Hell, no," Oralee replied. "I mean to take it out of the town treasury. Along with the cost of the vittles I'll be sending over regular-like."

Oralee jabbed a plump and purposeful finger in Sam's direction. "I'll have a word with you, in private, Mr. O'Ballivan."

"This is ridiculous," James protested.

"Oh, go foreclose on something," Oralee told him.

James reddened. "You have not seen the last of me," he told Sam and Rowdy and, presumably, the old yellow dog.

No one responded, so he stalked out, taking care to slam the jailhouse door behind him. Mungo grunted from his cell, then lapsed into snores again, loud as a freight train on loose track.

"I wouldn't mind seeing to my horse," Rhodes said. With a last, longing glance at the supper basket, he went out.

"You're playin' with rattlesnakes," Oralee informed Sam as soon as they were alone.

Sam lifted the cloth off the basket, helped himself to a biscuit and tossed a slab of what was probably venison to the dog.

"Somebody had to do something," he said.

THE MAN FROM STONE CREEK

"You got a take-charge way about you. That tells me there's a badge tucked away in your gear somewhere."

"We've already discussed that," Sam said, and took another biscuit.

"Not to my satisfaction, we ain't."

"Pardon my saying so, Miss Oralee, but your satisfaction is not one of my primary concerns."

To Sam's surprise, she gave a grudging little smile. "There are still two Donaghers out there, not countin' the kid. They'll either want to lynch their old pappy back there or set him free, but one way or the other, they'll come for him."

"Neither of them could find their ass with both hands," Sam answered.

"The stupid ones are the most dangerous," Oralee asserted. "They don't think overmuch about consequences."

"I'd have to agree with you there," Sam said, remembering the outhouse incident outside that cantina in Refugio.

"Thanks for that, anyhow." Oralee's voice was wry and sour as clabbered milk on a hot day.

"Good grub," Sam said.

"What happened to Bird?"

Sam sighed. Oralee had paid Rhodes's wages and brought supper. She deserved something in return for that. "She won't be back," he said.

"Sent her to Denver, did you?" Oralee's eyes flickered and she reached into her handbag. Brought out a folded sheet of yellow paper. "You didn't do her any favors, Sam O'Ballivan. Her people don't want her."

Sam felt a lurch at that, but he accepted the telegram with a steady hand, flipped it open. Sure enough, what Oralee said was true. The message was short and to the point. *Do not send her to us. We cannot put her up.*

"At least at my place, she had a bed and three meals a

LINDA LAEL MILLER

day," Oralee pressed as Sam read and reread the carefully printed lines. Maybe he was hoping it would change in front of his eyes. "What's Bird going to do when she gets to Denver and the home folks won't take her in?"

Sam didn't answer. Just handed over the telegram.

"She'll come back here, that's what she'll do," Oralee said. "It'll be the worse for her, too."

"Maybe," Sam allowed, and rubbed the back of his neck.

Oralee trundled to the door, took hold of the latch. "I warned you about the Donaghers as best I could," she re-iterated. "From here on, you're on your own."

With that, she departed, fairly running Rowdy down as he came back from tending to his horse.

Sam indicated the basket. "Better have some supper," he said. "It's going to be a long night."

Rhodes nodded. "We'll be all right," he told Sam. "The old dog and me." He hung up his hat, crossed the room and patted the mutt on the head. "You hungry, pardner?" he asked.

Sam's spirits rose a little. At least he didn't have to worry about the dog. "I'll be at the schoolhouse," he said. "If there's trouble, fire off a shot or two. I'll hear it and get here quick."

Rhodes simply nodded. His .44 looked like it was part of him and the leather holster was well-worn. "That's a good name for you," he told the dog. "Pardner."

Pardner gazed up at the new deputy with adoration.

Sam let himself out without a farewell.

Standing alone on the plank sidewalk, he turned his gaze toward the general store. It pulled at him, that place, but not because he wanted to buy anything.

Maddie was in there.

Practical, take-hold, half-again-too-pretty Maddie.

What would happen to the mercantile, and to her, now that Mungo Donagher was in jail?

THE MAN FROM STONE CREEK

Sam shook his head, rubbed the back of his neck again, hard enough to take off some hide. There was no sense in pining after Maddie Chancelor. He had a woman waiting for him up at Stone Creek.

Damn, but he wished he didn't.

CHAPTER
TWELVE

THREE THINGS happened on Wednesday.

The stagecoach came in, empty except for the driver.

Garrett Donagher was laid to rest in the churchyard, while Mungo stood by in handcuffs, his face expressionless. Undine wept prettily into a silk handkerchief, and Ben stayed close to Maddie, his eyes fixed warily on his pa the whole while. Oralee and her girls huddled together in a tight, defiant little cluster of brightly colored dresses and feathers that wafted in the warm breeze. The rest of the townspeople kept their distance, and there was no sign of Rex and Landry, a fact that both unsettled and relieved Sam.

He waited for the words to be said, leaning against a cottonwood tree with his arms folded across his chest. Watched as Oralee and her flock departed and the church ladies closed around the weeping Undine to spirit her away.

Mungo lingered, watching as the undertaker's sons began shoveling dirt back into the grave they'd dug the day before. If he'd noticed Undine at all, he gave no sign of it, nor had he spared so much as a glance for Ben, which was probably a good thing.

Finally, Rhodes took Mungo by one arm and ushered him back to jail.

Sam looked on as Maddie sent Terran and Ben back to the store, then approached him with purposeful steps. Drawing up a few feet short of the toes of his boots, she reached into the pocket of her trim black skirt. Even in solemn garb, she looked pretty, with her snow-white bodice and the cameo broach pinned decorously at her throat.

"There was a letter for you today," she said, and presented a vellum envelope. The scent of Abigail's rosewater perfume wafted up from it.

Sam liked Abigail, though he couldn't rightly say he loved her. Somehow, they'd fallen into an unspoken agreement, that was all. He usually welcomed her letters, which were generally lively and full of news, but this day he'd just as soon toss the missive into Garrett Donagher's grave and pretend it hadn't come.

"Thanks," he replied, and tucked the fat envelope into the inside pocket of his vest.

Maddie's eyes snapped with questions, but she was too much of a lady to ask any of them. At least, as far as Abigail's letter was concerned.

"How did you know Ben would hide behind the cookstove?" she asked.

Just like that, Sam was wrenched back to his boyhood. Crouched behind his ma's stove, every bit as scared as Ben Donagher had been the day of the shooting, but too curious not to look on from his hiding place.

"You knew right where he'd be," Maddie insisted quietly. Clearly she wasn't going to leave go of the subject until she had an answer, and one that suited her.

LINDA LAEL MILLER

He sighed, thrust a hand through his hair. "Stoves," he said, "deflect bullets."

She raised an eyebrow. Waited.

Sam looked away, looked back. "My ma was a widow," he told her. "She was pretty, and had her share of gentlemen callers. One day, two of them showed up at our place at the same time, and they were packing guns. They argued, each of them wanting the other to go, and neither one willing to give in. Ma told me to get behind the stove, quick, since they were blocking the door."

Maddie raised her chin. Swallowed.

"They drew and fired." Sam could see the whole thing playing out in his mind. Smell the gunpowder and the blood. He heard his ma scream, as clearly as if he were back there on that lonely homestead.

Maddie flinched, but she wanted the whole story and she was ready to wait for it. "How old were you?" she asked.

"Ten," Sam replied, and drew a deep breath to force the memory back into its proper place. "They killed each other, and my mother, too."

She put out a hand, rested it tentatively on his upper arm. She might have been laying it flat on a hot griddle, for the pain in her eyes. "I'm sorry," she said.

He didn't know if she was apologizing for asking, or expressing sympathy for the tragedy. In the end, it didn't matter. "It was a long time ago," he told her, but his throat was raw with the recollection and the words came out hoarse.

"Will you come to supper?" She wanted to know.

She sure had a way of rounding sudden bends in the conversation.

"I'd like that," Sam heard himself say.

"Six o'clock," she replied, and turned to go.

Sam went home, tended to the dog and the horse, took

a hasty bath in the chilly river and shaved. For all of that, he arrived right on time, tapping on the back door of the mercantile and wishing he'd thought to gather a few wildflowers.

That was when the third thing happened.

Esteban Vierra opened the door, easy in his skin and grinning.

"Supper's almost ready," he said, just as if he'd cooked it himself. Just as though he had every right to be admitting folks to Maddie Chancelor's kitchen.

MADDIE, WORKING DILIGENTLY at the stove, took a brief, secret and quite unbecoming satisfaction in the look on Sam's face as he entered her kitchen, having to pass by Mr. Vierra to do so. He'd received a perfumed letter from a woman that very day, after all. What right did he have to be disgruntled?

She sighed to herself, opening the warming oven to peer in at the biscuits she'd baked earlier. Sam O'Ballivan had plenty of things to be disgruntled about, she reminded herself, and it was vain to assume he cared one whit who her other supper guest was.

Ben and Terran were in the field behind the store, playing some boyish game, and Maddie was glad of that when Sam spoke right up.

"Oralee Pringle showed me a telegram from Bird's sister a few days ago," he said, hanging his hat on the peg next to the door, just like Warren used to do when he came visiting. "She isn't receiving, it seems."

Mr. Vierra's smile remained steady. "We didn't get ten miles before Bird took up with a bearded peddler, old enough to be her papa, bound for other parts. The last time I saw her, she was wearing a yellow cotton dress and waving goodbye from the box of a painted wagon."

LINDA LAEL MILLER

Of course, Maddie had inquired after Bird the moment Mr. Vierra had presented himself at her back door, just under an hour ago, but he'd said only that the girl was "all right." She felt the back of her neck warm, and stirred the sausage gravy with unnecessary industry.

"Maybe she'll write," Sam said, coming up alongside Maddie, all of a sudden, and giving her a start.

"Miss Abigail Blackstone?" Maddie asked tersely. "If I remember correctly, she's already written."

The moment the words were out of Maddie's mouth, she could have stuck her head in the gravy skillet, she was so mortified. Too late, it came to her that Sam meant Bird might write, not the woman who'd sent him a letter from someplace called Stone Creek.

"You noticed her name, did you?" Sam asked, and even though Maddie couldn't bring herself to look at him, she knew he was smiling that spare smile of his.

"I sort the mail," she said stiffly, whipping the gravy still harder. "I can't *help* noticing the occasional name."

"I see," Sam answered.

"Supper's ready," Maddie said. "Please call the boys inside, if you wouldn't mind."

She didn't actually hear Sam chuckle, but she felt a sort of subtle vibration in the air, recognized it as amusement and knew its source.

"It would be my pleasure," he told her, and left her standing there at the stove, wishing she could just evaporate like steam spewing from the spout of the teakettle. Good Lord. Now she'd given him the idea that she *cared* what letters he got, and she didn't.

She didn't.

And so it was that the five of them sat down to supper together—Maddie and Sam, Mr. Vierra, Terran and Ben.

Ben was understandably subdued, and it didn't escape

THE MAN FROM STONE CREEK

Maddie that he'd taken the chair closest to Sam's. Terran did most of the talking, and for once, Maddie was grateful. She had a headache and every time she glanced in Sam's direction, she wished she could live the last half hour over again.

She sure wouldn't mention the letter from Miss Abigail Blackstone if she could do that.

"So me and Ben are going to rig up some fishin' poles," Terran prattled, his face alight with eagerness. "Then we'll head straight down to the river and catch us a mess of trout—"

Maddie set her fork down with a bang. "You stay *away* from that river, Terran Chancelor," she said fiercely. "You can't swim a lick!"

Everyone stared at her, even Esteban Vierra.

For the second time that evening, Maddie yearned to disappear.

Sam broke the silence. "I could teach you," he told Terran solemnly. "To swim, I mean."

Terran's eyes glowed again. "Really?"

Sam glanced at Maddie, belatedly uneasy. "If it's all right with your sister, that is."

The river was treacherous, and full of swift currents. She didn't want Terran within a hundred yards of it; even if he learned to swim, he'd be certain to take reckless chances, showing off. If he were to drown—

It didn't bear thinking about.

"Please, Maddie?" Terran implored when the silence stretched taut.

Sam waited respectfully, watching her face, seeing too much.

"It's too late in the year," she said at last, and with no little relief. "The water will be cold."

"Come spring, then?" Terran pressed, anxiously hopeful.

LINDA LAEL MILLER

Maddie returned Sam's steady gaze. By winter's end, Sam O'Ballivan would be long gone, she thought, and was surprised by the bleak desolation the knowledge stirred in her. "Yes," she said, hating herself for offering false hope. "You may learn to swim in the spring."

"I'd like to learn, too," Ben put in rather timidly. "Pa never did know how. Rex and Landry don't, neither, and Garrett—" He paused, swallowed painfully. "He used to hold my head under water, down at the pond. Called me a tit-baby when I whooped."

Sam reached out, ruffled the boy's hair. "I promise I won't make you whoop," he said. Maddie noticed, though Terran and Ben probably didn't, that he hadn't said he'd still be around to teach them to swim, once the weather turned warm.

"Would you like more sausage gravy, Mr. Vierra?" Maddie asked, eager to head the conversation in another direction.

It didn't work. "On the other side of the river," Vierra said, "boys swim whenever they get the chance."

Maddie set her jaw.

Sam smiled.

"We're as tough as any of them," Terran said, cocky as a banty rooster.

Mr. Vierra grimaced. Pushed back his chair. "I'd better leave," he said, "before I wear out my welcome. Thank you for a fine supper, Miss Chancelor."

Maddie nodded, but didn't speak.

Sam excused himself to follow the other man outside.

"Clear the table," Maddie told Terran.

"We didn't have pie yet," Terran complained.

"Later," Maddie insisted, and got up to pump water into a kettle, so she could wash the dishes and be done with this interminable evening.

She shouldn't have invited Sam O'Ballivan to supper.

THE MAN FROM STONE CREEK

She'd done it on impulse, after he'd told her about hiding behind his mother's kitchen stove while she was gunned down, and because funerals always made her feel like she ought to do a kindness for somebody.

"Can't we have pie?" Terran persisted.

Maddie set down the kettle, got two plates, cut a slice of raspberry pie for each of the boys, and sent them upstairs with their desserts. She'd clear the table herself.

Like always.

When Sam came back in after talking to Mr. Vierra, he looked secretive, and there was a fresh-air scent around him that riled Maddie's nerves. He rolled up the sleeves of his white shirt, reached for a dish towel and immediately set to drying dishes as Maddie washed them.

"It's a good thing for a boy to learn to swim, Maddie," he said very quietly when they'd nearly finished the task.

She looked up at him, weighed her words carefully before she let go of them, so there would be no regrets. "Is it? Terran has a wild streak in him. He rushes in where no sensible angel would go. He'll head straight for deep water as soon as he can dog-paddle."

Sam raised a hand, as though he might brush away the tendril of hair Maddie felt sticking to her cheek from the steamy job of swabbing the supper dishes. Then he must have thought better of it, for he stopped. "There's a lot of deep water out there," he said, "and it isn't all in the river. Wouldn't you say it's better if he knows how to look after himself?"

Maddie bit her lower lip, wondered distractedly what Abigail Blackstone was like. If she was pretty, if she was smart. If she'd cried openly after Sam rode away from Stone Creek, or if she'd held her head high. If she'd ever gotten more than that brief, slanted smile out of him, made him laugh right out loud.

LINDA LAEL MILLER

Her eyes burned and her throat tightened. "Next," she heard herself say, "you'll want to teach him to shoot."

"Terran's growing up, Maddie. Let him be a man."

She turned away, busied herself putting away knives and forks and spoons. "I'd like to see him get that far," she said. "By my reckoning, learning to use a gun won't help his chances."

Sam laid his hands on her shoulders, gently turned her to face him. "Don't hold the boy too tightly," he told her with the tender pragmatism that made him rescue Bird, buy eggs from Hittie Perkins, take in the Donagher pup and God only knew what else. "He'll run, first chance, if you do."

Maddie wanted to pull away, but she couldn't seem to work up the will to follow through with it.

Sam tilted his head to one side and his mouth came within a hairbreadth of touching hers. Then he sighed and stepped back.

It was as if Abigail's shadow had passed between them. Maddie figured she shouldn't have been disappointed, but she was. Now she'd wonder, for the rest of her days, what it would have been like to be kissed by Sam O'Ballivan.

"School in the morning," he said. "I'll say good-night, and thank you kindly for one of the best meals I can remember."

Why did she want to cry?

Was it because there had been a funeral that day? Because there was a sad, lost little boy upstairs with Terran, right that very minute, with his eldest brother dead and his father in jail for doing murder? Was it because Bird's folks didn't want her, and Charlie Wilcox's poor horse had to stand out in front of the Rattlesnake Saloon, all day, every day, swatting at flies with his skimpy tail?

She shook her head slightly, flinging off the questions. The answer to each and every one of them was yes, and yet the sense of sadness and loss she felt went a lot deeper. It flowed beneath her heart like an underground river.

Sam hesitated, took her chin between his thumb and forefinger. "It's been a hell of a day," he said. "Get some sleep, Maddie. The world will go right on turning without your helping it along."

Maddie opened her mouth, closed it again.

Sam O'Ballivan crossed to the door, took his hat from Warren's peg and paused on the threshold to put it on.

She waited, expecting something, though she couldn't think for the life of her what it was.

He nodded and then he was gone.

Maddie stood rooted in front of the sink, staring at the closed door. At some length, she went to turn the lock.

ALONE IN HIS ROOM behind the schoolhouse, except for the pup, who was curled up on the bed bold as you please, Sam remembered Abigail's letter. Took it out of his vest pocket, broke the wax seal on the envelope and lifted the flap.

There were at least six pages, and Sam flapped them back and forth a little, trying to dispel some of the rosewater smell.

"This is a hell of a situation," he told the dog.

Neptune spared him a pitying look and went back to sleep.

Sam laid the pages on the table, walked away from them, went back. He and Abigail had a deal. It wasn't her doing that he'd met up with Maddie Chancelor, and his thoughts had snagged on her like fleece on a cactus thistle.

He forced himself to read the letter.

"My Dearest Sam," it began.

He sank into a chair at the table.

By the time you receive this, I'll be on my way to Haven. Papa says I oughtn't to come, because you're

LINDA LAEL MILLER

busy with important business, and a proper lady doesn't go chasing off after a man anyhow. I don't guess the place has a hotel, but I daresay I can find lodgings.

Sam stopped reading. Panic enlarged his throat, and if he'd been wearing a collar, he'd have unfastened it.

"Good God," he said. "She's coming here."

Neptune opened one eye. Evidently he didn't grasp the gravity of the situation, though he did make a low growling sound that might have been sympathy.

Sam bolted out of his chair to pace and curse.

Once, he even reached for his coat, planning to head right over to the telegraph office, get that sneaky little operator by the throat and make him send off a wire, telling Abigail, in no uncertain terms, not to come.

Problem was, if her letter was to be believed, and Abigail had never told a lie in her life, she could arrive on next Wednesday's stagecoach.

Damn it all to hell.

He stopped, rubbed the back of his neck. There was only one thing he could do, and that was to send Abigail straight back up north, where she belonged. She'd be put out by that reception, for a certainty, after spending a full week bouncing over dusty roads in a stagecoach, but there was nothing for it. She had cousins up near Phoenix. She could bide a while with them, take some of the strain out of a long trip made for nothing.

"*Damn* it, Abigail," he said.

Neptune raised the other eyelid.

Sam pictured himself meeting the coach in front of the mercantile, come Wednesday. He even imagined up a fistful of wildflowers, to make up a little for the return ticket he'd be holding in his other hand.

What he couldn't get clear in his mind was Abigail's

face, and that took him aback. He'd known her since he was a boy, not much bigger than Terran and Ben.

How could he have forgotten what she looked like?

CHAPTER

❧

THIRTEEN

IN SMALL TOWNS like Haven, death come in threes, clearly delineated because everybody knows everybody else, and with Garrett Donagher laid to rest and the shock of Mungo's confession subsiding, folks were uneasy. They began to murmur that a new round had begun.

Maddie heard the grim speculations, since the mercantile was the place where people congregated to exchange theories and gossip, but she was too distracted to give the matter any real credence. She had a business to look after, as well as an extra and very troubled youngster, and the weather had turned unseasonably warm, even for the southerly part of the Territory. The grass was dry, and everybody worried about wildfires.

Terran mentioned the swimming lessons Sam had promised him first thing every morning, last thing every night, and whenever he got the opportunity in between.

On Wednesday afternoon, with the stagecoach due in any minute and her young brother hectoring to go down to the river with a fishing pole, a drifter left the front door ajar, and flies bumbled in to buzz around the dry goods, bounce off the lid of the pickle barrel and whir at Maddie's ears. There was a strange, tremulous weight in the air— *when would it rain?*—and then Banker James put in an unexpected appearance.

She'd known *something* was about to happen. Well, here it was.

"Afternoon, Maddie," he said. The store was empty, except for two of Oralee Pringle's "girls" huddled in a far corner of the room and poring over a catalog, while she perched at the top of a ladder, dusting the tins of peas, green beans, corned beef and peaches that most people put up at home, during the harvest and at butchering time. She saved tables and lower shelves for things that sold better, staples like flour, sugar and salt, rope and nails, boots and cigars and dime novels.

Maddie made sure she wouldn't catch a foot in the hem of her dress and climbed down with careful dignity. "I'll have the books ready for examination on the first of the month," she said. "That's our regular day—"

Mr. James put up a pale and uncalloused hand. "I'm sure they're in good order," he said with unusual kindness. "They always are."

Maddie's heart, already skittering, lurched. She set aside the feather duster and wrung her hands once before she caught herself. With men like Elias James, one did not show weakness. "Then you must be expecting a letter." She glanced at the clock. "The stage should come in pretty soon."

James allowed himself a very slight, unnerving smile. "I've come about the store," he said.

Maddie's knees wobbled. She'd saved a reasonable sum of money, since she'd been hired to run the mercantile, but it wouldn't last long if she and Terran had to start over in

LINDA LAEL MILLER

a new place. Food and lodgings would gobble it up in no time, and then what would she do? This job had literally been a godsend, but such positions were rare, especially for a woman.

"Mrs. Donagher wishes to sell the establishment," Banker James announced, his gaze narrowed and speculative. "With Mungo in jail, and those two grown boys of his nowhere to be found, she's getting nervous. Wants an income, over and above what the ranch brings in. And, of course, she needs to hire a lawyer for her husband."

"But the store *provides* an income," Maddie said, trying not to look fretful and failing miserably. Dear God. It had been bad enough, being at Mungo's mercy. Being at Undine's would be beyond bearing.

James approached the counter, lifted the lid off a crock full of hard-boiled eggs and helped himself to one. "Mrs. Donagher and I have a proposition for you," he said, picking up the saltshaker and sprinkling liberally before taking a thoughtful bite. He made Maddie wait while he nibbled, every nerve in her body trilling with suspense.

To keep from going mad with tension, she went behind the counter, took up a pencil stub, and wrote, "E. James. One egg. 2 cents" on a scrap of paper.

"Mrs. Donagher would, of course, prefer a cash settlement, rather than a mortgage," the banker went on presently. He had the advantage, and he intended to press it.

Maddie felt heat rise under the high, prim collar of her second-best calico dress. "That's quite impossible," she said evenly. Mentally she was already packing her and Terran's personal belongings, such as they were, loading them into the battered wagon they had come to Haven in nearly six years before. Wondering if her decrepit horses could pull the rig even as far as Tucson without collapsing from old age.

"As a woman," James went on, after finishing the egg and licking the remaining salt off his fat fingers, "you would have a hard time securing a proper mortgage, of course."

Maddie seethed inwardly. What he said was regrettably true. Old Charlie Wilcox, who did odd jobs to support his drinking habit, could have borrowed against his signature. "I am aware of that," she answered.

"However," the banker went on, dragging the conversation out and clearly relishing Maddie's discomfort, "Mrs. Donagher is also very concerned for her stepson's welfare. Ben has been staying with you, as I understand it."

Everybody in town knew she was looking after Ben. Maddie bit down on her lower lip to forestall a rush of imprudent words. She nodded.

"If you'd be willing to serve as the boy's guardian until things settle down, Mrs. Donagher is prepared to offer you a very generous allowance toward the purchase price. The net cost to you would be fifteen hundred dollars."

Fifteen hundred dollars! It was a fortune. After more than half a decade of scraping by and making do, Maddie hadn't a tenth of that tucked away.

"I don't have that much," Maddie said. "And I can't raise it."

Mr. James sighed. "Then I guess I will have to place an advertisement in the Tucson *Gazette*. You may have a few months before we find a buyer." With that, he turned, headed for the door.

Maddie stopped him. "Mr. James," she said.

He paused, looked back at her, an avaricious glint flashing in his eyes. "Yes?"

"That will be two cents."

"Two cents?"

"For the egg."

He froze, and for a moment Maddie thought he was

LINDA LAEL MILLER

going to send her down the road right then, for insolence. He had the power, since he managed Mungo's affairs, to do just that. Instead, though, he reached into the pocket of his vest, walked past Maddie to the counter, where the register stood, and slapped down two gleaming copper pennies.

Without another word, he crossed back to the door, opened it and went out, closing it smartly behind him.

Maddie stared after him, watched as he walked by the front window.

In the distance she heard the familiar rumble of the Wednesday afternoon stagecoach, normally a signal to get ready for a rush of folks wanting to collect their mail or send things out last-minute, but Maddie didn't move. She *couldn't* move.

"Miss?"

The voice startled Maddie out of her stupor. She blinked and turned to see the dance hall girls standing close by, one of them holding the catalog they'd been so absorbed in during the interview with Banker James, with her finger marking a place.

"We want to order this frock on page sixty-three," the woman said shyly. "We mean to share it. Can we pay when it comes in?"

Maddie sighed. "Yes," she said, forcing herself to focus on the printed drawing they showed her. She noted the item number, size and price.

"Blue gingham," the quiet one said eagerly.

Maddie nodded, wondering where these two planned to wear a jointly owned blue gingham frock ordered all the way from Chicago, and promptly deciding that it wasn't her business. By the time it arrived, she'd probably be gone.

The bell over the door jingled and Maddie glanced in that direction. The stage was still a ways off, though by the racket it was making, it was getting closer.

THE MAN FROM STONE CREEK

Sam O'Ballivan loomed just that side of the threshold, and he looked agitated, tugging at his shirt collar with one finger. "I need a stagecoach ticket," he blurted. "And I need it fast."

Maddie had just lost everything she'd spent six long, hard years building, and she was testy over it. Besides, she hadn't seen Mr. O'Ballivan, except from a distance, when he stopped in front of the Rattlesnake Saloon to pat Charlie Wilcox's horse, since he'd come to supper a week ago, after Garrett Donagher's funeral.

"As you can see," she said, indicating Oralee's girls with a nod of her head, "I am presently occupied."

"This is an emergency," Sam insisted, and remembered to take off his hat.

"It's all right," one of the young women said. "We've got to get back to the Rattlesnake anyhow."

Maddie suppressed a sigh. Watched as the pair dashed out of the store, pausing to admire Sam as they went by him. The door slammed on their giggles.

"I need that ticket," Sam repeated.

Maddie moved behind the counter, in a swish of skirts, and got out her ticket book. "I'm not surprised that you're leaving," she said. "But I did think you'd take your horse."

"I'm not going anywhere," Sam said, watching that ticket book as though it meant admission to heaven and he would be turned away without it.

Maddie was too frazzled to be relieved, though something stirred in her heart at his words, muffled and sweet. She tapped the end of the pencil impatiently on the countertop. "What is the destination, please?"

"Flagstaff." He shoved a hand through his hair, raising his voice a little to be heard over the din of the rapidly approaching team and coach. "One way," he added anxiously.

LINDA LAEL MILLER

"Who is traveling?" That information wasn't actually required; Maddie just wanted to know, so she gave the question a businesslike tone.

A muscle bunched in Sam's jaw. "Abigail Blackstone," he said. "She may want to stop off at Phoenix on the way."

Maddie didn't dare meet his eyes; she was afraid he might see curious interest there, along with a glimmer of despicable and totally unfounded exultation. She reached for her official stamp and struck the ticket hard in three places. "Two dollars," she said.

Sam thrust the money at her as if it was about to catch fire in his hand. "Damn!" he swore.

Maddie started. "Is something wrong?"

"I need flowers," he told her, and dashed right through the curtain leading to her private kitchen and the back door beyond it.

Glad her prize peonies weren't in bloom, Maddie shook her head, put the two dollars into a cigar box reserved for the purpose, and prepared herself for the arrival of the weekly mail.

And Miss Abigail Blackstone. Who would, it seemed, not be staying long.

Maddie told herself the pleasure she took in that knowledge was downright unchristian, but it didn't help.

The stagecoach rolled up out front, in a billowing rise of dust, and Maddie straightened her hair, smoothed her skirts. She was grateful for Miss Blackstone's arrival, if only because it gave her something to think about besides Undine's decision to sell the mercantile out from under her.

She saw Sam pass the window, a bunch of hastily gathered weeds fairly crushed in one hand.

Curiosity drew her outside. She was usually too busy to greet the stage, and if anyone took notice and inquired, she would simply say she was eager to get the mail sorted.

THE MAN FROM STONE CREEK

Nobody noticed her presence at all, as it happened, let alone asked why she was there.

Sam opened the coach door before the driver could even get down from the box, and Maddie quelled the twinge she felt at that. He might be planning to send Miss Blackstone straight back to the high country, but he was eager to set eyes on her, too.

Silently lamenting the lingering flurry of dust that would soil her dress and settle in her hair, Maddie waited stalwartly, like Charlie Wilcox's horse.

Abigail Blackstone, dark-haired and lovely in a lavender traveling suit, unrumpled even after her long journey, flung herself straight into Sam O'Ballivan's arms.

Maddie's heart slipped down her rigid spine.

Abigail planted a smacking kiss on Sam's forehead. "You *are* glad to see me!" she crowed. "Papa said you'd be grumpy as a bear, but here you are, and you brought flowers!"

Weeds, Maddie thought uncharitably. A tug at her sleeve startled her.

She looked down into Violet Perkins's upturned face. The child was wearing the little muslin dress Sam had paid for; Maddie had told her it was a sample a salesman had left behind, way last spring. "Miss Oralee Pringle says to come," Violet said. "Soon as you can. She gave me a whole nickel to bring you word!" She held up the coin to prove the miracle. "See?"

Maddie smiled, patted the child's thin little shoulder. "Now what would Miss Oralee Pringle want with me?" she asked, glad of the distraction.

"She just said come see her, and be quick about it." Violet's forehead furrowed with thought. "I reckon I'd better go and ask Ma what to do with this nickel," she said, and scampered away.

Without looking at Sam and Miss Blackstone again,

LINDA LAEL MILLER

without worrying about the mail or the possibility of missing a customer, Maddie turned on her heel and headed for the Rattlesnake Saloon.

ABIGAIL STARED mutely at the stagecoach ticket Sam had placed in her gloved hand. It wounded him, seeing its meaning dawn in her whole countenance, but there was nothing for it. She was a proud woman, and when she met his eyes, he felt her injured confusion like a spear thrust.

"You're sending me away?"

The stage driver, having unloaded the mail bags and left them just inside the door of the mercantile for Maddie to see to, climbed the side of the coach to fetch down Abigail's belongings.

Sam signaled him with one hand and the man paused, puzzled, shook his head and stepped back to the ground.

"Sam?" Abigail prompted.

"You shouldn't have come here," Sam told her. He took her arm and led her a little way apart. "I'm *working,* Abigail, and besides, there's no fitting place for you to stay. You've got to turn right around and head back home. Now. Today."

Abigail, resilient as tempered steel, recovered her normal unassailable dignity. She lengthened her spine and tugged at the tops of her dusty traveling gloves. "You," she said, "are *always* working. And you've never minded before when I paid an unexpected visit. What, exactly, is different now?"

Sam had been aware of Maddie's presence, seen her walk away out of the corner of his eye, and wondered where she was headed. Not that Maddie Chancelor had anything to do with the subject at hand.

"There's been a killing, for one thing," Sam replied, forcing himself to concentrate. "A man named Mungo Donagher shot his eldest son to death."

THE MAN FROM STONE CREEK

Abigail blinked. "That's terrible," she said. Then, after a deep, measured breath, she added, "There's something more, Sam. Something you're not telling me. What is it?"

He thought of the map Vierra had given him that night in the graveyard in Refugio. Even then, as he and Abigail stood yammering on the sidewalk, there was a train rolling north, loaded with Mexican gold and unsuspecting passengers. If Vierra's information was sound, the outlaw gang would probably be waiting in ambush at the railroad trestle, and that was two days south of where he was, all of it hard riding.

"There's a *lot* I'm not telling you," Sam rasped, "because I *can't* tell you."

She pondered him, her wide-set eyes wise and watchful, her cheekbones flushed with color beneath a layer of trail grime. "You know you can trust me, Sam O'Ballivan," she said.

He sighed. "It's not a matter of trusting you. I have to leave town, right away, and I don't know when I'll be back. You'd be on your own."

"What about the children? Your students?"

"I'll just have to shut the school down until I get back." The stagecoach driver was checking his team, making sure the harnesses didn't rub anywhere. He must have seen the ticket, now crumpled in Abigail's right hand, because there was an air of lingering about him. Sam sensed the man's growing impatience and understood it. He had a route to cover and a station to reach before sundown.

Abigail smiled. "Or you could let me take over," she suggested, showing no signs of boarding that stagecoach. She'd gone to normal school, unlike Sam, who'd gotten the bulk his education from borrowed books, so it wasn't an empty threat. With Abigail, no threat was *ever* empty.

"How would I explain that? And where would you stay?"

"We'll simply make up some story," she said with

LINDA LAEL MILLER

growing eagerness. There were faint blue shadows under her eyes, and that worried Sam. For all her adventurous spirit, Abigail was delicate. "And I can stay wherever you're staying now. Surely you have a room somewhere."

A flush pulsed in Sam's neck. "It wouldn't be proper."

"Since when do you worry about what's proper?" Abigail countered, still smiling. Sam decided he'd liked it better when she was indignant.

"Since everything depends on my being the schoolmaster," he said.

"All aboard for Tucson!" the driver called hopefully. There were no other takers, so that meant Abigail, and she wasn't paying a lick of attention.

"You just said you were leaving," Abigail reasoned, "so it's not as if we'd be sharing your quarters."

Sam suppressed an urge to yank off his hat, fling it down on the board sidewalk and stomp on it in pure frustration. "Abigail," he said, *"get on the stage."*

Abigail folded her arms, but not before she tore the stagecoach ticket into tiny little pieces and flung it into the slowly settling dust. "No," she said flatly.

"Abigail—"

"You are not my husband, and therefore you have no authority over me. I choose to stay, and that's what I'm going to do!"

The driver shrugged, unloaded Abigail's trunk and valise, climbed into the box and took up the reins. Sam winced as the man wrenched at the brake lever.

He was desperate. *"Damn* it, Abigail—"

Abigail waved a cheerful farewell to the driver.

The stagecoach lurched into noisy motion.

She reached for a valise, and Sam took it from her, none too politely. He grabbed up the trunk with his other

THE MAN FROM STONE CREEK

hand and stormed off toward the schoolhouse, leaving Abigail to follow if she chose. Which, of course, she damn well did.

MADDIE STOOD OUT in front of the Rattlesnake Saloon, petting Charlie Wilcox's horse and trying to summon up the courage to march through those swinging doors and find out what Oralee Pringle had to say.

There were few secrets in Haven, and folks were out and about. They'd know the minute she stepped over Oralee's threshold, and they'd have plenty to say about it over their supper tables that night. She could go around back, but that would only intrigue them more.

The stagecoach passed, with a clatter of horses' hooves, a squeak of ungreased wheels and the inevitable cloud of choking dust. Maddie didn't turn around to see if Abigail Blackstone was inside it, but she hoped, with an unflattering intensity, that she was.

She took a deep breath and a step toward the saloon entrance. What did she have to lose? Undine meant to sell the mercantile, and once that happened, Maddie wouldn't have to worry about her reputation, because she and Terran would be packing up and leaving.

Oralee's plump face appeared like a painted moon above the hinged doors. "Come on in," she said, and there was a note of challenge in her voice. She'd registered Maddie's trepidation and the dare was implicit in her shrewd little eyes.

Maddie let out the breath she'd been holding in a determined whoosh and approached.

Oralee smiled, ever so slightly, and stepped back to let her pass into that cool, shadowy space where the floor was covered with sawdust. A scattering of drifters and local no-accounts looked up at Maddie's appearance, and the piano player raised his fingers off the keys and stared.

. LINDA LAEL MILLER .

Dance hall girls wavered, faceless, in the gloom at the edges of the room, their dresses like thin washes of water-color.

Maddie wanted to bolt, but she didn't.

"We can talk in my office," Oralee said. She paused to survey the clientele. "Back to your drinkin', you nosy bastards," she ordered, and to a man, they all retreated into their beer mugs and whiskey glasses. The piano player spun back to the keys and resumed his bawdy repertoire, and the dancing girls came to life.

Oralee proceeded, with all the purpose of a paddle-wheeler traveling downriver, making for an open door at the back of the room. Maddie, having come this far, gulped down the last of her misgivings and sailed in the other woman's expansive wake.

To Maddie's surprise, Oralee's private enclave was no cluttered burrow, littered with the detritus of sin. It was more like a parlor, graciously appointed, with elegantly painted glass lamps and fine furniture upholstered in pale green silk. The desk was ornate, and probably French, with decorative china panels, and a quill pen stood at the ready, beside a gold-filigreed inkwell. The floor was of highly polished wood—no trace of sawdust here—and the pictures on the walls were well-executed depictions of fox hunts, sleeping dogs and pink-cheeked children in hoop skirts and velvet knee pants.

The place gave Maddie an odd, disjointed sensation, as though she'd stepped out of one world and into another, totally unexpected one.

"Sit down," Oralee said, taking her place behind the desk.

Maddie hesitated, then took one of the silk-upholstered chairs. She folded her hands in her lap, lifted her chin. And waited circumspectly. When it finally occurred to her that

THE MAN FROM STONE CREEK

Oralee might have heard about the sale of the mercantile, and was about to offer her a job at the Rattlesnake, she bristled inwardly and kept her face impassive.

"I hear Undine Donagher's itchin' to get out of the storekeepin' business," Oralee said.

Maddie remembered that two of the girls from the Rattlesnake had been present when Banker James relayed Undine's offer. They must have carried the news straight back to Oralee. "Yes," Maddie said stiffly, braced for whatever might come next.

"And you turned down the chance to buy the place." Oralee paused thoughtfully, then fixed Maddie with another penetrating stare. "The store's a goin' concern. Only one between here and Tucson."

"I'm well aware of that," Maddie said.

"You've done a pretty good job runnin' it," Oralee allowed, with no trace of admiration. "Couldn't have been easy, fendin' off Mungo Donagher and those rascal boys of his all that time."

Maddie didn't answer. Her heart pounded and indignant tears burned in her throat and behind her eyes. She had herself and Terran to support, and she'd do whatever she had to do, but she hadn't reached the place where she was willing to sell her body, and it stung her pride that Oralee or anyone else thought she had.

"We're more alike, you and me, than a person might think," Oralee observed. "Two women in business, tryin' to make their way in a man's world."

Maddie gave a brief nod, clasping her hands so tightly that they hurt, and unable to let go.

Suddenly, Oralee smiled, genuinely this time. "By God," she crowed, "you think I want to hire you to work upstairs!"

Maddie's chin wobbled. She wanted to say she'd starve

LINDA LAEL MILLER

first, and that was true, but the prospect of seeing Terran go hungry was another matter entirely. If she couldn't find an honest job, or marry a man of means, modest or otherwise, she might find herself begging at the back door of this place or another one like it. She certainly wouldn't be the first woman to find herself in such desperate straits, or the last.

Oralee gave a shout of raucous laughter and tears of mirth glistened in her eyes. Her dyed-blond curls seemed to take on a life of their own, bobbing around her head.

Maddie waited rigidly for her to go on.

Presently, Oralee's amusement subsided to coarse chuckles. She dabbed at her eyes with a lace-trimmed handkerchief and studied Maddie for a few long moments.

"You didn't buy the store because you don't have the money," Oralee said, "and Banker James, in his infinite wisdom, wouldn't see fit to give you a mortgage."

Maddie's face was hot. She sat up very straight. "That's right."

"Well," Oralee said, "it just so happens that I *do* have the money. And I'm willing to make you a loan. We could be partners, or you could just make payments. With interest, of course."

Maddie's mouth fell open. She closed it again.

Oralee reached for a crystal decanter and poured herself a dose of whiskey. Took a sip while she waited.

"You can't be serious," Maddie said.

"Serious as bare feet in a thistle patch," Oralee replied.

"Why would you do this?"

"Partly to spite Elias James," Oralee answered bluntly, "and partly to put some of my money to honest work."

Maddie leaned forward, then sat back. "Land sakes," she said, stupefied.

Oralee refilled her whiskey glass, tossed back the contents and shuddered with satisfaction. "It's all right if you don't want to be partners," she reflected presently. "I'd understand that, right enough. I wouldn't cut anybody in on the Rattlesnake if I didn't have to. I like runnin' my own show."

The wings of Maddie's heart fluttered, preparing to spread and take flight. "What sort of interest rate did you have in mind?"

Oralee huffed out a breath. "Best one I can get away with," she said forthrightly. "That's probably around two percent, which is a hell of a lot more than I'd get out of Banker James. I'll have the papers drawn up, if you're agreeable. Mungo'd have to sign off on the whole deal, of course. He might not be amenable to Undine's plans."

"Mr. James seemed to think he would be," Maddie ventured.

"We'll see," Oralee said. "Have we struck a bargain?"

A smile welled up inside Maddie and took over her face. "I believe we have," she said.

Oralee stood, put out her hand. Maddie hesitated only a moment before she took it.

She practically danced back to the general store.

"There's a woman moved into the schoolhouse," Terran informed her the minute she walked in. He was sitting on the counter, bold as you please, nibbling on a peppermint stick.

Maddie stepped around the mail bags, locked the door and turned the Closed sign to the street. "Get down off that counter," she said. "And you know better than to help yourself to the stock."

"I paid for it," Terran said.

Maddie looked around, but the store was empty, except for the two of them. "Where's Ben?" she asked. "And where did you get a penny?"

"He's over to the schoolhouse, visiting Neptune. When he gets back, I reckon he'll have news about the lady."

LINDA LAEL MILLER

So Abigail Blackstone hadn't used that return stage-coach ticket after all. And she'd taken up residence at the schoolhouse. Maddie should have been pleased, since folks would be so busy with that scandal that they might even overlook her business venture with Oralee Pringle, but she wasn't. The thought made the pit of her stomach ache.

"That doesn't explain the penny," Maddie said.

Terran finished off the candy stick. "Mr. Vierra gave it to me."

Maddie frowned. Looked around again. "What? When did you see him? And why would he give you money?"

Terran grinned and jumped, belatedly, down off the counter. "I'm not supposed to tell anybody."

Maddie put her hands on her hips. "You'd better tell *me*," she said.

Terran thrust out a sigh that was bigger than he was. "He gave me a message," he said. "I'm supposed to take it to Mr. O'Ballivan as soon as the sun goes down."

"What message?" Maddie demanded. She noticed the folded slip of paper then, jutting out of his shirt pocket. "Let me see it."

Terran shook his head. "I can't. I'd have to give back the penny if I did."

"I might just take that penny out of your hide," Maddie warned. She advanced a step and Terran retreated, came smack up against the counter, rounded the far end and bolted.

"Come back here!" Maddie shouted.

No answer.

"Terran!" she called.

The rear door slammed in the distance.

CHAPTER
❧❧❧
FOURTEEN

THE NAMELESS HORSE watched curiously as Sam chopped and stacked more wood than he'd need for five winters.

"What," Abigail finally inquired from the back step, probably giving voice to the gelding's bewilderment, as well as her own, "are you doing?"

Sam surveyed the tops of the cottonwoods standing to the west. Their shimmering leaves wore a mantle of crimson and gold as the sun followed its slow, ancient path. Where, he wondered, was Vierra?

"That should be perfectly obvious, Abigail," he said dryly, for he knew the futility of ignoring her questions. It would have been truer to say he was keeping himself busy. "I'm laying in wood."

"I thought you were supposed to be leaving on some mysterious mission," she replied. She'd swapped her traveling garb for calico, brushed the dust from her black hair and pinned it into a tidy knot at the back of her head. The dog, Neptune, who had taken an instant liking to the ven-

LINDA LAEL MILLER

erable Miss Blackstone, sat at her feet, gazing upward in plain adoration.

"Why don't you just shout it to the entire town?" Sam asked, testy over the situation in general.

She bristled a little and straightened her skirts, the way she usually did when she was irritated. Sam had known her since he was sixteen years old and she was ten, and he read her expressions and mannerisms with the facility of long familiarity. "I was hardly shouting," she said, and folded her arms. "And I must say, I expected a more gracious welcome."

Sam felt a twinge of guilt and summarily put it aside. "When you barge in uninvited, Abigail," he said, "you can't very well *expect* a welcome, gracious or otherwise."

Abigail stomped down the steps and approached, the dog trotting beside her, practically tangling itself in the swirling hem of her dress. "Do we or do we not have an understanding, Samuel O'Ballivan?" she demanded when she got within spitting distance. From the look in her eye, she was working up to a good spew.

Sam sighed. It would have suited him better to pretend he didn't know what she was talking about, but it wouldn't do any good. Abigail was tenacious as a sow bear after a honeycomb, and about that easy to reason with. "I reckon we do," he allowed. He knew he sounded forlorn, and there was nothing for that, either. Maddie Chancelor had set up housekeeping in his mind, and that would have to be dealt with. Damned if he knew how to go about evicting her, though.

Sudden tears shimmered in Abigail's eyes, and that was cause for alarm. In all the years he'd known this contrary, cussed, fragile woman, Sam had seen her cry only twice— when her mama died after a fall from a horse, and when the coyotes got to a litter of barn kittens she'd named, dressed in doll clothes and squired around the countryside in her pony cart.

THE MAN FROM STONE CREEK

It still chafed a raw place in Sam's heart, that memory. Took the hide right off and scoured at the wound, the knowledge that he hadn't been there to save Abigail that sorrow.

"I am thirty years old," said the present-day, grown-up Abigail. "Either we're going to get married or we're not."

Another sigh built up inside Sam, but he didn't dare let it loose. Abigail was beautiful, she was smart and she was capable. She wasn't afraid of hard work or much of anything else, and she'd been pursued by every unmarried man within twenty miles of home, at one time or another. She'd turned them all down flat, too. Because of him.

He knew, with startling clarity, that he didn't love Abigail, not the way a man ought to love a woman he took to wife. He'd have fought every wolf, outlaw and devil in the territory for her, even at that moment, but his devotion wasn't husbandly...it was brotherly.

Still, the major expected him to marry his daughter, and he owed that man more than he could calculate on every abacus in China. Hell, he'd expected *himself* to marry Abigail—someday.

Always, someday.

The trouble with the future, Sam reflected grimly, was that it had a bad habit of turning into *now*.

"Sam?" Abigail prompted. She'd blinked back the tears, but she'd sunk her teeth into the question and she wouldn't be letting go before she got an answer.

"If I marry you," he said, "will you go back where you belong?"

Her eyes flashed and, for a moment, he thought she'd haul off and slap his face. He reckoned that was what he deserved.

"Do you love me?" she asked, and even though she spoke the words lightly, he could see that she held her breath after saying them.

He searched her face, the face he knew so well. Moved

LINDA LAEL MILLER

to caress her cheek, push a wisp of ebony hair back from her cheek, but stopped short and dropped his hand back to his side. "You know I do," he said.

Just then, Terran rounded the back of the schoolhouse at a dead run. Sam was at once concerned by the boy's apparent urgency and relieved that Abigail didn't have a chance to make him elaborate.

He barely stopped himself from demanding to know if something had happened to Maddie.

Terran pulled a small sheet of paper, loosely folded, from the pocket of his shirt. "I got a penny to bring you this," he said between pants, holding it out in one grubby hand. "Maddie wanted to read it, but I wouldn't let her." The boy glanced curiously at Abigail. "Evening, ma'am."

"Abigail Blackstone," Sam said without looking at her, "this is Terran Chancelor."

"Terran." Abigail greeted him, and there was something watchful in her voice.

"Mrs. Blackstone," Terran responded.

Sam's eyes were focused on the note, but he couldn't seem to get the words from the paper to his brain.

"That's *Miss* Blackstone," Abigail said.

Sam took another run at the scribbled message, and finally registered it. "Meet me at the graveyard in Refugio an hour after sunset, and be ready to ride south. The train is on schedule. E.V."

Abigail eased closer and Sam quickly folded the note and tucked it into his inside vest pocket.

"Thanks," he told Terran, who was staring at Abigail with a rapt expression, reminiscent of the dog's. Sam cleared his throat. "Miss Blackstone will be taking over the school for a few days. Maybe a week. Tell the other kids they'd better mind her, or they'll have me to contend with."

Terran's gaze sliced to Sam's face and widened. "Where

THE MAN FROM STONE CREEK

you going?" he asked, just as if it was his business. He put Sam in mind of Maddie that way, and a few *other* ways, too. Could be one of their ancestors was part mule.

"If I thought you needed to know that," Sam said evenly, "I'd have told you."

The boy flushed. "You'd better come back," he said.

Sam waited.

"Because you promised you'd teach me and Ben how to swim. You leave before we know that, we might drown sometime, and it would be your fault."

Sam checked the sun again and whistled for the horse. "I keep my word," he said, and felt Abigail's stare digging right into him. "Fetch my saddle and bridle from the shed, would you?"

Terran hesitated, then went off to do Sam's bidding.

"Do you, Sam?" Abigail asked quietly. "Do you *always* keep your word?"

He'd never actually proposed to her, never said he loved her. But he'd made a tacit promise to Abigail, just the same, and he'd honor it, whatever the cost. He looked into her eyes.

"Yes," he said.

She gave a little nod, made to touch his arm, and drew back her hand just short of contact, the way he had earlier, when he'd wanted to brush the backs of his knuckles along the length of her cheek.

VIERRA LIT a tallow candle at the feet of the Virgin, in the little chapel at Refugio, and looked up at the statue's placidly beautiful face. *I am a sinner,* he told her in silent Spanish. *I do not ask your grace for myself, but for the innocent ones. Let us get there in time, please, the* Americano *and me.*

"I didn't reckon you for a man of prayer," observed a familiar voice from somewhere behind him.

He turned, saw the Ranger framed in the arch of the doorway. O'Ballivan took off his hat, perhaps in deference to the Holy Mother, though if Vierra had had to venture a guess, he'd have said the man was not inclined toward religious devotion.

"I am a great many things you haven't reckoned on," Vierra answered. He turned again to the Lady, bowed his head as he made the sign of the cross, and reclaimed his hat from the front pew. It was really only a bench, with no rail to support the weary backs of the faithful, but then, worship was not meant to be a comfortable enterprise, was it?

"That," O'Ballivan said, "is what worries me."

Vierra grinned as he approached, but his spirit was heavy. He rarely offered a prayer to the Virgin, for he was the most unworthy of men, but there were times when only the indulgence of the Mother Herself would serve, and this was one of those times. "Where is your faith?" he asked.

The Ranger stepped aside to let him pass into the coolness of the star-scattered night. Music seeped from the nearby cantina, the plaintive thrum of guitar strings, ripe with some soft, inexpressible yearning.

Vierra thought of Pilar and felt ambushed. Her image always came to him in the most unexpected moments.

"I was beginning to think you'd gone to meet that train without me," O'Ballivan said, neatly sidestepping the philosophical question. His gelding stood at the water trough across the street, reins dangling, drinking noisily.

Vierra donned his hat. He'd left his own mount in front of the chapel, which was surely how the Ranger had known to look for him inside instead of in the cemetery, where he'd planned to wait. "And reserve all the *bandito*'s bullets for myself? That would have been selfish of me, not to mention foolish."

O'Ballivan's horse came to him, at some silent signal, and Vierra took note of the fact, to consider later. He'd learned long ago that such things defined a man more truthfully than anything he said.

They both took the saddle.

"Awful quiet around this town," the Ranger said. "Nobody's seen the Donagher brothers since the old man killed his eldest."

Vierra adjusted his hat, reined his horse toward the south. "And you thought they would be here, in Refugio? Perhaps in the cantina, swilling whiskey?"

"It crossed my mind," O'Ballivan admitted, spurring his mount to an easy trot alongside Vierra's.

"That is what troubles me," Vierra said. "Our friends, the Donaghers, are regular visitors, however unwelcome. There is one very obvious reason why they might be elsewhere."

"They've gone to rob that train," the Ranger concluded grimly.

Vierra nodded. "Their father is in jail. Their brother was buried, and they did not come to pay their respects. Even wolves will circle a fallen member of the pack, if only to make sure he is truly dead before they devour the carcass."

By now they had left the town behind and urged their horses to a gallop. The Ranger shuddered, then raised his voice to be heard over the clatter of hooves on hard ground. "I'm not sure they have the guts to stop a train and steal a shipment of government gold. Or the wits."

Vierra stood in his stirrups, stretching his legs for the long ride ahead. "Do you have another theory?" he asked.

"Not handy," O'Ballivan replied. "You've considered the possibility, of course, that Rex and Landry Donagher might be miles from that railroad trestle and up to something else entirely?"

LINDA LAEL MILL·ER

"I've considered it," Vierra said mildly. "But I think we'll find something a lot worse than a stick in the ground with a bloody rag tied to it if we don't get there before that train does." Out of the corner of his eye, he saw the Ranger's hat brim dip slightly as he nodded in grim agreement.

They rode in silence for a long time, leaving the dim and scattered lights of Refugio far behind them, following a thin, silvery trail of moonlight:

"If you'd been at Garrett Donagher's burying," the Ranger said presently, "I'd have seen you."

"Would you?" Vierra smiled to himself. They'd covered the better part of a mile since he'd mentioned the Donagher funeral. Clearly, O'Ballivan liked to chew on a subject for a while before he discussed it, and that might mean he was slow, which could be a good thing, in some ways. Not that Vierra was fool enough to underestimate the man.

"Yes," O'Ballivan said implacably. "I figure you've got somebody in Haven, keeping an eye on things and sending word across the river. If I had to hazard a guess, I'd say it was Oralee Pringle, or one of her girls."

"Perhaps," Vierra agreed. "Or perhaps it is Miss Maddie Chancelor."

The Ranger stiffened, almost imperceptibly, and Vierra indulged in another secret smile. Oh, yes, he thought with sly amusement. The truth was always hidden in the little things.

Vierra sighed. "She is very lovely," he said.

O'Ballivan didn't speak, but he was listening hard. Vierra could feel it, like a pulse in the air.

"If I had a heart to give away," Vierra went on, partly to pass the time and partly because he enjoyed baiting the Ranger, "I believe I would throw it at her feet like a flower."

"Good way to get it stomped on," O'Ballivan answered flatly.

THE MAN FROM STONE CREEK

Vierra laughed out loud.

He'd save his questions about the pretty lady who'd come in on the afternoon stage for later.

CHAPTER

FIFTEEN

A TAPPING SOUND at the glass door of the mercantile made Maddie lift her gaze from the account books and squint, puzzled. It was dark out and the store had been closed for several hours. Terran and Ben were upstairs, full of supper, and playing checkers—or at least, she'd thought they were. If they'd sneaked out and gone roaming, she'd give them what-for.

Another tap came, tentative, like the first, but a little more forceful.

Maddie glanced down at her shotgun, resting in its customary place under the counter, and a sense of unease shivered through her. "Coming!" she called, sliding off the high stool, patting her hair and heading for the main door.

As she moved nearer, she could make out a small, familiar shape on the other side. She peeked around the edge of the thin shade and recognized Violet Perkins standing stalwartly on the sidewalk.

Quickly, Maddie worked the lock and opened the door.

Perhaps the child's mother had sent her for some necessary item, but the streets of Haven weren't safe in the daytime, what with all the outlaws coming and going. At night, it was worse. "Why, Violet—what in the name of—?"

The tears on the little girl's upturned face shimmered in the strained fringes of light from the lantern Maddie had been working by, on her perch behind the counter,

Maddie pulled Violet inside and shut the door. If it hadn't been for the tears, she might have scolded her, but she knew this was no ordinary visit. "What is it?" she asked.

Violet sniffled moistly and squared her delicate shoulders. She reminded Maddie of a fledgling bird, just hatched and surely too fragile to survive. "I don't mean to bother you, Miss Maddie," she said. "I went to the school, but Mr. S.O.B. ain't there. Just some woman I don't know—I could see her through the window, and she looks pretty fancy, so I didn't knock."

Maddie felt a sting at the mention of Abigail Blackstone, however indirect, but she didn't take the time to follow it back to one of two possible sore spots—Sam being gone, or a pretty woman with a claim on him, taking up residence under his roof. She laid her hands on Violet's shoulders and leaned down to look into her face. "You aren't bothering me, Violet," she said patiently. "What's the matter?"

Violet sniffled again and Maddie suppressed an urge to wipe the child's nose with the hem of her apron. "My ma," she said miserably. "I think she's bad sick. She said fetch the teacher, so I tried—"

Maddie smoothed back a lock of Violet's thin, fine hair. "Just let me get the lantern and tell the boys I'm going out."

Violet's eyes, full of sorrow, widened with a forlorn

hope that tore at Maddie's heart. Was the child so accustomed to being refused that she couldn't trust simple kindness? "You'll come, then? Back to our place?"

Maddie took a moment to kiss the small, furrowed forehead. "Oh, Violet," she said. "Of *course* I will." She turned then, meaning to call out to Terran, but he was already standing midway down the stairs, with Ben hovering behind him. Poor, broken little Ben, always visibly braced for bad news, now that his father was in jail for the murder of his older brother, and who could blame him?

"You're going to the Perkinses' place?" Terran asked. His face, mostly in shadow, seemed curiously still, and his voice was flat.

"Yes," Maddie said, and started back to the counter to get the lantern. "I don't know how long I'll be gone. Lock the door behind me, and don't let *anyone* come inside before I get home."

"What do you want to go there for?" Terran persisted.

Maddie stopped, one hand resting on the wire handle of the lantern. "Hittie Perkins is ill," she said, unsettled by her brother's odd tone and chilly manner. "She needs help."

"You could get sick, too," Terran said. "Catch whatever it is she's got."

So that was it, Maddie thought with hasty relief. Terran was afraid for her, and little wonder. His world had been an uncertain place—first the loss of their parents, then the orphanage, then all his hopes of having a real family again dashed when Warren died so violently. She was all he had.

"I'll be careful," she said, hurrying to join Violet, who waited, poor little wisp of a thing, as if poised to flee, with one hand on the doorknob.

"They're not worth it," Terran called after her.

Maddie turned on her brother, her free hand resting on Violet's trembling shoulder. If she closed her fingers, she feared they might go right through the child's flesh and meet in the middle. "That," she said, "is *enough,* Terran. Lock the door when I've gone. I'll be back as soon as I can."

With that, she opened the door and stepped out, after Violet, who seemed to have taken a chill.

Terran's parting words echoed in Maddie's mind. *They're not worth it.*

"Terran didn't mean what he said, Violet," she told her.

"Yes," Violet replied with heartrending resignation, "he did."

Maddie bit her lower lip. "Let's go," she said, after taking and releasing a very deep, steadying breath.

The Perkinses' place—a shack, really—stood on the northern end of town, off by itself, putting Maddie in mind of a poor relation at a wedding party, yearning to join in, but not dressed for the occasion. A lamp glowed weakly in the only window, and Maddie walked a little faster, mainly because of a sudden and entirely shameful impulse to turn and run the other way.

The limbs of a lone oak clawed at the roof of the cabin, like fingers groping for a way in. John Perkins had hanged from a branch of that tree, and Maddie was afraid to look too closely for fear she'd see his shade still dangling there.

She shook off the fanciful feeling and straightened her shoulders. What had gotten into her?

Violet, clinging to Maddie's hand since they left the mercantile, fit to crush her bones, let go then and rushed ahead to push open the door. "Ma?" she called. "I couldn't find Mr. SOB, so I brung Miss Maddie in his stead!"

Maddie hesitated and then walked purposely forward. The threshold was high and she had to lift her skirts to step over it.

The stench of fouled bed linen, or a chamber pot in need

LINDA LAEL MILLER

of emptying, struck her first. There was a crude stove, fashioned from a metal barrel, two sawhorses with an old door laid across them for a table, and a single narrow bed shoved up against one wall. Hittie lay in a tangle of faded quilts, a wraith in the thin light from the lantern on the windowsill. Violet fluttered, like a little hummingbird, uncertain where to light.

Maddie brought her own lantern along as she approached the bed, eased Violet aside and touched the woman's pale forehead with a steady hand. She'd expected a raging fever, but Hittie felt clammy instead, and cold as a corpse.

"Violet shouldn't have troubled you, Miss Maddie," she said in a raspy, strangled voice. "I'm so sorry—"

"Hush," Maddie said. She'd never attended a sick person before, except for Terran when he'd come down with the grippe last winter. What was she supposed to do? "I'm here now, and it was no trouble." Not entirely true, but for the moment the assurance itself was all she had to offer the woman. "Do you hurt anywhere? How long have you been sick?"

"I hurt everyplace," Hittie said with a grim attempt at humor, and lapsed into a fit of coughing, covering her mouth with the bedclothes. "I been feelin' poorly for a couple of days now, but it didn't get real bad until tonight, long about suppertime."

Maddie set her lantern on the windowsill, beside the other, which flickered, about to gutter. "Violet," she said, without looking at the child, "do you know how to make tea?"

"No," Violet answered. "And we ain't got any, anyhow."

Maddie was getting used to the smell, but the poverty of the place seemed to loom in the shadows, another kind of miasma. Overhead, she heard the tree branches scratching, scratching, feeling for a crack in the crumbling roof.

"Have you eaten?" she asked, and hoped the pity she felt wasn't audible in her voice.

"We had eggs," Violet answered with some pride. "Ma didn't finish much of hers, though."

"I'm going to send somebody across the river for a doctor," Maddie decided out loud.

Hittie grabbed for Maddie's hand and caught it in a surprisingly strong grip, considering her emaciated state. "No Mexicans," she rasped, clinging. "I'm sore afeared of Mexicans!"

Inwardly, Maddie stiffened. "I don't think we're in a position to be choosey," she said. "You need help."

"I can't pay no doctor!" Hittie cried, and then lapsed into another coughing spell. The sound was racking, and Maddie felt the raw echo of it in her own lungs.

She turned to Violet. "Where is the water bucket?"

The child crossed the room, came back with a ladle, and, at Maddie's nod, held it to her mother's lips. Hittie sipped, and her coughing abated somewhat. She sagged back onto her bare pillow with a sigh.

The cabin felt as frigid as a springhouse, despite the relatively warm weather. Maddie used kindling and most of the firewood on hand to get the fire going. Fretful, she wondered where in blazes Sam was, and what he'd do if he were here.

It galled her that she was thinking such thoughts, and she tried to chase them away, but it was no good. If only Sam would appear. He'd know how to proceed, she was sure of that.

Violet appeared at Maddie's side, hovering like a feather caught in a downdraft. "Is my ma gonna die?" she asked in a breathless whisper.

Maddie stopped her fretful busywork and embraced the child fiercely. Violet had already lost her father, and in a

LINDA LAEL MILLER

brutal way. She and her mother scraped by on egg money and the too rare charity of others. "No," she said, and prayed that fate would back her up.

Violet began to cry. "She's worth it," she said. "I don't care what Terran says. *My ma's as good as anybody else.*"

"Of course she is," Maddie said with gentle conviction, still holding Violet close. "And so are you." She released the girl, bent again to look directly into that small, smudged, furiously despairing face. "Listen to me, Violet. I've got to find somebody to go across for Dr. Sanchez, and then stop by the mercantile for a few things. You stay here and try to get your mother to drink more water. I'll be back as soon as I can."

Violet clung to Maddie's skirt with one grubby hand. "You *got* to come back, Miss Maddie."

"I promise I will," Maddie said.

Violet looked up at her, blinking, and slowly released her hold on Maddie's dress. "Even if Terran says you oughtn't to?" she asked, her voice so small, Maddie could barely hear it.

"Even then," Maddie replied. She glanced at Hittie, now lying very still, with her eyes closed, and the two lanterns standing on the windowsill. As she watched, the first one flared and went out.

It was a dark night, with only a partial moon. She would have to leave her lantern behind, for Violet and Hittie, and make her way back to the center of town as best she could.

She knocked on three different doors before Henry Maddox, the town blacksmith agreed, over his wife's scathing objections, to ride across to Refugio and fetch the Mexican doctor. From there, Maddie hurried to the mercantile, climbing onto the wood box beside the back door to feel along the lintel for the key. Then light bloomed at the window over the kitchen sink and Terran opened the door. His face was stony as he watched Maddie get down, leaving the key where it was.

"Guess you came to your senses after all," he said.

Maddie stared at him. "I wonder when you'll come to yours," she replied, and swept past him into the kitchen. She took the lantern from the middle of the table and headed for the main part of the store.

After setting the light on the counter, next to the cash register, she went to work, pulling a tin of tea from a shelf, along with powdered aspirin and a brown bottle of laudanum. A woolen blanket came next and then a kettle, an enamel basin and a bar of soap.

"What are you doing?" Terran demanded.

Maddie didn't pause to look at him. She didn't want to think about her brother just then. "Go and hitch up the buckboard," she said, stacking things on the counter. "And when you've finished, load some firewood in the back of it."

"We *need* our firewood," Terran argued. "It'll be winter soon."

"Do as I tell you," Maddie snapped impatiently, straining to take cans of corned beef, fruit and vegetables down from a high shelf.

"You're takin' all these things to the Perkinses'!" Terran accused. "Just *givin'* them away! And you won't even let me have a stick of penny candy 'less I pay for it in cash money!"

Maddie walked over to Terran, met his defiant gaze and barely stopped herself from slapping him across the face. "Not another word," she warned, sick with shame at what she'd nearly done, while her brother glared up at her in full knowledge that she'd been about to strike him. *"Not another word."*

Grudgingly, Terran turned and walked away, presumably to do as he was told. Maddie watched him go, full of

LINDA LAEL MILLER

regret. In the morning, in the bright light of day, they'd talk, she promised herself. They'd come to an understanding and she would apologize for her outburst. He'd be the Terran she knew again, cheerful and mischievous, not this cold, uncaring stranger she didn't even recognize.

Plain as could be, she heard what Sam O'Ballivan had said about Terran, that first day, when they'd butted heads right here in the store.

Guess he's got a devious side, to go along with that mean streak of his.

Maddie put a hand to her stomach.

It wasn't true. It *wasn't*.

"I don't believe it," she whispered, just as if the clock had turned backward and Sam was standing in front of her again.

You don't choose to believe it. He'd said those words then, and he'd say them now, too, if he hadn't lit out for parts unknown.

Well, to *hell* with Sam O'Ballivan.

He was no help anyhow.

THEY'D RIDDEN HARD for two days, traveling mostly at night, he and the Ranger, stopping only to rest their horses and let them drink when there was water to be found. Fortunately, Vierra knew every *rancho* where a man could approach a trough or a well without catching a bullet for it, every stream and hidden spring. It was a relief when dawn came, though he usually favored the dark.

"How far to the trestle?" O'Ballivan asked, standing in his stirrups to stretch his legs.

"Maybe two miles," Vierra answered, doing the same. He nodded toward the peaks of the foothills they'd been climbing for the last few hours. "Most of it straight up."

"Obviously," the Ranger replied grimly.

THE MAN FROM STONE CREEK

That was when they heard the thin, distant shrill of a steam whistle.

"*¡Madre de Dios!*" Vierra gasped, giving his tired horse his heels. "The train!"

The Ranger kept up ably and shouted from alongside, "I thought you said it wouldn't get this far before noon at the earliest!"

Vierra didn't spare the effort to answer. He needed all his stamina to concentrate and to keep the horse moving. The trail was narrow now, and rocky, steeper with every lunging stride. He drove the animal on, and the Ranger stayed with him, though his gelding was puffing, lathered from the long ride, and close to winded.

Still, they'd covered the better part of that scant two miles before they heard the train whistle again, shrieking now. Just as they crested the last rise, the locomotive rounded a bend and came into sight, wheels screeching and throwing sparks as they grabbed at the track.

"What the hell?" the Ranger rasped as both he and Vierra reined in. A lone rider waited at the foot of the trestle, where it spanned a rocky chasm at least a hundred feet deep, facing down that speeding train as though it were a toy in a shop window.

"The engineer must have tried to outrun them, farther back along the line," Vierra said, every muscle in his body rigid, bracing for what was about to happen. For what he and the Ranger were too late to prevent. He drew his rifle from its scabbard, out of instinct rather than reason, but it was useless. The rider was out of range by at least three hundred yards, and as they watched, as the engineer at the controls of that locomotive laid on the brakes, he lit a fuse to what looked like enough dynamite to bring down the whole mountain, let alone a spindly trestle like that one. He tossed it onto the rails, waved his hat in triumph, and

LINDA LAEL MILLER

spurred his horse up a skinny trail alongside, as if the devil himself was after him.

Vierra wanted to close his eyes, but he didn't. Instead, he took off his sweat-soaked hat and pressed it to his chest, murmuring a prayer under his breath. Beside him, the Ranger struggled to control his horse, keep the terrified creature from whirling around and flat-bellying it in the other direction.

Smart horse, Vierra thought.

The blast came then, shaking the ground. Vierra felt the impact of the explosion, assaulting his eardrums, shuddering in the very air around him, saw the bright orange flash of flame and then the smoke. The trestle folded just as the locomotive cleared the edge of the slope, and he and O'Ballivan watched, helpless, as the engine plunged into space, pulling the other cars right along behind it.

Both horses went loco then, in the deafening aftermath, screaming with fright, tossing their heads, spinning on their hind legs. For all that it was a battle to stay in the saddle, Vierra never looked away from that wreck, and he didn't think O'Ballivan did, either. It wouldn't have been right to do that, even though it required a lot of grit to hold on to the sight.

"Sweet Jesus God," O'Ballivan gasped, when it was over. When the crashing stopped and the awful silence boiled up out of that ravine.

"Amen," Vierra said into the dreadful, trembling calm. They'd seen one man toss that bundle of dynamite onto the trestle, but he wasn't working alone. Any second now, the *banditos* would swarm out of the rocks on the other side, like tarantulas, and make their way down to collect the spoils.

"There might be somebody alive down there," O'Ballivan said, and started for the descending trail, snaking along that side of the ravine toward the river far below.

Vierra reached out and caught hold of the gelding's bridle strap.

"Not a chance," Vierra told him. "Wait."

The two men glared at each other.

"No one could have survived that fall," Vierra insisted, easing his horse backward, behind an outcropping of rock.

Reluctantly, O'Ballivan joined him. "Where the hell are they?" he mused, and Vierra knew he meant the outlaws who'd caused the cataclysm they'd just witnessed.

"Could be they spotted us," Vierra said, and spat. Bile kept rising in his throat. *Too late,* he thought, and fathomless despair yawned inside him like an abyss. He had to stay way back from the edge. *We were too late.*

"That won't keep the murdering sons of bitches from going after the gold shipment," O'Ballivan replied. "Maybe they're planning to bide their time until nightfall. Or ride around behind and get the jump on us."

Vierra swung down off his still-fitful horse, reached for his canteen and poured the contents into his hat so the gelding could drink. After a moment of deliberation, the Ranger did the same.

Vierra settled his sodden hat back on his head, once the horse had emptied it. The dampness was cool and soothing, though it didn't ease the dry ache that had opened up where his belly had been.

"Where are they?" he murmured, not really expecting an answer, watching the cliff on the other side of the river. There was no sign of movement, as far as he could make out, not even a jackrabbit darting out of the sagebrush.

O'Ballivan stared down at the wreckage. The top part of his face was shaded by his hat brim, but Vierra saw the tight, pale line of the Ranger's jaw. Saw the tension in his wide shoulders and in the way he gripped his horse's reins in one gloved fist. "Noon," he said. "The train wasn't supposed to reach this trestle before noon."

Vierra sighed. "Must have skipped a couple of stops— no freight or passengers to pick up, maybe. Engineers like to make up time wherever they can."

All of a sudden, O'Ballivan mounted up. "I've got to go down there," he said.

There would be no stopping him, Vierra knew. He put a foot in the stirrup and swung up onto his horse. "We'll be easy targets," he pointed out. "They'll see us for sure."

"We'll be out of range," the Ranger said, and started down the trail.

It was a path for mountain goats, not men on horseback, and a couple of times O'Ballivan almost pitched over the side, gelding and all. Vierra followed, more slowly, and much more carefully. All the while, he watched the other side of the ravine, his rifle resting across the pommel of his saddle, but nothing stirred over there, nothing at all.

And that made the hairs rise on the back of his neck.

ORALEE MARCHED RIGHT PAST Elias James's scrawny little clerk, and didn't so much as knock before she shoved open the door of his office and barreled over the threshold like a hay wagon pulled by a fast team.

"I've come to pay you cash money for that mercantile," she announced.

The skin under James's chin quivered like a turkey's wattle and his eyes went narrow. "What?" he demanded, standing and gesturing for her to shut the door in one motion.

Oralee smiled and opened her handbag, kicking the door closed with her right foot. She might have been hefty, but she was nimble, too. "How's your wife?" she asked, putting a trill to the words.

Banker James sat right down again and she heard the

breath rush out of him. "I offered to sell the property to Maddie Chancelor," he said, careful, like a man feeling his way over uncertain ground. "Not to you."

"Maddie'll be the owner, all right," Oralee said, making a show of catching hold of the wad of hundred dollar notes she'd taken from her private safe, not ten minutes before, and hauling it out for him to see. "I'm just financin' the deal."

"You can't be serious," James said, but when he got a look at all that money, he started to salivate. Fixed it with his eyes and didn't turn loose.

"Oh, I'm serious, all right," Oralee replied. She all but waved the bankroll under his nose before dropping it casually back into her handbag. "Are you plannin' to handle the sale, or do I have to ride all the way out to the Donagher place and make my pitch to Undine?"

James gulped. Reddened around his mutton-chop whiskers. "That won't be necessary. Anyway, it's Mungo who has to agree, not Undine."

"I reckon you'd better talk to him, then," Oralee said.

"You shouldn't be carrying around that kind of money, Oralee," James prattled, after clearing his throat a couple of times. "It's dangerous."

"There's nobody in this town that's as dangerous as I am," she countered. "My saloon ain't called the Rattlesnake for nothin'. When I coil and hiss, I mean to sink my fangs in, and that's that."

He looked longingly at her bulging handbag. It was her favorite, silk, with real pearls stitched on in the shape of a forget-me-not, but she didn't reckon it was the purse that held his interest. No, sir, it was money Elias loved, ill-gained or otherwise. "I'd be glad to put your funds into escrow," he offered, waxing friendly. "Just until I've spoken with Mungo."

"I'd just bet you would," Oralee retorted. She took in

LINDA LAEL MILLER

her surroundings with naked contempt. "And I'd sooner give it to old Charlie Wilcox for safekeepin' as let you get your fat paws on it." She smiled. "And you didn't answer my question. How's the missus these days? Still sufferin' from the vapors and those sick headaches of hers?"

James swallowed again. "Lenore," he said, "is very delicate."

"I reckon it would half kill her to find out that her fine, upstandin' husband pays double for Lulu's specialty every other Saturday."

A dull flush climbed the banker's neck. "I will not stoop to reply to that," he said indignantly.

Oralee smiled again, more broadly this time, and showing her teeth. "You stoop to plenty else," she replied.

"What do you want, Oralee?"

"Damn fool question," she said. "I just told you. I want the mercantile."

"You keep inquiring after my wife. I don't see what Lenore's health has to do with that. Unless, of course, you think you can blackmail me."

Oralee batted her eyelashes and put one hand to her bosom. Her derringer was tucked between her breasts, just in case she should have need of it. *"Blackmail?"* she repeated, suitably horrified. "I would never do such a thing." She paused, enjoying the banker's discomfort. To her, he wasn't just *one* banker, he was a whole string of carpetbaggers, going back as far as she could remember, each one a bigger thief than the last. It was folks like him that'd stole her papa's land and left her mama to die of the heartbreak. "On the other hand, I really can't say what my girls might let slip, maybe in the mercantile or some other public place."

Banker James rallied, but it was all bluster and Oralee knew it. She could read any man, though she had to admit, at least to herself, that that O'Ballivan fella stumped her a

THE MAN FROM STONE CREEK

little. He was about as male as a feller could get, but he hadn't come near the Rattlesnake Saloon, save to pat Charlie Wilcox's old horse and give it a handful of grain now and then. Something odd there, even if he was taken with Maddie, and darned if Oralee could work out what it was.

"It is highly improper for a lady like Miss Chancelor to do business with the likes of you," the banker said. "Her reputation will be in tatters by the time this is over. She'll be lucky if folks don't travel all the way to Tucson to do their marketing, just to avoid dealing with her."

"I guess that's more her concern than mine," Oralee said confidently. Up until now, she'd bought most of her own supplies in Tucson, mainly because the selection of goods was better and the prices lower. A few other towns-people had done the same. Most folks, though, preferred to buy at home, and the mercantile was thriving proof of that. "I'm just looking to earn a little interest on my money."

James spread his tallow-colored hands. "This whole thing was Undine's idea in the first place," he said. "For all I know, Mungo won't agree to any such transaction."

Oralee leaned in a little. "You'd better hope he does," she said.

The banker swore, but he pushed back his desk chair, stood and took his bowler hat off the rack on the wall behind him. He pushed past Oralee, making for the door.

"I won't keep you," she called after him, with plenty of sugar in her voice. "But give Lenore my best regards, won't you?"

MUNGO DONAGHER GRIPPED the rusty bars of his cell in both hands and stared, disbelieving, at the woman standing on the other side, a sheaf of what looked like legal papers

LINDA LAEL MILLER

in her hand. He'd had a bath and a shave and a change of clothes since the day he'd done the murder, but just looking at her made him feel dirty all over again.

Near as he could tell, it was late afternoon, but he was only guessing. He'd stopped marking the passage of time the moment he took Garrett's worthless life.

"Whore," he said just as the banker hurried in. Elias must have brought Undine here, then. Gone out to the ranch to fetch her into town for some business they'd cooked up between them. Drawn up those papers, too.

Mungo ignored him.

Tears sprang to Undine's eyes. Pretty as a picture, she was, in a flowered hat and a rose-colored dress. A matching beaded bag dangled from her wrist, and she had a parasol tucked under one elbow, like she was out for a stroll. All that frippery, bought with his money. She'd been down on her luck when he'd met her. Stranded, without a nickel to her name. Now, she looked like a Roosevelt.

It galled him severely.

"I know you don't mean that," she said brokenly. "You're just overwrought because you had to kill Garrett to save me."

Mungo blinked. For a moment he was in that accursed bedroom at the ranch again, putting a gun to his own son's head. He wrenched himself back to the grim present just before the trigger tripped.

"What?" he bawled, confounded.

She spoke up a little, maybe for the benefit of the cowpoke who'd been standing guard ever since the killing, but her eyes were clear and direct, as though she was trying to get a point across. "If you hadn't done what you did," she said, "well, who knows what would have happened to me?" She paused, sniffled again, but the tears had already dried, if they'd ever been there in the first place. Could be he'd imagined them. "I'm your wife. You protected me. I can't think what *else* you could have done."

Mungo opened his mouth, closed it again.

Undine smiled. "Soon as the judge hears my side of the story, you'll be out of this place. Back home, where you belong."

The thought of stepping over the threshold of that house gave Mungo pause. Hard as he'd worked all those years, he'd as soon burn the place to the ground as look at it, after what happened there. As he came back to himself, though, he felt a powerful yen for his old freedom.

"Maybe you'd like to go to California, after all," Undine suggested sweetly. Her eyes were still shrewd; she was looking straight into his head, unraveling his thoughts like so much tangled thread. Weaving the strands to suit her. "We could make a fresh start there. Put all this behind us for good."

Mungo felt himself being drawn like smoke to an open window. He gripped the bars harder, rested his forehead between them and shut his eyes tight. "What are them papers, Undine?" he asked in a thin whisper. After a few moments he glanced at the banker, saw the man tug at his celluloid collar with a nervous finger.

"Maddie Chancelor wants to buy the mercantile," Undine answered. "She'll pay fifteen hundred dollars cash."

"Buy the—?"

"Mercantile," Undine finished for him. She bit her lower lip, but her gaze held steady. Whole cloth, that was what her story was, and she was trimming it to fit. "We can use the money to hire us a Tucson lawyer, Mungo."

"There's *plenty* of money," he said, and looked past her to James for confirmation. He'd scrimped and saved for years, and he owned the ranch free and clear.

The banker nodded, and that was reassuring, but he kept his distance just the same. Meantime, the cowpoke looked on from over by the stove, sipping coffee from a blue enamel cup and not even pretending not to eavesdrop. The yellow dog lay snoring at his feet.

"We'll need all we can get together to make a go of it in California," Undine reasoned. "It might take a while to sell the ranch, too."

Sell the ranch.

Damn the house, but that land—that *land*—had soaked up his blood and sweat for thirty years. How could he leave it? Who would he be, anyhow, without that patch of ground, stretching as far as the eye could see, in every direction?

"I can't bear to go on living here, after what's happened," Undine said, and her voice took on a fretful note, though her eyes still didn't change. Mungo was reminded of a rattler he'd run afoul of one time, out on the range. It had sprung at him from some rocks next to the creek, when he squatted to drink, sunk its fangs into his thigh and, even as the venom surged through his system like so much molten lead, he'd drawn his pistol and shot that snake into little chunks of quivering flesh. "Folks will talk."

Mungo didn't figure he'd ever see the outside of that jail, except maybe to stand trial in Tucson or Tombstone, and then, like as not, he'd hang. Still, there was that fierce longing, wandering inside him like a wraith, feeling its way from window to door, pounding and wailing to be let go.

Mungo wasn't stupid. He knew Undine might take the money from the sale of that store and light out for California or elsewhere without him, leave him to face his come-uppance on his own. But the truth was, he didn't give a damn about the mercantile. If Undine took to the road, well, he'd know the truth of her feelings, at least. If she stayed, that might be reason enough to fight for his life.

"Get me a pen and ink," he said.

Undine's cheekbones went pink with pleasure, and maybe triumph. Rhodes produced the requested items from a desk drawer and Mungo signed the papers. Before the ink was dry, Undine had snatched them back.

"You won't be sorry," she said.

Mungo wasn't sorry about much of anything, including the fact that he'd shot his firstborn in the back of the head, at point-blank range. Undine claimed he'd saved her, and he knew that wasn't precisely true, but a man had a choice about what he believed. Might as well be the easier thing as the hard one.

"You run off," he warned as she turned away from him, "and you'd better pray to every saint in heaven that I hang."

Undine stopped cold, looked back at him. "Why, Mungo," she scolded prettily, "if I didn't know better, I'd think you were *threatening* me. And here I am, ready to tell the truth about what happened and save your stubborn neck from the noose!"

Mungo scowled. "California ain't such a big place that I couldn't find you," he said. "You just remember that."

"I never forget anything," Undine said coolly. "Not anything at all."

A moment later she was gone, with the banker trotting at her heels like a blind sheep.

"I reckon a lot of folks would believe you were just protecting your wife," the cowboy jailer observed thoughtfully when the door closed behind Undine and Banker James. He set the ink bottle down on the desk and laid the pen next to it. "Yes, sir, I reckon they'd believe it."

Mungo sat on the edge of his cot, buried his face in his hands and waited—not for the circuit judge, or some

LINDA LAEL MILLER

fancy lawyer come from Tucson to take his part, not even to be set free.

No, sir. Mungo Donagher was waiting to see what his lovely bride would do once she got her mitts on that money.

CHAPTER
SIXTEEN

THEY WERE ALL DEAD, piled up in those upended railroad cars like the last few matches in a box.

Eight passengers. Two conductors. Six *federales*, apparently guarding a strongbox Sam assumed was filled with government gold. While Vierra stood watch on the riverbank, Sam brought the bodies out, one by one, starting with a woman and two little girls in flowered bonnets. He laid the three of them in a row on the rocky shore; surely somebody was waiting up ahead somewhere, to gather them in and celebrate some long-awaited arrival. Now, there would be tears instead of joyful greetings.

Something ground deep and hard inside Sam.

Vierra scarcely glanced at the corpses, but he was sweating as if he'd carried them himself. "Did you find the gold?" he asked after visibly struggling to contain the question for a few moments.

It was a reasonable thing to ask, and offered quietly, but it made Sam's jaw tighten just the same. He looked at the

LINDA LAEL MILLER

trestle, part of it standing, a spindly, wooden thing, part dangling like splintered bone from a severed arm. "It's in there," he said, filled with bleak determination, steeling himself to go back.

"Where the hell are they?" Vierra fretted, presumably referring to the outlaws, turning in a full circle to take in the surrounding terrain. "I know they're here."

Sam headed back toward the single passenger car, trying to be thankful that there weren't a hundred corpses, instead of sixteen. Except for the locomotive, which had plunged nose-first into the river, the rest of the train lay in a pile in about eighteen inches of water. "Like I said before," he called in reply, fixing to climb through a hole in the side of the car, "they're waiting for dark."

"They have to know there are only two of us," Vierra said as Sam looked back at him through the opening. The Mexican moved to look down at the bloody bodies of the woman and her daughters, made the sign of the cross.

"For all they can tell," Sam replied, buying a few moments before he had to wade through all those dead folks again, "we're scouting for a posse. Half the U.S. Cavalry could show up any minute, or a hundred *federales*."

Vierra didn't answer, just shook his head.

The grim work went on, and all the while, Sam knew he wouldn't be able to bury the bodies. There were no shovels, the ground was stony, and it was getting late in the day. When night came, he and Vierra would probably have all they could do to stay alive themselves.

He had brought the last *federale* out—a boy no older than seventeen—slung over his right shoulder like a sack of grain, by the time the sun started to dip behind the rocks to the west. The outlaws hadn't shown themselves in all that time, but Sam knew they were watching by the prickle under his hide.

He wished he had blankets, or even coats, to cover the remains of those unfortunate wayfarers, but except for a few lap robes, which he'd spread over the first woman and her daughters, there was nothing. He did find a crate of dead chickens in a freight car, along with bags of mail and some staples, like sugar and flour and rendered lard.

On the shore, well away from the line of corpses, he busied himself plucking and cleaning two of the birds, as best he could, using his pocketknife and the muddy river water, a little ways upstream from the wreck. Vierra gathered a pile of driftwood and plucked some sagebrush from the hillside for a fire, but Sam noticed the other man's gaze kept straying back to the train, and he didn't have to wonder what he was thinking.

Vierra's mind was fastened tight on the gold.

Meanwhile, the horses grazed on patches of grass sprouting between river rocks. Though they weren't tied or hobbled, they didn't stray within twenty yards of the bodies.

The sun slipped lower in the sky.

The chicken carcasses roasted, succulent and snapping, on a spit over the low fire. Sam wasn't hungry, but he knew he had to eat to keep his brain alert and his gun hand steady. He had a powerful hankering for coffee, made strong on his little stove in the room back of the schoolhouse, and waited resolutely for the desire to pass.

"How much gold do you think there is?" Vierra asked. He was lounging next to the fire, watching the chicken cook, but he had his pistol drawn, resting on the ground beside him. Every once in a while, he felt for it with one hand, as though he thought it might have grown legs and sneaked off.

"No idea," Sam said evenly, stirring the fire with a stick. "I saw a strongbox. I didn't open it."

Vierra assessed him. "Why not?"

LINDA LAEL MILLER

"I was a little busy. Anyway, it's got a lock on it. One of those dead *federales* probably has the key in his pocket."

"You sure were in a hurry to get the corpses all laid out neat and tidy on the riverbank," Vierra observed. "It's not like it was going to make any difference to them."

Sam had been keeping his body busy, so his mind could work unimpeded, but he felt no compunction to explain that, or anything else, to Vierra. They'd been thrown into this assignment together, for reasons Major Blackstone hadn't bothered to clarify when he'd issued Sam's orders, but they were still strangers. Sam didn't trust Vierra much more than the outlaws who had done this horrendous thing, and now, with nightfall less than an hour away, by his estimate, he was prepared for just about anything—including the possibility that Vierra might have been in on the robbery all along. That could be why the others had yet to come after the gold. And it could be why he and Vierra hadn't gotten here on time to stop the disaster in the first place; Sam only had Vierra's word for it that the train wasn't due to reach the trestle before noon.

The theory that Vierra might be a member of the gang had one hole in it, though. Why involve an Arizona Ranger? Vierra knew who he was. Granted, he, Sam, was just one man, but it still didn't make sense. He was a complication, and it would have been far simpler to leave him out of the equation in the first place.

Just then a rock rolled downhill behind them and Vierra was on his feet in an instant, crouched, his pistol in one hand. Sam had drawn his .45 without rising from his seat by the fire, and thrust it back into his holster when he spotted a jackrabbit skittering across the wall of the ravine.

Maybe Vierra was what he claimed to be, Sam reflected.

And maybe he was putting on a show.

"We ought to haul that gold out here," Vierra said when he'd calmed down a little. "Where we can keep an eye on it."

"The gold's fine where it is," Sam said evenly. "The water's shallow, and that car's sunk as far as it's going to." He tested the chicken with the point of his knife, figured it for done, and took the spit off the fire. Kicked river dirt over the flames to douse them. A fire in the daylight was one thing, and it was another in the dark. No sense providing a beacon.

The two men ate in silence, both watchful, both listening.

The shadows thickened as the sun finally dipped behind the top of the ravine.

Sam fetched his ammunition belt from the pile he'd made when he unsaddled the gelding. He was going to have to name that animal one of these days; couldn't just keep addressing it as "Horse."

Vierra watched curiously, his hand resting on the butt of his pistol, now holstered. Sam smiled to himself, figuring his companion might be having some of the same thoughts he'd had earlier, only in reverse. Maybe he reckoned Sam for one of the robbers.

"What are you doing?" Vierra asked, his eyes narrow as he watched Sam check his bullet supply.

"We're likely to live longer if we do our shooting from inside that railroad car," he said, eyeing the chamber of his pistol even though he knew it was fully loaded.

"What about the horses?" Vierra asked, but his face relaxed a little, it seemed to Sam. He surely saw the sense in taking cover behind all that iron, crumpled as it was, but it was probably the chance to get close to the strongbox full of federal gold that smoothed his feathers. Neither man mentioned the obvious: that the car would provide shelter from the outlaws's bullets, but it might also turn out to be a trap. Taking cover was the lesser of two evils.

LINDA LAEL MILLER

"We'll stake them on the other side of that pile of boulders," Sam said, pointing downriver, "and hope to hell they don't get caught in the crossfire if there's a shoot-out."

Vierra looked around again, straightened his shoulders and set about taking care of his horse. Sam did the same for his own, grateful for the solace of ordinary tasks.

After that, they made their way into the passenger car, standing on seats torn loose from the floor in the crash so they could look out through broken windows.

"There's something wrong," Vierra advised when they'd been keeping watch for the better part of an hour. It was full night now, though twilight still played at the top of the ravine, and the inside of the car was dark, smelling of fear and death and something foul in the water. It came to Sam, with a chill, that there might be more bodies pinned underneath the car, a lookout, maybe, crouched on the catwalk on the roof, or someone with the misfortune to be moving between cars when the trestle gave way.

"You sound," Sam observed, thrusting those images forcibly out of his head, "like a man with reason to expect things to go a certain way."

He felt Vierra's sudden stillness. "You think I'm one of *them?*"

"I've seen stranger things happen," Sam said.

"If you weren't a lawman, I believe I'd shoot you right here and now, just for defaming my character like that."

"You could try."

Vierra chuckled in the gloom. "You think you're faster than I am, *gringo?*"

"Might be that I am," Sam allowed. He'd been in plenty of skirmishes in his time, and he was still alive, which said all that was needed about his prowess with a gun. On the other hand, the same could be said of Vierra.

"That would make things too easy for the *banditos,* if

THE MAN FROM STONE CREEK

we shot each other," Vierra surmised. A brief wisp of moon glow illuminated his profile. "I am not one of them." He paused and spat, as if the idea had caught on his tongue and soured there. "But some of that gold is mine, if I bring *los diablos* back to a certain *rancho* alive."

"You told me it belonged to the Mexican government," Sam pointed out. "And given that I carried six dead *federales* out of this passenger car, I believed that much of your story."

Vierra stiffened, gazing out the window, and cocked his pistol, a cold, decisive click in the dark. "Here they come," he whispered, and, sure enough, four riders were making their way down the cliff trail, shadow creatures, part man and part horse.

Sam's palm sweated where he gripped his .45. *Dead or alive. Just bring the bastards in. But put a stop to the thieving and killing.* Those were the major's orders, but even after what the gang had done, the worst of it lying still on the shore in mute witness, Sam couldn't bring himself to shoot those men out of the saddle.

As he and Vierra watched, the riders gained flat ground. Three of them held back, cloaked in darkness, their hat brims down over their faces. The fourth man rode to the forefront.

"We been watching you," he said. "You might just as well come out of there and let us have what we've come for."

Sam didn't recognize the voice, but he thought he should have. All he knew for sure was that whoever the ringleader was, he *wasn't* Rex or Landry Donagher. He was too slightly built for that, though he sat a horse as though he'd been born to it.

Vierra spewed a stream of Spanish invective and fired a shot over the bandits' heads, striking the ravine wall and bringing down a shower of small stones.

The trio at the rear scrambled down off their horses and

LINDA LAEL MILLER

took cover in the rocks, and Sam waited for a volley of retaliatory gunfire, but it didn't come. The man up front had raised a hand to forestall it.

"Save your bullets, you damn fool!" Sam rasped at Vierra.

Vierra cursed again, but he didn't fire. "Women!" he shouted to the men on the bank. "Little children! Look at them, lying there, you bloodthirsty cowards!"

The man still on horseback turned his head in the direction of the bodies. He reined his mount toward them, and Sam thought he might have ridden right over the lot if the animal hadn't balked. Except in a blind panic, no horse would deliberately step on anything, lest it lose its footing.

"We tried to stop the train in a canyon," the rider answered, "a mile or so south of here. That engineer kept right on coming, pouring on the coal. His bad luck that we'd posted a man up ahead, in case of that very eventuality. At a signal from us, he blew up the trestle."

In case of that very eventuality, Sam repeated in his head. He'd never known a cowpoke or a drifter who talked like that. Who the hell *was* this, and why did he figure he ought to know the answer to that question already?

"Just give us the gold," the man called, "and we'll be on our way. Leave you to bury these good dead. Say a few kindly words over them, if you please, as a favor to us."

Vierra shouted another insult.

Dead or alive. Sam went so far as to take aim on the man in the lead before his conscience snagged him. The major didn't give a damn how he accomplished the task, he reminded himself, and neither did the Territorial government, as long as the murdering, rustling and robbing ended, north of the border. But Sam wanted to see the four of them tried, sentenced and hanged, and he'd bring them in for the purpose, if he had to whip the lot and Vierra in the bargain to do it,

"We're not inclined to do you any favors," Sam replied.

Another faint wash of moonlight swept the riverbank, and Sam strained to recognize any or all of the men, but it was too dark. They were mere shapes, clad in long coats. He did make out that they'd all drawn rifles.

"There are only two of you," the leader said with cold cordiality. "How long do you think you can hold us off?"

Sam had been considering that question all along, and no answer was forthcoming. "It would be easy enough to even the odds," he responded. Damn, but it *would* be easy. Shoot the sons of bitches, drape them over their own saddles and lead their burdened horses out like a pack string. Leave the gold for Vierra to do with as he chose.

Trouble was, unlike the killers, Sam had a conscience, and he knew his own mind. If he shot those men without real cause, he'd see them falling in his mind, over and over again, for the rest of his days, whether his eyes were open or closed. And he'd wish he'd done things differently.

It would be burden enough that he couldn't bury those bodies.

"Just throw that strongbox out here," the leader cajoled, "and we'll ride out. No harm done."

No harm done. All those corpses lying on the bank, and at least one more in the locomotive. Vibrant, flesh-and-blood lives, cut short, stolen. Sam could barely comprehend the kind of fear those people must have felt when the train plunged into midair; just thinking of it made his stomach churn. And God knew how many others had been left behind to mourn and to imagine what their loved ones must have gone through in those last terrible moments.

"I'll rot in hell first," Sam vowed.

"Then I guess we have a standoff," replied the spokesman with resignation. He swung down out of the saddle and,

LINDA LAEL MILLER

seeing only the outline of him in the darkness, Sam was struck, once again, by a frustrating sense of familiarity.

The man bent over one of the bodies, and Sam heard the tearing of cloth.

"We got more dynamite, boss," one of the men in back said. "We could blast them out of there." Rex or Landry Donagher for sure, Sam thought, though he couldn't have said which one.

"Shut up, you damned idiot," answered the boss man. In the moonlight, Sam saw him tie a bit of bloody cloth to the stick they'd used to roast the rabbit, and jam it into the ground. After that, he took to picking up driftwood from the bank.

Sam had considered the possibility that the outlaws might have more explosives, but it didn't worry him. Sure, they could blow up the car easily enough, and scatter Sam's and Vierra's body parts from here to kingdom come, but the contents of the strongbox would go up with them and rain down in that river like salt. They'd play hell gathering it all up if that happened, and the gold, after all, was the whole point of the enterprise.

"We buried your brother the other day," Sam called to Rex and Landry, hoping to get a rise out of either of them. "Your old man is in jail for it. Came into town with Garrett's blood and brains splattered all over his clothes, Mungo did, and admitted to the whole thing."

A thrumming silence ensued and Sam knew he'd struck a chord. Waited.

One man stepped out from behind his rock. "You're lyin'," he accused.

Dead-center, Sam thought.

The leader paused in his firewood-gathering to curse.

"It's the God's truth," Sam pressed. "According to Mungo, he caught Garrett with Undine, put a pistol to the back of his head and pulled the trigger. I saw the body myself."

The man who'd spoken seemed to cave in on himself. Even in the gloom, Sam saw how his shoulders slumped and his fists slackened at his sides. "That can't be," he said.

"Shut your trap, Landry!" Rex, no doubt. It was a confirmation of sorts, and satisfying for that reason, though Sam couldn't see where it made much difference in the moment. He'd suspected all along that the Donaghers were involved in the spree of robberies and murders plaguing citizens on both sides of the border, and he and Vierra were sweating in an upended railroad car with limited ammunition, no food and no water. Sam wasn't about to drink from that river.

The leader whirled on his men in a rage. "If either of you says another word, I'll shoot you myself!"

Landry moved to take shelter behind his rock again, then found some new resolve among his undoubtedly meager inner resources and stepped forward instead. Went right past the boss and waded into the water. "Give us that goddamned gold!" he shouted.

Vierra's response was Anglo-Saxon in origin.

Landry, having left his rifle behind, reached for his pistol, drew and fired. The bullet pinged off the side of the railroad car and Vierra shot him in the right foot for an answer.

Donagher bellowed with pain and affronted rage, and would probably have emptied his pistol on Sam and Vierra if the leader hadn't reached out and slammed down his gun hand.

Landry cursed and limped, bleeding, back to his hidey-hole.

"Nice shot," Sam told Vierra. "Stupid, though."

Vierra chuckled grimly, lowering his gun to his side. "The *patrons* said they wanted these sidewinders alive. They didn't specify that they couldn't be crippled in the process."

LINDA LAEL MILLER

There had been a shift on the riverbank. The boss squatted to build a fire on the spot where the first one had been, and the other three must have been busy with Landry Donagher's wounded foot. Sam braced a shoulder against the wall of the railroad car and relaxed a little, though he was still watchful. He and Vierra had another vulnerability—their horses, and while the idiot trinity back of those rocks probably hadn't thought of it, he was sure the boss man had. He was just biding his time, that was all; knew it was on his side.

"What do you plan to do with your reward?" Sam asked idly without glancing at Vierra. "Provided you manage to get the drop on me and take in all four of those outlaws, that is."

"There is a woman," Vierra answered, surprising Sam by his direct response. "Her name is Pilar Montoya. I want to marry her, and she wants the same, but her papa—well, he is of a slightly different opinion. He prefers a man of means for his Pilar, and I, at present, do not qualify."

Of course there's a woman, Sam thought, counting his intelligence a notch above Landry Donagher's, if that. Maddie assembled herself in his mind and he tried to put her aside for Abigail, without success. Maddie might as well have been standing at his elbow, giving advice. "And you figure you'll change his mind—Papa's, that is—if your saddlebags are full of gold?"

Vierra sighed. "Nothing will change his mind. But if I can offer Pilar a home and all the attendant comforts, I can claim her honorably."

Sam checked the cylinder of his .45 again. *Still full,* he observed with grim humor. "This Pilar—you're sure she *wants* you to claim her, honorably or otherwise?"

"Sí," Vierra said fiercely. Then he sighed again. "There is one small problem, however."

Sam arched an eyebrow. "Like what?"

"She's getting married in three weeks."

"That *is* a problem. I'm not sure I'd consider it small, though."

Just then an altercation broke out back of the rocks on the riverbank. Both Sam and Vierra stilled themselves to listen.

"He's gonna bleed to death if I don't get him some help!" Rex shouted.

"You're not goin' anyplace!" the third man retorted, and he sounded as if he was willing to defend his viewpoint with a bullet or two of his own. "We came here to get that gold, and we ain't leavin' without it!"

The leader threw up his hands and turned his face heavenward, as if offering a silent, beleaguered prayer. Not that God ought to be sympathetic, for Sam's money, but you never knew with God. In Sam's experience, He was just as likely to throw in His lot with whoever had the best cards in their hand as take the part of the underdog.

"You shot off three of his toes, you bastards!" Rex hollered, enraged.

"Not to mention ruining a perfectly good boot," Vierra admitted as a quiet aside to Sam.

Sam thought of Garrett, moldering in the churchyard at Haven. Like as not, he'd have considered the loss of a few toes a minor inconvenience, compared to having his brains spilled all over Mungo and Undine's bedroom floor.

The leader left off praying or whatever he'd been doing, drew his own pistol and fired it into the air, ostensibly to restore order. Before the first flare of discharged powder faded, it was followed by second and then a third.

Rex, Landry and their unknown compatriot had all gone silent.

"Shit," Sam whispered as the boss reholstered his pistol and headed straight for the spot where he and Vierra had left their horses.

LINDA LAEL MILLER

Vierra caught his breath.

Sam watched helplessly as the man took one of the bridles from the pile of tack, tossed it expertly over the horse's head and led the unnamed gelding into plain view.

"This is a fine animal," the outlaw said. "It would be a shame to put a bullet through its head." He drew the pistol again and jabbed the barrel up under the gelding's throat. "I'll do it, though, if you don't let us have that gold."

Sam wanted to close his eyes, but out of respect for the horse, he didn't.

"They say horse meat is tasty," the leader went on. "I guess we could butcher and roast him right here. I've got the fire going already."

Sam broke out in a sweat and his gorge rose into the back of his throat. He could shoot the bastards, probably hit all four of them, but the horse would still be dead.

"You can have the gold!" Vierra shouted suddenly.

Sam slanted a glance at his companion, at once confounded and deeply relieved. "How do we know they won't shoot the horse anyway?" he rasped.

"We don't," Vierra answered. "But they'll do it for sure, the way things stand." He went for the strongbox, tried with a mighty effort to lift it, and failed. Looked at Sam with exasperated impatience.

"Hold on!" Sam yelled through the window. "We'll throw the gold out the door at the end of car. Just remember that we've got guns, and plenty of bullets, and we won't hesitate to drop any or all of you in your boot tracks if any harm comes to either of those horses!"

"I knew we could come to a reasonable agreement," the leader said cheerfully. To show goodwill, he released the gelding and swatted it on the flanks to send it trotting, reins dangling, back to its grazing place.

Sam and Vierra each took one end of the strongbox by

its rope handles, lugged it to the end of the car, and flung it through the open door. It landed with a splash in the river and sank a foot or so to the bottom.

The leader, Rex Donagher and the fourth man waded in to fetch it, while Landry stayed back. Every once in a while, he gave a strangled wail of pain and residual fury.

Hoisting that strongbox out of the water was a Herculean task, even for three men, since all of them kept a pistol at the ready, leaving only one hand free for the effort. They managed it, though, while Sam and Vierra watched, crouching near the door and careful to stay out of the line of fire.

"We thank you kindly," the leader said when they'd regained the shore with the spoils and Sam and Vierra had gone back to their former posts at the windows. The murdering thief didn't bother to search the pockets of the slain *federales* for a key to the strongbox. A bullet served the same purpose.

"*¡Madre de Dios,*" Vierra whispered when the lid of the small trunk was raised. Maybe he was expecting the gold to be lying in there loose, gleaming in the scant and intermittent moonlight, like pirate's treasure, but it was in bags, as Sam had known it would be. The heavy cloth sacks rattled musically as the boss doled out four to each man, with orders to put them in their saddlebags, and kept at least twice that many for himself.

"The weight of it ought to slow them down," Sam mused, pistol in hand. Conscience aside, if any of them raised a hand to his horse, he'd put a bullet through them without so much as a blink.

"Donagher will probably leave a nice trail of blood for us to follow, too," Vierra added.

"They'll kill him if he proves to be deadweight, and Rex, too, since he's likely to put up a fight," Sam said.

The outlaws mounted up and the two able men rode

LINDA LAEL MILLER

back up the ravine trail without a backward glance. In the flickering light of the fire lit for horse-roasting, Sam watched as Rex helped a moaning Landry into the saddle, where he bent low over the pommel.

Rex rode to the water's edge, facing the railroad car. "I don't know which one of you done this to Landry," he called, "but I'll kill you for it, after you've suffered a while first. Kill both of you, just to make sure I got the right one."

"It ain't true what they said about Pa and Garrett," Landry said, choking out the words as though they were little wads of barbed wire. "It ain't true, is it, Rex?"

"It's true, all right," Sam replied. "And I wouldn't give two whoops in hell for your chances, either, now that you've become a liability. Throw down your guns and turn yourselves in, and you might live to see the sunrise."

Rex spat for an answer, leaned to grip the reins of his brother's horse and made for the steep trail the others had taken.

Vierra started for the door, but Sam grabbed hold of his arm and held him back.

"You'll be no good to Pilar draped over the back of your horse with your head in a sack," Sam said.

Vierra, who had stiffened to shake loose, stood still instead. "You're right," he said grudgingly. "The boss and his sidekick are probably waiting up there to pick us off as soon as we set foot outside this car."

"Once Landry and Rex catch up," Sam told him, "they'll ride on in a hurry. For now, though, I'd just as soon not make a target of myself."

Vierra gave a great sigh and sank onto one of the other seats. He took a few moments settling himself, and then his grin flashed in the dark.

"So," he began, "who is the lovely lady who came in on the Wednesday afternoon stage?"

CHAPTER
SEVENTEEN

VIOLET LAY CURLED at the foot of the narrow bed, a small, fusty ball of sorrow and pride, felled by utter exhaustion and the hasty supper Maddie had patched together after she got back from the mercantile. Hittie, too, was asleep, though fitfully so, tossing and turning, whimpering as she dreamed.

And still the oak tree searched the roof with its many twisted fingers.

Maddie kept her helpless vigil seated on an upended crate, dragged over to the bedside from the door-and-sawhorse table, her chin propped in her hands. If the Perkinses had owned a timepiece, she might have taken some comfort in the rhythmic ticking, pushing the night along, from second to second, but there was none.

Dawn was just breaking when she heard riders in the dooryard and got up to open the door. The neighbor she'd sent across the river to fetch the doctor was just reining toward home, while a squat man carrying a physician's kit climbed wearily down from the back of a burro.

LINDA LAEL MILLER

Maddie's tired heart swelled with relief. She hadn't dared to consider the distinct possibility that the doctor would refuse to come. Folks in Haven rarely summoned him, preferring the services of a white man from Tombstone or Tucson, and when desperation forced their hand, received Dr. Emilio Sanchez coolly.

Going out to greet him, Maddie was conscious of her crumpled dress and tumbledown hair. "Dr. Sanchez," she said. "Thank you for coming."

He merely nodded, assessing the odd little house and the skinny chickens already pecking the sparse ground outside their coop as he started toward the open door.

Maddie was just turning to follow him when she saw Abigail Blackstone approaching purposefully from the direction of the schoolhouse. Miss Blackstone's tidy hair and neat sprigged muslin dress made an unsettling contrast to Maddie's general dishevelment, and it shamed her how glad she was that no one was here to make a comparison between the two.

"You're out early," Maddie said, and tried to smile.

"You must be Maddie Chancelor," Miss Blackstone said. Her eyes were kind, with a note of deep sadness in them, but they took Maddie's measure just the same.

Maddie nodded. "And you're Abigail Blackstone."

"Yes," Abigail said, and moved to stroke the doctor's burro, standing nearby.

"There is sickness here," Maddie told the other woman. "It might be best to keep your distance."

Abigail turned her head, regarded Maddie with one eyebrow raised and her hand resting lightly on the burro's shaggy neck. "Whatever it is," she said quietly, "I've either had it already or nursed someone who did. I came to offer my help, if you'll take it."

Maddie swallowed. She couldn't have said what she'd

expected from this unknown woman, but it hadn't been this quiet, competent generosity of spirit. "I guess word got around pretty fast," she said.

Abigail smiled, though her eyes were still pensive, even somber. "Your brother came knocking on my door as soon as it was light. He's worried that you'll take sick."

Maddie felt a pinch of concern. She wasn't ready to think about the things Terran had said about Violet and her mother the night before, or the way he'd acted. Still, he was her only blood relation and just a boy, and he and Ben had been alone at the mercantile all night long, probably scared. She needed to see him, know that he was safe.

She nodded, more to confirm her own thoughts than Abigail's remark. "I'll wait to see what Dr. Sanchez says, then go on back to the store." She wanted to ask about Sam O'Ballivan—oh, she had so *many* questions about Sam O'Ballivan—but she was too proud.

Abigail must have guessed her thoughts. "We don't have to be enemies, Maddie," she said.

Maddie had been about to turn and lead the way into the cabin, but Abigail's words stopped her. "Enemies?" she echoed, but she knew all too well that the other woman was referring to Sam. Some things didn't have to be spoken out loud to be understood.

Miss Blackstone merely smiled. "He's a wonderful man. I can't blame you if you're taken with him."

Maddie started to protest, stopped herself and tried again. "I'm not 'taken' with Mr. O'Ballivan," she said. She'd spoken truthfully. Why did the words sour like a lie on her tongue?

"I wish I believed you," Abigail reflected with a small sigh. For the next few moments she regarded Maddie with thoughtful intensity. "But you don't even believe *yourself,* do you?"

"Nothing has happened between Sam and me," Maddie

LINDA LAEL MILLER

said. At least, *that* was the truth. He'd never made any sort of overture, romantic or otherwise. It was the way she felt in his presence, or when she thought of him, especially late at night, that worried her.

"Some things," Abigail observed, "happen on the inside, where no one can see."

Maddie didn't respond, but the idea of Sam loving Abigail Blackstone or any other woman left a bruise on her spirit. From the first day she'd met him, she'd known he was just passing through, and so ignored the fact that her heart seemed to lean toward him, somehow. Now he'd installed Miss Blackstone in his room behind the schoolhouse, and that said all there was to say.

"Go look after your brother," Abigail said. "I'll take over here and send word if there's any change."

Maddie hesitated, glanced toward the shack and saw Violet watching from the doorway. The child looked so small, and so forlorn, standing there in the dress Sam had bought for her. Maddie approached, while Abigail held back.

"Who's that lady?" Violet whispered suspiciously.

"That's Miss Blackstone," Maddie replied. "She's come to look after you and your mother for a while, so I can see to Terran and Ben and make sure things are all right at the store."

A tremor moved visibly through Violet's stiff little body. "I don't know her," she said.

"She's Mr. O'Ballivan's good friend," Maddie answered. "And she knows about nursing."

"You won't come back," Violet accused. "Terran will make you stay at home."

Maddie reached out, touched the child's uncombed hair. "I *promise* I'll come back," she said. "As soon as I possibly can."

Violet gnawed at her lower lip and her gaze strayed to

Abigail as the other woman stepped up beside Maddie, who introduced the two, murmured a few reassuring words to Violet and turned to go.

Violet caught up with her in a few steps, clutched at her hand. "Miss Maddie!" she cried, tugging. "Miss *Maddie!*"

Maddie blinked back tears of exhaustion and sorrow. "Yes, Violet?"

"Thank you. Thank you for comin' to watch over Ma the way you did. Even if you don't come back like you promised, I'm obliged."

Maddie smiled, bent and kissed the top of the little girl's head. "Try to rest, Violet," she counseled softly. "It won't do if you wear yourself out and fall sick from it."

Violet peered up into Maddie's carefully controlled face for a long moment, trying to read her. Then she nodded, let go of her painful grip on Maddie's hand and rushed back to the cabin.

Terran was in the kitchen, dropping an armload of wood into the box beside the stove when Maddie stepped wearily through the open back door. He regarded her stonily but said nothing.

"Where's Ben?" she asked to break the uncomfortable silence.

"He's lit out," Terran replied. He wouldn't meet her eyes and tried to push past her to escape into the yard. "We got into it."

Maddie laid a hand on his shoulder to stop him. He stiffened but didn't try to get free. "I have many things to say to you," she said, "but I'm too tired to start, and I've got a full day's work ahead of me." She paused, sighed. "What happened between you and Ben?"

"He said if he had a sister like you," Terran said, flushing defiantly as he finally looked up to meet Maddie's gaze, "he'd treat her nice."

LINDA LAEL MILLER

Maddie waited.

"I said I *do* treat you nice, and he called me a liar. So I told him to get out and not ever come back."

She sighed. "Go find him, please. He needs to be here with us right now, Terran."

He glared up at her, recalcitrant to the bone. She had herself to thank for that, and no one else. In her desire to protect him, she'd indulged him too often. "What about breakfast?"

Maddie frowned. "It'll be ready and waiting."

Terran stood still. "I won't tell him I'm sorry, because I ain't," he said.

Maddie ruffled his hair. "'Because *I'm not*,'" she corrected.

He swallowed, nodded once and bolted.

Maddie didn't move right away. She felt as though she'd somehow rushed ahead of herself, leaving the Perkinses' place, and had to catch up. When she did, she moved quickly, ladling hot water into a basin from the reservoir on the stove, fetching a flour-sack towel and a bar of soap and scrubbing her hands and face until they stung.

She put on a pot of coffee, then assembled the ingredients for hotcakes—Terran's favorite—made a batter and whipped it to a bubbly froth. By the time her brother returned, with a stoic Ben in tow, the table was set and the meal was waiting in the warming oven.

The three of them ate in silence.

When Terran had cleaned his plate, he carried it to the sink, which was, Maddie figured, as close to a voluntary apology as she was likely to get.

She sighed.

A loud knocking at the front of the store stirred her to action. She and Ben put their own dishes with Terran's, and then she smoothed her hair and passed resolutely through the curtain into the main part of the mercantile.

Oralee Pringle was peering through the display window, looking concerned.

Maddie hurried to open the door.

"We won't make us any money if you're going to lollygag half the morning," Oralee said. She sounded impatient, but there was something that might have passed for kindness in her eyes.

"It's Sunday," Maddie said reasonably.

Oralee smiled. "So it is. You'd think I'd remember, with Saturday bein' the biggest night of the week for business."

Maddie didn't comment.

"I know you spent the night tending the Perkins woman, and you look all done-in," Oralee said. "You ought to lie down awhile."

Maddie must have looked confounded, because Oralee laughed.

"Lordy," she said, "I think you're half again as stubborn as I am, and that's saying something. How's the Perkins woman faring this morning? Hittie, isn't it? And how's that poor little kid of hers?"

"They're in a desperate way," Maddie said, conscious of Oralee's gaze as she reached for the broom, but unable to look at the other woman until she'd blinked a few times. She wondered if anyone else would ask about Violet and Hittie over the course of the day, and feared they wouldn't. Mostly, folks just pretended the Perkins family didn't exist.

"I'll send a couple of my girls over there with some vittles," Oralee announced.

Maddie stopped sweeping.

"What're you starin' at me for?" Oralee demanded too loudly and too cheerfully. "Ain't you never heard of a whore with a heart of gold?"

LINDA LAEL MILLER

"I will thank you to watch your language, Oralee Pringle," Maddie heard herself say. But she was smiling.

"If we wait for them 'good Christians' over to the church to do something, those folks'll starve. Too afraid of gettin' sick themselves, I reckon. And probably tellin' each other this is what comes of bein' a Perkins."

"There are a lot of kind people in this town," Maddie had to say. "They're just scared, that's all."

Oralee huffed out a scoffish breath. "Might as well believe what suits you," she allowed.

Just then two of Maddie's regular customers paused on the sidewalk out front, peering in through the display window. Seeing Oralee, they recoiled, fanned themselves industriously and rushed on by.

"Guess I'm not good for business, on Sunday or any other day," Oralee remarked, and though the words were stoutly uttered, Maddie heard some sorrow in them. "Best I get back to the Rattlesnake, anyhow. I'll send somebody by with my grocery order tomorrow. No sense shoppin' in Tucson anymore, now that I've got a stake in your fortunes."

Before Maddie could respond, Oralee opened the door and trundled out into the crisp morning sunlight.

"NEVER MIND WHO came in on that stage," Sam said impatiently when Vierra put the same question to him for what must have been the hundredth time since they'd left the railroad car to saddle up and go after the Donaghers and the rest of the outlaw gang. They'd started right away, but it was hard, tracking at night, and now that the sun was up, Sam was beginning to wonder if they'd flat-out lost the trail.

They'd come to an abandoned adobe, walls still standing, roof caved in, and Vierra dismounted to squat, lift the wooden lid off a cistern and peer in. His grin flashed up at Sam, bright as a new watch case in a splash of sun. "She's pretty, whoever she is," he said.

Sam resettled his hat, exasperated about many things besides Vierra's hectoring and the hard travel. "Is there any water in that hole?" he rasped, scowling.

Vierra scooped out a hatful as an answer and poured it over his head. His horse took a step forward and nuzzled his back, wanting a drink.

Sam swung down from the saddle. He wondered what Abigail was up to, back in Haven, and what Maddie thought of her coming to town and moving right into his quarters like a common-law wife. It took him a few moments more to get beyond that tangle to consider, once again, where the outlaws might be.

Vierra straightened, found a pair of wooden buckets alongside the old house, probably no sturdier than the roof, and filled them from the cistern. Set one down for each of the horses. They drank with sloppy thirst.

"We'll find them," Vierra told Sam, hooking his thumbs in the back of his gun belt and standing there on the tilt, with one hip cocked.

"I didn't say we wouldn't," Sam said, snappish from the frustration and the long night.

Vierra gave a low whistle through his teeth. The grin didn't waver. "But you're fretting about it, just the same." He scanned the landscape, barren and hilly, with a scrub of a tree here and there, clinging to the sandy soil for its life.

"There must be a thousand places to hide out here," Sam muttered.

"We'll look in every one of them, if we have to," Vierra said. He crouched next to the cistern again, his dark hair still dripping from the first dousing, dipped his hat in a second time and drank from it. "In the meantime, we ought

LINDA LAEL MILLER

to do what they're probably doing. Lay up and let the horses rest. I'm hungry enough to eat the north end of a southbound rabbit."

Sam went to the cistern at last and knelt, tossing his hat aside. He splashed his face with both hands, then drank cautiously. The water was lukewarm and woody tasting with debris, but it was wet and he'd drained his canteen a couple of hours back. "You hunt down that rabbit," he told Vierra, "and I'll see what I can rustle up for the horses."

"At least tell me her name," Vierra said. He surely was a persistent bastard, which boded well for rounding up the outlaws and not so well for Sam's overtaxed patience.

"Abigail," Sam spat. "Abigail Blackstone."

Vierra's grin broadened, bright as a signal from a pocket mirror. "I'd have sworn you'd taken a fancy to Maddie Chancelor," he said.

Sam scowled, got to his feet. "If you're not going to find us some breakfast, maybe I'd better do it."

The Mexican laughed. He rose with more ease and languor than Sam had managed, saddle-sore as he was. "Perhaps," Vierra said, laying splayed fingers to his chest, "I will court Maddie myself."

"What about Pilar?" Sam asked, a little quicker and more sharply than he'd have liked.

Vierra sighed eloquently, turned his dark gaze to the horizon. "Yes," he said. "What about Pilar?"

"Go get the goddamned rabbit," Sam said.

Vierra laughed again, put on his wet hat, checked the cylinder of his pistol and set out on his mission. Sam found a patch of sparse grass behind the adobe and staked the horses there. He refilled the water buckets, put them within range of the lead lines and, shading his eyes with one hand, looked out over the landscape for any sign of smoke from a campfire. A new and prickly feeling, just beneath the hide on the back of his neck, told him the gentleman outlaw, the Donagher brothers and the fourth man were closer than common sense would dictate.

The first shot didn't worry him. Vierra had picked off a rabbit. The second made him bolt for his exhausted horse, but before he got the cinch tightened, the Mexican was back, carrying a couple of quail in one hand.

"No rabbit this morning," he said.

Sam unbuckled the cinch and pulled the saddle and blanket off the gelding's back. The animal quivered at the reprieve and went back to snuffling up dry grass.

While Vierra cleaned the birds, Sam built a low fire. They ate without speaking, then spread their bedrolls in the shade on the western side of the adobe and stretched out.

"Lonely place to live," Vierra said.

Sam hoped his companion wasn't fixing to chat. Now that he'd appeased his raging stomach and laid himself down on the cool ground, he felt a need to sleep. He didn't offer a response, hoping that would be the end of the conversation. An hour or two looking at the backs of his eyelids and he'd be ready to ride.

"What do you suppose happened to them?" Vierra mused.

Sam covered his eyes with his hat. He said nothing, not because he was optimistic that Vierra would shut up, but because he was already going under.

"The people who settled out here, I mean," Vierra said, just as if Sam had asked. "It's a lot of work, putting up an adobe, the kind of thing a man wouldn't do just for himself, so there must have been a woman. Maybe even some kids."

"Christ," Sam growled.

Vierra made settling sounds, shifting around on his bedroll, and Sam knew without looking that he'd cupped his hands behind his head and was grinning up at the hard blue sky like the damn fool he was. "I'm still hungry," he confided.

LINDA LAEL MILLER

"Vierra?"

"What?"

"Shut up before I stuff both your boots down your throat."

Vierra laughed.

The report of a rifle brought them both upright, surging to their feet, scrambling for their horses. They left their bedrolls behind, along with most of their gear, and rode bent low over the animals' necks, racing in the direction of the shot.

The rider lay sprawled facedown in the brush, arms wide of his body, blood already seeping through the dusty canvas of his coat. Sam jumped down off his horse without reining it in and cursed when Vierra charged on without him.

He drew his .45, just in case, and bent to roll the man onto his back.

Landry Donagher stared upward, vacant eyes still bulging with shocked effrontery. His last thought was etched so plainly on his face that it might have been written in India ink. *Christ Almighty, I've been shot.*

"Hell," Sam said. He didn't like leaving a dead man for the buzzards, even if that dead man happened to be a murdering waste of air like Donagher, but as before, on the riverbank, there was no other choice. He mounted up again and heeled the gelding into a full run, after Vierra.

Dust billowed all around him, from Vierra's horse and the men ahead of him, and Sam pulled his bandanna up over his mouth and ducked his head slightly to keep his eyes clear. He was only a few lengths behind when another shot ripped through the mud-thick atmosphere and Vierra spun backward off his mount and rolled twice, head over heels, before coming to a hard stop. Sam managed to rein the gelding to one side moments before it would have trampled Vierra into a gruesome mash of blood and bone.

THE MAN FROM STONE CREEK

Sam swore and landed running, for the second time in five minutes. Vierra was shot through the right shoulder, and he grinned up at Sam with a strange, happy regret, like some idiot who'd just slid down the greased pole at a carnival before gaining the prize on top. "I'm all right," he said. "Go after them—the gold—"

With that, Vierra passed out. Probably a mercy, if the injury was as bad as Sam feared it was.

He crouched, cursing under his breath, and tore Vierra's shirt so he could get a good look at the wound.

It was deep, all right, and bleeding like a son of a bitch.

Sam used Vierra's bandanna to stuff the hole, caught the man's terrified horse and settled it down with a few gruff words. Then he hoisted Vierra off the ground, draped him over the saddle he'd just been shot out of, and held on to the reins of the horse while he mounted the gelding again.

While the outlaws rode in one direction—there must have been a dozen of them now, from the dust they were raising— Sam and Vierra headed in the other, back to the adobe.

Sam laid Vierra on his bedroll, letting the horses wander, still saddled and fitful, reins trailing.

Vierra came to long enough to grin again. "You should have gone after them," he said.

"You're damn right I should have," Sam retorted grimly, pulling the blood-soaked bandanna out of the hole in Vierra's shoulder, rinsing it out in one of the horse buckets and pushing it back in again.

Vierra gasped at the pain. His eyes rolled back into his head and closed.

"Goddamn you, Vierra," Sam said.

Vierra broke out in a clammy sweat, but at least the bleeding had slowed.

Sam watched him for a while, then decided he'd better do something useful. He gathered sticks and sagebrush and

LINDA LAEL MILLER

bits of wood left from an old shed, long-since collapsed, and built a second fire. After digging around inside the adobe for a few minutes, he found a battered cast-iron kettle, filthy with mice leavings and almost rusted through on the bottom. He washed the pot in the cistern, filled it with water and set it at the edge of the flames to heat.

Vierra was still unconscious, but he'd taken to shuddering, as if a man taken with a fever, and Sam braced himself for the hard reality of the situation. They were two days' ride from Haven, the outlaws were getting away, and he wouldn't have bet a solitary nickel that Vierra would make it till morning.

When the water in the kettle was good and hot, Sam dunked the bandanna again and cleaned Vierra's wound as thoroughly as he could. He took a flask of rye and a spare shirt from his saddlebags, ripped the shirt into strips for a bandage, and hunkered down to pour two fingers of good whiskey into the other man's gaping flesh.

Vierra came up screaming Spanish curses, and Sam pushed him back down, so the whiskey wouldn't spill out before it could do any good.

"Lie still," Sam ordered. "You go thrashing around like that and there's no telling what you'll do to your insides."

Vierra blinked. His skin was pale and slick with sweat, his lips drawn tight across his teeth. "What happened?" he choked out.

"Well, that's a stupid question if I've ever heard one," Sam said. "You got shot, that's what happened."

"*¡Madre de Dios!*" Vierra groaned, and tried to cross himself. His arm fell to his side in the attempt. "My shoulder feels like it's on fire."

"That's the whiskey," Sam said.

"You poured it in the wrong hole," Vierra complained, gasping out the words.

THE MAN FROM STONE CREEK

Sam chuckled, in spite of their predicament, which was not promising, and would become less so when night fell. He reached for the flask, unscrewed the stopper and handed the rye over to Vierra, who took a couple of gulps, gave a violent shudder and gave it back.

Sam bandaged the wound, spread his own bedroll over Vierra and stood.

"Are you planning on going somewhere?" Vierra asked, squinting up at him with a peculiar combination of accusation and hope.

"I saw a shovel inside the adobe," he said. "I'm heading out there to bury Landry Donagher before the coyotes and the wild pigs get to him. Like I couldn't do for those others, by the river." He leaned down, placed Vierra's pistol in his hand, atop the blanket. "If you need help, fire a shot."

"Where's that whiskey?" Vierra wanted to know.

Sam laid the flask on Vierra's chest, checked the fire to make sure it wasn't about to jump the circle of stones containing it and start a wildfire, and caught his horse. He carried the shovel in his hands as he rode.

Donagher was right where he'd left him, of course, and the critters hadn't discovered him yet. Sam got down off his horse, left it to graze on the sparse desert grass, and started digging. The ground was hard, and he hit a thin layer of bedrock three feet down, but he kept on, sweat-drenched and aching in every muscle. The sun was dipping low when he rolled the dead man into his grave, said a few distracted words meant to pass for a prayer and covered him over with dirt and a mound of stones.

When he got back to camp, he half expected to set right to work on another grave—he'd seen a lot of men die of lesser wounds than Vierra's—but the Mexican was sitting up in his blankets, with his back resting against the wall of the adobe, smoking a roll-your-own and finishing off

LINDA LAEL MILLER

the whiskey. Watching Sam approach, he dragged a blood-streaked forearm across his mouth.

"There's a village half a day's ride over that ridge," Vierra said, pointing to the northeast.

Sam tossed the shovel aside, got down off the horse and filled buckets at the cistern to water both animals. "I guess you must have some reason for telling me that," he said when he damn well felt like saying something.

Vierra shook his head, disgusted. He moved as though he meant to stand but failed in the attempt. Sam thought briefly of Tom Singleton, the former schoolmaster, trying to get to his feet after the well-dangling incident at the school. "I could die out here, you know," Vierra said.

"I reckon you'd have done that already, if you were fixing to," Sam said. He wasn't going out hunting, so they'd have to make a supper of hard tack and jerky, scrounged from the bottom of their saddlebags. Sam wished heartily for a cup of coffee, hot enough to sear his tongue and strong enough to float a horseshoe. Could have done with a creek bath and a book, too, but except for the cistern, there probably wasn't a watering hole within twenty miles.

Vierra looked aggrieved, then lodged another complaint. "We're out of whiskey, too."

Sam pulled a second flask from inside his shirt, half full of cantina rotgut, almost guaranteed to make a man go blind. It was the only thing he'd found on Landry Donagher before he buried him. If Donagher had held on to his share of that gold, the others had relieved him of it, along with his horse and gun.

He wondered if Rex had tried to defend his brother, or if he'd turned on him, in the end, like a slat-ribbed wolf. Wondered if Mungo would grieve for a second dead son, once word got back to him.

Vierra's gaze tracked the whiskey. "Give me that," he said. "I'm in pain."

Sam sniffed the contents of the flask, reminded himself that he might have need of his eyesight for some time to come, and carried it over to Vierra, who snatched it from his hand, took a gulp and practically choked to death. Sputtering and spitting, he looked up at Sam as if he'd given him kerosene, and done it on purpose, too.

"Bad stuff," Sam said. "Don't pour it out, though. We'll need it to disinfect that wound of yours."

"I'd sooner let you cauterize it with a hot poker," Vierra countered, his eyes red with fury and rotgut.

"I could do that," Sam offered mildly.

The hard tack and the jerky, served up a few minutes later, didn't fill him up, but he consoled himself with the negligible belief that it was better than nothing.

MADDIE SPENT the rest of the day dusting and rearranging stock. She was untying her apron when Terran spoke from just behind her, nearly startling her out of her skin.

"You planning to make supper?" he asked.

Maddie moved to touch his shoulder, but he stepped back, out of reach.

"Are you?" he persisted.

"There's bread and cheese in the pantry," Maddie said. "You and Ben can help yourselves. I'm going over to the Perkinses' place to look in on Violet and her mother."

"That schoolmarm's there," Terran argued. "Miss Blackstone."

Maddie stifled a sigh and hung her store apron on the peg next to the curtained doorway behind the counter. "Yes," she said as moderately as she could, "and she must be ready to go over to the schoolhouse and get some rest. Besides, I promised Violet I'd come back."

LINDA LAEL MILLER

"Violet," Terran scoffed. "What about me?"

Ben watched the exchange from a few feet away, his eyes large and troubled.

"What *about* you, Terran?" Maddie countered, impatient.

"I'm your *brother*," he said.

"I'm well aware of that," Maddie answered. She moved past him to enter the pantry, came out with the bread tin and the cheese and slammed them both down on the tabletop. "There's your supper," she said. "Eat."

With that, she stormed out the rear door, and she hadn't traveled two steps before she hated herself. Terran was a child. He was scared. And he *was* her kin.

She stopped, torn between going back and keeping on.

The door sprang open and Maddie's heart leaped, but it wasn't Terran coming after her to say he was sorry, to say he understood that she had to go to the Perkinses and do what she could. It was Ben, barreling earnestly toward her, clutching a cloth napkin in one hand, thrusting it at her.

"It's my supper," he said.

Maddie accepted the bundle with a trembling hand. "Ben—"

"I'm not hungry anyhow," Ben said stalwartly.

"There's more food in the pantry," Maddie said, at once touched by Ben's sacrifice and heartsick that the gesture hadn't come from Terran. "You help yourself."

"I'd rather go with you," the boy replied, and fell into step beside Maddie as she started for the shack at the edge of town. It would be dark soon, she thought with a shiver, and those tree branches would claw at the roof again, if a breeze came up.

"Ben, Mrs. Perkins is very sick," Maddie protested. "Suppose it's catching?"

"I reckon if it is," Ben reasoned, keeping pace, "it's already too late."

THE MAN FROM STONE CREEK

Maddie shivered again. She'd been worrying about that very thing all day, busy as she'd kept herself, but she'd shoved the thought away whenever it surfaced. She couldn't simply abandon Violet and Hittie, whatever the risks.

"Just the same," she said as the Perkinses' shack came into sight, "don't you go near that house." Violet and Abigail were squeezed together on the high threshold in the doorway, their heads bent over a book. Even from a distance, Maddie recognized it as the one Sam had bought in her store.

"Did she come here to take Mr. O'Ballivan away some-place?" Ben asked when Maddie paused to try to find a smile within her weary self. Failing, she looked down at the boy and saw with a vague sense of relief that his gaze was fixed on Abigail.

Still, the question pierced Maddie's middle like a dart and quivered there, and she had to take several deep breaths before she dared answer. "I don't know, Ben," she said, and wished Sam would come back from wherever he was and, well, just be Sam. He might be aggravating, and even in-sufferable, but there was something about his sturdy presence that made hard things easier to bear.

"I hate her," Ben said just as Abigail looked up and smiled.

"No, Ben," Maddie protested.

"I do," he insisted. "Terran does, too. She's come to fetch Mr. O'Ballivan home!"

"Shh," Maddie said, and reached for Ben's shoulder, the way she'd done with Terran, and with the same disheart-ening results. He dodged her touch and ran off, hurtling through the tall grass, away from her, away from Violet and her mother, away from the woman who'd come to lay claim to Sam O'Ballivan. For one disturbing moment, Maddie felt like running, too.

LINDA LAEL MILLER

If Violet had noticed the exchange, she didn't show it. She seemed to have just spotted Maddie, standing there on the road, with Ben's donated supper in her hand, squashed inside a blue-and-white-checkered napkin. Her whole face alight, the child dashed out to meet her.

"Miss Oralee sent some of her fancy women over, and they're in there right now, feeding Ma soup out of a silver spoon!" The words spilled from Violet's mouth like a litter of puppies tipped out of a wheelbarrow.

Abigail approached, wearing a tired smile and holding the book she and Violet had been poring over under one arm. Sure enough, it was Sam's. "I waited here so I could give you the news myself," she said to Maddie. "Hittie seems to be on the mend, and Oralee's 'fancy women' have the situation in hand."

Maddie nodded, stricken mute with relief.

"They mean to keep coming *all night*," Violet marveled. "Two at a time, taking their turns."

Abigail smiled again at the child's delight, but she looked pale and a little fragile. "It's not every day you get such interesting visitors as these," she said.

Maddie smiled back. It was a spindly smile, but it was all she had to offer. "You go see to your mother," she told Violet, who immediately scampered off toward the house. Ben had vanished from his perch on the chopping block, and a slight breeze rustled the branches of the hanging tree.

Maddie met Abigail's steady gaze. "Would you like a cup of tea, Miss Blackstone?" she asked. She decided to throw in supper, which would be an odd repast, cobbled together from this and that, whatever might be found on the pantry shelves. Abigail's eyes danced at the offer.

"I would be delighted," she said.

CHAPTER
EIGHTEEN

"HOW FAR AWAY is that village you mentioned?" Sam asked. He hadn't planned on traveling by night, but Vierra, intermittently conscious, was clearly in a bad way.

His traveling companion, still leaning against the adobe wall and watching the dying fire, clenched his jaw while he worked up an answer. Sam reckoned Vierra's pain would be enough to make a lesser man scream, and he felt a cautious respect, mingled with an abiding mistrust.

"Probably ten miles," Vierra finally said. "Rough country, too. Dangerous for the horses."

"No doctor, I suppose," Sam observed, rubbing his chin. He'd grown a stubble of beard since setting out on this journey, and suddenly he wanted a shave as much as he wanted strong coffee and a meal cooked on a stove, in some woman's lamp-lit kitchen.

That the woman who came to mind was Maddie, not Abigail, did not escape his notice.

"No doctor," Vierra confirmed. "There's a medicine man, though."

LINDA LAEL MILLER

"I guess we'd better go there anyhow," Sam decided. Vierra needed a decent bed to lie on and more tending than could be had on the trail.

"I guess so," Vierra agreed.

Sam saddled the horses, gathered the bedrolls and other gear, and helped Vierra mount up. The Mexican bent low over the pommel, gripping the horn with white-knuckled hands and breathing hard from the exertion of mounting, something he usually did without using a stirrup.

"You reckon you can stay on that horse?" Sam asked.

Vierra considered the question grimly, then shook his head. "Not likely," he answered, and Sam knew the answer had cost the other man a substantial hunk of his pride.

Without further comment, Sam took his rope from the leather catch on his saddle, unfurled it and bound Vierra to horse and saddle, like a deer carcass to be brought home from the hunt. Vierra endured the humiliation, his pain-darkened eyes daring Sam to make a remark.

Sam said nothing, since he knew it might as easily have been him wounded and trussed up like that. He mounted and turned his gelding in the direction the Mexican had indicated, leading the other horse by the reins.

The ride was necessarily slow, partly because of Vierra's deteriorating condition and partly because the moonlight was thin and the trail, winding up into the hills, was perilous. As Sam rode, he kept one ear open for any sound other than the plodding footsteps and occasional puffing exhalations of their two horses. Those outlaws were out here somewhere, and though they were probably more interested in putting as much ground between themselves and that blown railroad trestle as possible now that they had their gold, they knew they were being pursued, knew one of those pursuers was badly hurt and therefore easy pickings. In some men's

THE MAN FROM STONE CREEK

minds, that would add up to unfinished business, and they might well decide to double back and deal with the situation, once and for all.

In their place, Sam figured he would have tied up that loose end. No witnesses that way. Nobody to catch up, by some miracle, and make trouble.

They rode doggedly on.

Vierra drifted in and out, now prattling on about Pilar, now bent almost full-out over his horse's neck, held to the saddle only by the net Sam had made with his rope.

It was almost sunrise when they reached the village, a dusty little collection of hovels, fashioned of mud and stone. A good rain would wash the whole place down the hillside, but the smoke from those chimney holes was a welcome sight to Sam.

A few skinny dogs barked to announce their arrival and Vierra stirred then, sat up in the saddle. An old man, hardly taller than a rooster, came out of one of the huts, ducking to pass through the low doorway. Sam watched as he sized up the visitors and felt relief when the fellow didn't slip back inside for a rifle. Instead, he approached.

His eyes were on Vierra, but he put his question to Sam, in Spanish. What had happened?

Sam answered in kind, making the explanation brief. After all, it would have been obvious to anybody that Vierra had taken a bullet.

The old man inquired if Vierra was a prisoner, given the rope binding him to his horse.

Sam shook his head.

Vierra spoke to the villager in a wheedling, shallow-breathed voice. His face gleamed with sweat, though it was still cool, with the last of the night just passing. "Don't you remember me, Pablo? It is Esteban."

Suddenly a broad grin of recognition spread over

Pablo's dark, suspicious face, but it was quickly replaced by concern. He shouted over one shoulder, calling a stream of heretofore hesitant villagers out of the huts and causing another uproar among the dogs. Before Sam could dismount, Pablo was untying Vierra, easing him down from his perch with the help of several other men.

Sam got to the ground, spotted a spring at the edge of the tiny village and led the horses toward it. Here, then, was one reason for the location of the settlement—water. Another was clear visibility, in all directions. If he and Vierra had been traveling by day, Pablo and the others would have seen them coming long before they'd even begun the climb.

Leaving the horses to drink thirstily, directly from the spring, Sam walked the perimeter of the hilltop, one hand shading his gritty eyes from the fierce light of the new sun, scanning the surrounding countryside for the band of outlaws.

If they were still in the area, they'd gone to ground and doused any campfire at first light so the smoke wouldn't rise and give them away to an observer. They might be holed up someplace, but they could just as well have ridden deeper into Mexico—or back toward Haven.

Sam stiffened, vexed that the latter possibility hadn't occurred to him, at least consciously, until now.

Haven. Rex Donagher was still alive, as far as Sam knew. He'd learned of his elder brother's murder and his father's imprisonment. He might well have gone back, to mourn Garrett, break the bad news about Landry, even try to spring his pa from the jailhouse. This last possibility was a concern to Sam, but there was a greater one.

Maddie was in Haven.

Terran and Ben and Violet and all the other kids in the school were there.

And so was Abigail.

THE MAN FROM STONE CREEK

Sam shifted his hat, eyed his horse. He couldn't ask that gelding to travel another mile without rest, and he wasn't in much better shape himself. If he rode for the border now, as he was sorely tempted to do, he'd be lucky to get there at all, and he'd be of little use even if he did.

As much as he hated the idea, he'd have to stay in this hilltop village, at least until nightfall, and give both himself and the horse time to recover.

A boy came, barefoot and skinny as the dogs, and offered to put the horses to graze. Sam nodded in agreement, pulled some change from his pocket, and picked the pesos from among the nickels, dimes and quarters, giving them to the kid. A smile white as a high-country snowfall slashed across the lad's dark, dirt-smudged face and he went to tend the animals.

Sam made his way back to the center of the village, where a great fuss was being made over Vierra. A rough-hewn bowl, filled with a mixture of beans and what passed for rabbit meat, was thrust into Sam's hands. He ate numbly, tasting nothing, interested only in filling his empty stomach.

Vierra was taken in hand by the village women—in spite of his pain, he clearly relished all that female attention—and Sam left him to it. He found his canteen with his other tack, where the boy had left it in a pile, filled the canteen from the spring, drank it dry and filled it again. Then, at the invitation of a woman old enough to be God's first cousin, he made his way into one of the huts, stretched out on a pallet and slept like a dead man.

The low, steady beat of a drum finally awakened him many hours later. He'd been vaguely aware of the sound all day, steady and rhythmic as his own heartbeat, but he'd been too tired to rise to the surface of thought, far above his head. Instead he'd settled into the silt in the depths of his mind and given himself over to exhaustion.

LINDA LAEL MILLER

Now, with twilight a dull purple at the door of the hut, Sam sat up on the pallet, stretched mightily and reached for his hat. Midway, he realized he wasn't alone, and met the patient gaze of a young Mexican woman, on her knees and resting back on her haunches, a bowl held carefully in both hands.

She smiled at Sam, extended the bowl.

It grieved him to take it. He'd seen enough, on his arrival that morning, to know the village was a poor one, scrabbling out an existence in a hard, inhospitable land. He was ravenously hungry, though, and there was the matter of the girl's pride. God knew how long she'd been waiting, just to give a stranger food she couldn't spare.

Sam took the meal, with muttered thanks. More rabbit, roasted this time, and a little more palatable without the beans.

"How is Señor Vierra?" he asked in Spanish after a few bites, half fearing the answer. He still didn't trust the Mexican, but he'd come to like him, just the same.

The girl's eyes were luminous in the light of the single tallow candle burning on top of a crude crate. "He is too sick to ride," she said. "There is fever and much pain."

Sam nodded, grateful for small favors. He wouldn't have been surprised if the drumming had turned out to be part of a mourning ceremony, with Vierra either on a pyre or already buried.

He finished the rabbit, handed back the bowl and wiped the grease from his mouth with one sleeve. "Where is he?"

The girl rose, set the bowl down next to the candle and beckoned for him to follow.

He found his friend in another hut, stretched out on a pallet and stripped to the waist. A poultice of some sort covered the wound, and women of every age hovered like eager servants, the youngest of them holding a gourd-ladle

THE MAN FROM STONE CREEK

of spring water to Vierra's lips as Sam straightened, just inside the door.

Vierra grinned.

"I've seen livelier tree stumps in my time," Sam observed, "but you seem content with your fate."

"You're planning to ride on without me," Vierra said. The grin faded, but there was a reluctant affability in his manner.

"You'll be all right here until you can mount a horse," Sam replied after a spare nod of acknowledgment. "I'm heading back to Haven." He knew he didn't need to explain his reasoning; Vierra was no fool. He'd have worked it out by now, as Sam had, that at least one of the robbers—Rex Donagher—was bound to head for home territory. The others might or might not be with him, but Sam reckoned he could find them, after a little palavering with Donagher.

"Look after Maddie," Vierra said. So he'd gone beyond Sam's theory, then, and straight to the heart of the matter. "I'll be along when I've got the strength to travel." He paused. "And, O'Ballivan?"

Sam, in the act of turning to leave, paused. Waited.

"That gold. Part of it belongs to me, so if you happen to recover it, don't go turning it over to the *federales*."

"No promises," Sam said.

Fifteen minutes later he was riding a rested horse downhill and due north.

MADDIE AWAKENED after a restless night and the first image that came into her mind was Sam O'Ballivan's. She shook that off, yawning, and sat up in bed, deliberately shifting her thoughts to the recent visit with Abigail.

They'd sat in Maddie's kitchen, sipping tea and nibbling at leftover biscuits, and talked about everything *but* what Maddie was most interested in: Miss Blackstone's association with the schoolmaster.

LINDA LAEL MILLER

She'd learned that she and Abigail had several things in common. Both loved the piano and collected songs, with ballads preferred. The difference was, Abigail owned a spinet; Maddie had nothing but a few pieces of her mother's tattered sheet music and a handful of poignant memories. Both women loved flowers, and neither attended church regularly, Abigail because it was too far to travel from her father's ranch outside of Flagstaff to town just for a few hours on a Sunday, and Maddie because her parents, so faithful and so devout, giving over their whole lives to spreading the Gospel, had been snatched away. She'd never forgiven God for that. It seemed like a lack of appreciation on His part.

Abigail had a flower garden and Maddie nurtured a few spiny peony bushes out behind the store. They only bloomed for a few weeks in the spring, and she passed the rest of the year yearning for the sight of their lush, fragrant red blossoms.

A rap sounded at Maddie's bedroom door and Terran called her name. She pulled on her wrap, smoothed her hair, anxious at the prospect of another crisis, and said, "Come in."

Terran stepped cautiously into the room. "Ben's gone again," he said.

Maddie stared at him. "What?"

"He must have taken off sometime during the night," Terran told her. "There wasn't any note."

Maddie closed her eyes for a moment, to get back to her center. Lately she'd been quite literally beside herself. "Land sakes," she murmured. "Where could he have gone?"

Terran shook his head. "Don't know," he answered. "I went over to the jailhouse, figuring he might have wanted a word with his pa, but Mr. Rhodes said he hadn't seen him."

"What about the schoolhouse? Could he be there?"

Again, Terran shook his head. "He wouldn't want any

truck with Miss Blackstone, seeing's how she's fixing to take Mr. O'Ballivan back home with her one day soon."

Maddie felt a pang at the reminder. Most likely, Sam was planning to marry Abigail, or he wouldn't have installed her at the schoolhouse. Best she quit mulling that over in her thoughts, like butter in the bottom of a churn, and accept it. The sooner, the better.

For the life of her, she couldn't think why she cared, one way or the other, what Sam did or whom he chose to marry, but the fact of it was, she *did* care, and to a most disturbing degree.

"Abigail," Maddie said reasonably, "is a very nice woman. It isn't right to hold Sam—Mr. O'Ballivan's affections against her. You go and look for Ben some more, while I get dressed. Stay in town—and keep *away* from the river."

Terran was already backing toward the door. "What if that's where he's at, though? Ben, I mean. What if he's gone down to the river to fish or think or maybe just throw some rocks in the water?"

Maddie narrowed her eyes. "You know a lot about things a boy might do at the river, for somebody who's been forbidden to go near it," she said.

Terran ducked out into the short, narrow corridor that led to the sitting room. His chamber, even smaller than Maddie's own, was on the other side, under the eave.

"If you don't find Ben right away," Maddie called after him, "you round up some people to help you!"

The answer was the rapid clatter of Terran's boot soles on the back stairs, soon followed by the slamming of the kitchen door.

Maddie made her bed, hastily donned a practical calico dress, brushed and braided her hair into a single heavy plait, not wanting to take the time to pin it up properly, and went downstairs. She had an hour until time to open the

LINDA LAEL MILLER

store, so she brewed a pot of coffee, toasted some bread in the oven and fretted over Ben.

Where could he have gone?

The urge to leave the mercantile and join Terran in the search was almost overpowering, but Maddie resisted it. Boys went wandering all the time, and Ben had more reason for it than most, with his father in jail and his eldest brother in a fresh grave. She knew she ought to close the store, but with the ink barely dry on the purchase contract, and a mortgage payment to Oralee Pringle looming, she couldn't afford to do it.

After choking down what would have to pass for breakfast, Maddie put on her apron, scanned the account books, checked to make sure the shotgun under the counter was loaded, and stood anxiously at the display window in front, peering this way and that, hoping to catch a glimpse of Terran or Ben.

Instead she saw Oralee approaching, clad in a mass of lace-trimmed pink ruffles and carrying a parasol to match. She trundled up to the door just as Maddie turned the lock to let her in.

"If it ain't one thing, it's another," Oralee said without preamble. "I sent my girls out beatin' the brush for that little Donagher kid after Terran told me he was missing—them I could raise from their beds, anyhow. Night work, you know."

Maddie felt a blush warm the skin over her cheekbones. "Yes," she said. "I understand. Has there been any sign of Ben?"

"Not so's I've heard," Oralee allowed, and gave a sigh that made her copious ruffles move in a fascinating, undulating sequence. "That Perkins gal is a little better today, though. Just looked in on her myself. Sittin' up in bed. I dare say it was my Estella's hen soup that heartened her. She and that kid are skinny as fence rails. I've a mind to

THE MAN FROM STONE CREEK

offer 'em a place under my roof, but a body can't take in every stray and, besides, there's no room."

The idea of little Violet living at the Rattlesnake Saloon made Maddie's blood cold as creek water, but she knew Oralee's intentions were kind, so she said nothing. "I could use a bowl of Estella's hen soup myself," she told Oralee, to make conversation. Oralee's cooks came and went, and Estella, a black woman who had mostly kept to herself since her arrival six months before, was the latest in a long procession.

Oralee straightened her spine and more quivering of ruffles ensued. "I came here on business, anyhow," she said. "Got wind that Undine means to come by for a shopping spree sometime in the next couple of days, and I wanted to warn you that she'll expect credit and you oughtn't to give it to her."

Inwardly, Maddie sighed. She didn't give credit except in the most dire circumstances, and the fact was widely known, but Undine Donagher was used to being the store owner's wife and getting whatever she wanted because of it. She was bound to put up a fuss, and while Maddie wasn't afraid to say no, she wasn't looking forward to Undine's inevitable reaction, either.

"Maybe she'll know where Ben's gotten off to," Maddie said speculatively.

Oralee gave a skeptical huff. "She don't give a damn about that boy," she said. "She mostly ignores him, and I reckon that's his good fortune."

Bleak sadness washed over Maddie and for a moment she was back in the orphanage in Kansas City, scrubbing pots and scouring floors till her hands were raw from lye soap and hot water, just so she could stay close to Terran, the only family she had left. Although Ben's circumstances were a little different, she understood how lonely and

LINDA LAEL MILLER

confused he must be, and how much he must yearn to belong to someone.

"I'm afraid Terran might go down to the river, looking for him," Maddie said distractedly, thinking out loud.

"Boys do favor such things," Oralee agreed. "I'd offer to tend the store so you could go and see for yourself, but it might run you to bankruptcy, having a madam back of the counter." Her face brightened behind its coat of skillfully applied paint. "No reason I couldn't have the buggy hitched up and take a gander myself, though."

Maddie was buoyed by gratitude, and she went so far as to clasp both Oralee's hands in her own and squeeze them. "Thank you," she said.

Oralee flushed with surprise and, for the briefest of moments, her fingers tightened around Maddie's. In the next instant, though, the front door slammed open and Isaiah Parker, from down at the feed and grain, poked his bald head in to impart the news.

"Charlie Wilcox's horse just came to town without him!"

Both Oralee and Maddie froze, staring.

"I been here since this town was a wide spot in the road," Oralee said finally, "and that horse ain't *never* come all this way by itself."

Parker nodded vigorously. "Some of the boys from the Rattlesnake headed right off to see about Charlie," he said. With that, he retreated to the sidewalk, intent on spreading the tale.

Maddie didn't know Mr. Wilcox very well, but she'd certainly developed a fond sympathy for that old horse over the years. Once in a while, she'd even fed the poor creature a lump of rock candy, paid for out of her own sparse resources, and though most of the townswomen crossed the street to avoid passing so close to the saloon,

THE MAN FROM STONE CREEK

Maddie never did. She liked to stop and pet Dobbin, offer him a kind word or two.

"What do you make of this?" she asked Oralee.

"Nothin' good," Oralee said, and took her distracted leave without another word.

Maddie's brother burst in by the back way before Maddie had a chance to wonder if Oralee would remember her promise to drive her buggy down to the riverside, looking for both Terran and Ben. His eyes were huge, seeming to take up most of his face, which was white as a sun-bleached sheet.

She expected him to blurt out something about Charlie Wilcox's horse showing up riderless. Instead he cried, "Ben's down by the river, soaked to the skin. He told me he fell in, and Miss Blackstone must've gone right in after him, because she's as wet as he is, and she's just lyin' there on the bank! Maddie, I tried and I tried, and I couldn't get her to wake up!"

Maddie's heart seized in her chest. "Dear God," she gasped, rushing for the door. "Stay here!" she called back as she bolted out onto the street. Everyone in town, it seemed, was gathered around Mr. Wilcox's horse. Maddie shouted for help even as she lifted her skirts and ran for the river, but no one seemed to hear.

She sprinted down the road, through the shrubbery in front of the schoolhouse, across the grounds. Ben's little dog, Neptune, came running from the direction of the river, barking frantically.

Maddie's throat closed with fear. "Ben!" she screamed.

"Over here, Maddie!" the boy cried.

Maddie followed the dog, rather than the sound of Ben's voice, and when she came to the riverside, terror boiled up inside her like steam in a lidded pot.

Just as Terran had said, Abigail lay still on the bank,

LINDA LAEL MILLER

sprawled facedown, as though she'd been flung there by a great tide, while Ben knelt, shivering, beside her, in tears. His clothes were still dripping with water, and Neptune whimpered, put both front paws up on the boy's back and tried to lick him.

Maddie dropped to her knees and turned Abigail over with a forceful wrench of both arms. Her eyes were open, staring blindly upward, and Maddie knew before she bent to listen for a heartbeat that she was dead.

A fearful sob escaped Maddie. She gripped Abigail by both shoulders and shook her hard, desperate to awaken her, all the while knowing it was hopeless.

"Maddie," Ben said uncertainly. "Maddie?"

"Go," Maddie rasped, swatting at the boy with one hand and weeping. "Go back and get someone!"

"Who?" Ben asked.

"Anybody!" Maddie cried, and slapped one hand over her mouth lest she start screaming and never stop.

Just then she heard the sound of an approaching wagon. Men's voices, raised and anxious, more than one, Maddie thought, and Terran's among them.

Out of decency, and because she had liked Abigail, and because Sam loved her, Maddie reached out and gently closed the woman's eyes with the tip of one finger.

"What happened?" Maddie whispered to Ben. *"Tell me what happened."*

Ben dashed at his face with a wet sleeve. "I was crossing on that log over there." He paused and pointed. "I took a spill, and Miss Blackstone must have seen or heard me yell, because all of the sudden, she was there. She came in the water after me. Good swimmer, too. She got hold of me, and we was to the place where we could stand when she just went under—for no reason that I could see—and didn't come up. I pulled her out, once I caught hold,

THE MAN FROM STONE CREEK

and her eyes was open, but she wouldn't answer when I called her name!"

Maddie heard the men coming through the brush, heard Terran's voice, too, but she didn't look away from Abigail's still and perfect face. She might have been hewn from alabaster, a statue of some Grecian goddess.

Mr. Callaway, head of the school board, crouched to rest his fingertips against the hollow of Abigail's throat, where there should have been a pulse. Maddie saw him shake his head, and she began to shiver as violently as if she'd been into the river herself. Someone laid a suit coat over her shoulders, helped her to her feet.

Terran came to her side, put an arm around her waist. He'd disobeyed her, hadn't stayed behind at the store like she'd told him to do, and she was glad.

"What's Sam going to say?" she whispered. Maybe nobody heard her, because nobody answered.

SAM HAD BEEN ON THE TRAIL for the best part of two days when he rode into Haven on that Wednesday morning, and those who saw him coming pretended not to notice him. He thought that a curious thing, but he was too tired to reason it out, and too anxious to make sure Rex Donagher and the rest of the bunch hadn't gone through the place on a rampage to ask questions.

He spotted Terran and Ben, standing on the sidewalk, watching him, both of them owl-eyed.

Sam looked around.

Everything seemed normal enough. Charlie Wilcox's horse stood in front of the Rattlesnake Saloon, like always, and the jailhouse was still standing. In fact, smoke curled from the chimney, which meant the stove was going and there might be hot coffee on hand.

Sam turned his attention back to where the boys had been

LINDA LAEL MILLER

standing, but they'd vanished, and now Maddie was walking toward him, dead down the center of the road. Her chin was high, but she was pale, and as she drew nearer, he saw her eyes. They looked like two burned holes in a blanket.

Something twisted in Sam's gut. He swung down from the gelding and strode to meet Maddie.

She stopped and looked up at him, sorrow in every inch of her, but bravery, too. Out of everybody in that town, she'd been the one to come out and say whatever had to be said.

Sam braced himself, even as Maddie wobbled, and he took hold of her upper arms to steady her. "What is it?" he asked, and the words came out raw, scratching at his throat hard enough to tear the flesh.

"I can't tell you here," she said, and took a deep breath. Having done that, she took hold of his hand. Led him down the road, past the mercantile and the feed and grain, past the woodlot and the church. His horse followed obediently.

When she paused at the undertaker's gate, he knew.

Abigail.

"No," he said, as if by refusing to hear what happened he could turn back the great, crushing tide of truth that was about to crash down over him.

"I'm so sorry, Sam," Maddie whispered, and there were tears standing in her whiskey-colored eyes as she gazed up at him.

He pushed past her, slammed open the gate, barreled into the house without stopping to knock.

Abigail lay on a long table, in what would have been the parlor in an ordinary home. Her hands lay folded, bluish-white upon her chest, and pennies weighted her eyes.

Sam threw back his head and bellowed in useless protest.

CHAPTER

NINETEEN

MADDIE, STILL STANDING at the undertaker's gate, closed her eyes when she heard Sam's cry of outraged grief. The sound went through her like a cold shock, and reached deep into the ground like roots, reverberating there, leaving her trembling and weak-kneed. When she could move, she turned and walked slowly away.

Back at the store, she tried to concentrate on the tasks at hand—unpacking the dozen crates of merchandise delivered that morning from Tucson by freight wagon, pricing shirts and bullets and tins of ground coffee, entering each individual item in her inventory book. But her thoughts kept straying back to Sam, alone with the terrible fact of Abigail's death. Finally, Maddie gave up, went to the kitchen and brewed herself a pot of strong tea. If she'd owned any whiskey, she probably would have poured a generous portion into her orange pekoe.

Customers came and went, and Maddie saw to their needs, going through the motions of tallying the cost,

LINDA LAEL MILLER

writing up the receipts, making change. All the while, she kept one eye on the front door, watching for Sam O'Ballivan.

"It's a shame about Charlie Wilcox, isn't it?" asked Mrs. Walter Crosby, after selecting three dime novels. "And that poor Miss Blackstone, too. It seems that tragedy is our lot these days." She paused. "Do you think it will rain soon?"

Maddie blinked back uncharacteristic tears. The same day Abigail perished, Mr. Wilcox had been found dead in his shack, most likely of heart failure, and his horse was standing in front of the Rattlesnake Saloon at that very moment, patiently awaiting a master who would never return.

No. She did not think it would rain.

"Maddie?" Mrs. Crosby prompted in a kindly tone when Maddie didn't speak right away. "Are you all right?"

Maddie swallowed. "There's been too much death around here lately," she said softly. "Garrett Donagher and now poor Charlie and Abigail—"

Mrs. Crosby nodded her agreement. "Makes a body want to crawl under her bed and hide there till better times come along."

The bell over the door jingled and Maddie's heart rushed up into her throat. Sam O'Ballivan stepped over the threshold, looking gaunt and befuddled, as though he was certain he had business at the mercantile but couldn't recall precisely what it was.

Maddie remained behind the counter, though everything in her longed to go to him, put her arms around him, tell him it would be all right.

She had no right to do the first two things, and the third, by her reckoning, would have been a lie, so she stayed put.

Mrs. Crosby dropped her change into her large handbag, along with the books, and hurried out of the store, giving Sam a sympathetic nod as she passed.

THE MAN FROM STONE CREEK

He didn't seem to see her, though. He stood still as a pillar in the middle of the store, his gaze fixed on Maddie, bleak and desolate and wholly confounded.

The tick of the big clock intruded on the thick silence, so loud that it seemed to echo off the walls.

"How did it happen?" Sam asked finally.

Maddie explained as simply as she could. Ben had gone to the river before school started for the day and fallen in. Abigail must have heard his cries, or seen him slip off the log—nobody knew for sure. She'd rushed to save the boy and drowned in the process.

"She didn't drown," Sam said when Maddie had finished. "Abigail was a strong swimmer."

Maddie offered no comment. She leaned on the counter, braced with both hands, to keep from slipping to her knees.

"It must have been her heart," Sam went on.

"Her heart?" Maddie repeated.

"She had spells, all her life," Sam said, like a man talking in his sleep. He, like Maddie, hadn't moved. "Couldn't get her breath sometimes. Other times, she'd swoon, for no reason. Just crumple to the floor." He paused. "She always came around, though."

"I'm so sorry," Maddie said, wondering if he'd hold the tragedy against Ben. Give up on whatever he'd come to Haven to do and head back to Stone Creek, taking Abigail's body with him, for a proper burial on home ground. "What now?" she asked, dreading the answer.

"I've got to send a wire to the major," Sam replied. "He'll want to come and collect Abigail's remains himself."

"That's been done," Maddie said. "I found his name among Abigail's things over at the schoolhouse. I hope you don't mind my taking the liberty."

Sam smiled oddly and shook his head. "I don't mind," he said. "Did he send a reply?"

LINDA LAEL MILLER

"Not yet," Maddie answered. Her throat felt painfully dry and she reached for her teacup, then set it down again. She knew she wouldn't be able to swallow the smallest sip.

"The undertaker told me about Charlie Wilcox," Sam said, and turned his head in the direction of the Rattlesnake Saloon, frowning as if he could see clean through the walls of the mercantile, see that poor horse keeping its hopeless vigil at the hitching rail.

A tear slipped down Maddie's cheek. "They took Dobbin over to the livery stable the first night, the second night, too. Somehow he got out of his stall each time and headed straight for the saloon."

Sam looked her way again. "Thanks for meeting me with the news about Abigail," he said gruffly. "I wouldn't have wanted to hear it from anybody else."

Maddie swallowed once more and followed up with another nod. She couldn't have spoken just then to save her life.

"Well," Sam said when the silence stretched to the breaking point, "I'd best get on with things." With that, he turned, crossed to the door, opened it and went out.

Maddie groped for her stool and settled herself on the seat, making no further effort to keep from crying.

SAM CAUGHT HIS HORSE, left to fend for itself when Maddie met him in the street and he'd dismounted to hear what she had to say. Leading the animal by the reins, he walked to the Rattlesnake Saloon and stepped up beside Dobbin.

The ancient horse nickered a greeting.

"We've both lost a friend," Sam told Dobbin, stroking his neck. "You come on home with me, now, and we'll ride this out together."

With that, Sam turned toward the schoolhouse, still leading the gelding he'd rode hard from Mexico, and set out.

Charlie Wilcox's horse plodded along behind him.

Back at the school, Sam groomed the gelding, left both horses to graze and drink from the stream, and forced himself to go inside.

Abigail's things had been put away, packed into her trunk, and Sam was grateful for that. He reckoned Maddie deserved the credit; she'd known the gathering up would be a painful task, and she'd spared him the doing of it. She'd left a note on the table, too.

Neptune is with us, at the store. M.

Sam had forgotten Ben's little dog, and he supposed that was a mercy. He'd have worried about the critter if he'd remembered, and he surely didn't need another problem to gnaw at in his mind.

Now, he stood alone in the room behind the schoolroom, with Abigail's scent faint in the warm, dusty air. He was numb with sorrow and no little guilt. He'd cared so deeply for Abigail that her absence left a carved-out place inside him, but he hadn't loved her. Not in the way she'd wanted, not the man-woman way she'd loved him. She'd known how he felt, of course. Known he'd have gone ahead and married her, because of the understanding between them, because he was a man of his word, even when it went unspoken.

Still, it must have tried her spirit sorely, wanting what he couldn't give.

Sam rubbed his eyes between a thumb and forefinger and wished he hadn't left all the whiskey with Vierra. He felt raw, inside and out, and he surely could have used some numbing.

Because he needed something to do, he brought the copper tub in from the shed, then got a fire going in the stove. He carried in water, put it on to heat and went back to the well for more. The process kept him busy, and when his bath was ready, it was deep, if lukewarm.

LINDA LAEL MILLER

He stripped, got into the tub and scrubbed till his skin was raw.

Once out of the bath, and wearing clean clothes, he filled a basin, lathered his prickly beard and shaved. By the time he'd dragged the copper tub to the door and dumped it, he felt almost human.

He wondered if there'd been a telegram from the major yet, or if the old man would just show up on the afternoon stage, or driving a wagon so he could take Abigail home and lay her to rest next to her long-dead mother. Sam would have bet on the latter.

He'd go along, of course. He couldn't let the major make a trip like that by himself.

But there was still the matter of the outlaw gang, and Vierra, lying wounded in that hilltop village in Mexico. There were the schoolkids to think about, too. Violet and the others. He'd come to care about those little rascals, and it didn't set well, the idea of leaving them.

And there was Maddie.

What of Maddie?

She was a strong, independent woman, and she'd gotten by just fine without his help all these years. She'd coped with the loss of her betrothed, raised her brother and run a thriving business. She didn't need him.

Still, when Rex came back to Haven, as he surely would, bent on either killing Mungo with his bare hands or setting him free, all hell was bound to break loose. Maddie and the rest of the townspeople, with no real lawman to protect them, would be vulnerable to Rex and most likely the rest of that murderous bunch, too. Sam was under no delusion that just because he'd only seen five men so far, and knew for a fact that one of them, Landry Donagher, was dead, there weren't more. He'd seen the dust raised by their horses, out where Vierra was shot.

THE MAN FROM STONE CREEK

The gang had struck in a lot of places, on both sides of the border. A handful of men couldn't have managed that—the distances were too great. It was a possibility, of course, that he was dealing with more than one outfit, but his gut said different.

He went out to sit on the back step, waiting for something. Or somebody.

He didn't know which.

When Terran bounded around the corner of the schoolhouse with a covered basket in one hand, Sam wasn't surprised.

"Maddie said you must be hungry," the boy announced, pausing a few feet away and taking Sam's measure with his eyes. "She sent these vittles."

"I'm obliged," Sam answered.

Still, Terran kept his distance. "You blamin' Ben for getting Miss Blackstone drowned?"

Sam looked toward the horses, watched them for a few moments, then shifted his gaze back to Terran. "No," he said. "It wasn't Ben's fault."

"He shouldn't have been down there by the river," Terran offered cautiously.

"No," Sam agreed quietly. "He shouldn't have been. But you tell Ben for me that I've got no hard feelings."

Terran came close enough to hand over the basket, but he still looked wary, and there was a tension in him that troubled Sam, though he couldn't quite get hold of the reason why. "There's a whole strawberry pie in there," the boy said. "We were going to have it for supper."

Sam managed a smile. "I guess I'd best save you a piece, then," he replied. "You can have it right now if you want to."

Terran relaxed a little. "Maddie gives stuff away all the time," he confided.

LINDA LAEL MILLER

"Does she?" Sam spoke lightly. He lifted the cover of the basket and glanced inside. A jar of Christmas pears floating in red nectar. Ham in a tin. Half a loaf of bread. And the pie.

"When Violet's mother got sick, Maddie took groceries right off the shelves for them, knowin' they couldn't pay. And she made me take them some of our firewood, too."

Sam tore off a chunk of the bread and felt an anticipatory clench of hunger in the pit of his stomach. "When folks have trouble, it's good to help them out whatever way you can," he said.

Terran's jawline hardened. "Nobody ever helped Maddie and me," he said. "We've had to make it on our own. It's been that way since we left the orphanage."

Sam moved over on the step to make room for Terran. "Sit down, if you've a mind to talk awhile," he said: Then, to sweeten the offer, he added, "I'll share the pie."

Terran hesitated, then perched beside him, but he was ready to bolt. Sam could feel his readiness, coiled inside the boy like a hissing snake stuffed into a matchbox.

The pie had been cut into eight slices and Terran reached inside the basket to help himself to one of them.

"Tell me about the orphanage," Sam said.

Terran shrugged, already gobbling pie. Between swallows, he answered, "It was like a big school, only you had to stay there all the time. Maddie worked for her keep, so we could be together."

Sam felt a pinch in his heart, and it had nothing to do with Abigail or the vast new landscape of sorrow her loss must have opened up for the major once the news reached him. "What became of your folks?"

"They got a fever and died. After that, it was just Maddie and me. Maddie was too old to live at the orphanage. They'd have turned her out on the streets if she hadn't begged them for work."

THE MAN FROM STONE CREEK

It made Sam ache inside to think of Maddie begging for anything, let alone being turned out to make her own way in a harsh world. "Those must have been hard times for both of you," he said moderately and, having finished the bread, took a piece of strawberry pie. "How'd you wind up in Haven?"

"Maddie saw an advertisement in a newspaper. She wrote and sent her picture, and Mr. Donagher hired her. Sent us the money to come out here."

Sam considered that. Mungo must have figured on snaring himself a pretty new wife, but he hadn't reckoned on Maddie's pride and that streak of independence. "It was a brave thing to do, coming so far. Were you scared?"

Terran's spine stiffened. "No," he replied. "I knew Maddie would see to things. Right away, she took up with Warren, anyhow. He was going to build us a house. We'd have been a family, then. Warren and Maddie and me."

"You miss him a lot?"

The boy's chin trembled. "Yeah. I should have known somebody'd kill him, though. That me and Maddie would be on our own, just like before."

Sam lowered his half-eaten slice of pie, waited for his throat to open up again. His eyes burned and he fixed his gaze on Charlie Wilcox's old horse, just in case he didn't succeed at keeping them dry. "People die, Terran," he said hoarsely when he'd caught his breath. "But that doesn't mean you and Maddie will always be alone."

"She says we're a family already, just the two of us."

"I reckon that's so," Sam said. Out of the corner of his eye he saw Terran's face crumple and his thin shoulders began to shake with the effort to contain his emotions.

"Maddie could have got sick, taking care of Mrs. Perkins. She could have died. And then what would have happened to me?"

LINDA LAEL MILLER

Sam waited a long time to answer, struggling with a few emotions of his own. He'd been an orphan himself, after his mother had been killed. Abigail's mother had died early, too, and that had been a bond between them. He'd gotten his raising from bunkhouse cowboys, working on ranches as a roustabout, and then from the major, who'd taken him in after he signed on to ride for the Stone Creek spread, treated him like a son, sent him away for a stint in the cavalry, and finally made a Ranger out of him. For all he'd been through, he knew he'd been damn lucky.

"Maddie isn't going to die anytime soon," he said. "And even if she did, you'd be looked after."

"I wouldn't go back to that orphanage or any place like it," Terran said.

"No," Sam allowed. He'd been on his own a long while at Terran's age, and he remembered how it was. He'd fallen in with kind companions, but that hadn't kept him from grieving in his bunk at night. It hadn't made the shadows any less threatening, or soothed the ache in his midsection when he saw families headed to church of a Sunday morning, sitting cheek by jowl in their wagons, speaking a heart language he didn't understand.

"I'm twelve," Terran went on with staunch bravado. "I reckon I could make my way if I had to." He didn't look like he reckoned that at all, but Sam saw no point in calling him on it.

"You won't have to," he said instead. He rested a hand briefly on the boy's shoulder. "Anything happens to Maddie, you just get on the stage to Flagstaff. From there, you hitch a ride to Stone Creek. That's my ranch."

Terran's eyes widened. "You've got a ranch?"

Sam nodded.

"Then what are you doing down here in Haven, teaching school?"

THE MAN FROM STONE CREEK

The question, logical as it was, caught Sam off guard. He could lie with the best of them, but he didn't like doing it, especially to a boy. "Man's got to earn a living," he said.

Terran studied him suspiciously. "Seems to me ranching would pay better than schoolmastering," he observed. "Town council couldn't even get a *woman* to do it."

"There are some things," Sam replied, stifling a sigh, "that you just have to take at face value."

Terran was silent for a long time, wrestling with something inside, Sam figured. In time, he spoke, and startled Sam all over again. "Now that Miss Blackstone's dead," he said, "I guess you could marry Maddie. She's cussed, but most folks would say she's pretty."

"I suppose Maddie would have something to say about that," Sam said carefully. "A fine woman like your sister could marry anybody she wanted."

"She likes you," Terran said.

"I like her, too," Sam answered. "But it's more complicated than that. Getting married, I mean. Maddie's got her store, and I've got a ranch up north, a long ways from here. One of us would have to give some important ground, if we were going to be together."

"Maybe you don't want her because she ain't a virgin," Terran speculated.

Sam was careful not to react visibly, but it took some real doing. He held his tongue, figuring anything he might say right then would surely come out wrong.

Terran waited, as though he was letting the announcement sink in. "Warren said so, once. It was the only time I ever heard them argue."

It was like a burr in a fresh wound, knowing Maddie had lain with another man, and he had no right to feel the way he did. Sam groped for speech, roused his tongue, which had grown thick and tried to slither into the back of his

LINDA LAEL MILLER

throat. "It's a private thing, Terran," he said. "What happens between a man and a woman."

"I never told nobody but you," Terran replied. "I figured you might be willing to overlook it, but I guess I was wrong."

Sam had never even kissed Maddie Chancelor, though he'd wanted to right enough and he'd thought about it a thousand times since they'd met. Even now, in the midst of sorrow, he imagined how it would be, and he was ashamed of the turn his mind took from there.

"Now you probably figure Maddie for a loose woman." Terran's freckled face reddened with obstinate conviction. "She isn't. Any man who married her would be plain lucky!"

"I'd have to agree with you there," Sam said thoughtfully.

Terran got to his feet. "I guess I'd better get back to the store. Maddie wants me to sweep the sidewalk, and anyhow, I've got to keep an eye on Ben, so he doesn't take off again."

Sam nodded. "You tell Maddie I'm obliged for this food," he said.

Terran nodded and took his leave.

THE NEXT MORNING, when Sam got out of bed and looked out the window to see what kind of day it was going to be, he noticed right off that old Dobbin had vanished.

It didn't take much to figure out where he'd gone.

Sam put on his clothes and headed for the Rattlesnake Saloon, on foot.

Dobbin stood out front, like always, swishing his sparse tail and waiting. Sam's eyes commenced to burning again, and he was trying to make sense of that when along came Maddie, crossing the street, slant-wise, from the mercantile. She was wearing a blue chambray dress and her hair was plaited, the single heavy braid resting over her right shoulder. She gave Sam a tentative smile and held out her hand to Dobbin, offering a glimmering chunk of rock candy.

"Poor old horse," she said.

Sam looked away, blinked, and looked back. "I wish there was some way to tell him Charlie's gone," he said to Maddie when he trusted the words to come out steady.

Dobbin took the rock candy from Maddie's palm and chomped.

"I wonder if it would do any good," Maddie said quietly. "Knowing, I mean."

Sam looked toward the undertaker's place. Abigail was there, waiting to be taken home and buried, and all the knowing in the world wouldn't change that. "Jesus," he said on a ragged breath. "I wish she hadn't come here in the first place."

Maddie withdrew her palm, now that Dobbin was through with the rock candy, and laid it lightly on Sam's arm. "It isn't your fault, Sam."

He met her eyes, but it was an unaccountably hard thing to do. "Isn't it?"

She didn't answer.

Sam thrust a hand through his hair. "Guess I'll stop by the telegraph office to see if there's been any word from Abigail's pa. After that, I'll ring the school bell. You tell Terran and Ben I mean for them to learn something today, and to fetch Violet on their way there."

Maddie smiled, softly and sadly, but the sight of it soothed something in Sam, warmed him a little. "I'll tell them," she said. And only then did she lift her hand from his sleeve. She patted Dobbin once more, then turned and headed back across the street.

Sam came up dry at the telegraph office, so he went back to the saloon, told Dobbin he was leaving and he ought to follow, and the horse heeded him.

LINDA LAEL MILLER

When the two of them got back to the schoolhouse, Sam gave both animals a pan of grain, scooped from the sack in the shed, and made good on his word to Maddie, hauling on the bell rope until the peals seemed to echo off the farthest hills.

The major showed up at noon, when the kids were in the schoolyard, working off a morning of pent-up energy. He was driving a wagon, with a plain rosewood coffin in the back, and his grizzled, craggy old face was a mask of stalwart mourning.

Sam approached, nodded his greeting, since all of a sudden, he was too choked up to speak. The children went still and silent behind him, like a storm wind suddenly dissipated.

"Where is she?" the major asked.

"I'll take you there," Sam said, about to turn and tell the children that school was dismissed for the day.

The old man stopped him with a stout, "No."

Sam moved a step nearer. "It's a long way back to the ranch," he said quietly. "You'll require company."

"We're only going as far as Phoenix in this wagon," the major answered with a decisive shake of his head. "Catch a train north from there." He paused, cleared his throat. His eyes, hollow with despair, never left Sam's face. "She brought some things with her. I'd be obliged if you'd fetch them out here so I can get my daughter and make for home."

After a moment's hesitation, Sam sent Terran and Ben inside for Abigail's trunk and handbag.

"I ought to go with you," Sam insisted.

"You ought to stay right here and finish what you started," the major countered firmly.

There would be a funeral, and even though he dreaded it more than anything in the world, Sam couldn't imagine

THE MAN FROM STONE CREEK

not attending. Abigail had been his closest friend. "I want to pay my respects."

"Time enough for that when your work is done."

"Don't you want to know how it happened?"

"I got a long telegram from a Miss Chancelor. I don't need any more explanations. All I want is to take my daughter back to the ranch, where she belongs."

Terran and Ben returned, lugging the heavy trunk between them. Violet brought the handbag.

Sam took the trunk from the boys and hoisted it into the back of the wagon, alongside the varnished coffin, most likely procured in Phoenix, along with the two-horse team and the wagon.

Meanwhile, Ben scrambled up into the box, on the side opposite the major, pale with some private determination.

"She died savin' me," the boy said solemnly. "It's my doing that she's dead."

Sam went around to stand behind Ben, meaning to lift him down to the ground.

"Who do you belong to?" the major demanded in a booming voice.

A shudder went through Ben's small frame, but he didn't push away and run, like a lot of kids would have done. "Nobody in particular," Ben said. "My pa's in jail for killin' my brother Garrett." The boy didn't know he'd lost a second brother, Landry, because Sam hadn't found a way to tell him. "I've been livin' with Miss Maddie and Terran, over at the general store, but I don't imagine they can keep me long."

Sam reached for the boy in earnest, but the major stopped him with a scowl. "Don't you have a ma?" the old man thundered.

"No, sir," Ben replied. "She died havin' me." He took a deep breath; Sam saw it rack its way through the kid's narrow back. "Anyhow, I'm sorry for what happened to your daughter. I had a part in it, and I'd do anything to go back and do things different."

"I can tell you this," the major said after a few moments of pensive reflection. "There isn't any changing the past. You did what you did, and Abigail did what she did, and that's the way of it. I don't mind asking a favor of you, though."

Ben waited.

Sam tried to swallow his heart.

"Don't you go wasting a perfectly good life feeling bad over what you can't do anything about. I don't want that, and neither would Abigail. She wasn't the kind to hold a grudge, or to stand idle when somebody was in trouble. If you'd honor her remembrance, then you do right. Learn your lessons and make something of yourself."

"Yes, sir," Ben said.

"Go on, now," the major ordered. "I need a word with your teacher, and it's got to be private."

Ben nodded and leaped to the ground. He and the rest of the kids went inside the schoolhouse, on the march. The major could turn just about any bunch into a platoon, just by being who he was.

"Is it true that boy's on his own, Sam?"

Sam nodded. "For the most part. His name's Donagher. He's got a stepmother who probably won't want to bother with him, and an outlaw for a brother."

"Part of that gang you're after?"

Again, Sam nodded.

"The boy's got no other kin?"

"Not that I know of," Sam said.

The major absorbed that, cleared his throat and poised his hands to bring down the reins and get the team and wagon moving. "If nobody takes him in, once the dust settles, you bring him to me. I'll fetch him up just the way I did you."

If the offer had come from any other man in Creation, Sam would have pointed out that raising a boy was a hard job for an old coot, but this was the major. There was nobody quite like him on the face of the earth, and if he said he'd make a home for Ben, he meant it.

"I'd still like to ride along with you," Sam said. "At least as far as Phoenix."

"Well, I won't have it," the major retorted in a tone of finality. "I gave you your orders before you left Stone Creek. And when I give an order, I expect it to be followed."

Sam gave a halfhearted salute. "Yes, sir," he said.

With that, the major released the brake level, slapped down the reins and was off toward the main part of town, the wagon jostling over bumps and ruts as he went.

Sam watched him out of sight, and wondered if he'd ever lay eyes on the old man again.

MADDIE WATCHED through the display window as the wagon passed, driven by an old man. She saw the casket in the back and recognized Abigail's trunk. Sadness surged up into her throat and made her dizzy with grief. She was drying her eyes and about to turn away, when Undine pulled up in front of the mercantile, at the reins of her smart buggy.

Oh, Lord, Maddie thought, not now. Oralee had warned her that Mrs. Donagher was in a mood for marketing, but with all that had gone on, she'd forgotten.

Undine secured the buggy brake and wrapped the reins neatly around the lever before straightening her elaborate feathered-and-flowered hat and climbing daintily down from the seat.

Maddie moved away from the window and pretended to be busy straightening a stack of denim trousers as

LINDA LAEL MILLER

Undine whisked into the store, tugging at her gloves and smiling with anticipation. Nobody would have guessed, to look at her, that her husband was in jail, a stone's throw away, for murdering his own son right in front of her eyes.

"Who's that old man I just saw driving down Main Street?" Undine asked.

Maddie wondered if Undine was already looking for another elderly, prosperous husband, and brought herself up short. She had no way of knowing what was going on in the other woman's mind and, besides, it was an innocent question. "I think it's Major J. P. Blackstone," she said with dignity. "He's come to get his daughter."

Undine pulled a folded fan out of the sleeve of her lavender day dress and flicked it open to flutter it under her chin. "It must be a relief to you. That's she's gone, I mean."

Maddie was so stunned that, for an interminable moment, she couldn't speak. She just stood there, stricken, staring at Undine in disbelief.

"Don't try to tell me you're not taken with Sam O'Ballivan," Undine warned lightly. "I saw the way you looked at him when you were out at our place for supper."

Maddie's right hand clenched into a fist. She'd never struck another person in her life, but she wanted to then. Oh, how she wanted to land a haymaker in the middle of Undine Donagher's smug, china-doll face.

"I'd go after him myself," Undine went on blithely, fanning herself and making her way toward the stack of dress books Maddie kept at the far end of the counter, "if I wasn't a married woman."

Maddie opened her mouth, closed it again. Unclenched her fist.

Undine glanced back, over her shoulder. "Is something wrong?" she asked sweetly.

"What's going to happen to Ben?" Maddie heard herself ask.

"Well, I thought *you* were going to keep him," Undine answered, sounding puzzled. "At least, for the time being."

Maddie swallowed. "I can't give you credit," she said.

Undine blinked. "What a strange thing to say!" The fan went faster. "I'm still Mrs. Mungo Donagher, you know. And I sold you this store for a very good price."

"Cash only," Maddie said. "That's the rule."

"Well, I never!"

Maddie stood her ground, half expecting Undine to either come at her with her claws bared or to storm out of the store in an indignant flurry of costly lavender.

"Oralee Pringle is behind this, isn't she?" Undine asked. "Hateful woman."

"Business is business, Undine. Oralee has nothing to do with it."

Undine slapped open one of the dress books, huffed out a sigh and began to peruse the fashions she'd looked at a dozen times before. "Very well, then," she said in the tone of one graciously overlooking a gross injustice, "I'll pay cash for whatever I buy. It's not as if I'm poor, like you."

Maddie set her jaw. She'd have liked to send Undine packing, in no uncertain terms, but the truth of it was, she *was* poor. She had Terran to support and a payment to make to Oralee, come the first of the month, and she'd need every sale she could make in the meantime to do it.

"Your last order ought to be in soon," Maddie said, and took refuge behind the counter, for Undine's protection, not her own.

Undine nodded distractedly, pulling off a glove to wet an index finger on the tip of her tongue, the better to flip pages. "It would serve you right, Maddie Chancelor," she said without looking up, "if I waited to make my pur-

LINDA LAEL MILLER

chases in California. Things take forever here. In San Francisco, there are real dress shops. A person can walk in, try on what they like, and walk right out again with it. Nobody there would wait weeks and weeks for their clothes to roll in on a dusty old stagecoach."

"I'm sure you're right, Undine," Maddie said.

Undine looked up at her, her eyes suspicious.

"How is Mungo?" Maddie asked cheerfully, reaching for her feather duster and wielding it with a passion, nearly toppling a pyramid of tobacco tins in the process.

"I want this blue sateen ball gown, the one from Paris, France," Undine said, jabbing a finger down onto the page in front of her. "*If* you can promise it will be here before Christmas."

Maddie paused. She knew the dress Undine was referring to; she'd yearned over it herself, in idle moments. As if a storekeeper in a town like Haven would ever have need of such a thing. "It costs twenty-five dollars," she said. It was an exorbitant price; a spinet could be had for less, or a good pony cart.

Undine opened her handbag, reached inside and brought out several gold coins.

Maddie stared. Of course she'd seen gold before, but only rarely. Folks around Haven traded mostly in small change and paper money.

"Twenty—five—dollars," Undine said pointedly, laying the coins down, one by one, in a shiny row on the counter.

Maddie peered at them. Blinked. "These are Mexican," she said.

"Oh, for heaven's sake!" Undine cried on a gust of exasperation. "They're *gold,* aren't they? Take them across the street and give them to Banker James. He'll trade them for American currency, I assure you!"

Maddie didn't touch the coins. They glowed like small

pale suns, though, against the dark, polished wood of the countertop. "Where did you get these?" she asked, honestly puzzled.

Undine hesitated. Her eyes darkened ominously and her mouth tightened. "I sold some of the cattle," she said at last.

Maddie frowned. In her experience, ranchers *bought* cattle on the other side of the river and sold them in the Territory. "In Mexico?"

"It's none of your business how I conduct my personal affairs!" Undine snapped, and then blushed at the unfortunate choice of words. Garrett Donagher's ghost might as well have been standing right there in the store with them.

Maddie waited tactfully.

"Do you want to sell me this dress or not?" Undine demanded.

Maddie weighed one of the coins in her palm, decided it was roughly the equivalent of a five-dollar gold piece, and scooped up the other four. "I'll send in the order by wire," she said.

"Good," Undine said. "And remember—it has to be here before Christmas."

"Is it a gift?" Maddie asked innocently.

"Yes," Undine replied tautly, wrenching her glove on and closing the dress book with a force all out of proportion to the task. "For me."

"Happy Christmas," Maddie said.

Undine reddened, though not in her usual fetching way. In fact, she looked downright florid, and somehow, coarse. "I'm going to visit my husband," she said as forcefully as if Maddie had asked, then swept to the door in a rustle of skirts and crisply starched petticoats.

"Give him my regards," Maddie called after her.

Then she opened her hand and looked down at the gold coins.

LINDA LAEL MILLER

The profits from that one enormous sale would nearly cover her first payment to Oralee.

So why did she feel as though she wanted to fling them into the street?

CHAPTER
TWENTY

SAM WAS SITTING on a river rock, near the place where Abigail was found, when the night sounds suddenly ceased and he heard a horse on the other side. He laid a hand on the butt of his .45, but he was too late. A gun barrel pressed into the back of his neck.

"Some Ranger you are," Vierra said, and leather whispered as he holstered his pistol. "I could have killed you three times over."

Sam let out his breath, stood slowly and turned. If he hadn't known Vierra was wounded, he'd have knocked him into the scrub brush. "You didn't waste much time getting back here," he said after he'd unclenched his jaw. "I thought you'd still be lying around in that hut, letting some pretty woman ladle springwater down your gullet."

Vierra laughed, but there was an edge to the sound. "I couldn't stop thinking about that gold," he said. "If I don't get my hands on it soon, I'm going to have to kidnap Pilar."

LINDA LAEL MILLER

Sam started for the schoolhouse. There was a light burning inside, on the table, and coffee cold on the stove, left over from a lonely supper of canned ham, cinnamon pears and more strawberry pie. "I'll have no part in that," he said as Vierra fell into step beside him. "Why'd you leave your horse on the Mexican side?"

Vierra's grin flashed in the night. "He doesn't speak much English."

Well, Sam thought, disgruntled, he'd heard the *horse,* anyway. He'd be a while getting over the chagrin of letting Vierra sneak up on him like that, though.

They stepped inside, Sam in the lead. He turned to look back at Vierra, who'd paused on the threshold.

"Where's that good-looking woman you had stashed here before we headed south?" he asked.

Sam tensed, then bent to put yank open the stove door and throw some wood on the fire. In a sidelong glance, he saw Vierra's smile fade. His arm was in a sling, but otherwise he didn't seem much the worse for wear.

"Something's wrong," he said.

"Abigail's dead," Sam told him. Some things had to be said bluntly.

Vierra stared at Sam as he straightened and took the coffeepot by the handle, checking its weight. Still enough for the two of them, though there'd be plenty of grounds floating around in the bottom.

"What?" the Mexican demanded, none too promptly.

Sam set the coffeepot down on the stovetop with a clunk. "Mungo Donagher's youngest fell in the river. Abigail went in after him. She was a good swimmer, so I figure her heart must have given out. She had spells."

Vierra hauled back one of the chairs at the table. "Sit down," he said.

Sam wasn't in the mood to argue, so he sat.

THE MAN FROM STONE CREEK

Vierra pulled a flask from inside his shirt and shoved it at Sam before taking the other chair, turning it around backward and straddling the seat. "Drink," he ordered.

Sam unscrewed the top, poured a good dose of Mexican whiskey down his throat and nearly died of strangulation. "What is this?" he demanded when he stopped coughing and caught his breath. "Kerosene?"

Vierra ignored the question, leaned forward and crossed himself with his good hand. "*¡Madre de Dios,*" he muttered. "Dead. Did you love her?"

Maybe it was the bad whiskey that made Sam answer an inquiry that personal; he didn't know. "No," he said, screwing the lid back on the flask and sending it skittering across the tabletop to Vierra. "That's the hell of it. I didn't. Not like I should have."

Vierra waited.

Sam wiped his mouth, had second thoughts about the flask, but didn't reach for it. "The major came and got Abigail today. Took her back home for burying."

"If you didn't love her, what was she doing here in Haven?"

Sam didn't speak.

"She loved *you,*" Vierra guessed out loud, and crossed himself again.

"I don't want to talk about Abigail," Sam said stonily.

A long silence ensued. The fire took hold in the belly of the stove and heat rushed audibly through the coffeepot. Vierra rose from his chair, scouted for a mug and poured the lukewarm brew into it, adding what seemed like half the whiskey in the flask before setting the cup in front of Sam.

"Then talk about Maddie," Vierra urged.

Sam shook his head, eyed the concoction warily and took a cautious sip. He felt the muscles in his shoulders slacken suddenly and the sensation was both pleasant and unsettling.

LINDA LAEL MILLER

"I told you about Pilar," Vierra reminded him.

"You're acting like some old spinster at a Lonely Hearts Club meeting," Sam growled. "I *told* you—I don't want to talk. Not about Abigail. And not about Maddie, either."

Vierra smiled wanly, but his eyes were solemn. "Life is very short," he said quietly and in his own good time. "If you want Maddie Chancelor, you'd better do something about it."

"If you're going to carry on like this," Sam said after a second, still-cautious sip of the doctored coffee, "you might as well go back across the river." The stuff didn't taste as nasty, diluted by stale coffee, as it did straight.

"Now that's not very neighborly, as you *gringos* say," Vierra answered. "And I'm not going anywhere. The men we're looking for came through Refugio late last night, headed this way."

Sam sat up straighter and pushed the mug away. "Why didn't you say so in the first place?"

Vierra shrugged. "We have plenty of time."

"Before what?" Sam snapped.

"Before they try to break Mungo Donagher out of jail."

Sam glowered. "What the hell are you talking about?"

Vierra sighed. "I stopped at the cantina to water my horse," he said. "One of the girls told me the gang had been there the night before. There were more than a dozen of them, according to her, and they were in a real cheerful frame of mind, except for Rex. He was morose, and real put out with his old man for gunning Garrett down. Drank more than his share of rotgut and did some fancy talking."

Sam got to his feet, made sure his gun was loaded and there were plenty of spare bullets in his belt. He wasn't a hasty man, but he felt an urgent need to be doing something, just the same.

Vierra took a gold watch from the pocket of his vest

and checked the time. "They're planning the raid for midnight," he said. "That means we have almost three hours to make a plan."

"What is there to plan?" Sam demanded. "We have to stop them."

Vierra indulged in another sigh. "You're a schoolmaster, O'Ballivan. Do the arithmetic. There are at least a dozen of them and two of us. Anyway, who cares if they take Mungo Donagher and string him up from a tree? I say we lay low for now, follow them back to wherever they're hiding out, and watch for a chance to get the gold."

"*Damn* the gold!" Sam raged. "Even a son of a bitch like Donagher deserves a fair trial. Maybe you're willing to stand by while they lynch him, but I'm not!"

Vierra raised both hands like a man shielding himself from a burst of flame. "Calm down," he said.

"The hell I will!" Sam snapped, and started for the door.

"What are you going to do?" Vierra called after him.

Sam didn't trouble himself to answer. He whistled for the gelding and strode toward the shed, where his tack was stored.

Out of the corner of his eye he saw the light wink out inside the schoolhouse, and Vierra came down the steps. As if summoned by some silent command, the Mexican's horse trotted out of the brush, dripping river water.

Silently, but with the air of a man much put upon, Vierra put a foot into the stirrup and swung into the saddle.

The two men rode without speaking, through the cottonwoods and scrub brush, and pulled rein behind the jailhouse.

"Stay here with the horses," Sam ordered in an undertone as he dismounted.

Keeping to the shadows, Sam made his way around to the front, looked up and down the deserted sidewalk, and stepped into the dim light from the jailhouse window. When he went inside, there was no sign of Rhodes, or the

LINDA LAEL MILLER

yellow dog, but Mungo stood watching him, his big, gnarled hands gripping the bars.

Sam riffled the desk drawers until he found a pair of handcuffs and the keys to the cell. "Facedown on the floor," he told Mungo, "and put your hands behind your back."

Mungo frowned. "What—?"

"Just do what I tell you," Sam said. "Unless, of course, you'd rather be lynched."

The old man hesitated, obviously weighing his options. "What—?"

"Do it," Sam snapped.

Mungo eased himself to his knees, then sprawled on the floor.

Sam unlocked the cell door and cuffed Mungo with the dispatch of long practice. "Where's Rhodes?"

"Gone down to the Rattlesnake for supper," Mungo said as Sam helped him to his feet. "What the hell's going on here?"

"I'll explain later," Sam replied, giving the other man a shove to get him moving. "Right now, I'm trying to save your worthless hide."

"Suppose I let out a holler, once we're outside?" Mungo asked, stumbling a little as Sam gave him another push, this one harder than the first.

"You'll get the butt of my .45 in the back of the head," Sam answered. "That'll shut you up right enough. Or I could just leave you here, and let Rex and his bunch put a noose around your neck."

"Rex is my son," Mungo said, gaining the sidewalk.

"So was Garrett," Sam answered. He took Donagher by one arm and hustled him around the side of the jailhouse.

"You plannin' to turn me loose?" Mungo asked hopefully.

"Not a chance in hell," Sam told him.

Vierra leaned on the pommel of his saddle, watching

the proceedings with interest. "We seem to be short a horse," he said.

"We're not going far," Sam replied. He helped Mungo get a foot in the stirrup and hoisted him onto the gelding. With the old man's hands cuffed behind his back, it was an awkward enterprise, and Vierra maneuvered his horse to block Donagher from falling off the other side.

Sam took the horse by the reins and started back the way they'd come, through the brush, careful to keep to one side of the path. Donagher might have been old and bound at the wrists, but that didn't mean he wouldn't try to get away, and run Sam down in the process. The rancher was an able horseman, after all, and if Sam had been in his place, he'd have given the gelding his heels and worried about getting out of the handcuffs later.

Vierra must have had the same thought, because he drew his pistol and kept it trained on Mungo the whole way back to the schoolhouse.

Once they arrived, Sam wrenched Donagher down off the horse.

Mungo lost his balance and landed hard on the ground, cursing under his breath. Sam pulled him up by the back of his shirt and flung him toward the ramshackle storage shed. Mungo crashed through the doorway and there was a clang as he struck the copper bathtub.

"Goddamn it," Donagher grumbled, hitting the dirt floor, "I'd rather be lynched than treated like this!"

"Be careful what you wish for," Sam said, taking his rope down from a peg on the wall. He crouched and bound Mungo from his shoulders to his ankles, like a haunch of pork netted in string.

"Suppose I need to piss?" Donagher demanded.

"Reckon you'll get wet," Sam answered. He tugged at the rope to make sure it was secure.

LINDA LAEL MILLER

"You're gonna wish you hadn't done this," Mungo warned.

"Maybe," Sam agreed. "In the interest of letting you breathe, I'm not going to gag you. One sound out you, though, and I'll stuff one of my socks halfway down your throat."

Mungo cursed Sam, all his ancestors and all his descendents, but he did it quietly.

"Now what?" Vierra asked reasonably when Sam stepped out of the shed and latched the flimsy door.

Sam didn't answer until they were too far away for Mungo to hear. "You go back to the jailhouse and make sure Rhodes doesn't raise the alarm, if he hasn't done it already. I'm headed for the telegraph office." He got back on his horse, and Vierra did the same, but not without putting in his two cents.

"The telegraph office is closed."

"I plan to open it again," Sam said.

They parted ways at the edge of town.

Tucson was an hour away, on a very fast horse, and Tombstone was half again as far. The marshals of both towns would need time to get up a posse, if they were inclined to help at all—Sam wasn't sure they would be, but he had to try.

There was a light burning in the quarters above the telegraph office, but Sam had to do a lot of pounding before the operator came downstairs and, after peering at him around the door shade for a few precious moments, finally let him in.

"Is this an emergency?" the clerk asked, peevish, his Adam's apple bobbing up and down the length of his scrawny throat.

"As far as you're concerned, it is," Sam answered. "Get on the wire."

THE MAN FROM STONE CREEK

The clerk winced and moved behind the desk, dropping into his wooden swivel chair.

"No tricks, either," Sam warned. Last time he'd sent a telegram, it had been to Bird's sister, up in Denver. He'd paid a dollar extra to keep it secret, and the sneaky little bastard had gone straight to Oralee as soon as Sam turned his back.

"It'll cost two dollars," the clerk said with tremulous audacity.

Sam leaned across the desk, got the man by his shirt-front and yanked him partway to his feet. "I reckon it won't," he countered.

BEN DONAGHER LAY STILL upon the cot Maddie had moved into Terran's room just for him, staring up at the ceiling and listening as the structure of the mercantile settled around him, nail by nail, board by board. He didn't want to close his eyes just yet, because every time he did that, Miss Abigail Blackstone's still-white face loomed up in his mind, filling the whole of it.

Her lips were blue and her eyes stared like they were made of glass. He'd seen eyes like that before, once, when he'd ridden to Tucson with his pa, in a brand-new wagon, to visit a taxidermy shop, only they'd been looking out of a bobcat's head. Pa had hunted down and shot that critter himself, after it killed two calves, right in the corral. He'd ordered its big head stuffed and its tawny hide tanned, and nailed it up over the barn door as fair warning any cat, wolf, coyote or stray dog that might be inclined to raid his livestock.

Ben swallowed, remembering how he'd hated walking underneath that dead bobcat, watching him with its empty eyes, when he went to do his chores. All the time he was mucking out stalls, milking the cows or pitching hay down

LINDA LAEL MILLER

from the mow where it was stored, the hairs had stood up on the back of his neck, prickly as hog's bristles.

When Undine came to live at the ranch, Ben had marked her for a troublemaker right away, but she'd raised such a fuss about that bobcat that his pa finally took it down and burned it with the parts of an old shed that had collapsed after a hard rain. When the ashes were cool, Garrett sifted through them until he uncovered those glass eyeballs, and after that, Ben never knew where they'd turn up.

He'd found one in his stew one night at supper, when Undine was upstairs, with a cold cloth on her head, feeling peakish. They'd all laughed, his pa and brothers, when he bolted from the table and threw up as soon as he got outside.

Another time, in the dead of night, he'd gotten up after a bad dream to go downstairs for a drink of water. When he came back, one of those eyeballs was resting square in the middle of his pillow, gleaming in a stray beam of moonlight.

He'd shuddered and broken out in a sweat, too, but he hadn't made a sound, because he knew Garrett was listening, and he was damned if he'd give his brother the satisfaction of getting a rise out of him again. He'd taken that eyeball, carried it outside and dropped it down the well.

Garrett had boxed his ears for it, and ever after, Garrett had carried its partner in his pants' pocket, like it was a good-luck piece, and brought it out whenever he wanted to get Ben's goat.

Ben wondered if Garrett had had that eyeball on him when Pa put a pistol to the back of his head and pulled the trigger. Maybe they'd buried it with his worthless carcass, the way they sometimes buried folks with pocket watches or wedding bands.

He hoped so. The only thing worse than seeing that eyeball again would be seeing *Garrett* again.

THE MAN FROM STONE CREEK

Garrett was dead, he reminded himself. Gone forever. Hallelujah.

Ben shifted, and the pup, curled at his feet, whimpered in protest. He'd seen Garrett go into his pa and Undine's room that awful morning, Ben had, and headed straight out to the barn, where Pa was saddling up, to tell on them. He'd never forget the look on his pa's face, or what had happened after that.

Ben hated Garrett and wished him dead more than once. Same with Rex and Landry, and Pa, too.

He shivered. He hadn't wished Miss Blackstone dead, exactly. Just far away from Haven. He'd hated her because he knew she meant to marry up with Mr. O'Ballivan and spirit him back to the north country, but she'd been kind to him, and all the other kids, over the two days of school she'd taught. And then he'd gone and fallen in the river and she'd died saving him.

Ben's eyes burned. He bit his lower lip and blinked hard. Maddie said it was an accident, Miss Blackstone's dying like that, and Mr. O'Ballivan agreed, according to Terran. Ben would have liked to believe that, but he knew different.

It was his hatred that had killed her, same as it had brought Garrett to a bloody end.

He heard footsteps outside in the corridor and his breath froze in his lungs even though he knew it was only Maddie, on her way to her room. She paused, like always, and then went on. It was a comfort to Ben, the way she stopped to listen like that, same as if she'd touched him.

"Terran?" Ben whispered a few moments later when he heard Maddie's bedroom door close.

His friend stirred and made a *hmm* sound, but he didn't wake up. Terran was a sound sleeper, one of the many things about him Ben sorely envied. He'd have given

LINDA LAEL MILLER

anything, save his dog, for a sister like Maddie——though he'd heard Undine say, more than once, that Maddie probably wasn't Terran's sister at all, but his mother.

As far as Ben was concerned, all that meant was that Terran was even luckier than he'd thought.

Maddie was gentle. Ben liked the way she smelled and the sound of her voice, and the way she hummed when she was marking prices on things with a grease pencil. He liked the warm feeling he got when she looked at him, and he knew she really *saw* him, standing there.

Most of the time, he felt invisible.

He slipped out of bed, and the pup stood, stretching and curious.

"You stay," Ben whispered, pulling on his clothes.

Neptune lay right down again, with a dog sigh, his muzzle resting on his paws, watching Ben's movements with a rolling motion of his eyes. When Ben raised the windowsill, Neptune stood and, for a moment Ben was afraid he'd commence barking, wake up Terran and Maddie.

"Shush," Ben warned, putting a finger to his lips.

Neptune cocked his head to one side and perked his ears, as if he was trying to work out whether he ought to make noise or be still.

"You *shush*," Ben repeated firmly as he put one foot out the window, onto the steep pitch of the mercantile roof.

Neptune made a whiny sound, but then he settled back down in the blankets. Ben was relieved, but it left him with a hollow feeling, too. He had things to do, but it would have been nice if Neptune had raised a ruckus, rousing Terran and bringing Maddie on the run. She'd have made Ben stay, taken him downstairs for a cup of cocoa and given him what-for.

He wouldn't have minded considerable what-for, if it came from Maddie.

Carefully he made his way down the slant of the roof,

over to the sturdy water spout, where hard summer rains drained into a barrel in July and August. Maddie liked to save that water for hair-washing, she said.

Ben shimmied down the spout, balanced on the rim of the barrel and jumped to the ground.

WHEN THE JAILER finally wandered back in, followed by his dog, he found his prisoner gone and Vierra sitting behind the desk, his feet up and crossed at the ankles. Sam was still down at the telegraph office.

The cowpuncher went for his gun, but Vierra was faster and had him in his sights before he could clear leather.

"I wouldn't," Vierra advised after the fact.

"Who the hell are you?" Rhodes demanded. Privately, Vierra agreed with Sam's assessment. Rowdy Rhodes wasn't the kind of name a mother gave a son; he'd fashioned it himself. A lot of men did that, some for good reasons, others because they had something to hide.

Vierra didn't give a damn which it was, with Rhodes or anybody else. He smiled benevolently and introduced himself, but he didn't lower the pistol.

Rhodes's gaze swiped to the empty cell again, as though he might have missed something the first time he looked, then back to Vierra. "Where's Donagher?"

"The devil came and got him," Vierra answered easily. "Said they were one voice short in the hell chorus."

Rhodes narrowed his eyes. "I was charged to see that he stayed put," he said. The yellow dog sat at his feet, panting, and Rhodes gave him a distracted pat on the head.

"Nobody argues with the devil," Vierra said, checking his pocket watch. It was getting on toward ten o'clock. He sighed and snapped the case shut with a motion of his thumb.

"You may have gotten the drop on me," Rhodes said, loosening up a little, now that he wasn't in immediate

LINDA LAEL MILLER

danger of getting shot, "but I still have a badge. Your name don't mean shit to me. What's your business here?"

Vierra felt a surge of respect. He didn't let it show, of course. Didn't like to tip his hand. "That depends," he said.

Rhodes scowled, picked up the coffeepot, gave it a shake and set it down again with a disgusted thump. The little tableau put Vierra in mind of the Ranger; he had a way of doing the same thing. Liked his coffee, and when there was none in the pot, he took it as a personal affront.

"This was the easiest damn job I've ever had," Rhodes complained, going to the threshold with the pot and flinging the dregs into the street. "Sit around and watch an old man sleep. That's all I had to do to collect my pay." He ladled water into the pot, along with fresh coffee, and banged the thing down on the stovetop again. The hinges on the metal door squealed as he wrenched it open to jam in newspaper and kindling. "Thanks to you, I'll be shown the road for sure now."

Vierra smiled. "Maybe not," he said.

Rhodes struck a match, lit the crumpled newspaper in the stove, and crouched to blow on the flames. Took his time answering, which was another thing Vierra was inclined to like about him. "What do you mean, 'maybe not'?" he asked, shutting the stove door again and rising from his haunches. "I'm plain running out of patience with you."

Vierra did a parody of stricken alarm.

Rhodes simmered as he went on about his coffee-brewing. It was a complicated task, Vierra reflected, with as many steps as shoeing a horse or hitching up a wagon.

Whiskey was a lot less trouble.

"What's your real name?" he inquired.

The other man left the stove, rubbing his palms down his thighs in clear vexation, then hauled a crate from against the wall, upended it and sat. "What's yours?" he countered.

"I told you. Vierra."

Rhodes looked skeptical. The dog leaned against his right leg and he stroked its back with long, slow motions of his gun hand. Vierra always kept an eye on another man's gun hand, *especially* when he'd put it to some ordinary, innocent task.

"So you say," said the lawman. "All I know for sure is, my prisoner is gone and you surely had a part in it."

"Where you from?" Vierra asked, and thought to himself, with some amusement, that he was getting the knack of sounding like a *gringo.* If it weren't for his dark hair and eyes and his Mexican hide, he probably could have passed. Not that he wanted to. He'd have to spend too much time brewing coffee.

"Montana," Rhodes answered after a long, stubborn silence.

"You're a long way from home," Vierra observed. Where the hell was O'Ballivan? If the Ranger didn't turn up soon, he'd have to assume he'd found some trouble and go looking for him.

Rhodes shrugged, but there was a challenge in his blue eyes when he looked squarely at Vierra. "So are you," he said.

Vierra indicated a southerly direction with his pistol. "Just across the river," he answered. He thought of Pilar, living outside Refugio with her papa. Wherever Pilar was, was home.

"Handy," Rhodes observed. "You break somebody out of jail, and all you have to do is cross that wide stream they call a river. Up home, that would be a creek."

Vierra raised an eyebrow.

"You ever seen the Missouri?" Rhodes pressed. "*That's* a river."

LINDA LAEL MILLER

Just then Sam came through the door, which was standing open to the tense and quiet night, looking irritated. Rhodes made a sudden move and Vierra almost shot him before he realized Rhodes was reaching for the damn coffeepot.

"You got another cup?" the Ranger asked.

Inwardly, Vierra sighed. Then he cocked the pistol and spoke to Rhodes. "Don't get any ideas about throwing that boiling coffee on anybody."

Rhodes looked horrified, even as the pot boiled over and sizzled on the hot stove. "And take a chance on hitting the dog?" he asked.

"Ah, yes," Vierra said, lowering the .45 again. "The dog." That was another thing about *gringos*. They were sentimental about critters Indians and Mexicans boiled up with beans when game was scarce. He turned his gaze on O'Ballivan. "Did you send the wires?"

"Yes," the Ranger replied, still exasperated. "Waited for the replies, too. That was what took so long."

"Are they coming?" Vierra asked, referring to the Tucson and Tombstone marshals, who would, hopefully, bring sizable posses along with them—provided they were willing to make the ride to Haven, that is.

"Yes," O'Ballivan answered after a troubled glance at Rhodes. No doubt he was wondering how much Vierra had told the other man.

"*Nada,*" Vierra said without being asked.

Disgruntled, Rhodes scouted up two mugs and filled them, handing off the first one to O'Ballivan, who took it with both hands. "I sure wish somebody would tell me what the hell's going on around here," the cowpoke grumbled.

The Ranger savored his coffee for a few moments, though Vierra figured it must have been hot enough to strip a layer of skin off his tongue, coming right off the boil like that. "We've got reason to believe there might be a raid on this place, around midnight," he said after a couple of hard swallows. "Some folks are of a mind to spring Mungo from the hoosegow."

"Imagine that," Rhodes said, and made his *gringo* eyes go wide.

O'Ballivan laughed.

"Guess there could be some shooting," decided Rhodes.

"Imagine that," Vierra said.

BEN FOLLOWED THE RIVER, though he stayed well clear of it, three miles to where it took a southerly bend. From that point, it was maybe another hour of hard trudging to where he'd buried his Christmas and birthday money. He'd need it to get him and Neptune up north, on the stagecoach, to where the old man lived.

He took to the road, figuring to make better time, and that was his mistake. The riders must have come overland, traveling alongside the river, where the ground was soft enough to muffle the sound of horses' hooves. They were on him before he could dive for the brush.

"If it ain't my little brother," taunted a familiar voice. Rex. Ben didn't hate him or Landry near as much as he had Garrett, which was probably why they were still alive.

Rex leaned in the saddle, caught Ben by the back of his shirt and yanked him right up onto the pommel. The horn jabbed hard into his tailbone, but Ben didn't flinch.

"What are you doin' out here, anyhow?" Rex gave him a hard shake and, not for the first time, Ben wished he wasn't so small for his age. Folks usually thought he was eight or nine, instead of twelve, like he was.

"Pa's in jail," Ben said instead of answering Rex's question. "They're gonna hang him, on account of he shot Garrett in the back of his head."

LINDA LAEL MILLER

Rex was filthy. His breath stank and he'd grown a beard. In the time he'd been gone, he'd gotten meaner, which was hard to credit, given that Ben had known desert rats with a better temperament.

"That ain't the half of it," Rex growled, as though he knew the whole thing was Ben's doing. He'd as good as murdered Garrett, and Pa, too, for all practical intents and purposes, he'd hated them so hard and so long. "Landry's dead, too. And you know why it happened?"

Ben did know, of course, but he wasn't fool enough to say so. Rex and Landry had been close, like a pair of idiot twins with their heads stuck together, Pa said. Claimed you could drop one of them in China and one of them in New York City, and they'd find each other.

"No, sir," Ben lied, barely able to get the words out, he was so scared of that look in Rex's eyes. "I don't."

"Because of that so-called schoolmaster and his Mexican sidekick, *that's* why. One of them shot off half Landry's foot, and the time came when we had to put him down like a dog!"

"Rex," a familiar voice put in, "shut up."

Ben blinked, let out his breath and methodically counted the other riders in his head as a way to calm himself. They'd had time to pull their bandannas up, covering the lower halves of their faces, but he recognized most of them, just the same. They rode for the Donagher brand. But the one who'd spoken...

"We can't take him with us," one of the other men said.

Ben reckoned the insides of his ears must have swollen almost shut, for some reason. The riders were bunched close in, like cattle trying to weather a blizzard, yet the voices seemed to come from some far place.

"I'd as soon break his neck as look at him," Rex said.

Ben believed that.

"No," said another voice, and that one he knew.

He tracked it to a slender rider, off to his left. "Undine?"

"Let him go, Rex," Undine said. Her words echoed queerly, like those of the others, but she nudged her horse right in close, and Ben would have catapulted into her arms if his brother hadn't had a fierce grip on the back of his neck, fixing to snap it right in two, no doubt.

"We can't," Rex argued. "He'll hightail it straight for town, spout off to Maddie or that schoolmaster how he's seen us, and that'll be the end of it!"

"You wouldn't tell on us, would you, Ben?" Undine asked, and the sweetness of her tone scared him more than anything Rex had said.

"No, ma'am," Ben said.

"Because we're going to get your daddy out of that awful jail." Undine's gaze glittered in the night, just like that glass cat's eye Garrett had put on his pillow to scare him. "You wouldn't want to ruin that. I know you wouldn't."

"No, ma'am," Ben repeated, because he seemed to have forgotten how to form any words but those two.

Rex's hand tightened on the back of Ben's neck. "'No, ma'am, no, ma'am,'" Rex mocked, his breath hot and stinking on Ben's cheek. "You weasely little bastard! You'd say anything to save your worthless hide. Then, first chance you got, you'd have the law on us. Kin don't mean *nothin'* to you!"

"Undine," said the man Ben thought he ought to know, "if you want the kid to live, you'll have to stay back and keep an eye on him. Until we finish off O'Ballivan and Vierra, we'll not know a peaceful moment, no matter where we may wander."

Ben's eyes widened. Except for Mr. O'Ballivan, he didn't

LINDA LAEL MILLER

know another man who talked fancy like that. Not even Banker James, who'd been to college back east someplace.

"You said we were going to get Mungo out of jail!" Undine shrieked. "What's this about killing Sam? I won't let you—"

"You can't stop us," Mr. Thomas P. Singleton broke in, having uncovered his face to speak.

Ben gaped.

"There's a lot of gold involved here," Singleton went on mildly. "You get in our way, Undine, and we'll have to kill you, too."

"You'd murder your *own* sister?" Undine retorted.

Sister? Ben thought, dazed. How could Undine be Mr. Singleton's sister? Her name hadn't been Singleton before she married Pa.

Mr. Singleton doffed his hat, pressed it to his heart. His wild red hair was ruffled and seemed to move on its own, rising off his narrow head like threads of flame. "Only if she made it necessary," he said. "And, remember, you're only my half sister."

Undine hooked an arm around Ben's waist and pulled him off Rex's horse and onto hers, with a strength he wouldn't have imagined she had. She slackened her hold just as quickly, though, and Ben scrambled to keep from tumbling to the stony road. They'd have trampled him for sure if he did, or shot him so he couldn't run away.

"You'd better have Mungo with you when you get back!" she warned.

"Why, Sister," Mr. Singleton purred, "I'd swear you'd developed an unseemly fondness for that old fool."

"There are papers only he can sign, and you know it!" Undine retorted, nearly unsettling Ben in her agitation. "And don't you dare try to leave me behind, Tom, because

THE MAN FROM STONE CREEK

if you do, I'll tell every lawman I can find who you are and where you mean to go with all that Mexican gold!"

Ben's hands sweated, where he clung to the saddle horn. Undine shifted back a little, and he let go long enough to swing a leg over her horse's neck. There were only two thoughts in his head; the rest had scattered like hens with a fox in their midst.

The first one was, he was glad he hadn't brought Neptune.

The second, he didn't want them to kill Sam O'Ballivan.

"He's just a schoolteacher!" Ben blurted. "Like you! You've got no call to hurt him!"

Mr. Singleton leaned in so close that all Ben could see of his face was his big, watery-blue eyes. "He's not a schoolteacher," Singleton said, almost breathing the words instead of saying them. "He's an Arizona Ranger. Now, you be a good boy, Benjamin, and mind your stepmother. If you do, I might not have to turn you over to your brother here. Let him do whatever he wants."

Ben went as cold as if he'd been laid out for burial.

Singleton's threat was not an idle one. He knew that for sure. And he knew Rex had gone crazy. He'd kill him, all right, if given the chance, and take his time doing it.

"I'll mind Undine," Ben choked out. "I *swear* I will!"

"See that you do," Singleton crooned in that voice that made you want to go to sleep. The one he'd used to talk about Romans and arithmetic and proper grammar, when he was teaching school. Ben had nodded off more than once, back then, and gotten his knuckles rapped for it. They'd smarted something fierce from that ruler.

It seemed a tame punishment now.

"Take the boy back to camp, Undine," Singleton told his sister. "I know you'd prefer the comforts of your dear husband's ranch house, but if something happens to go wrong in town, that's the first place they'll look for you."

LINDA LAEL MILLER

Ben turned his head, saw Undine bite down on her lower lip, then nod.

"If he's foolish enough to try anything," Singleton added, reining his horse away, toward town, "you kill him."

Undine hesitated, then nodded again.

Rex lingered a moment, even as the others rode off. He took Ben by the hair and jerked his head back. "You be good," he said, pressing the words between his teeth.

The letting go hurt almost as much as the taking hold.

Ben gulped down a cry of pain, watched with relief and hatred as his last remaining brother spurred his horse to catch up with the rest of the gang.

Ben had counted thirteen men.

What chance would Mr. O'Ballivan have against so many?

"This better not end up costing me my share of the gold," Undine said. "I've got plans for it."

Ben knew he could take her, strong as she was, but she'd yell for sure, before he got a hand over her mouth, and Singleton and the others would surely hear.

No, he'd have to wait, whether he wanted to or not, until they'd reached the camp, wherever it was.

CHAPTER
TWENTY-ONE

MADDIE TRIED TO SLEEP, but there was an oppressive sense of—what *was* it?—great and ominous forces, converging, sweeping into Haven, huddled fearfully on the banks of the river, from all the vastness of the four directions. Though her room was warm, even stuffy, she shivered.

She sat up in bed, groped for the lamp on her bedside table and struck a match to the wick. It was still early. Perhaps she would read awhile, and if that failed, she might put on her wrapper, go downstairs, brew a soothing pot of tea. If she became truly desperate, there was always the account book. The very dullness of adding and subtracting, multiplying and dividing all those carefully entered figures was almost guaranteed to weight her eyelids and set her to yawning.

She reached for her book, a worn volume of John Donne's poetry, plumped her pillows and settled back to open to the page she'd marked with the colorful band from a cigar, carelessly discarded by a customer. Maddie was not one to waste any useful item, especially one that was pleasing to the eye.

LINDA LAEL MILLER

She sighed and attempted to focus her attention on the singular music of Mr. Donne's offering, each word a note in a silent sonata. But Maddie's heart was playing another tune and her mind remained uneasy.

She closed the book and set it aside, listening not just with her ears, but the whole of her being. Was it the weather? Maybe *that* was what she felt humming in the air, that inexplicable charge that always heralded a rare storm, the kind that brought ground-shaking thunder and flashes of lightning fit to rally the four horses of the Apocalypse. The grass around Haven was frightfully dry; there hadn't been a good rain in months.

Oh, God, she prayed silently, *let that be it.*

But Maddie heard nothing, save her own shallow, rapid breathing and the spritely, audacious music spilling through the doorway of the Rattlesnake Saloon.

The clink of Oralee's badly tuned piano, catching her ear in unguarded moments, invariably stirred yearnings she couldn't hope to fulfill. A spinet of her own, to play whenever she felt the inclination. A man to caress her body in the night and challenge her mind during the day.

Sam O'Ballivan.

Her throat ached with the poignancy of what she felt.

Sam O'Ballivan.

The man had never kissed her, never bared her flesh to his hands and his mouth. In point of fact, he had never touched her, except in the most innocuous ways, helping her down from a horse. Gripping her shoulders to steady her.

When had she come to love him?

For she did love him, though it was her own despairing secret, nestled safe in her soul, and while there might be some who had guessed, she had never confessed the truth to anyone. She was only now admitting it to herself.

When, though? When had it happened?

THE MAN FROM STONE CREEK

Perhaps that very first day when he'd come into the store to collect the package mailed from Stone Creek. He'd seemed to fill the whole place with the quiet power of his presence.

Tears burned behind Maddie's eyes. Tears of frustration and sorrow.

She might as well love one of the flickering figures from those moving-picture boxes she'd seen once in a Tombstone ice-cream parlor. She'd dropped a penny into a slot and watched a brief melodrama, marveling at the jerky way the images moved. A handsome cowboy, with a kerchief at his throat, saving a woman from a stagecoach robbery. Sweeping her up onto his horse and carrying her off into a sunset etched in shades of gray.

She'd been fascinated, especially by the kiss at the end, and shamed by her extravagance. If Terran hadn't demanded the ice cream she'd promised, she might have watched the whole silly thing over again. Wasted another perfectly good penny.

"Way of the future," the man behind the counter had claimed, his huge black mustache quivering as he scooped the frozen vanilla concoction into a bowl for an eager Terran. "You just wait and see."

Maddie shook off the memory. Moving pictures were a passing novelty, and Sam O'Ballivan might just as well have been a character in one of them. He'd be gone that quick and, besides, he still belonged to Abigail, even if she *was* dead. He'd loved her enough to risk all kinds of scandal, or he wouldn't have let her move into his room in back of the schoolhouse.

"Stop it!" she scolded herself, and was grateful for the strange scratching that sounded at her bedroom door.

She got up, donned her wrapper.

"Who's there?" she asked.

The scratching came again.

LINDA LAEL MILLER

Terran or Ben would have knocked.

Maddie opened the door and looked down to see Neptune sitting there, looking up at her with plaintive brown eyes. She smiled wanly at her fanciful interpretation. Neptune *always* looked plaintive.

She crouched to ruffle his ears. "What is it, boy? Do you need to go outside?"

Neptune whimpered.

Maddie straightened, frowning. She'd had a brief respite, thinking about moving pictures, but now her uneasiness was back. She went back for the lantern on her bedside table and hurried through the small sitting room to Terran's door.

The latch hadn't caught properly and Neptune had pushed it open. That, she was sure, was why it stood ajar.

She peeked inside, holding the lantern aloft.

"Terran?"

"Hmm-mmm?" Her brother stirred in his narrow bed, but didn't awaken.

Maddie's gaze slid to the cot where Ben slept. It was empty, and the window above it was raised. The flour-sack curtains shifted, almost imperceptibly, in the slow, heavy breeze.

"Terran!" Maddie cried.

Neptune, all but tangled in the hem of her wrapper, gave a soft, earnest whine.

"Terran!" Maddie repeated. She set the lantern on the wide windowsill and bent to shake him by one shoulder.

He opened his eyes, partly at least, and regarded Maddie with that baffled irritation common to those who've had their slumbers interrupted. "What?" he asked, stretching the word even as he stretched his body.

"It's Ben. He's gone."

Terran groaned and tugged the pillow over his face. "Not again."

THE MAN FROM STONE CREEK

Maddie pulled the pillow off and tossed it aside. "Get up. We've got to find him."

Another groan from Terran. "Why? He'll come back on his own. He always does."

"Terran, *get up!*"

He raised himself as far as his elbows, hair tousled, eyes narrowed to skeptical slits. He shook his head once, from side to side, as though throwing off the effects of sleep. "All right," he said. "All right. But you've got to give me some privacy, Maddie. I'm not decent."

Maddie looked down at her wrapper and bare feet. She wasn't "decent," either, not for the street, anyway. "Hurry!" she urged, and then turned, on the fly, to head back to her own room.

Five minutes later she was downstairs, fully dressed and waiting impatiently for Terran.

She went to the bottom of the steps and shouted his name.

"I'm coming!" he yelled back.

Neptune stood on his hind legs to scrabble anxiously at Maddie's skirts with his forepaws.

"You'll have to stay here," Maddie told him with some regret. He might be handy, finding Ben, but it was dark out and he could so easily get lost. Too, there were the coyotes and the big dogs that sometimes got loose and ranged the town. Neptune would be easy prey to them.

The dog cried.

Maddie's heart twisted. She leaned down to pat his head. "I'll find him," she said. "I promise."

Terran thundered down the stairs just then, his shirt misbuttoned and his hair atangle. Under any other circumstances, Maddie would have admonished her brother, sent him back to his room to attend to his appearance, but Ben's absence, coupled with the eerie niggling of her intuition, lent an urgency to the situation that she couldn't ignore.

LINDA LAEL MILLER

"If we just wait," Terran reasoned pettishly, "he'll come back."

Maddie ignored the protest, already opening the back door. "You fetch Mr. O'Ballivan. I'll start at the other end of town and walk every street if that's what I have to do."

Terran sighed. "All right," he agreed.

They stepped outside and Maddie shut the door on poor Neptune before he could dash out to join them. As she headed in one direction, Terran went toward the school-house.

Neptune's yelps made Maddie want to cover her ears with both hands, but she quickened her pace instead of going back for him.

BEN RECOGNIZED the camp right off, even though it was dark. It was tucked away in a little arroyo, a mile or so from the ranch house. Ben knew the place because he'd gone there so often, when he was just a kid, to hide from his brothers and, sometimes, his pa. Once, he'd made a fire and passed the whole night there, and when he got back in the morning, expecting a beating, nobody but Anna even knew he'd been gone.

Anna hadn't said a word to betray him. She'd just put a little extra on his breakfast plate, because she'd known nothing would have brought him back save the kind of hunger that eats up the belly and then gnaws at the backbone for good measure.

"Mr. Singleton called you his half sister," he said to Undine as they dismounted in the middle of the camp, next to the dead fire. He wanted to keep her mind busy—it wouldn't do at all if she figured out that he meant to escape first chance he got.

Undine sighed. She was wearing trousers, like a man, and boots. Suspenders, too, and a loose cotton shirt. Ben

THE MAN FROM STONE CREEK

knew the whole getup for his own. They were things he'd outgrown, two summers ago, and Anna had put them away in a box. Said somebody might need them one day.

"That's right, Ben," she said. "We had the same mother but different fathers." She didn't look him in the eye; just stood there, with her hands on her curvy hips, surveying the countryside. Most of which was invisible, because the moon was still scant and the stars seemed to have receded, as though they wanted to distance themselves from earth and from all the people who lived there.

"You're part of that outlaw gang," Ben said. "The one Pa's been talking about." There had been accounts of the raids in the papers for months; his pa got the *Epitaph* sent over from Tombstone and the *Gazette* from Tucson. He liked to compare the two; said if a man only read one newspaper, he was likely to get slanted accounts of what was going on in the world. Now, Ben remembered how Undine's mouth used to tighten whenever his pa read out loud about cattle prices or something the politicians were up to back in Washington City. She'd especially disliked accounts of the robberies and murders that had been so common of late.

"You'll have to promise not to tell anybody what you know," Undine said. "Otherwise—well, Tom's right—you'll be a real problem."

Ben was *already* a problem, and he knew it. Singleton might have *said* he could stay alive, but like as not, he'd only been appeasing Undine, so he and Rex and the others could get on with all they meant to do in town.

Kill Mr. O'Ballivan, for a start.

Ben's stomach growled, just like it did when he was real hungry, but he *wasn't* hungry. He was afraid—for himself, yes, but more for Mr. O'Ballivan and that Mexican he rode with, the one with the good boots. For Maddie and Terran

LINDA LAEL MILLER

and the whole town of Haven, come to that. He'd seen the look in Rex's eyes; his brother wanted folks to be sorry for what had happened to Landry, and Garrett, too, and he'd see that they were.

"They'll kill me when they get back here," he told Undine calmly. "And maybe you, too."

Undine took a few moments to think, then nodded once, briskly and with decision. "What we've got to do is move that gold," she said.

"What gold?" Ben asked, stalling. He could make it to Undine's horse, but she was carrying a pistol, stuck in the waistband of her pants. Something about the angle of it made Ben believe she'd be fast on the draw, even if she was a woman.

"Never mind *what* gold," Undine snapped. "What we'll do is, we'll help ourselves to as much as we can carry, and then we'll move on. By the time they get back, we'll be down the road. Might even have time to stop at the barn and get you a horse of your own. You'll slow me down too much if we ride double."

Ben merely nodded, waiting.

Undine paused, as though she was listening for something on the wind, then started riffling through the bedrolls and saddlebags scattered on the ground. When she tossed the first bag to Ben, it proved so heavy as to almost knock him over. She found another and hurled that one at him, too, but this time he was ready and caught it easily.

She took four more bags, besides the pair she'd entrusted to Ben, and headed for the horse.

"Come on," she said, stashing the clinking sacks in her saddlebags and putting out one hand for what Ben was carrying. "We haven't got any time to waste."

Ben paused, biting his lower lip. "I gotta make water first," he said.

THE MAN FROM STONE CREEK

Undine's whole body tightened with exasperation. "Well, hurry up about it," she said. "And give me that gold before you make for the brush." She stopped, watching him intently. "Don't get any fancy ideas about running away, either. I've got a fast horse here and I'll be on you before you've gone a hundred yards."

Ben nodded, handed over the gold and slipped into the bushes. There, he relieved himself, both because he urgently needed to, had since Rex had grabbed him, and because he knew Undine would listen for the sound. Then, after he'd buttoned his pants, he bent, picked up a flat stone and tucked it into the back of his shirt. It felt cold and hard against his bare skin.

Undine had already mounted up when he got back to her. She didn't say anything, just shifted one foot out of the stirrup on the left-hand side so Ben could climb up behind her.

"It's hard to believe a woman would be part of an outlaw gang," he said when they'd ridden a little way. Meanwhile, he was fidgeting to pull out his shirt tail in back and get hold of the rock before it fell to the ground.

Undine laughed. "Is it?" she teased in a mean voice, talking loud so he'd hear her over the beat of the horse's hooves. "Well, land sakes, Ben Donagher, there's more to life than a twelve-year-old-boy can imagine."

"I'll be thirteen in seven months," he said.

She turned far enough in the saddle to look square into his face. "Quit that squirming around," she said. "That gold is deep in those saddlebags, and if you try to get to it, I'll know."

Ben made himself look meek. He even swallowed, so she'd see. He had the rock in his right hand, but he couldn't bring himself to whack her in the face with it. She might be kin to a killer, and part of a robber gang, but she was

LINDA LAEL MILLER

pretty, and she'd been kind to him sometimes, in her calculating way.

"I wouldn't do a thing like that," he assured her, keeping his fist, with the rock tightly clasped in it, back of his thigh. "Steal, I mean."

"Holier than thou," Undine said in the kind of voice St. Peter might call up to turn somebody back at the Pearly Gates. "That's what comes of spending so much time with a prude like Maddie Chancelor."

Ben kept his face still until she turned around. Then he hit her square in the back of the head, not as hard as he could have done, but hard enough.

Undine sagged in the saddle and blood gushed through the back of her hair, which was pinned up just above her nape. After he'd reached around to catch the reins in his left hand, he steered for softer ground and then shoved her off.

She lay moaning in the dirt, face turned to the sky.

"Don't you die," Ben told her. Then he reined the horse around and rode for town.

THERE WERE LANTERNS burning inside the jailhouse and the door was wide open. Terran stopped on the wooden sidewalk, thinking Ben might have come to pay a visit to his pa. Sure, it was practically the middle of the night, but Ben did crazy things like that sometimes. Hadn't he tried to cross the river, walking a slippery log, and nearly drowned himself, along with Miss Blackstone? Hadn't he made a habit of running off whenever the mood took him?

Terran felt a certain relief. If Ben was here, at the jailhouse, he'd take him back to the mercantile. Get him by the ear, if he had to. Then he'd give a yell for Maddie, to let her know all was well, and quick as you could say "Jack Robinson," he'd be in his own bed again, sound asleep.

He was growing. Maddie said that all the time. And a boy that was growing needed his rest.

He stepped up to the threshold.

Mr. O'Ballivan was there, and Rhodes and Vierra. The big old yellow dog, too. No sign of Ben, though, or Mungo, either.

Mr. O'Ballivan frowned. "What are you doing, roaming the street at this hour?"

If he'd had a father, Terran figured he would have said something just like that. It pleased him a little, hearing it from Sam, and made him sad at the same time. "Maddie sent me to tell you Ben's gone again."

Mr. O'Ballivan set his mug of coffee aside and approached, still frowning. "Where do you reckon he's gotten off to this time?"

"I thought maybe here," Terran answered glumly. The way things were going, he'd be lucky if he saw his bed again before morning. Maddie would make him go to school, too, no matter what. "Where's Mr. Donagher?"

Sam laid a hand on Terran's shoulder. Sometimes, when he felt the need, Terran liked to call Mr. O'Ballivan by his first name, inside his head. "Never mind that. You go and tell Maddie that the two of you ought to stay inside the mercantile and keep to the back."

"But what about Ben?"

"I'll find him," Sam said. A look passed between him and Vierra, who was seated behind the desk Terran still thought of as belonging to Warren, but it was a look he couldn't make sense of.

"Maddie said—"

Sam's grasp tightened on Terran's shoulder, not painfully but hard enough to hold his attention. "I don't care what Maddie said. Just do as I told you, Terran."

"She won't like it."

"I'm not concerned about that, either. *Go.*"

Terran went. He walked along the sidewalk first, then he darted onto the road and ran right down the center.

If Mr. O'Ballivan said they were to go back to the mercantile and keep themselves away from the front, where there were windows, that meant there would be shooting.

TOM SINGLETON RODE at the front, like always, and drew rein when the band reached the little rise overlooking Haven. Rex tried to ride past him, eager to get to his pa, but Tom reached out and grabbed hold of the bridle strap, fair tripping Rex's horse.

He was little, Tom was, but he was strong, and he was mean. Rex looked forward to shooting him in the back one day soon, but it wasn't likely the other men would take Rex's part in a gunfight, should one break out then and there, so he had to bide his time and mind his manners.

Tom had drawn his pistol, and he shoved the barrel tip hard into Rex's temple. There'd be a bruise by sunup—if he lived long enough to greet the light of a new day.

"Hold up," Tom said, though it was clear to everybody that Rex had already done that. "I know you want to call your daddy to account for what he did to Garrett, but only fools go plunging into a situation where they don't know what's waiting for them."

Rex put down a suicidal urge to spit in Tom Singleton's prissy-assed, womanly face. He swallowed instead, but a charge went through him, just like he'd gripped a lightning bolt with both hands. His throat went tight and dry as the Mexican desert, and he couldn't get a word past it.

"You're not a fool, are you, Rex?" Tom asked in that croony way he had that made a man's skin crawl up his back like a whole army of ants.

Rex couldn't get the answer out, but it pounded inside his head. No, damn it, he wasn't a fool. Furthest thing from it.

He had his share of the gold, and plans to hightail it north, all the way to Canada, where he'd make up a new name for himself and start over fresh. He planned to sleep, drink and chase women for a while, but in time, he reckoned he'd buy some land and a few cattle and take himself a wife.

No, sir, he wasn't a fool.

"Maybe you ought to wait right here," Tom said, thoughtful-like, and before Rex had a chance to catch his breath, Tom had cocked a bullet into the chamber of that pistol, and the tip of the barrel bit deeper into Rex's temple. "You're a hothead, Rex, just like that brother of yours."

Rex tensed. Every time he remembered what happened to Landry, down there in the badlands on the other side of the border, it hit him fresh. Landry was gone. By rights, he should have been riding with the outfit right now, with a share of the gold to show for all he'd suffered. Making plans to head up to Canada, his horse traveling alongside Rex's.

But it wasn't to be, and Tom Singleton was the main reason. Oh, they'd shot off half Landry's foot, the Ranger and that Mexican he was riding with, but it was Tom who'd put Landry down like a crippled cow. Rex knew that for sure, even though the others had made sure he wasn't there to see.

"I got to go with you, Tom," Rex choked out. Tom and the others were set on killing O'Ballivan and the other man so they could enjoy the fruits of their labors in peace, and Rex wanted to see those two dead more than anybody did, but he had something else in mind, too. He had to tell his pa about Landry, and once he'd done that, he'd put a bullet square between the old man's eyes.

He owed that much to Garrett.

"I don't like that idea," Tom said pleasantly. "O'Balli-van and Vierra aren't the sort to give up. Track a man to the end of his days, just for the sheer orneriness of it. I mean to see that they stay put for good, and I can't do that if you're going to do something crazy."

"I won't do nothin' crazy," Rex promised, his heart hunkered in his throat and expanding so as to burst.

"No," Tom said quietly, "you won't."

Rex felt hopeful. Especially when Tom lowered the gun, though a glance downward showed his finger was still on the trigger. In the next instant, though, Tom flipped that pistol end over end and the butt of it came at Rex's face.

A burst of pain blinded him.

His last conscious thought, as he toppled to the ground, was that Tom Singleton had split his skull wide open, like a melon at a summer picnic.

SAM WALKED the river's edge, picking his way along in the darkness, reminded of Abigail at every step. He called Ben's name, over and over, but there was no response. He checked the schoolhouse, for the second time, and it proved fruitless, as before.

He paused at the door of the shed, where Mungo Donagher lay bound on the floor. "Old man," he said, "I'm looking for your youngest boy. He lit out from Maddie's place sometime tonight. If you know where he might go, you'd better tell me."

"Why should I tell you any damn thing at all?" Mungo retorted.

Sam drew his pistol and opened the shed door slowly, in case Donagher was poised to jump him.

Mungo lay curled on the dirt floor, just where Sam had left him.

"Ben's your own flesh and blood," Sam said evenly. "He's just a kid, and he's probably in danger. Not that I think you've ever paid him much attention, but even you ought to have some idea where he'd hole up."

"He'd go to his mama's grave, most likely," Mungo allowed, but grudgingly. "He was always mooning over Elsie, even though he never knew her. I told him she wasn't coming back, that she was nothing but bones by the time she'd been a year in the ground, but he didn't listen."

"He'd be at the cemetery, then?" Sam was running out of time. He thought back to Garrett's funeral and the spot where he was buried, and hoped to God he'd find Ben there. He was shutting the door when Mungo finally troubled himself to answer.

"Elsie ain't buried in town. She's on the ranch, next to Hildy."

Sam considered that. Ben had no business wandering abroad at night, but if he'd gone to the ranch, he was five miles or better from Haven. Considering what was coming, he was probably safer there, for all the dangers he might encounter.

"Untie me," Mungo drawled. "Let me go. I'll take to the road and nobody'll be the wiser."

"Save your breath, old man," Sam said, and shut the door.

"I'll see you're paid for your trouble!" Mungo pressed. "Right handsomely, too!"

Sam turned and walked away.

He heard the horses, a dozen or more, just as he rounded the bend in the road, the one that would take him back into Haven. And he knew by the direction that it wasn't the posses coming from Tombstone and Tucson.

Ducking into the brush at the side of the road, Sam bolted for the jailhouse, one hand on the butt of his pistol even as he ran. He got inside just before the first spray of bullets peppered the facade.

LINDA LAEL MILLER

"Put out that goddamned lantern!" he bellowed as Vierra and Rhodes scrambled to get ready for the fight.

The lantern flame winked into darkness.

TERRAN TOOK A MAN'S GRIP on Maddie's hand when the shooting broke out, and she was distracted, for one blessed moment, by his strength. They landed hard behind a horse trough, too far from the store to take shelter there.

"Stay down!" Terran rasped.

It was her instinct to protect him, but something had shifted. *He* was protecting *her.* "What's happening?" she whispered as they clung to each other.

"I don't know," Terran answered, breathless, his arm across Maddie's back, keeping her down, out of the way of bullets. "Sam—Mr. O'Ballivan—told me to find you and take you home. Said to keep ourselves to the back of the building."

Maddie struggled to orient herself and Terran in relation to the gunfire. "The *jailhouse!*" she croaked, and tried to rise. Sam was there, she knew it, and he was fixing to get himself killed, just like Warren had. She wasn't about to stand for that.

But Terran, a scrawny boy of twelve, would not be moved. "Maddie," he barked, "you *stay put!*"

She began to tremble. Sam couldn't die. He *couldn't.* "Dear God," she choked out. "What if they kill him?" *They,* she realized, in the space of a moment, meant the Donaghers, Landry and Rex. They'd assembled a gang of drifters and bandits and gone to the jail to break Mungo out.

"Right now," Terran said reasonably, "we've got enough to reckon with. I mean to see that they don't kill *us!*"

A splintered silence fell, but it was all too brief. Gunfire erupted again, with a vengeance, and it sounded to Maddie like two armies clashing on a battlefield.

THE MAN FROM STONE CREEK

"Sam is there," she said, wanting to weep.

"Yes," Terran replied, confirming her worst fear. She'd hoped against hope he'd say no, say he'd seen Sam last at the schoolhouse, where he'd be safe. "And the best thing you can do to help him is keep out of the way!"

"Shouldn't we try to get back to the store?" Maddie wasn't used to deferring to Terran. It felt strange, and she did not want to make a habit of it.

"When there's a lull," Terran agreed.

But the lull was a long time coming.

Maddie broke free of her brother's grasp just long enough to peer over the edge of the trough. It was dark and yet she could see plainly all the way down the street to the jailhouse, as though by some otherworldly illumination.

Terran wrenched her down again.

"We can't stay here," Maddie told him.

"We're not moving," Terran argued.

Maddie looked behind her. Only a few feet of sidewalk separated them from the sheltering space between the telegraph office and the feed-and-grain. From there, they could dash to the alley and take the back way to the store. If she could just get to her shotgun…

She heard riders then, dozens of them, it sounded like, coming from the south. Maddie held her breath, assembling every stray smidgeon of strength. She could break away from Terran, but if she did, he'd surely follow, none too carefully.

"Terran, listen to me," she pleaded. "We *must* get off the street!"

He turned his head, studied her solemnly, and for a long time. Meanwhile, the shooting intensified to a new pitch. A bullet struck the other side of the trough and water gurgled out.

Maddie couldn't help thinking of it as life's blood—

LINDA LAEL MILLER

Terran's, Sam's, her own. "Come on!" she cried. Clasping Terran's hand, she got partway to her feet, pulling him after her. They ran, half crouched, for safety.

Heart pounding, Maddie paused between the two buildings to drag in great, gasping gulps of air. Terran, too, was breathing hard, but he recovered more quickly than Maddie and took the lead again, hauling her through to the alley.

When they reached the back door of the mercantile, it was all Maddie could do not to fling herself down on the kitchen floor. Instead she let go of Terran's hand and ran for the front of the store to fetch her shotgun.

She was vaguely aware of Neptune, barking at the top of the stairs.

Just as she reached the counter, the front door exploded inward, crashing against the wall. The glass shattered and a man wearing a bandanna over his face burst inside, looking wildly around him, failing to notice Maddie in the darkness. She watched, frozen, as he went for the boxes of bullets and began grabbing them up.

Maddie's palms sweated on the stock of the shotgun.

"Stop!" she ordered.

The intruder whirled in her direction and she saw the glint of a pistol barrel. At the same moment he fired, Maddie was jerked off her feet. She landed hard on the floor behind the counter and the shotgun went off, blowing a hole in the ceiling.

"What—?"

Terran glared at her and jerked the shotgun out of her hands. Cocked it hard. Where had he learned to do that?

"Shut up, Maddie," he said.

The robber rounded the end of the counter just then, pistol at the ready, but he never got a chance to fire because Terran beat him to it.

The roar of that shotgun was deafening. The smells of gunpowder and blood filled Maddie's nostrils and the smoke made her blink. Maybe it was a mercy that it all happened so fast, that she didn't see the man's chest explode.

"I had to do it," Terran said.

Maddie didn't answer. *Couldn't* answer.

SLOWLY, CAREFULLY, Rex Donagher raised his head. It hurt like holy bejesus, and he figured his nose was broken. He put a hand to his face and it came away bloody. Turned onto his back with a groan.

He was still a man, living and breathing. Not a carcass, but a man.

An unexpected blessing.

It was then that he registered the sound of gunfire— distant pops, flying fierce and fast.

The fog clouding Rex's vision began to clear a little. He bestirred himself to sit up and failed, fighting the dizziness that swooped down on him like some big, dark bird, beating its wings, pecking at his skull, talons bared to tear flesh.

Reason, never swift in coming, assembled itself slowly in Rex's pounding head.

The bastards. The *bastards*. Tom and the others, they were down there right now, shooting up the jailhouse, maybe the whole piece-of-shit town, robbing him of the just pleasure of vengeance. They'd left him behind. Probably reckoned him for dead.

He tried to sit up, but the motion was like an ax-blow to his skull. Bile scalded its way up his windpipe and he rolled onto his belly again to vomit in the dirt.

When the spate had passed, he spat and wiped his mouth on the sleeve of his coat. After a few deep breaths, he made another attempt to get to his knees, and this time he succeeded.

LINDA LAEL MILLER

There were shouts from below and the beating of horses' hooves.

By now, his pa was surely dead, along with a lot of other folks.

And he'd missed the whole damn party.

He spotted his horse, wandering fitfully nearby. Grazing on the dry grass. He whistled once, twice. Low and easy, so's not to scare the animal off.

The horse came, finally. Rex grabbed hold of one stirrup and hauled himself to his feet. He knew he'd pass out again, if he tried to mount up, let alone ride, and if that happened, he'd be a sitting duck when the others came back.

He fumbled for his saddlebags, murmuring to the horse.

The animal wanted to shy but was well trained by years of range work. Or maybe the horse just knew Rex would shoot him if he didn't settle down. For all Rex's kindly words, he would have. He surely would have, if it came to that.

At last, he got one of the bags open, reached inside, found his pouch of tobacco. He fumbled past that, going deeper and deeper until he finally closed a hand over what he really wanted—the small box of matches he carried for lighting up a smoke or starting a campfire.

He dropped the matches, fell to his knees to recover them. The horse pranced nervously, nearly trampling him. He shoved at the animal with one hand, got hold of the little box with the other.

He muttered to himself as he struck the first match.

They'd brought it on themselves. All of them. Tom and the others. His pa. Sam O'Ballivan and the Mexican, Vierra. Oralee Pringle and that snooty Maddie Chancelor, who turned up her pretty nose at the likes of him. Once, he'd asked her to dance, at a party behind the Cattleman's Bank, and she'd turned him down. She'd spoken kindly enough, but he'd seen the contempt in her eyes. Oh, yes, he'd seen.

She thought he'd killed Warren Debney. Well, the joke was on her, Rex thought, because it was Pa done that. He'd believed she'd turn to him in her sorrow, the old fool.

He tossed the match into a thicket of sagebrush and it went up with a satisfying burst of heat and flame, just like that bush in the Good Book. Only the Lord wouldn't be talking out of this one. No, sir. It was Rex Donagher talking now, and the message was plain enough.

They could go to hell.

The whole bunch of them could just go straight to hell.

CHAPTER
TWENTY-TWO

THE SHOOTING DWINDLED, then stopped.

Sam, crouched just inside the jailhouse door, the .45 grasped in his right hand, waited a few beats before he dared peer around the frame to take in the scene in the street.

Men lay sprawled everywhere, their horses long since scattered for parts unknown. The air was acrid with smoke, and the silence seemed to pulse with echoes of the battle.

"You men all right in there?" a voice called.

Vierra, on his haunches under the window, glanced in Sam's direction.

A form took shape, out of the darkness, followed by another, and then another. Light caught on a star-shaped badge.

"No casualties," Sam answered after looking over his shoulder. Rhodes was just putting his pistol away, and the dog was in one piece, too. "Did you fare as well?"

"One man winged," the marshal answered, coming toward them. He was tall and thin, with a handlebar

THE MAN FROM STONE CREEK

mustache and the quiet competence of an able gunman. The brim of a round black hat shadowed his features. "He'll be all right, once we get him back to Tombstone so he can be tended."

Sam holstered the .45 and went out to greet the other man.

"You got more problems than these here dead outlaws," the marshal said.

Sam saw it then. The red glow of a wildfire racing downhill toward the town.

"Holy Christ," he breathed.

The marshal turned to address his men, who'd been moving among the bodies, checking for pulses, or maybe loot. "Start knocking on doors," he told them calmly. "Rouse folks and tell 'em to run for the river. Leave their belongings behind."

A second lawman appeared from the gloom. "Get over to the livery stable," he said to his own posse. "Turn them horses loose."

Maddie, Sam thought, and bolted for the mercantile.

He found her kneeling beside a dead man, while Terran crouched opposite. The dog was there, too, holding back, sniffing anxiously at the night air.

"There's a wildfire coming!" Sam yelled, hauling Maddie to her feet. "Get down to the river as fast as you can!"

Maddie struggled, pulling toward the stairs. "Mama's sheet music—my money—"

"No time!" Sam retorted. A hellish glow shone at the window now, and folks and horses were fleeing through the streets, making plenty of noise while they were at it. The fire, a distant hum only moments before, was roaring toward them. "You've got to run for it, Maddie—as hard and as fast as you can!"

"Terran!" she gasped, coming to herself, glancing wildly around until she spotted her brother.

LINDA LAEL MILLER

Terran scooped Neptune up into his arms, shoved him at Maddie. "The horses are tied up out back!" he cried, and turned to run for the rear of the store.

Sam caught him by the back of his shirt, flung him toward the front door. "I'll get them!" he said when Terran hesitated.

Maddie stared up at him blankly, clutching the dog in both arms, her heart in her eyes. "I'm not going anywhere without you, Sam O'Ballivan," she said.

Sam cursed, because he knew she meant it. Knew, too, that there were implications he'd want to examine later, if he survived this accursed night. Short of carrying her over his shoulder, he couldn't make her move, and he couldn't let that sorry old two-horse team of hers burn to a crisp in the lot behind the store, either.

He ran past the curtain, through the kitchen beyond, out the back door. The horses were screaming in fear, their eyes rolling.

Sam cut the lines with his pocketknife, thanking God for old, frayed rope, and threw open the wire gate. He swatted the panicked animals hard on the flanks to drive them out. From there, they'd have to fend for themselves.

The fire was less than a hundred yards away, hot enough to raise blisters on Sam's back as he dashed, coughing, into the store again. Maddie, Terran and the dog were still standing in the middle of the floor, as if they'd turned to stone. Terran clasped what looked like the cash box under one arm and a shotgun in the other.

"Violet and Hittie!" Maddie blurted.

"It's too late!" Sam retorted, and lifted Maddie right off her feet, dog and all. He sprinted for the front door, Terran close behind, and they joined the rushing throng of people and horses and bawling milk cows headed for the river.

The fire pursued them, even as it gobbled at walls and danced on roofs. The sound was like nothing Sam had ever heard. The heat seared his flesh, right through his clothes.

And still he ran.

Past the bodies of the outlaws, scattered in the street.

Past the bend in the road, and the schoolhouse, with the red glow of the fire glaring on its face. Sam grieved for his books; knew he couldn't save them. He went on and put Maddie down at last, on the riverbank, sent her stumbling toward the water with a hard push. Went back to turn loose Charlie Wilcox's old horse, tethered behind the school, and despaired of his own, left behind at the jailhouse.

He'd never even given the gelding a name.

He might have forgotten all about Mungo Donagher, if the old man hadn't thrown his weight against the inside of the shed door and come tumbling out, still bound from head to foot.

Sam got out his knife again, severed the bonds at Mungo's ankles, and dragged him toward the river, with his hands still cuffed behind his back and his ropes making him hobble like a turkey with its feet tied together.

MADDIE SAT, dazed, on the wet, smooth stones next to the river, amid horses and dogs and stricken people, watching as the flames lashed, angry and crimson-orange against the night sky, consuming Haven. Consuming everything she knew, everything she owned.

And still it moved closer, that ravenous, flickering beast.

Mexicans began to cross the river, on horseback, on burros, on the rickety rafts they used for fishing.

"Come," they said in anxious Spanish, gathering up sobbing women, wandering children, old men enervated by smoke and heat and sorrow. Over and over, they ferried back and forth, back and forth, stolidly carrying bewildered humanity to the other side.

LINDA LAEL MILLER

Maddie waited stubbornly, still clutching Neptune to her bosom, watching anxiously for Sam.

The fire drew nearer, and hotter. It consumed the schoolhouse and the woodshed behind it. Only when Terran pleaded did Maddie allow herself to be taken. Only then. And she would not let go of the dog.

She crossed the river on the back of a burro, with Terran riding behind her, his arms tight around her middle, while she still clutched Neptune.

"Miss Maddie?"

Maddie slid down off the burro's back, on the Refugio side. Her eyes burned from smoke and heat and pure despair, and at first, she did not trust them. She blinked.

"Violet?"

The little girl grinned up at her, face sooty, clothes blackened, but apparently unhurt. "You better put down that dog, Miss Maddie," Violet said practically.

Dr. Sanchez appeared, took Neptune gently from Maddie's embrace, set him on his feet, gave her a hasty examination. Then he went back to his work among the rescued, tending burns, offering what comfort he could.

"Oh, Violet," Maddie said on a sob, and gathered the child close against her. "I thought you must surely have perished!"

"A man came and got Ma and me, on a big horse," Violet answered when Maddie released her. "He's from Tucson. Real strong, too."

Maddie smiled wanly. "Have…have you seen Mr. O'Ballivan?"

Violet shook her head. "I reckon he'll be along, though."

"He's probably dead," Terran said flatly. They were the first words he'd uttered since they'd come over the river, and Maddie wanted to slap them right back down his throat. She might have, too, if she hadn't remembered

Warren and how Terran had looked up to him, loved him like a father.

Terran couldn't afford even to hope Sam had survived. He was already bracing himself for another cruel loss.

A priest approached, touched Maddie's arm. "You rest," he said in careful English. "Safe here."

Maddie was too spent, emotionally and physically, to resist. She let herself be led along a Mexican street, into a little adobe springhouse, where she lay down, in her singed calico dress, and succumbed to sleep.

When she awakened, it was still dark.

"Maddie?"

She opened her eyes. Strained to see.

Sure enough, Sam O'Ballivan knelt beside her, blackened and blistered, but entirely whole, as far as she could tell. She gave a small, strangled cry and sprang upright to fling both arms around his neck.

"Shh," he said, but he held her. Kissed the top of her head and her temple, then her mouth. "Where's Terran?"

Maddie nestled close to Sam's chest. Clung to him. "He's safe," she said. The priest had taken Terran and Neptune with him, after seeing Maddie safely settled in the springhouse. She was afraid to think where Ben might be. "Hold me, Sam. Hold me real tight."

He chuckled. "Glad to oblige," he said.

Something primitive took Maddie over then. Some celebratory impulse, some need she would have sublimated at any other time. She put her hands tight to either side of Sam's head and pulled him into a feverish kiss, as hot and as hungry as the fire that had swept through Haven that night and finally burned itself out at the edge of the river.

Sam hesitated, then groaned and deepened the kiss. Their tongues joined and Maddie's loins sparked.

LINDA LAEL MILLER

He was the one to break away first. "Maddie—"

She began unfastening his shirt buttons, slipped frantic hands inside to feel his chest, find the drumbeat echoing from his heart. "Please, Sam," she whispered, but she wasn't begging. She was demanding.

"There'll be no going back, once it's done," he warned, his voice low and hoarse from passion and smoke.

Maddie grasped at his belt buckle for an answer, and he closed his hands over hers.

"You have to be sure of this," he said.

"Damn you, Sam, I'm sure," Maddie gasped, and pulled free to open the front of her dress. Her breasts pushed at the thin fabric of her camisole, aching, the nipples already straining for his touch.

His tone was typically pragmatic. "All right, then," he told her. He unfastened his gun belt and set it aside. Then he caressed Maddie's breasts, as delicately as if they were holy things, treasures found at the end of some long, difficult pilgrimage. He laid her down and straddled her, on his knees. "All right, then," he repeated, and bent his head to suckle her, right through her camisole.

She cried out and arched her back, and their bodies touched where they most wanted to join.

Sam groaned again and fumbled with the ribbons, laid her camisole aside. "If you want having, Maddie Chancelor," he said, "I'll have you."

He lowered his head to her breasts then, and made free with them. At the same time, he bunched Maddie's skirts up, reached inside her drawers to find the moist, tender place.

Maddie went wild, clawing at his back, his shoulders, his hair.

He slipped his fingers inside her, while his thumb worked the nubbin of flesh where her womanhood centered. It seemed to Maddie, in those heated, frantic moments, that the whole of creation had shrunk to that one, tiny, pulsing part of her.

"Oh, God," she whispered. "Sam—" He played with her. Teased her. *"Sam!"*

The pressure built and built, until Maddie thought she couldn't bear another moment of it. He gave her no choice but to bear it.

"Next time," he said, close to her ear, between nibbles at her lobe, "I'll use my mouth. I'll part your legs, Maddie, and I'll put my head between them and I'll suck on you until you come apart."

"I don't know—what that means—to come—apart—"

"You're about to find out," Sam told her.

She erupted then. Exploded. Fire shot through her, from her very core. She sobbed with the force of the release, thrust her hips upward for more and still more, and he gave it. He stroked her and plucked at her with his fingertips, until she fell trembling to the floor of that Mexican spring-house.

He pulled her bloomers down and off, tossed them aside. Opened his trouser buttons.

"Are you sure, Maddie?" he asked.

She nodded. The need was already building inside her again.

"Is it the first time?"

She shook her head, too needy for shame. All she wanted, in all the world, was Sam O'Ballivan inside her. Deep, deep inside her.

He touched his member to the entrance of her body and she grasped at him, tried to pull him to her.

He entered her then, in a hard, swift motion, and Maddie welcomed him with the whole of herself, met his every thrust, writhing fitfully beneath him, seeking. Seeking.

LINDA LAEL MILLER

Finally, Sam took her wrists in his hands and pressed them to the floor, on either side of her head. He drove into her, with all his strength, and she splintered, her throat raw with cries as she rode a fiery sword into shattering, incomprehensible bliss.

She was drifting down, like a feather caught up in a whirlwind, when suddenly he stiffened, with a gruff moan, and spilled his seed into her.

Afterward they lay entwined and silent, with no breath to speak, as the world slowly awakened around them.

A rooster crowed.

Voices murmured in quiet Spanish.

Maddie's head rested on Sam's shoulder as daylight crept into their small hiding place.

"Was it Debney?" Sam asked very quietly.

Maddie had known the question was coming, and she was prepared to answer with the full truth. He'd leave her once he knew, of course, but she'd had him for a part of one night, and she'd be the rest of her life marveling at all she'd felt, all she hadn't dreamed it was possible to feel.

She shook her head. "His name was Jimmy," she said.

Sam waited. There was no tension in him, as far as Maddie could tell, but that didn't mean he'd understand.

Maddie's throat was dry and she swallowed. It didn't help. "He came to one of Papa and Mama's revivals. He was older—I was just fourteen and he was seventeen—and I thought I loved him. He followed us the whole of that summer, from town to town, and one day, in a haystack, in the middle of a field—"

"He was Terran's father," Sam guessed.

Maddie nodded. "He promised we'd get married, and I was to meet him at the train station in Kansas City. We'd go live with his folks, he said. They had a farm, outside of Independence. So I waited, and the train came and went, but

THE MAN FROM STONE CREEK

Jimmy never showed up. Finally, around sunset, Papa came and got me in the wagon and took me home." She paused. "If you can call another camp, beside another river, 'home.'"

Sam shifted, and for a moment Maddie thought he was going to put her from him, but he didn't. He slipped his arm around her and held her loosely against his side. "Go on," he urged when she struggled to find more words.

"I stayed out of sight whenever we had a revival, until Terran was born. After that, Mama and Papa claimed him as their own. They never judged or condemned me— they were such good people—but it was clear I wasn't to tell another living soul what happened, and I didn't, until Warren."

"How did he take it?"

"He was angry at first. Claimed I'd misled him. But Warren was a good man, and he loved me. He said what was past was past, and we'd just go on from there. A few days later, he was shot to death."

Sam was silent for a long time, pondering. "Does Terran know the truth?" he asked finally.

Tears came to Maddie's eyes. "I can't imagine how I'll tell him," she said. "I've always been his sister."

"Maybe he'd rather have a mother than a sister," Sam suggested.

Maddie raised herself onto one elbow, so she could look down into Sam's face. He was awfully calm about this. Maybe, she thought, with a stab of despair, because he didn't care, one way or the other. About any of it.

About her.

Sam caressed the side of her cheek with one index finger. Then, with the pad of his thumb, the same thumb he'd used to drive her to sweet distraction only a little while before, he brushed away her tears. "Terran knows you're not a virgin," he said. "He heard you and Debney

LINDA LAEL MILLER

arguing about it. If I were you, Maddie, I'd tell the boy as much of the story as would be fitting."

Maddie didn't answer.

Sam sat up, began straightening her clothes, methodically, matter-of-factly, like a man putting the table to rights after supper. Maddie permitted it, but her face burned, because now that the passion had ebbed, she knew he'd used her, just the way Jimmy had.

She kept her head turned away and wouldn't look at him when he spoke again.

"I've got to go, Maddie," he said.

No surprise there.

"Look at me."

She shut her eyes tight, kept her face averted, but she couldn't help ask the question that swelled up in her heart and tumbled over her tongue. "Where are you going?"

He'd say back to Stone Creek, she decided.

There was nothing left of Haven, and Abigail was dead, and whatever he'd come to do, he'd done it.

"I want to find Vierra," he said with resignation, "before he does something stupid."

Maddie's eyes flew open and she stared mutely at Sam.

Sam smiled down at her. He looked weary and filthy and damnably satisfied. Easy in his skin. "What did you think I was going to say?"

She was almost too proud to tell him. "That you were leaving these parts for good," she said, her voice small. *Leaving me,* she added silently.

"I surely plan to do that," he answered.

"Oh," Maddie responded. Most of the time, she liked being right, but on this occasion, she wished she hadn't been.

"You might as well wait for me," Sam reasoned. He nodded then, as if to approve his own decision. Got to his feet, reached down to help Maddie to hers.

THE MAN FROM STONE CREEK

She stood shakily, unsure of her balance.

Sam laid a finger to the tip of her nose. "You'd best scout up something to eat," he said. "I'll be back as soon as I can."

CHAPTER

TWENTY-THREE

SAM FELT SHAME, when he left Maddie behind, at the door of that springhouse, along with a curious, desolate exhilaration, but he couldn't afford to dwell on it.

God knew, it would catch up with him soon enough, but in the meantime he had things to do.

He'd turned Mungo Donagher over to the marshal from Tucson during the night, so that was one matter resolved. Most of the outlaw gang was dead, lying blackened and twisted in front of whatever might be left of the jailhouse, but he couldn't be sure of that, so he'd go across the river and have a look at them.

Maybe they'd be recognizable and maybe they wouldn't. Their number would tell him something.

He mounted the only horse he had—Charlie Wilcox's old nag—and headed for the far shore.

He rode past the ruins of the schoolhouse, the pyre where his cherished books had been consumed, and between the smoldering stumps and skeletons of cottonwood trees. Coming up behind the jail, which was nothing but a blackened pile of boards, he was relieved to see that the gelding wasn't there. He rarely prayed, but in those moments, Sam hoped a benevolent God had taken mercy on that horse.

Going on past, to the road, he took a few moments to comprehend the destruction all around him. The whole town had been wiped out, reduced to rubble. The mercantile. The Rattlesnake Saloon. The telegraph office.

Sam dismounted, shaking his head, and went to look at the bodies.

He counted twelve, and most were barely recognizable as men, let alone individuals. But when he saw a thatch of red hair atop one charred head, he crouched.

Tom Singleton. The former teacher, the man he'd come to Haven to replace and hauled up out of the schoolyard well. He'd been the leader of the outfit, Sam realized. The one whose voice and countenance had been so familiar, back there in Mexico, beneath that broken trestle.

He'd been clever, Singleton had. He'd been ruthless in pursuit of that *federale* gold.

And it had all come down to this.

Sam lingered a moment, then got to his feet.

He didn't give two hoots in hell about the gold, but he knew Vierra did. Knew, too, that his traveling companion had never crossed the river last night with the others fleeing the ravages of the fire. That meant he was either dead or looking for the gold.

Vierra was too quick to have burned, Sam concluded, so it must be the latter.

He patted the bedraggled old horse and was about to mount up when two things happened.

The gelding appeared at the far end of the street, trotting right down the middle. He was covered in soot, but none the worse for any trials of the night just past, as far as Sam could tell. At the same moment Ben Donagher came riding in from the opposite direction. He, too, was blackened, his eyes wild in his face as he took in the wreckage.

"Where is everybody?" Ben asked, reining in.

Between finding his lost horse and seeing the boy alive and well, Sam's throat was thick with jubilation. His eyes burned, along with the space behind his nose, and for a few moments he couldn't say a word.

"Other side of the river," he finally managed to say. "As far as I know, everybody's safe."

"Maddie?" Ben demanded. "And Terran?"

Maddie. Sam recalled her, sweet and vibrant and fierce beneath him, and ached. She'd be regretting what she'd done with him, once she came to her senses. She'd been in shock over the fire, that was all. "They're fine. Neptune, too."

Ben let out a sigh that seemed to come from the soles of his boots. "Rex done it," he said. "He set this fire. I found him up on top of the hill, burned to death."

"I'm sorry," Sam said, and laid a hand on the boy's leg. "You get on across to the Mexican side. There are folks over there to look after you."

Ben didn't move. "What about you? What do you mean to do?"

"I've got some business to attend to," Sam said. "I'd count it as a favor if you'd see that old Dobbin here gets across. Otherwise, he's likely to stand in front of the Rattlesnake, what's left of it, till somebody comes to fetch him."

"I got things to tell you," Ben said, but he took Dobbin's reins when Sam offered them. "Undine was part of the gang." He sat up a little straighter in the saddle. "I had to hit her in the back of the head with a rock to get away, but I don't reckon it was hard enough that she's kilt. She and Mr. Singleton were in it together. He said she was his half sister."

Sam nodded. "Where is she, Ben?"

Ben told him where the camp was, and mentioned the gold, too. Had some of it right in his saddlebags. He finished with, "You don't need to go after her. Mr. Vierra's on his way out there right now. I told him what I just told you, not five minutes ago."

Sam checked the gelding over, found him sound if singed, and mounted up. "Go on, now," he told the boy, cocking a thumb toward the river. "Marshal Rhodes is on the other side. You give that gold to him for safekeeping."

Rhodes could have ridden out during the night, but he and the yellow dog had stayed on to help. In Sam's mind, that meant he could be trusted.

Ben nudged his horse into motion, then paused again. His eyes were haunted as he ran them over what remained of the jailhouse. "Did my pa burn up in there?"

Sam shook his head. "He's on his way to Tucson, with a U.S. Marshal. Like as not, he'll be going to the federal prison at Yuma from there."

Ben merely nodded, but his relief was plain, along with the kind of bearing up a boy his age shouldn't have been faced with. After a long while, he asked, "You reckon that old man who come for Miss Blackstone would take me on as a ranch hand?"

Sam smiled. "I reckon he would for certain," he said.

"Guess I'll go and see to Neptune, then," Ben decided.

"Look after Miss Maddie, too," Sam urged. "She'll be in a state once she realizes the store is gone. Right now, she's probably telling herself there's some hope it was spared."

Once again Ben nodded, and they parted.

UNDINE DONAGHER SAT ALONE in the middle of the camp, watching as Vierra rode in. She held a rifle across her knees, but made no move to take aim. The gold lay around her, like stones circling a fire pit, in a score of grimy bags.

"I guess something must have burned," she said in an odd, disjointed voice. "The sky looked red, to the south."

Vierra kept an eye on the rifle, even as he dismounted. He'd tossed his sling aside, sometime during the night, which he'd spent in a hayloft with Pilar, and his wounded shoulder pained him severely. "The whole town of Haven went up," he told her. "There's nothing left."

Her purple eyes widened. Approaching cautiously, Vierra noted the blood on her shirt. "The bank?" she asked. "All Mungo's money was in that bank!"

Vierra spread his hands, suppressed a wince at the protest in his shoulder. "Gone," he said.

She absorbed the word like a blow. Sighed philosophically. "There's still the gold. When Tom comes back, we'll make for California."

Ben had told him about Tom, and the others, and he'd passed Rex Donagher's dead body on the way to the hidden arroyo. "They're gone, too," he said quietly. "All of them."

"Not my brother, Tom!"

"Dead in front of the jailhouse. We were waiting for them when they rode in, and there was a shoot-out. They might have gotten away with it, but for the posses from Tucson and Tombstone showing up when they did."

Undine blinked rapidly. Her eyes were at once blank and alert, like those of a predator. Her throat moved visibly as she swallowed. "That's a lie."

Vierra didn't move or speak. He knew she was thinking about shooting him, and he wondered if he'd let her do it. He'd never shot a woman, and he wanted to keep it that way.

He heard the horse approaching from behind, and knew it was Sam O'Ballivan without turning around to look.

THE MAN FROM STONE CREEK

Undine raised the rifle, and Vierra drew, as quick as if his gun had been greased.

"Throw it down," he told her.

Undine hesitated, probably figuring the odds, and tossed the rifle aside just as the Ranger rode in and dismounted beside him.

"You're under arrest, Mrs. Donagher," O'Ballivan said.

Undine swallowed. Her gaze darted from Sam to Vierra and back again. "I didn't do anything wrong," she replied.

"That's for a judge to decide," O'Ballivan told her. "I'll take you to Tucson, if you're fit to travel. Ought to please you to know you'll be reunited with Mungo."

"What about the gold?" she demanded.

"Yes," Vierra said, studying the Ranger. "What about the gold?"

To his surprise, O'Ballivan shrugged. "I've been thinking about that all morning," he said. "And on the way out here, I concluded that it belongs to the Mexican government. My orders were to see the gang dead or arrested, not recover what they'd stolen."

Vierra opened his mouth, closed it again.

O'Ballivan slapped him on the back. "If you ride hard," he said, "you can still get to Pilar before she marries the wrong man."

"That's it? That's all you have to say?"

"No," O'Ballivan answered, going around behind Undine to inspect the wound to the back of her head. It must not have been too bad, because in the next instant, he hauled her to her feet by one elbow. "If you do marry up with Pilar, I'd like to know about it. I'll be at Stone Creek ranch, outside of Flagstaff."

"How am I going to carry all that gold?"

"I reckon that's your problem," O'Ballivan said.

"What about Maddie?"

LINDA LAEL MILLER

O'Ballivan arched an eyebrow. "What about her?"

"She's going to need looking after."

The Ranger laughed, even as he bound Undine's hands behind her with a bandanna. "Maddie needs a lot of things," he said. "But looking after isn't one of them."

Hardly daring to believe his luck, Vierra stooped, picked up a couple of bags of gold, carried them to his horse, tucked them away in his saddlebags. As he went back for more, O'Ballivan lifted Undine onto the horse, then swung up behind her. He gave Vierra a salute.

"Adios," he said. "And thanks."

Vierra merely nodded, watching as O'Ballivan rode away with his prisoner, never once looking back.

MADDIE TRAVELED BACK across the river in the middle of the afternoon, astride a burro, leaving a concerned and fitful Terran behind at Refugio. She rode past the schoolhouse, past the jail, past the Rattlesnake Saloon, the hem of her skirt dripping river water.

There were others in town—folks had come from the surrounding countryside, as well as Tucson and Tombstone, to help. They'd brought wagons and food, medicine and blankets and clothing.

But Maddie might as well have been all alone when she came to a stop in front of what had once been the general store.

The roof had caved in and the walls were burned to cinder.

She'd grieved before.

For her parents, for Warren. Even for Jimmy.

But this was something different.

An ending of another sort.

"Maddie?" She looked down, saw Oralee standing alongside the burro, looking up at her, one hand shading her eyes from the sun.

"I don't know how I'll pay the mortgage now," Maddie said.

Oralee smiled. "Oh, I got my money back," she answered. "So don't you worry about that part."

Maddie frowned. The whole town had been destroyed. How could Oralee have recovered the fifteen hundred dollars she'd invested in the mercantile?

Oralee laughed at her expression. "Practically the only thing in Haven that could stand up to a fire like that one was the safe in the Cattleman's Bank. Elias James opened it right up, soon as the dial was cool enough to touch, and handed it over."

"Why would he do that?" Maddie asked, mystified.

"He owed me," Oralee said cryptically. "That's all you need to know about it, Maddie Chancelor."

Maddie sighed. Tried to smile and failed. "I guess your safe must have come through the fire, too," she mused.

Oralee nodded. "I mean to rebuild," she said. "First chance I get, I'm going to order me some lumber and hire some workers. I could put up another mercantile, too. Probably not till next year, though. There won't be much of a town here for a long while."

Maddie said nothing. Nor did she try to hide the tears that sprang to her eyes.

"What are you meaning to do?" Oralee asked kindly.

"I don't know," Maddie admitted. "It's as if the world came to an end."

Oralee reached up, patted Maddie's hands where they gripped the reins. "Sometimes," she said, "an ending is just what a body needs to make a new beginning."

Maddie was still taking that in when the sound of an approaching wagon distracted her as well as Oralee. Both women watched as a peddler drove into town, and, sitting straight and proud beside him, was Bird.

LINDA LAEL MILLER

They pulled up and Maddie reined the burro around, staring. Bird was plump with well-being, and her face was scrubbed clean of bawdy house paint. She wore a red calico dress with a bonnet to match.

"I ain't comin' back to work for you, Oralee," she announced first thing. The man beside her, who must have been half again her age, wore a bowler hat and an open smile. "This here's my husband, Albert J. Hildegarde," she said.

Albert J. Hildegarde tipped his hat. "Best regards of the day, ladies," he said.

Bird took in the ruins of the mercantile. "You need a ride someplace, Maddie?" she asked.

"I just might," Maddie replied, squaring her shoulders and lifting her chin. "Where are you headed?"

"North," Albert answered. "Got to pick up some supplies in Phoenix. Looks like folks around here will be needing goods."

Maddie let her mind rest on Sam O'Ballivan.

She loved him, all right. She wouldn't have given herself to him, even in the aftermath of a disaster, if she hadn't. If she pressed him, he'd probably marry her, take her and Terran back to Stone Creek with him.

But she knew he didn't love her. He hadn't had time to get over Abigail.

It was curious, but she could have married another man, even without love, just to put a roof over Terran's head, and her own. With Sam, things were different.

It would kill her to look into his eyes, day after day, night after night, and see duty there, and unflagging honor, but not love.

Not love.

"If you meant it," she said to Bird, "Terran and I would be obliged for a ride as far as Phoenix."

"What will you do there?" Oralee asked. She sounded worried.

"Survive," Maddie said. She looked back at the store again, took it all in, so she could remember not only what it was, but what it became. "Just survive," she finished.

FOLKS STREAMED INTO Tucson from Haven, brought there by kindly friends and strangers, in the backs of wagons, mounted on borrowed horses. All of them looked stunned.

As Sam came out of the marshal's office, he reckoned the same thing was happening over in Tombstone. People had a way of putting aside their own concerns when calamity struck, and doing what needed to be done.

A tug at his sleeve deflected his attention and he looked down to see Violet Perkins standing next to him, with an ice-cream cone dripping in her free hand.

"Hullo, Mr. SOB," she said cheerfully.

Sam smiled, ruffled her hair.

"I guess that was Ben Donagher's stepmama you just put in jail."

He nodded. "You look real pretty today, Violet," he said, noting her clean face and ruffled dress.

She shoved the ice-cream cone upward. "Want some?"

Sam grinned. "No, thanks," he said.

"My mama's getting married," she told him. "To the man who rescued us from the fire."

"That was quick," Sam commented, but he was pleased. Women had to make their way in the world as best they could.

"His name is Seth," she went on. "He bought me this dress and this ice cream, too. He has a house with a porch and a yard. His wife died three years ago and he's been right lonesome."

"Do you like him, Violet?" Sam asked gently. He didn't

LINDA LAEL MILLER

know what he could do about it if the answer was no, but he had to find out, or the child's well-being would prey on his mind from that time forward.

She nodded. "Mama does, too."

"That's good," Sam said.

Violet looked back over her shoulder, nearly spilling the ice cream to the sidewalk. "I guess I better go. Mama and Seth are in with the justice of the peace. They ought to be hitched proper by now."

Sam leaned down, kissed the top of her head.

She took the opportunity to hook an arm around his neck, stood on tiptoe and smack him on the cheek with ice-cream lips. "Thanks for the dress and the storybook, Mr. SOB," she whispered. "I knew all along they was really from you. And thanks for letting me go to the outhouse whenever I wanted, so I didn't wet my bloomers."

Sam blinked hard. Before he could bring himself to say "You're welcome," or anything at all, she'd turned away, skipping off down the sidewalk.

He crossed to the telegraph office, sent a wire to the major.

"Assignment done. Coming home. Bringing some people with me. I've got a boy and a dog to spare. Do you still want Ben Donagher?"

He was across the street an hour later, paying for a team and a wagon and a whole passel of other things, when the telegraph operator tracked him down with an answer.

"Damned right I do," the major had replied. "Think I know who else you're bringing along. Will have your place readied up. Come on home."

Come on home.

Sam meant to do just that.

It slowed him down considerably, traveling by wagon, with his gelding tied behind, and it was past nightfall when he pulled up alongside the river on the Haven side. He rode the gelding across and was met on the shore by none other than Ben. The dog was beside him.

"Maddie wanted me to leave with her and Terran, but I said I'd stay," the boy told him, his face full of hope. "Go on up to Stone Creek with you."

Sam froze halfway between the saddle and the ground. Let himself down slowly. "Maddie left?" he asked when he thought he could get the words out without tripping over any of them.

Ben nodded. "With Bird and her peddler husband," he said.

Sam swore. "You know where they went?"

"Phoenix," Ben said helpfully.

Sam rubbed his chin. He needed a bath and a shave, but between taking Undine Donagher to jail in Tucson, buying the wagon and new clothes for everybody but Neptune, he hadn't had the time. "How long have they been gone?"

Ben shrugged. "Left this afternoon," he said.

"You still got your horse?"

"Yep," the boy answered.

"Well, get him. If we're going to catch up to that peddler's wagon, we'd better be on the move."

Ben hesitated only a moment. Then he fetched his horse and crossed the river with Sam. The dog rode with Sam.

On the other side, Sam put Neptune in the back of the wagon, with the crates and packages, and hoped he wouldn't chew anything up. Ben climbed into the box alongside Sam, after they'd secured their tired horses behind.

They'd traveled less than an hour when they came upon the camp.

Maddie came out to meet them, looking tired and dirty and forlornly surprised. Sam didn't speak to her. He just got down from the wagon, turned Ben's horse and the gelding loose to graze, and then unhitched the team. Ben and the dog had long since gone to greet Terran, but Maddie lingered.

"That's a fine team and wagon," she said when the silence got too long and too uncomfortable. "I gave our horses to Mr. Maddox, the blacksmith."

Still, Sam said nothing. He didn't trust himself.

Maddie seemed bent on starting up a conversation. "I guess I should have waited to say goodbye, and thank you for all you did," she said softly, "but Bird and Albert were heading out right away."

"Guess so," Sam said.

A tear slipped down Maddie's cheek. "You'll be going on to Stone Creek, I suppose."

Sam finally faced her, set his hands on his hips. "It's home," he replied.

"Ben tells me you're an Arizona Ranger."

He thrust a hand through his gritty hair. "I think I'm through with rangering," he allowed. "I just want to settle down at Stone Creek and concentrate on ranching." Then, carefully, "What are you meaning to do, once you get wherever it is you're going?"

"I'll look for work."

"What kind of work?"

She shrugged. Spread her hands. "Whatever I can find," she said.

"I'm in the market for a wife," Sam heard himself say. In the next moment he wished the ground would open up and swallow him without a trace. *I'm in the market for a wife,* he'd said. Like he planned on buying a cow off the auction block.

"What about Abigail?"

The question startled Sam right out of the tangle of embarrassment he'd gotten himself wound up in. "Abigail," he said, "is dead."

"But you loved her."

Sam looked away, made himself look back. "I *should* have loved her," he said. "But I didn't. Oh, I fooled myself for a long time, but once I met you, I knew the truth of it."

Now it was Maddie who was flummoxed. "Once you...met me?" She almost whispered the words, and put one dirty, tremulous hand to her throat.

"I love you, Maddie."

She just stood there, without saying a word.

"I'm an old-fashioned man," Sam said, moving to take her upper arms in his hands. "When I lay down with you, it was because I wanted to make you mine. Not just for one night, either. For always."

She cried harder, and he wondered if he'd insulted her somehow, mentioning their lovemaking, or if she still cared for Warren Debney and didn't know how to go about telling him.

"Oh, Sam," she said finally. And she put both her arms around his neck. "Sam."

He kissed her, tentatively at first, and then with everything he felt for her. She responded with a fervor that made him wish they were back in that Mexican springhouse. But the fact was, they weren't. They were within a hundred feet of another wagon, and Terran and Ben had to be considered.

Sam lowered his hands to Maddie's waist and held her away, but he kept the distance slight.

"I love you, Sam O'Ballivan," Maddie said, smiling up at him, even though she was still weeping. "I love you."

He caressed her breast, felt her nipple harden deliciously against his palm. "Then I suppose you ought to marry me, before the both of us wind up with bad reputations."

LINDA LAEL MILLER

She laughed, and the sound made Sam's heart swell.

"The sooner the better," she said when she'd recovered. He kissed her again.

Then he gave a whoop of joy, lifted her right off her feet and spun her around in a circle. Neptune had rejoined them, and he ran 'round and 'round, barking with delight.

Ben and Terran were drawn by the festivities, too, their faces bright with curious pleasure.

Sam set Maddie back on her feet and nibbled lightly at her ear. Felt a shiver go through her.

"I wish we could make love," she whispered. "Right here and now."

He nibbled again. "Next time I have you," he promised, "it will be in a real bed, and we'll be married."

Her eyes twinkled with mischief as she looked up into his face. "Will it be like before?" she teased.

"Better," he said. He looked over his shoulder at Ben and Terran, who were standing at a little distance.

She trembled again. Stroked his cheek with the backs of her fingers. Practically made his knees buckle, as easy as that.

"Come and have some supper," she said. "Bird's got enough rabbit stew in that pot for all of us."

They sat around the peddler's fire, eating and talking quietly.

When it was time to bed down, Maddie and Bird retired to the interior of Hildegarde's well-equipped wagon, with Albert in a bedroll beneath. Ben, Terran and Neptune stretched out in the back of Sam's buckboard, among the parcels, and Sam lay underneath, tired to the bone and grinning like a damn fool.

It would be several days before they got as far as Flagstaff. Once there, he and Maddie would find a preacher and make it legal.

THE MAN FROM STONE CREEK

Overhead, Terran and Ben began to snore out a soft chorus of exhaustion. Sam listened for a while and then he dozed off himself. When he woke, it was daylight, and Maddie was crouched beside the wagon, beaming.

"Wake up, Sam O'Ballivan," she said. "The coffee's ready."

"You sound like a wife," he teased.

She laughed. "I'm practicing."

He pulled her down beside him, kissed her until they were both breathless.

"You kiss like a husband," she said.

Sam grinned. "I'm practicing," he told her.

CHAPTER
TWENTY-FOUR

THE HIGH COUNTRY lay blanketed beneath a dazzling snow, virtually untouched, as far as the eye could see, and sprinkled with diamonds. The air was cold and bracing, and Maddie O'Ballivan sat straight on the wagon seat, beside her husband, taking it all in. Down at Haven, even as far north as Phoenix, the ground was bare and dry. This was like another world.

"Stone Creek," Sam said with quiet pride.

Maddie saw two houses, smoke curling, home-scented, from their stone chimneys, a variety of outbuildings and a partially frozen stream running through, like a long strand of sky-blue thread. Hereford cattle grazed on summer hay, scattered from wagons by men with pitchforks. Great, towering pines stood sentinel on the sloping hillsides and, in the distance, at the end of a twisting trail, a town nestled, brave and remote and new.

Sam had told her about the town. Said what it needed was a general store, and he'd build one, if she'd run it.

Maddie's heart swelled into her throat. It was hard to believe, looking upon that pristine expanse, that she and Terran and Ben were going to live there. She felt as though she'd died and been reborn.

In the back of the wagon, Neptune began to bark. It was an exuberant, hopeful sound. Ben and Terran, bundled in the coats Sam had bought for them in Flagstaff before the wedding, fairly jumped up and down with excitement.

"Which house is the major's?" Ben asked, poking his head between Maddie and Sam. His breath made a white plume in the thin air.

"That one," Sam said, pointing, to Maddie's surprise, to the smaller of the houses. He'd told her a few things about the setup at Stone Creek, that he and Major Blackstone were partners in the ranching business, as well as rangering, though he reckoned the latter would slow down, now that he had a wife and a boy to raise. But he'd wanted the rest of it to be a surprise, and it was.

Maddie's gaze turned naturally to the larger house, a long, two-story structure of stone and timber, with windows gleaming at the front. From now on, she thought, this would be her home. Come the spring, she could plant a vegetable patch, and flowers, too.

It was a miracle.

"You'll be glad to sleep in your own bed again," she said because she was afraid she'd forget how to speak if she didn't say something, no matter how mundane it might be.

Sam had followed her gaze, and now he grinned, the reins resting lightly in his gloved hands. The team sputtered and tossed their heads, anxious for feed and rest and the warmth of a barn. "Actually," he said, "I've never lived in that house, so it'll be as new to me as it will be to you."

Maddie looked into his eyes, forgetting the boys, the

LINDA LAEL MILLER

dog, the horses tied behind, everything but Sam. "You built it for Abigail," she mused, with no rancor.

He kissed the tip of her nose. "I built it for you," he said, and then he set the wagon moving again. "I just didn't know at the time who you'd turn out to be, that's all."

Major Blackstone waited, the collar of his coat pulled up around his ears, on the porch of the first house. With a shy smile, he made his way out to the gate as Sam reined the buckboard to a halt.

"Welcome to Stone Creek, Maddie O'Ballivan," he said, catching and holding her gaze.

"Thank you," Maddie answered. She too felt shy; the major was Abigail's father, after all. It must have seemed strange to him, seeing Maddie as Sam's bride, taking a place he'd surely imagined for his lost daughter.

The major seemed to see right inside Maddie's mind. He reached up and patted her hand. "It'll be a fine thing, having you here," he told her, gruffly gentle. "A fine thing indeed."

Ben leaped down from the back of the wagon, Neptune barking at his heels. "Where's the bunkhouse?" he asked.

Major Blackstone smiled. "You won't be living in the bunkhouse," he said. "I've got a room ready for you upstairs."

Ben's eyes widened. "My dog, too?"

"Your dog, too," the major said. His wise eyes swung to Terran, still in the back of the buckboard. Took him in in a way that made him part of things. "You'd best stay a spell, too. Help your friend get settled in." He looked at Maddie again, then Sam. "Let the newlyweds have some time to get used to each other."

Terran, subdued since Maddie had taken him aside, the first night in Flagstaff and told him the truth about the both of them, let out a heartening whoop, grabbed his things and jumped down just as Ben had.

The major rounded the wagon, untied Dobbin and Sam's gelding. "We'll see to these critters," he said. "Won't we, boys? Nice barn waiting for them."

Sam shifted on the seat to watch. "Obliged," he said.

"The old fella," the major noted, examining Dobbin with a practiced eye, "looks ready for the pasture." He patted the tired horse fondly, but looked at Sam. "You ever name the other one?"

"Apollo," Sam answered. He and Maddie had agreed on the name on their wedding night, between bouts of love-making. Apollo, he'd said, was the sun god. There had been enough darkness in their lives up to then, and now it was time for light.

The boys, neither of whom had seen more than a skiff of snow in their lives, had already figured out how to bunch the stuff into balls and fling it at each other, and their laughter rang like music, with Neptune contributing joyous yelps.

They'd be starting school in town in a few days, but for now they could play. They'd been through so much, both of them.

"What are you sitting here for?" the major demanded good-naturedly, his eyes resting with affection on Sam. "Seems to me, you could think of better things to do."

Maddie blushed. Sam laughed and turned the team toward the other house, perhaps a mile away.

A few minutes later they pulled up to the door of a barn, so new that the wood was still unweathered and fragrant with pitch.

"You could go on inside the house if you want," Sam said.

Maddie smiled. "No, sir," she answered. "You're not getting out of carrying me over the threshold, Sam O'Ballivan."

He chuckled. "It was worth a try," he said.

Maddie swatted at him, laughing.

They unhitched the team together, put the weary horses in their stalls, groomed and fed and watered them. Sam took a while to groom Dionysus, too, and to check the animal's lame foot, now healed. When the work was done, Sam said he'd fetch their belongings from the wagon later, took Maddie by the hand and led her around to the front porch.

At the door he paused, placed his hands on either side of Maddie's face, and kissed her gently.

"This is *your* house, Maddie. Yours and Terran's and mine. Let's remember Abigail and Warren—they'll always be part of our lives—but under this roof, there will be no ghosts. Agreed?"

Maddie swallowed. Nodded.

Sam swept her up into his arms, so suddenly that it took her breath away. He opened the door and they were over the threshold.

A spinet gleamed, next to the fireplace, though there was, as yet, no other furniture.

Maddie took in an audible breath at the sight of it.

"Wedding gift from the major," Sam said, setting her on her feet.

"How did he know? How did *you* know?"

Sam rested his hands lightly on either side of her waist. A charge went through Maddie, and much as she wanted to sit at that spinet and let loose all the music she'd been storing up inside since the last time she'd played, she wanted something else more.

"Terran talks a lot," Sam told her, and grinned.

Maddie felt flushed, even though they'd just come in from a cold, snow-spread day and the fire on the hearth was burning low. "Do we own any furniture at all?" she asked practically.

Sam's blue eyes twinkled. "A table, a bathtub and a bed."

Maddie's tongue tied itself in a tidy knot.

Sam look her hand, led her into the kitchen at the back of the house. There was another fireplace there, with flames flickering inside, a big wood stove with a tap on the hot-water reservoir, and a long, plain table with benches on either side.

Maddie pictured herself cooking there, pictured all of them, her and Sam and Terran, at the table, laughing as they shared a meal.

Meanwhile, Sam went out the back door and came back shortly with a large, round tub. He set it down close to the stove, which was already pumping delicious warmth into the spacious room, and turned the tap to let hot water flow into it.

"You first," he said, picking up a bucket and carrying it to the sink, where he began pumping cold water into it.

Maddie looked around. "You mean—undress?"

"Unless you want to bathe in your clothes," Sam said, lifting the lid on the reservoir and emptying the bucket into it. He went back to the sink, when Maddie just stood there, and commenced to pumping again.

"Undress?" Maddie echoed stupidly. "Right here?"

Sam grinned at her, over one shoulder. "Right here," he said.

Maddie took off her bonnet first, then her heavy cloak. Laid them aside on one of the benches lining the table. She wanted a bath; she was cold, at least on the outside, and they'd traveled a long way from Flagstaff. On the inside, she felt feverish, and a familiar tension was building.

"You're going to—watch?"

"I certainly am," Sam said.

"Sam," Maddie choked out, "this is a *kitchen*."

He stopped his filling and carrying and emptying to run

LINDA LAEL MILLER

his gaze over her. It scorched as it passed, and made her nipples harden against her camisole and the bodice of her new woolen dress. "There is no room in this house," he said, "where I won't make love to you, sooner or later."

A delicious shiver went through Maddie. She began unbuttoning the front of her dress, but she fumbled so that it took forever. Sam, usually eager to help with the process, stood back, watching with a possessive heat in his eyes.

Maddie stripped until she was naked, waiting for Sam to take her.

Instead, he gestured rather grandly toward the tub.

Maddie stepped in, sank down into the water with a sigh. Sam brought her soap and a towel, and fetched some of her things from the wagon. Then he went back for more while she bathed.

When she'd finished, she stood, dripping, and he admired her for a long moment before wrapping a towel around her.

"Venus," he murmured, "rising from the sea."

Maddie's heart fluttered its wings.

She wanted Sam to kiss her, make love to her. Instead he helped her out of the tub and pointed toward the rear stairs.

"Our room is at the far end of the hall," he said. He dragged the tub to the back door and Maddie felt a rush of cold air as he emptied it.

She nodded, covered in gooseflesh, and started for the steps, looked back to see Sam turning the tap on the stove. Hot water steamed into the tub. When he began to peel off his clothes, Maddie turned strangely shy and bolted.

Sam's laughter followed her to the second floor.

Their bedroom, like the kitchen and the parlor, boasted a fireplace. A blaze had been laid, and Maddie struck a match to it, stalling. The bed was huge, a mahogany four-poster with fluffy pillows and a colorful quilt, turned back to reveal white linen sheets.

Maddie swallowed. The light shifted and fat snowflakes began to drift past the windows.

She moved closer to the fire, wishing she had a nightgown, but the towel would have to do. There was no way she was going back down those stairs to the kitchen for her valise. Sam was there, and he was naked in the bathtub.

"Silly," she said, impatient with herself. It wasn't as though she and Sam hadn't made love before. Why, practically the minute they'd exchanged "I do's" in Flagstaff, he'd dragged her off to a hotel-room bed and ravished her so thoroughly that even the recollection of it aroused her.

She paced.

She added wood to the fire.

She watched the snow.

She looked at the big, inviting bed.

She added more wood to the fire.

And then the door opened and Maddie's breath caught.

Sam came in, naked except for a towel tied loosely at his waist.

He held out a hand to Maddie, and she went to him, tentatively, for all the world like a blushing virgin bride.

He kissed her. Tugged at her towel until it dropped away. Let his own fall to the floor.

"Do you remember what I told you that first time?" he asked in a ragged, sleepy whisper, stroking her with his hands, nibbling lightly at her earlobe. "In the springhouse in Refugio?"

Maddie remembered, all right. Her blood sang with the recollection.

She swallowed, nodded. She'd waited for that particular promise to be fulfilled, nerves jumping with anticipation every time she thought of it, but Sam had withheld it.

Not that she'd gone unsatisfied, because she hadn't.

Oh, she certainly hadn't.

LINDA LAEL MILLER

"I wanted it to happen here," he said.

He guided her to the bed, laid her down gently on the sheets, cross-wise, with her hips on the edge.

Maddie moaned.

Sam knelt, parted her knees, set her heels on his shoulders. He chuckled when she shivered at the feel of his warm breath on the nest of moist curls between her legs.

He stroked the insides of her thighs, slowly, making the flesh quiver in the wake of his fingertips.

Maddie bit down on her lower lip, raised her hips slightly, instinctively offering herself to him.

He slid his hands under her buttocks, lifted her higher still, a man preparing to feast. When he burrowed through and took her full in his mouth, she cried out.

He withdrew, teased her with his tongue.

She began to writhe, and a fine sheen of perspiration dampened the hair at her temples, the space between her breasts, the smooth skin of her belly.

"Slowly," he said.

"No," Maddie pleaded, breathless. "Fast."

She felt the shake of his head between her legs, and groaned in desperate frustration. He meant to take his time with her, and the thought of that made Maddie beg.

He lapped at her. Kissed the insides of her thighs. Long, light, trailing kisses that made her whimper and plunge her fingers into his hair. He reached up, caressed her breasts, one at a time. Held her apart with the fingers of his other hand.

"*Sam!*" she gasped when she could bear the wait no longer.

He fell to her then, took her greedily, voraciously, granting her no quarter.

The release was cataclysmic in scope; Maddie dug her heels into Sam's shoulders and flew, and cried out again

THE MAN FROM STONE CREEK

and again, until she was hoarse. At last, at last, she fell trembling to the bed, dazed with pleasure, wanting him inside her. Wanting him to put his baby in her.

The craving was fierce, elemental as a wildfire or a torrential rainstorm.

Sam held her apart with his fingers and began kissing her, and the sweet horror of it struck her all at once.

He was going to make her do it again. Climb to those heights, flailing like flotsam atop a boiling geyser. She would burn in the unseen flames and, finally, leave herself completely behind.

"I can't," she whispered.

"You will," he replied at his wicked leisure.

And she did.

Again.

And then again.

After that, they made love, and by the end, Maddie was so exhausted, she tumbled into the most profound slumber of her life.

When she awakened, the room was dark, and Sam slept, his head resting on her stomach, his breathing deep and even.

She smiled, twisted a tendril of his hair lightly around her finger.

So this was what it was like, belonging somewhere. Having a real home.

And home wasn't a town, or a house, the way she'd always thought. It was a person.

Home, for Maddie, was the brave, spacious heart of Sam O'Ballivan. A heart big enough to take her in, and Terran, as well. Come the spring, Terran's name would be O'Ballivan, too.

Tears of pure joy filled Maddie's eyes. Then she snuggled in and went back to sleep, where dreams awaited, almost as sweet as reality.

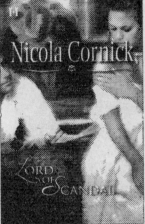

REQUEST YOUR FREE BOOKS!

2 FREE NOVELS
FROM THE ROMANCE/SUSPENSE
COLLECTION PLUS 2 FREE GIFTS!

YES! Please send me 2 FREE novels from the Romance/Suspense Collection and my 2 FREE gifts. After receiving them, if I don't wish to receive any more books, I can return the shipping statement marked "cancel." If I don't cancel, I will receive 4 brand-new novels every month and be billed just $5.49 per book in the U.S., or $5.99 per book in Canada, plus 25¢ shipping and handling per book plus applicable taxes, if any*. That's a savings of at least 20% off the cover price! I understand that accepting the 2 free books and gifts places me under no obligation to buy anything. I can always return a shipment and cancel at any time. Even if I never buy another book from the Reader Service, the two free books and gifts are mine to keep forever.

185 MDN EF5Y 385 MDN EF6C

Name _____ (PLEASE PRINT) _____

Address _____ Apt. # _____

City _____ State/Prov. _____ Zip/Postal Code _____

Signature (if under 18, a parent or guardian must sign) _____

Mail to **The Reader Service:**
IN U.S.A.: P.O. Box 1867, Buffalo, NY 14240-1867
IN CANADA: P.O. Box 609, Fort Erie, Ontario L2A 5X3

Not valid to current subscribers to the Romance Collection,
the Suspense Collection or the Romance/Suspense Collection.

Want to try two free books from another line?
Call 1-800-873-8635 or visit www.morefreebooks.com.

* Terms and prices subject to change without notice. NY residents add applicable sales tax. Canadian residents will be charged applicable provincial taxes and GST. This offer is limited to one order per household. All orders subject to approval. Credit or debit balances in a customer's account(s) may be offset by any other outstanding balance owed by or to the customer. Please allow 4 to 6 weeks for delivery.

Your Privacy: Harlequin is committed to protecting your privacy. Our Privacy Policy is available online at www.eHarlequin.com or upon request from the Reader Service. From time to time we make our lists of customers available to reputable firms who may have a product or service of interest to you. If you would prefer we not share your name and address, please check here. ☐

BOB07

LINDA LAEL MILLER

77194	MCKETTRICK'S HEART	___ $7.99 U.S. ___	$9.50 CAN.
77190	MCKETTRICK'S PRIDE	___ $7.99 U.S. ___	$9.50 CAN.
77185	MCKETTRICK'S LUCK	___ $7.99 U.S. ___	$9.50 CAN.
77101	MCKETTRICK'S CHOICE	___ $7.99 U.S. ___	$9.50 CAN.

(limited quantities available)

TOTAL AMOUNT $ _____
POSTAGE & HANDLING $ _____
($1.00 FOR 1 BOOK, 50¢ for each additional)
APPLICABLE TAXES* $ _____
TOTAL PAYABLE $ _____

(check or money order—please do not send cash)

To order, complete this form and send it, along with a check or money order for the total above, payable to HQN Books, to: **In the U.S.:** 3010 Walden Avenue, P.O. Box 9077, Buffalo, NY 14269-9077; **In Canada:** P.O. Box 636, Fort Erie, Ontario, L2A 5X3.

Name: _____
Address: _____ City: _____
State/Prov.: _____ Zip/Postal Code: _____
Account Number (if applicable): _____

075 CSAS

*New York residents remit applicable sales taxes.
*Canadian residents remit applicable GST and provincial taxes.

HQN™

We *are* romance™

www.HQNBooks.com   PHLLM0607BL